NECTAR
from a
STONE

A Novel

Jane Guill

A TOUCHSTONE BOOK
PUBLISHED BY SIMON & SCHUSTER
New York   London   Toronto   Sydney

TOUCHSTONE
Rockefeller Center
1230 Avenue of the Americas
New York, NY 10020

TOUCHSTONE and colophon are registered trademarks
of Simon & Schuster, Inc.

For information regarding special discounts for bulk purchases,
please contact Simon & Schuster Special Sales at
1-800-456-6798 or business@simonandschuster.com

Designed by Jan Pisciotta

Manufactured in the United States of America

1   3   5   7   9   10   8   6   4   2

Library of Congress Cataloging-in-Publication Data
Guill, Jane.
Nectar from a stone : a novel / Jane Guill.
p.   cm.
"A Touchstone book."
1. Wales—History—1284–1536—Fiction. 2. Soldiers—Fiction.
3. Revenge—Fiction. 4. Widows—Fiction. I. Title.
PS3607.U485N43   2005   813'.6—dc22   2004056574
ISBN 0-7432-6479-7

Acknowledgments

My sincere appreciation goes to Nat Sobel and the patient souls at Sobel Weber; the inimitable Dr. Loren Logsdon; Ally Peltier, Amanda Patten, and Trish Todd at Touchstone Fireside; Peg Haller; and to the Barrington Writers Workshop, especially Miriam Lykke. To my parents, my two children, and my steadfast friends—thanks and ever thanks for being as remarkable as you all are.

Of course, this book would never have been possible without the encouragement and counsel of my extraordinary husband, Andy Lewis. *Rydw i'n dy garu di.*

Foreword

Every age presents men and women with its own peculiarities, pains, and pleasures. In 1351, when this tale begins, the world still reeled from a sweeping and horrific visitation of the bubonic plague. People named the disease the Great Mortality, or the Pestilence. Educated guesses put the death toll in Europe at somewhere around one-third of the population, perhaps more. Certain places were luckier than others, but doomed villages here and there succumbed completely.

The Church of the Middle Ages, God's omnipresent intermediary in the Western world, had proven all too clearly unable to stop the spread of the affliction. More worldly opinions had to be sought. In October 1348, learned doctors in France decreed the disease was caused by a triple conjunction of Saturn, Jupiter, and Mars in the fortieth degree of Aquarius, an event they said had taken place on March 20, 1345. Their opinion was accepted as state-of-the-art scientific wisdom. Like the Church's call for unceasing prayer and contrition, the doctors' astral verdict did nothing to deter the Mortality. The pandemic took its own unimaginable course, leaving in its wake stunned and disheartened survivors.

The Black Death was by far the most grievous tribulation of the fourteenth century. But there were other conflicts and troubles.

Edward I, grandnephew of Richard the Lion-Hearted, conquered Wales in 1282. When Llywelyn ap Gruffydd, the last true Welsh prince, was killed in battle against Edward's forces, his head was stuck on a pole and displayed in London as a trophy and unambiguous warning to the defiant.

Edward was an effective and ambitious ruler, but ruthless. His son, Edward II, was the first English-appointed Prince of Wales. But Edward II came to a famously bad end, deposed and murdered by his wife, Isabella of France, and her English lover, Roger Mortimer. However, Edward and Isabella did manage to produce an heir before they grew completely estranged. It was their son, Edward III, who ruled Britain in the days of this story.

A war with France was instigated by Edward III and had already been raging for fourteen years by 1351. England felt entitled to huge chunks of France. Of course, France disagreed. There was also fierce disagreement on trade issues. In the end, England won most of the battles, but France won the war. The conflict lasted until 1453. It is now called the Hundred Years' War, a more euphonious but less accurate appellation than the Hundred and Sixteen Years' War.

It's likely people on both sides of this contest often set out to do battle with patriotic zeal. Joan of Arc, perhaps the most famous teenager in history, comes to mind. But some participants certainly hungered for plunder more than anything else. Others had no say at all in their military careers but were dragged unwillingly into duty. This was probably the case with many Welshmen.

Women faced battles of their own. A woman in the fourteenth century dealt with customs and abuses so familiar to her she may not have even given them any particular thought. Unless she was wealthy, her legal status was on par with a madman's or a sheep's. Her husband could beat her if he took the notion, as long as he didn't cripple or kill her—and provided her screams didn't disturb the neighbors.

A thirteenth-century (male) encyclopedist called woman "a hindrance to devotion." Original sin was traced by the Church to Eve. Naturally it followed that all women, with a few saintly exceptions, were the Devil's temptresses and his lusty recruiters. Of course, not every male embraced that prickly assumption. Surely many men adored their mothers and daughters, their good wives, and did not suppose them to be demonic seductresses.

The Welsh places and byways mentioned in these pages are not fictional. The Trackway of the Cross can still be traced or even walked for a large part of its sixty-mile length. Sylvan quiet reigns over much of it. A medieval man or woman dropped there now through some glitch in time might find sections of the track little changed. Birds still sing high in the oaks. Bees flit and buzz. But if the modern pilgrim

hears monks' chants or lepers' clackers, or glimpses lost ladies in the mist, it's only a trick of the imagination.

Sarn Elen too—the Roman Road in Wales—can be followed for a long way. Ghostly legionnaires do reveal themselves there, now and again, as they do on many of the Roman roads in Britain. Perhaps these indefatigable soldiers are still looking for a way back to Rome. Or maybe they're only eternally marching back to their British outposts, hungry for dinner and evening wine. The lonely ruin of Dolwyddelan Castle can be visited, also the church at Llanrhychwyn, and of course, Edward I's imposing castle at Conwy.

The Welsh language, one of the oldest in Europe, flourishes.

And the Honey Fair still takes place in Conwy, every September.

On Welsh Pronunciation

A very brief key, with some approximate English sounds:

a as in "bath" or "hard"
ae rhymes with "high"
c always pronounced like the hard *k*
ch always as in "loch"
th always as in "thick"
d as in "dog"
dd as *th* in "that"
e as a long *a* as in "sane" or "echo"
f as *v*
ff as *f*
g as in "go"
h as in "hat"—never silent
i as *ee* in "peer" or as *i* in "tin"
l as in "love"
ll see below
u as in "hit"—but when accented, as a rounded *ee*
w as *oo* in "pool"
y as *u* in "but"—preceding a vowel, as *y* in "yet"

Welsh names and words can look formidable. But any reader can learn to pronounce most with reasonable exactness. In Welsh every letter is pronounced. With few exceptions, the accent is on the next-to-last syllable. The most difficult sound is the *rh*, but a well-trilled *r* will do instead. The consonant *ll* is another matter and has to be acquired. You can get near to it if you prefix the liquid *l* with the *ch* sound in *loch*, or if you put *th* in front of *l*. Thus Llan = Chlan or Thlan.

Another example of pronunciation: Ysbyty Ifan = Us*butty* Ee*van*.

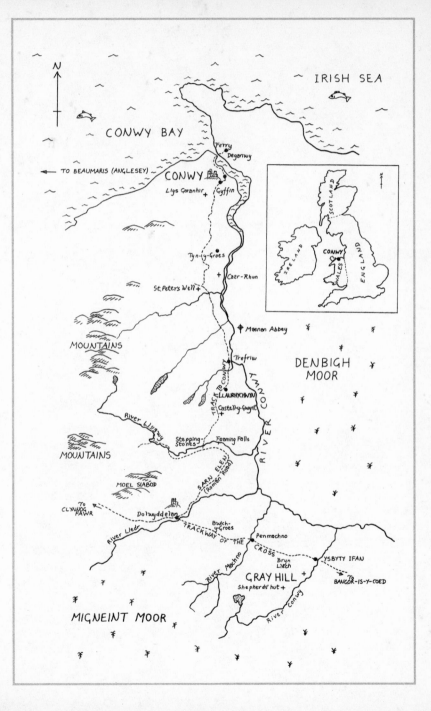

NECTAR
from a
 ## STONE

I

Gray Hill

Maelgwyn's "husbandly attention," as he called it, went on and on. Strange, how time could creep and crawl.

The room grew darker as the fire died.

"Have you no answer, Elise?"

Had he posed a question? Lying there, all she'd heard was the sighing of the wind, outside, and the faint rush of blood in her ears.

He stared down into her face. "Or is this unamiable silence yet another sign of your waywardness?"

This required some reply. "I have never studied to be wayward to you, sir," she said.

"Hah. You require no study, being a born mistress of the art." He reached down to pinch her thigh, his usual way of emphasizing a point. She bit back a cry but knew there would be a bruise. "Had you been attending, wife, you would have heard me say your constant lack of response is vexing. Nor am I able to fathom your ingratitude. Who are you to be ungrateful? Better souls than you suffer every hour. As we speak, worthy Welshmen bleed on French battlefields. In the course of the Great Mortality, thousands of good Christians fell. Yet *you* survived, Elise. Then you were so fortunate as to come here to me. *Deo dilecti.* But why?"

Deo dilecti. Chosen by God. When had she so offended her Maker that she had been chosen by Him, for this?

"It is as great a mystery to me as it is to you," she said, without equivocation.

"So I should imagine. But are you happy to be alive, rejoicing in my protection and devotion? No, I fear you are not. The pitiful dowry you brought with you does not compensate me for your relentless ingratitude, I assure you."

She closed her eyes for a moment, considering that dowry. It had not been pitiful, she knew. But she also knew there was never anything to be gained by contradicting Maelgwyn. So she opened her eyes and said, "Merely I am worn from the demands of the day and the household. There's only Annora to aid me." Then she lied. "But I am not ungrateful."

Would the reasonable excuse of fatigue stem a more grueling interrogation? The truth would never do. She couldn't tell this cruel man how she loathed and feared him, how the very sight of him—his long, muscled trunk and ox's neck—had become so abhorrent to her it was almost past bearing. Further, the truth could finally tip the scales of his volatile temper, a temper grown increasingly vicious in the two years since she had come to his rambling old house, Bryn-llwyd. Gray Hill.

"I confess," he was saying, "I forget from time to time that you are but a woman, the worst sort of stinking rose. The holy philosophers tell us all we need know of the sorry origin of women."

He continued, providing endless unwanted instruction even as he resumed his "husbandly attention."

She turned her head away to look down at the wooden floor, hoping to will her mind to some less hurtful place. A large black spider, speckled with yellow dots, crossed a rough plank near the hearth. It stopped and reared two of its legs, as if searching for some invisible passage. Then it lowered its legs and scurried toward a wall.

What tales had she heard of spiders? What had her servant and friend, Annora, told her? Elise pondered the question to divert herself. Soon she remembered Annora's words: to their webs spiders entice fallen souls who only appear to poor human eyes as trapped moths or mites, before herding them to Purgatory. But hadn't Annora also said the creeping things were a blessing in the house, because they could miraculously absorb the poisonous Pestilence vapor, bind it to the spots on their backs? Could these tales be true?

The evening wind grew stronger and shifted. Timbers objected. On one wall of their chamber three extravagant new glass panes, Maelgwyn's proudest acquisition and the first, he boasted, of many more to come, had been set into a triptych of branches hacked from a young oak. Still tall in its place but condemned to wither limb-stripped and then tumble down too early, that oak could no longer soften with its used-to-be leaves the view south to the empty Migneint Moor. It was Elise's fancy that the triptych, stolen from the tree's living body, would never contentedly cradle its fragile burden. And so it moaned softly with complaint.

A fierce gust brought the faint scent of the garderobe to the solar. The privy had been corbeled out over the river next to the chamber, and often stank when gales blew from the west.

"Fah, it reeks of cess in here," said Maelgwyn, for once echoing his young wife's thoughts.

But she flinched, for his harsh voice had startled her.

"You're skittish as a maiden, girl. Does my affection overwhelm you, or are you merely in the throes of yet another of your unholy visions?"

This jibe targeted a susceptibility to trance, hers since the season of the Gemini moon in 1343, eight years past, when she was eleven. Terrifying or glorious, her visions came unbidden, mostly eluding interpretation. To the past frustration of her loved ones, and now Maelgwyn, they often featured absolute strangers. Often, but not always.

In trances, sometimes only vaguely remembered by her once they'd passed, she had rightly foretold a rain of dying stars and spoken, most eerily, with the forgotten voice of the bard, Taliesin, who passed to Rapture in the days of Arthur and Myrddin. She had described strange landscapes and revealed to a lonely maiden the secret love of a neighbor. Likewise, many times she had predicted pregnancy. Or death.

That final item, predicting death, could not be thought remarkable. Death had lately stopped in many houses. It had thrown its dark cloak over every valley and knoll in Britain.

On the island of Anglesey, where Elise was born, three or four days north from Gray Hill, the gift of prophecy was regarded as God's favor. When she was a child, her parents refused coins from neighbors hoping to crouch nearby, their ears cocked for any mystic rambling that may have chanced to fall from Elise's young lips as she worked the spindle or sorted her mother's herbs.

Deep mystery was in her spells. Among a world of betters, why had God chosen her to deliver even the least vital word? Or was it God who had chosen? Elise understood there was no tisane or trick to calm her doubt on this. Was she God's herald, or only Satan's fool?

High wrought by what he called immoral superstition, Maelgwyn rebuked her for her trances without fail, and the previous winter he had lashed her with a studded whip one morning as she sat enthralled in a vision. Elise had felt no pain but had revived to the sight of three bright welts across her inner wrist. She had smiled down at the marks and said, unexpectedly to herself, "Father, Son, and Holy Ghost."

Her husband's face had grown chalky white before he added more wounds, blurring the crimson edges of the original three. "Blasphemy!" he cried and flung himself from the room.

His ill temper had not softened since, but she preferred it more than she could say to his monstrous ardor.

Now, in their solar, he pulled her up by her arms and dragged her from the bed without warning. She made an effort to stand upright but stumbled backward. Only a wooden chair behind her kept her from sprawling. At her seeming retreat, Maelgwyn's hands dropped to his sides. His blue eyes glinted in the light of the tallow candle flickering on the table near the chamber's closed door. Cast into ghostly relief by the candlelight, a dark vein pulsed at his temple.

He swooped down to catch her wrists with one large hand and squeezed so hard that her fingers grew quickly numb. "You choose so blithely to defy my wishes? Then kneel," he said, forcing her to her knees. "Like so. Only now do you strike the proper posture for supplication, Elise."

When she tried to pull away, he tightened his hold and seized the neck of her summer shift. She gasped as he ripped downward, rending the fine cloth. With a soft hiss, the ruined shift fell to the floor around her.

"Didn't the great thinker Boethius tell us that woman is a temple built upon a sewer?" he said, breathing a bit harder, but smiling. "Was he not a godly man?" He reached around her and ran the blunt fingernails of his unoccupied hand down her spine. "Some of your gender will call that an overly harsh edict, of course. But what is a righteous man to do? I must align myself with the Church's precepts and declare every woman an Eve."

Face hot, legs icy, Elise ceased any effort to free herself and sagged into his grip. "I am only fatigued, Maelgwyn, and addled by weariness. I will not fight you anymore," she said, staring up at him. "Let me rise so we may go on. I'm too aroused to kneel." She essayed a coy smile but knew it must be ghastly.

"No, Elise. Your wan smile and gray eyes can't dupe me further tonight. I mistrust women with gray eyes, you know, for they always, always prove to be sinful. In any case, *I* am a prophet now. And I foresee the most practical way for a willful wife to absorb a husband's teaching will be low and mean, so she may more easily comprehend it. That thought is balm for my distaste. I only pray my righteous seed is steered by Heaven to a smooth passage down your throat, toward your wicked soul."

He released her and inclined his head. "Move to me now, to ingest my probity."

Stronger hints of the privy assailed her as mounting winds buffeted the old manor. Some creature, mouse or bat, disturbed the thatched roof above. Drifting to the floor beyond Maelgwyn, the resulting halo of fine dust shone in the candle's glow.

Not a soul would come if she called. No one would hear her cries, except perhaps her friend Annora, Gray Hill's only other human inhabitant. Meanwhile her bare-chested husband stood between her and the door, hosen around his knees.

"For shame, woman," he finally said, as she gave no sign of obeying.

Another gale shook the manor. Hail pinged against glass. With more urgency than grace, she tried to rise but tangled her feet in her torn shift. Maelgwyn yanked her up by her hair.

"Any bleating ewe would be less trouble," he said, dragging her back toward the bed.

Twisting away at the last moment, she ran to the window. There, after two long years of cowardice, her caution deserted her. It dissolved like a tattered shadow. But in its stead it left a wild, quick-blossoming rage. Her head fairly swam with rage.

"A ewe? I recommend one, sir," she said, breath uneven. "Or an ass. A fine great ass for your mighty probity." Without conscious thought she began to laugh like a madwoman.

His thick brows drew together to form one black line. "Yet more shame, Elise."

Her laughter ceased as abruptly as it had begun. "Maelgwyn, can you not feel it? Something taints you. Some evil. In this house you are the fountainhead of everything unholy, for your pleasure can only be bought with pain. How sad and rotten your soul must be, how endless your fear. Indict me if you must"—she wrapped her arms around herself, covering her breasts—"but you know full well your own foul craving will condemn you straight to Hell."

A sickly half smile played at the corners of his mouth, and his nostrils flared.

Forcing herself to look into his face, she was shocked to catch a glimmer of fear, fear she had discerned in him only once before.

He drew back slightly, as if sensing her discovery.

"You're frightened," she said.

He took a breath; his broad chest swelled with it. And the fear disappeared from his eyes.

"Afraid?" he said. The word dripped with scorn. His teeth showed in a wider, crueler smile. "Of a godless female? You're a greater fool than I supposed."

"Likely I am. But I saw it. You had that same look another time, one other time only, just after I came here."

"Poor Elise. It's almost amusing to witness your attempts to evade my wrath, and God's."

Her eyes did not leave his face. She would *will* him to answer, will him to pay for his violent gratification with one small moment of truth. "You know it's true. That first time, I described a vision I'd had. It was before I knew to keep my visions secret from you when I could. I told you I saw a woman. She stood naked by a river and she wore a necklace of tiny starfish. She called your name. She—"

"Your tactics pall."

"Who was she? Your first wife? Your mother?"

Silence fell, absorbing any warmth remaining in the room. Gooseflesh climbed her limbs. Her dark hair spilled down her back to her waist. Outside, the hail stopped, and the wind grew less violent.

After a near eternity of quiet he spoke. He brought his hands to his chin, palms together as if in prayer. "What do you hope to gain by spewing your wicked tales, Elise? You and I both know your visions are only a sorry plea for my attention. We both know you never prattled of any woman."

"I did, Maelgwyn."

He went on as if she had not spoken. "But by mouthing your lies, your evil fantasies, you have damned yourself with words. Finally, Elise. Finally you cause me to kill you, as I've imagined I might since we wed, if only to do God and other men a service."

He took a step toward her, and another.

She shrank back with a cry.

He stopped and gazed past her, to his new panes and the darkness beyond, to the unseen rushing river. "Who will weep? I'll say you fell to a revisiting of the Mortality. I'll say you divined it yourself from a glimpse, in a vision, of a lake burning with brimstone. Is that not prophetic? Tomorrow morning or the next, what fool would burrow into your grave to confirm the dreaded symptoms?"

Without moving his head he shifted his focus, regarding her from the corner of his eye. "Let she who is ripe . . . fall."

"You're mad," she whispered.

He lunged.

Slammed back against the window, her knuckles hit a pane. Glass shattered, scoring uneven red lines down her arm. He struck her across the face with the side of his broad hand.

As blood dripped from her elbow to her foot, he struck again.

Shielding her head with her sound arm, she fell to the floor. "If I am to die," she cried, "at least let me say a prayer of contrition."

He loomed over her, breathing hard. "My dear," he said, with sudden real dismay, "I fear you are in the right. Yes, you must pray to Mary Magdalene. You must ask her to petition Heaven on your behalf—although I suspect it will be futile."

She cringed when he reached out, obscenely gentle, to stroke her hair. "Poor girl, where is my Christian compassion? Yes, yes, you must certainly pray."

She looked up at him as he bent over her. "I already have," she said—and drove a sharp glass dagger upward, hard, into his groin.

He crashed to the floor, but then staggered up at once to his knees. "Satan's bitch," he gasped. His arms shot out. His hands closed around her throat.

As a gray mist swirled up before her, she lashed out blindly with the shard and heard him curse again. His hands dropped away from her neck.

Once more the room grew still.

2

LOYALTY, AND A SHROUD

Her sight cleared.

Maelgwyn lay sprawled, face up, hosen still around his knees. Blood oozed from the first wound and from a second in his neck. He breathed irregularly, with a faint wheezing sound.

She squatted across the room, poised to flee, naked except for her wedding ring and the silver ankle bracelet her mother had given her before she died.

Shameful truth to tell, she was pondering whether to stab him again to hasten his reunion with his Maker.

Behind her the door creaked.

She sprang up and spun around, glass dagger raised.

It was Annora. Brown-eyed, pink-faced, seemingly more wide than tall, she stood uncertainly at the chamber's threshold. Then she uttered a muted exclamation and hurried to Elise's side to stare down at Maelgwyn.

"I've killed him," Elise said, lowering her arm. "I've murdered him with this." Offering the red, jagged shard, she noted that her bloody hand that held it was as unsteady as her voice. "He told me he'd murder me and say it was the Pestilence. I think he feared some trance of mine might send him to damnation. He said to pray to Magdalene. To Magdalene, Annora." She heard her own gibbering, and forced herself to stop. Taking a steadying breath, she glanced at her friend. "But Annora, why are you not yet sleeping?" she then said. Her words were the slightest bit less strained but lapsing toward the doubtful comfort of inanity. "Why are you still in your clothes?"

It was indeed so. The plump, rosy woman wore one of the only two dresses she possessed. They were identical, those dresses, both a faded, ashy brown. Each had at one time been golden yellow.

"I couldn't rest." Annora looked at the weapon, then back down at Maelgwyn. "I was so fearful for you. Every day at sunset," she said. "Because I knew."

Elise closed her eyes.

"I'd hear you crying in the night," Annora went on.

So strange was her demeanor, so opposite her usual bluff acerbity, that Elise was roused from her haze. "You heard me?" She turned to regard the other woman.

"A hundred times or more. And I was told such things in Ysbyty Ifan, when he sent me to the shops, tales of his strangeness and cruelty. The villagers warned me, bade me beware, called him an evil man." Annora's gaze fell before Elise's as a demon of self-loathing passed across her round, lined face. "Yet I did nothing," she whispered, beginning to cry.

"No, don't weep. What course could you have taken?" Elise reached out her hand toward her old friend. "Don't fault your silence, for I swear I never will."

She prayed Annora would believe her. She was so fine and loyal. She'd stayed with Elise's family, on Anglesey, all through the days of the Pestilence, after the other servants had fled. She was too righteous to charge herself with any imagined wrong.

Annora ignored Elise's hand. She went to the bed, pulled the fox coverlet from it, and flung it around the naked girl—all the while avoiding her gaze, as if ashamed. Next she took her bloodied arm in her calloused hands, gently appraising.

"This looks worse than it is, cariad, and will heal without a sign," she told her, with some of her old hearty manner. She touched Elise's face. "But your eye may swell shut by morning."

Then Elise was enfolded in a convulsive, sobbing hug.

"I knew, I knew he hurt you," Annora cried, rocking them both. "But I've grown too old and fainthearted to be brave. Can you forgive me? Can you ever regard me without contempt?" Her face was wet against Elise's shoulder as the girl's cheek rested on her gray curls. Annora's always unruly hair had escaped from her frayed beige wimple.

"Hush, darling. You've never been a coward and there's nothing to forgive." Elise returned her embrace with what strength she could summon. "You're as dear as a mother to me."

Standing secure in the circle of Annora's love, she became an innocent child once more and leaned her weight into the past. She allowed herself the sweet luxury of remembrance, for those moments, remembrance of her childhood days on Anglesey.

She imagined again the pearly mists at dusk and saw a ring of willow trees and silver birch swaying in a column of moonlight. There were cromlechs of pitted rock raised by mourners who had dwindled to dust long before the Romans came. And the sea's lost creatures came scuttling back to their mother across her cold sandy hem. There—Elise's two young brothers, shouting, whirling, their faces lit by morning, too glowing and good, surely, to encounter anything but joy. Mother, Father, arms outstretched, waiting on the hillside.

Oh, then . . . 1349. But these clouded images came less gladly.

By that year Elise had taken simple delight in seventeen summers and winters but still had found no man she would contentedly have for husband. Mother and Father did not urge her. Their good home was too happy to shake their eldest from it, if she was not yet prepared to be shaken.

That autumn arrived oddly warm and wet. Its dregs found Annora at the hearth, grim, but seemingly impervious to time or puny illness. She laced gruel with hope and herbs. All to no avail. For on a feather-stuffed mattress nearby, beneath embroidered sheets, lay Elise's brothers. Their wide-open eyes were milky and unseeing. Their limbs stretched straight and still forever.

Muffled prayers, muffled weeping. A fierce downpour.

Who would be next to die?

Elise's English mother, blonde, serene, a privileged beauty full of happy tales of lords and ladies she had known; on the Sabbath following her sons' deaths, she crept to her bed and did not rise again. "*Salva nos,*" she sang to the wall. Five nights. Swollen, stinking, black. *Salva nos.* Save us.

On their fine carved door a crimson cross, its new paint bleeding in the rain.

Father. Brave, strong Father next fell to the weight of grief and fever. He flung terrible epithets skyward as Annora tried, vainly, to spoon gruel into his wild mouth.

Elise? She was hale enough at first. But she shrank at the cry of any gull too near their window, any hiss of damp wood on the fire. Selfishly, so she thought, she studied to benumb herself before Father's end. Before Annora's. And her own.

All the while Death and his wife, so the saying went, perched on the eaves and cantered by each evening on their fine ebony stallions.

Father's handsome face grew gray, grotesque. But then, near the end, he brightened a little as he told Elise of his correspondence, when the Pestilence had first begun, with the prosperous distant cousin of a recently dead friend. On the mainland of North Wales this unknown cousin, one Maelgwyn, pious widower, was needful of a wife.

Father had smiled weakly. "*Mi a'th roddais i wr,*" his dying voice told her, observing, even then, the niceties of a proper Welsh betrothal. "I have given you to a man."

Lovingly, he'd meant to provide for her future. Understanding this, she cradled his heavy, swollen hand and thanked him. But she knew his final hope would come to nothing. She knew she too would soon be dead.

Indeed, after taking Father, the Pestilence bore down savagely on her. It raced molten through her blood. A suitor with mortal intentions, it offered oozing buboes, dread, and agony that could never be made malleable by any human language—not Welsh, not the English she'd spoken with her lovely mother, and not the tormented tongue the soul learns but the mouth can never utter.

She wept to God to let her join her family. But her prayers must have been too leaden to rise through a sky already choked with beseechings.

Finding her, she surmised, too difficult or paltry a bride, or perhaps glutted temporarily by its greedy feast of death, Pestilence withdrew its hand. Blue smoke coiled to the ceiling as the sickness raced off toward the moon.

Deo dilecti. Somehow, Elise had been chosen to survive.

Near her old home the bells at Penmon Priory tolled without ceasing. Three times three for the death of a man. Three times two for a woman. Three times one for a child.

The Augustinian monks at Penmon put their sturdy faith in the curative powers of Saint Seiriol's Well, there in the shadows of the priory. But they fell in droves, just like sinners. While Elise lay healing, running her fingers over her fading wounds and railing against the miracle that had dragged her back from the edge of Heaven, she imagined the monks in a dead circle. Tonsured heads met at Seiriol's indifferent pool. Chaste limbs splayed out to imitate the rays of a chilling sun.

"There is nothing the Devil detests more than the ringing of a church bell," a Penmon monk had told her once, in kinder times. She wondered if the Augustinians worried, with their final breaths, who on Anglesey would be left to toll the bells for them.

Scars bloom on memory. While this sad tale was two years past, crisis racked the present. Elise had killed a man. So she stood away from Annora, away from her steadfastness and affection.

She stared silently down at Maelgwyn.

Annora's gaze joined hers. Even as they watched, his manhood— which had been, surprisingly, still somewhat erect—drooped to one side. It shriveled and lost ruddiness before their eyes.

Annora mopped her face with her apron, then clicked her tongue. "Fie," she said, in a heartier voice than before. " 'Twas that not a mea- ger mallet to cause such consternation?"

"Twig or trunk, the townsfolk at Ysbyty Ifan will hang me. Or they'll rip me apart at the crossroads like a wishbone for the Devil."

"But the sodomite's not gone yet, Elise." She gestured to the slight rising and falling of Maelgwyn's chest. "He hangs by a thread. Likely he malingers to stave off his own reckoning."

"You're right. Oh, you're right." Elise brightened. Indeed, the man still breathed. "Then I'm duty-bound to fetch a priest from the hos- pice to administer the sacraments."

"What story will you give the fellow?" Annora's lips curled without humor. " 'My poor husband, there in a puddle of blood, has suc- cumbed to . . . unusually located piles. Only see the signs of them, there on his neck and—'"

"Stop." Elise pressed her palms to her eyes as panic threatened to engulf her. "Shall I just let him bleed to death?"

"Tempting." Annora nudged Maelgwyn's knee with the scuffed toe of her goatskin slipper. "But if you must, fetch the sheet and spread it beside him," she all at once instructed.

Elise asked, "Why?" but still hurried to do as she'd been bid.

"Think, girl. Who will tell of this? His own servants have all died or run off. The village and hospice are half an hour north. Besides, monks and villagers alike despised him, that's clear from everything I've heard. Child, they all pitied you. Tell me honestly, met you ever a soul, one single soul, who held Maelgwyn in esteem?"

Always strong for her slight stature, Annora bent, and rolled him without particular effort onto the sheet. Wrinkling her nose, she pulled his gray hosen completely down, past his white shanks and long-nailed toes, and she flung them to a corner. Then she straightened, while Elise stood by wringing her hands.

"We'll put him in the river," Annora said, huffing a little, "in that deep pool. The current will carry him off. Let the Lord decide if wild beasts should have him for tomorrow's breakfast, leagues away from here. Meanwhile we'll make his plan our own and say he fell to Pestilence."

"No. Oh, no." Elise knelt to chafe his hand. "There's a chance I can save him still. And so save myself."

"Yes? Then maybe he'll be so pleased to see you when he revives, he'll gift you with further proof of his love."

Elise released his hand as if it had burned her. As it dropped to his chest, she noticed a speckled spider, motionless, in a shadow near the door. Whose soul did it wait to collect?

Shaking her head to banish the thought, she turned again to Annora. "Don't you see? What I did was hideous, but I did it without forethought, to save myself from murder. This way is too considered. It will damn us as surely as all his sins damn him."

"Fine." Annora folded her arms across her chest. "Nurse him until he's strong enough to finish his deed. After that he can kill *me* lest I give word against him. Then if he still has inclination, he can acquaint some other sweet girl with his tender mode of love, take a third joyous bride."

" 'Thou shalt not kill.' Oh, Annora, we can't—"

Annora's lips became a thin line. She would not be bested with mere Scripture. She drew the sheet up and over the length of Maelgwyn's body, one side, then the other. Then she rose, gray head held high.

Exhausted, bewildered, Elise considered the makeshift shroud.

Could she agree to this desperate scheme? If she did not, could she allow Annora to take matters into her own hands, as she surely would, and bear responsibility for her crime?

In the shadows, the spider waited.

Elise raised her head to meet the eyes of her old friend, and needed no vision to know she would regret her work of this night.

3

WHAT THE RIVER KNOWS

Stopping for breath whenever their burden grew too heavy, they dragged Maelgwyn—draped in the wool sheet, bound with leather cords—down the stairs, across the firelit great hall, past the carved screens that shielded the hall from the front and rear doors, through the winter parlor, the buttery, and out the door by the kitchen court. Then, more slowly because of the rough, wet ground, they went on, past the neglected bakehouse, the brewhouse, along the path to the river. Elise had thrown on an undertunic and a brown surcoat, tied her hair back with a green ribbon, and donned cordwain shoes. Battered wooden clogs kept her above the mud.

The fitful wind had settled to a constant breeze and blown the clouds away. A thousand stars and a full yellow moon shimmered on the water, and on Maelgwyn's barely breathing form. Death would likely take him before the first or second bend.

Swollen by the heavy rain of that cold summer, the Conwy River sang over rocks and shoals as the women stood on its bank.

"May God have mercy on the soul of my husband, Maelgwyn," Elise said, crossing herself. An icy draft slid up her spine.

Observing her, Annora said, "Be dauntless, cariad. This night won't last forever."

But Elise feared it might.

Together they rolled Maelgwyn over the bank. He hit the opaque river with a startling splash, and the echo of the splash chased itself to the edge of the Migneint Moor. Beyond.

But as soon as the echo faded, one corner of the shroud was captured, peeled back by an eddy. Bent at an unnatural angle, Maelgwyn's elbow broke the surface of the water. Next, his white face. Annora turned away, looked to the sky, and shrugged. Then she nodded to herself.

But Elise was unable to take her gaze from her husband's gently bobbing form. She continued to stare after him. As if to punish her morbid regard, a malicious beam of moonlight landed directly upon his ghostly lips. It showed them curving upward. Then its beam spread to encompass his eyes.

Did one pale eyelid flutter?

Elise blinked.

No. No, his face was still as stone. It was only a trick of the moon, or the river.

The current finally captured the body and carried it away.

All the while the Conwy rippled and moaned.

Annora sprinkled pebbles into the water as Elise stared downriver. The scent of damsons was borne on the breeze, along with the ever-present stink of the privy.

"Just hope," said Annora, wiping her hands on her apron, "no ale-swigging priest wanders off from the hospice to empty his bladder into the river when that son of Beelzebub floats by."

Elise gasped at this somehow unconsidered possibility.

Seeing her alarm, Annora turned fully toward her, hands on her hips. "Elise, where has your brain gone begging? A body, even partly unshrouded—what would anyone but a simpleton assume, still yet, seeing it go drifting by?"

Elise drooped with relief. "Pestilence."

"Aye, most likely. Or they might suppose he's a poor soldier, lately shipped home to die of hurts inflicted in France. Either way, they're sure to let him go on drifting. There would be no profit in fishing him out."

An owl hooted just across the river. Not long after, there rose a sharp little scream that ceased mid-cry—a star-crossed vole or rabbit.

"Is no creature safe tonight?" Elise wondered aloud, then gazed down again at the water.

"No creature is ever safe, child, and we'd be fools to imagine else. Since there's nought to do to change that, we'll think of more hopeful things." She cocked her head and gave her unhappy friend a considering look. "Has it occurred to you yet that you're free, a widow? In fact, it would be a good idea to throw your wedding ring into the deep. You won't need it anymore."

Moonlight bathed them. It washed away all color as they stood by the singing river.

"Widow," Elise said. "And murderess." But she tugged off the ring with alacrity and threw it in the Conwy.

"Doesn't that feel better? But Maelgwyn doomed himself, cariad. You're no murderess."

"I am." Looking down at her clogs, she gave a bitter laugh. "Murderess, widow. How could it be so, in the space of one single day?"

"I tell you, you've rid the world of a beast."

"With my whole heart I wish I could believe you."

"It's pure righteousness, sometimes, to strike. If any man in your family had survived the Pestilence, he would have killed Maelgwyn for you. Readily, with God's wrath in his sword arm."

"Truly? Don't the priests always say we women should submit ourselves to our husbands?"

"Even husbands who torment their wives, and use them worse than swine?" It was Annora's turn to cross herself. "There are men in this world who aren't monsters, child."

"So I once believed . . . but I've been dreaming of the cloister."

"Cariad." Dismay was writ large upon Annora's moonlit face. "Sweaty wimples, hellish food. All those brides of Christ under one thwarted roof. And what abbess in Britain would take kindly to your visions? Child, we cannot."

Her "we" almost made Elise smile. It meant Annora had no intention of letting her fend for herself, in a convent or anywhere else. But harder truth lurked beneath their words. They both understood without saying that they'd be obliged to quit Gray Hill by the morning.

They trudged up the path to the old house, to its shadows, its blood-stained floor, and its spiders. How could they stay? How could they linger in a house that harbored so many nightmares?

Ten paces from the worn stone steps Elise faltered, then went on, pretending she might indeed be dauntless. She prayed Maelgwyn's ghost would slumber peaceful with his corpse, that body and spirit both would flow with the Conwy River past the places of men, unhindered, to oblivion.

Before mounting the manor steps she stooped to pluck three damp sprigs of rue from a clump growing wild near the path. She would weave a green and yellow bracelet and wear it tight against her skin so she would not be tempted to forget the thing she had done.

But already she sensed Maelgwyn's essence fading, and every trace of his dark memory with it.

Though she tried her best to quell it, a tiny flame of joy, in her secret heart, would not be quite extinguished.

4

HOSTAGE

While he lived, the titles Count of Eu and Constable of France rested upon the shoulders of one and the same man: Raoul de Brienne. In the second week of November 1350, this noble gentleman crossed the heaving water from Dover to Calais, in a humble, unobtrusive vessel. As he set foot on his native French soil for the first time in five years, his mood was not initially as buoyant as he had often dreamed it might be; he suffered lingering effects of an unpleasant case of mal de mer.

The count was a military hostage. Taken for ransom at the sack of Caen five years earlier, he had been borne west across the Channel and rather comfortably confined outside London near Windsor Castle since that time. Regrettably, his prolonged captivity had resulted in the amassing of hardly any of the eighty thousand gold écus Edward III of England was demanding for his release.

Disembarking at Calais, he was taken into civilized custody, as had been prearranged, by a tall British nobleman who spoke impeccable French and dressed with simple elegance. This new minder, Gwydion ap Gruffydd, was to accompany de Brienne to Paris with half a dozen unassuming but able British soldiers. The French government had been earlier apprised of the group's route and its peaceable and important raison d'être and so allowed it to move southward unmolested through the chilly November countryside.

The homecoming Frenchman had no cause for complaint with his escort. Gwydion ap Gruffydd had been in France for four years performing a variety of undisclosed and unheralded diplomatic tasks for the English government. He was civilized, discreet, and gracious in his temporary guardianship of de Brienne. He readily allowed his prisoner to make several halts at snug inns and brothels along the way from Calais to Paris. He even gladly joined the count in his repasts and carousings.

The whole party was nevertheless aware of the need to hasten on
to Paris. Raoul de Brienne had an important appointment there with
his illustrious family's legal representatives. Cash-poor but rich in
land, the count had arranged to sign away his castle and some acreage
at Guines, six miles south of Calais, to the English king. In lieu of the
eighty thousand écus, land would thus purchase his freedom at last.

This bargain was hardly unique in the long-running war between
France and England. Wealthy hostages were the stuff of lucrative
barter and bribe that oiled the war machines on both sides of the conflict. Hostages were often allowed to come and go in their own or their
enemy's land if their movements accomplished the gathering of funds
or the securing of desirable property to help obtain their release. It
was an honorable combatants' system that had worked satisfactorily
since the war began in 1337.

But in France's capital city, things went disastrously wrong.

By virtue of his unlamented father's natural death, King John II
had been ruler of the French for less than three months by November of 1350. In the regular course of such matters, he'd been advised
of the famous and affable Count of Eu's intention to trade land and
a castle for freedom. But far from considering it business as usual,
the fledgling monarch apparently believed the exchange would
gravely jeopardize French security. King John was furious. What had
seemed to Raoul de Brienne a reasonable transaction, not much different from a dozen others before it, was suddenly decried as the
worst sort of treachery.

John II's wellborn advisor and crony, Charles of La Cerda, a
twenty-four-year-old Castilian political exile, was rumored to be the
real force behind the new king's extreme reaction to de Brienne's intended bargain. Charles was ambitious and intelligent, but ruthless
and arrogant as well. Cynical observers said he saw a place for himself
as constable of France if the existing constable could be eliminated.

On November 16, 1350, Raoul de Brienne was arrested, along
with his English minder, Gwydion ap Gruffydd. The charge given was
treason.

The next morning the count was executed at John II's rambling
Parisian mansion, Hôtel de Nesle.

Gwydion ap Gruffydd, as a ransomable member of a noble and

wealthy British family, was offhandedly given as prisoner to King John's accommodating friend, Charles of La Cerda, to keep as Charles saw fit until a ransom payment could be procured from across the Channel.

The extravagantly dressed Castilian took an instant dislike to his new hostage. Though perhaps a mere five or so years separated them—Charles being the younger—the tall Briton regarded his warden with a disquieting gaze. Remarkably, considering the great admiration in which Charles held himself, that gaze soon made him feel small and even gauche. The man's dark eyes took in Charles's sparkling rings and medals and his fashionable clothes, and those eyes seemed amused, perhaps even contemptuous.

How could that be? the Spaniard wondered. Did he not know with whom he dealt? Should his foreign insolence be endured for one moment by a close and increasingly powerful friend of the king of France?

On the east side of Paris, near Porte Saint-Antoine, Charles of La Cerda maintained a fortresslike mansion he rarely visited. From its upper windows the old Roman Road leading to Melun could be glimpsed. Inside this well-guarded house Charles imprisoned Gwydion ap Gruffydd.

On the first morning of the internment, the two men stood at opposite ends of the small, cold room that would serve as Gwydion's cell.

"You are fortunate, my friend," said Charles, standing at his ease near the room's only door while a flat-faced guard hunkered outside in the hall. "For this is rather a homey chamber, is it not? With its own little window too. I realize there are no furnishings, but it has a certain austere charm, yes? And while you're my guest, my men will faithfully bring you slop for your dinner and perhaps an occasional bottle of France's most abominable wine. Something special."

"I will be in your debt," said Gwydion, his eyes hooded.

"Undoubtedly. Although it will create extra work for me, I'll endeavor to personally select the vintage. I trust that will be sufficient for such a great lord as yourself." This sneering speech reflected Charles's rapidly mounting wish to humble his patently overproud captive.

Through the narrow, unglazed window Gwydion considered the view toward the Roman Road. "Thank you again. But now I'd like ink and parchment to send word to my people so they might make arrangements for my ransom." He spoke without heat and betrayed no outward sign of concern for his predicament.

His calm demeanor further goaded Charles, who was much more accustomed to being shown slavish respect than to being waved off for writing supplies like a servant. He gave a spiteful response. "You're in too sad a rush to escape my hospitality, I think. But no, Gwydion ap Gruffydd. I'm afraid it won't be quite as painless as that. I've decided your lack of proper respect has now earned you a lengthier sojourn in Paris."

His prisoner did not reply. Merely he turned from the window to fix his host with his dark unreadable gaze.

Charles hated the unusual but undeniable sensation now assailing him that *he*, who clearly ought to be master of this situation, was being overtly judged and found wanting. "What sort of English name is it that you possess?" he suddenly asked, to repel this displeasing notion. He infused his voice with as much disdain as he was able, and it was considerable. "Gwydion ap Gruffydd. It has a remarkably crude and discordant sound, I think, even for an English name."

The tall man leaned his shoulder against the wall and once more gazed out the window. "My father is Welsh."

"Welsh?" La Cerda's eyes all at once gleamed with a mixture of malicious amusement and relief. "But now I understand. Suddenly it's all quite clear. You're Welsh. So you really can't help your lack of grace or manners, since you hail from a wretched patch of dirt known by all as a breeding place for filthy whores, whoresons, and hovels. I can picture your greasy hearthside, now that you've told me."

Gwydion stifled a yawn. "Can you?"

Inoffensive in themselves, these two words nevertheless incensed Charles afresh. "I can," he said, gripping his sword's hilt and taking a step toward his hostage. "You're not really a nobleman at all, are you, Gwydion ap Gruffydd? You're only an inconsequential barbarian."

"Since I am at your mercy, Charles, every word you utter must necessarily be true."

"You're wise to realize it." The Castilian took a steadying breath and fought down his rage. "But as you've now unveiled yourself as such a negligible fellow, I see no need to rush to help you secure your freedom. You'll linger here, Welshman. Permit my clumsy but earnest guards to entertain you in my absence. Mayhap I shall come from time to time to assure myself you are well looked after."

"Your adopted king might not appreciate having a sizable ransom delayed by personal umbrage, or whatever strange emotion it is that now overwhelms your judgment."

Charles knew this was true, but the knowledge only caused him to rush suddenly forward and strike Gwydion across the face with his leather-gloved hand. "No, he might not," he said, panting a little as he backed away. "But who will tell him? Do you suppose the king can spare a thought for your existence now you're gone from his sight?"

With the back of his hand, Gwydion wiped a trickle of blood from his cheek. "I begin to understand your methods. But is this some peculiar Castilian code of honor you follow, or is it all your own invention?"

A flush started at Charles's neck and crept to his high cheekbones. "I doubt you'll be so bold after you've languished here for weeks. Perhaps eventually your manners will improve."

"I doubt it. We filthy Welsh are damnably bloody-minded."

Charles moved to the doorway. "Then I'll instruct my men to try to wear down your rough edges in my absence. But I'll save your final lesson in deportment for myself, of course. I anticipate the day."

"I will still be unarmed, naturally."

Charles smiled. "Naturally. A true gentleman need not trouble himself with whimpers of disparity from the more vulgar classes."

The Castilian departed, banging the door shut behind him. A key grated in the lock.

Gwydion ap Gruffydd sighed and immediately began a thorough inspection of his cell, of the window too narrow for an infant to squeeze through, and the thick walls and door. Seeing no obvious means of escape, he made an inadequate bed of his long black cloak and stretched out on it. He was weary. He stared up at the ceiling and considered the events of the past week.

Poor de Brienne. Well, at least his final days had been happy. Gwydion half smiled, picturing in his mind's eye his likable hostage at an inn near Cambrai. Raoul had supported a pretty mademoiselle on each knee, as had he. A plate of cakes and three bottles of wine sat on the table before them. Only four days ago that had been. Now the count was dead.

What sort of king did France find itself ruled by? What sort of man chose to be advised by such glittery, spiteful popinjays as Charles of La Cerda?

More importantly, at least to Gwydion—where were his six comrades? He hoped they had managed to evade French justice, and Castilian. He hoped his old friend William, the most wily and audacious of the lot, would discover his whereabouts and learn the character of the man who held him hostage. William had never been one to abandon a friend to trouble.

Gwydion closed his eyes and slept.

5

OMENS

Back inside Gray Hill, Annora took two rush bundles from the wooden box by the entrance court door and bustled across the great hall. Mid-room, she bent to ignite the bundles from the hall's central fire. As she did, a glowing cinder spit itself over the iron firedogs and landed between her feet. Holding the now flickering rushes away from herself, she rose, and kicked the cinder back toward the raised hearth.

"A good omen, cariad," she called over her shoulder. "If a cinder drops at your feet, it means a journey will go safely."

Discreetly slipping the rue bracelet over her wrist, Elise tried to answer lightly. "If it burnt a hole in your hem, Annora, you'd say it meant we could expect a fine, warm summer. Or a feast with gilded, baked swans. Have you never encountered a bad omen?"

"One or two only. But I don't have your gift for prophecy."

"If gift it is, then it's haphazard and nearly useless." On the open-timbered ceiling high over the hall's circular fire, smoke-drawing louvers rattled in the breeze. Elise shivered, drifting nearer Annora and the hearth. Looking into the flames, she shifted to the subject most oppressive to her mind. "If we leave, what will happen? Chance visitors will find this place empty, even of bodies. Won't they wonder why we've all vanished? Won't there be an alarm raised in the countryside?"

"I think not," said her friend, tossing a thumb-sized bit of kindling into the fire. "Not if we mark the doors with painted crosses and let them swing on their hinges. Not if we leave a trail of fouled sickness rags from the solar, down the stairs, all the way to the river."

"Rags and crosses?" Elise tucked a strand of hair behind her ear. She noted that her fingers had not finished with their trembling. Then she remembered her most hellish glimpse of a red-daubed door; it had been on Anglesey, at her old home.

"I'll mark them the last thing, after you're well down the path. So you needn't see," said Annora, as if she had read her young friend's mind. "Next week or next month, anyone passing this blighted place will think we've been swallowed by Pestilence. The lot of us." She smiled grimly. "They'll think our boils drove us mad and we've leaped into the river. Or that we staggered weeping to the moor. After seeing such talebearing rags as I shall fashion, who would search out our noxious bones for a proper Christian burial?"

Elise's throat felt much as it had when Maelgwyn's hands ringed it. "This scheme sits badly on me," she said. "Might it not alert Death he has unfinished business with us both? You came away untouched by the Pestilence. A rare enough thing, everyone says. By another twist of fate, I managed to survive. But now I'm not so eager to die as once I was."

"You think I've forgotten those days, Elise? But surely you comprehend, our need is too dire for scruples. We can't pretend there's not the smallest risk of discovery of our sham. We have no choice. We can't go back, only forward," she said, more briskly, offering Elise a smoking torch. "Go, child. Light up the edges of the buttery. Hurry there now and gather provisions for a journey. You'll be happier with a task."

Elise accepted a bundle reluctantly. "What will you do?"

"Take what is yours from the solar. A dress or two, the hip-belt, the silver crucifix and chain." She had already crossed the hall to the foot of the stairs. "Then I'll erase signs of Maelgwyn's excess spillage from the floor."

"Wait," Elise called. "The crucifix and hip-belt are mine, for I brought them with me here. But I want nothing of Maelgwyn's. No money he has touched or brooch or fine cloth. Everything he touched is tainted. Annora, do you understand me?"

The gray-haired woman started up the steps. Hearing the solar door creak open in a moment, Elise turned away, sighing.

In the buttery she lit three candles she found pushed to the back of a shelf. Mere stubs, they burned fitfully in old brass holders. But any light was welcome, for she wanted no dark corners.

A cupboard yielded most of what they might need for their flight. On the work table she had soon collected a leather beaker, two knives and a spoon, two goats' bladders filled with ale, a hunk of ripe cheese, and the remaining three loaves of heavy brown bread she'd baked earlier in the week. Forests they would likely pass through might provide further sustenance—herbs, nuts, and berries.

Taking her torch, Elise walked back out to the passageway between the great hall and the wooden screens. From an alcove there she drew out two stout yew staffs where they waited upright beside the idle meat skewer. They would need the staffs to test the depth of streams or rivers they might cross, perhaps also to protect themselves from wild boars or dogs—or from robbers and other lawless men.

Bearing two folded dresses, and with Elise's belt and silver chain dangling from her fingers, Annora joined her a little later in the buttery as Elise packed tools and provisions into two gray sacks sewn of rough carry-marry. Just then one of the candle stubs burnt out, expiring in an adder of smoke. Moving more swiftly by unspoken agreement, they secured the sacks with thick strings looped for carrying and went out to the great hall.

It was brighter there. On the walls hung old tapestries, their once-upon-a-time scenes faded by soot and neglect to almost nothing. At the dais end of the room, raised one step, sat the long feast table. It was visibly warped and bowed at its center. Elise had never seen that poor table laden with any fare. Maelgwyn had certainly dined in the hall, but he preferred to eat alone—"away from the gnaw of female chatter"—using a narrow stone bench as both table and seat. Annora and Elise always took their meals in the buttery.

Though large and well appointed, Gray Hill was not a house that welcomed merriment. At least not under Maelgwyn's regime. His father had been a good man, an open-hearted man. So it was said. Elise often wondered what had happened to make Maelgwyn so opposite, so bent toward misery.

If she had spoken, the woman in her vision, the woman by the river, would she have provided an answer to that question? Who was she? What could have caused the fear in Maelgwyn's eyes?

Now that he was dead, those questions would never be answered.

Elise's gaze fell to the filthy rushes scattered over the dirt floor. On Anglesey her mother had had rushes swept away with every new moon, for she had not favored their burgeoning ripeness. But Maelgwyn hadn't been inclined to waste money on fresh rushes too often. "Once a year is sufficient. The day before Easter, to honor the Resurrection," he had said. "Only a house-proud woman would squander her husband's coin more frequently than that, just for the sake of show." With his usual arbitrariness, he had not considered his glass windowpanes frivolous, though he had bragged of their expense and proclaimed them the only ones for miles around.

Even as Elise remembered that bit of meanness, a gray mouse scurried across the floor. It made a rustling sound and a little path through the rushes as it ran toward the screens.

"Aha," said Annora, as the mouse disappeared. "Mayhap that was the new lord and master. He can't fail to be an improvement."

Elise rounded quickly on her, preparing to object.

Annora forestalled her. "Child," she said, raising a hand, "you have the look of a hobbled cow before the fall slaughter. Would you have us sing dirges, dust ourselves with ashes, and never laugh again?"

"My husband is dead. I stabbed him with broken glass and rolled his body into the river. He has had no priest to comfort him, no blessed sacrament. What easy jest can alter that?"

"What sacrament would have made him acceptable to Heaven?" Annora pursed her lips. "Would it pretty away every rape you suffered, every cruel thing he did to you in these two years?" Her voice grew thick with angry new tears. "You know the particulars of your union better than I. I only cowered in my corner and allowed you to suffer. So instruct me. Would a marble effigy bearing a scroll at its edges— here lies Maelgwyn, of famous reputation—would it change him to a saint?"

"I don't know." Elise shook her head as if to ward off Annora's logic. "But however Heaven deals with Maelgwyn, what tale will *my* effigy tell?"

Annora pulled Elise gently into her arms for the second time that night, and Elise did not resist. "Heaven will know you for its own, child. You'll join your family there. Oh, but not for years and years."

Elise held tightly to her old nurse, her friend. She savored her warmth and breathed in the familiar scent of lye rising off her flanella dress. "You'll be waiting with them, won't you?" she said. "Will you be standing at the gate, all shining gold and beautiful?"

"Shining gold and beautiful?" Annora gave a watery chuckle. "That will be one of the Maker's better tricks."

After a moment Elise pulled away, as another question niggled. "Do you think anyone will ever live here again? Or will this house sit haunted and sad forever?"

"A few weeks, more like. They say prostitutes, halfwits, and runaway friars live now in abandoned manors all over Britain."

"Why?"

"Rich and poor alike died of the sickness, Elise. As we know too well. Why wouldn't a person claim an empty house fifty times grander than their own, if they ever had one, when there's no one left in that house to say nay?" She gave an indelicate snort. "Likely there are scores of such new dwellers. Scullery maids tarted up in dead ladies' silks, and never-bathed louts astride fine stallions, on jeweled saddles."

"What of Bron-haul?" Hillside of the Sun, their old home on Anglesey. "Could that be its fate?"

"It was a fine house, a temptation for any wretched wanderer. You weren't thinking of going back, child? Living with the shades of old hours all around us?"

"I do think of Bron-haul sometimes. So empty and cold. But truly, though I know you mislike the idea of the cloister, it—"

"Bah!" Annora shook a pink fist at the ceiling. "The cloister will not do. I've already told you it will not do."

"Then where? Sad to say, we have no protector. Since when does the world take kindly to poor, unattached females?"

"The world has changed, I think. With so many dead, there must be everywhere a clamor for workers. Or young wives."

Elise shook her head. "If I must be a bride again, I will only wed the Church. At least then I will be certain to share a bed with no one but the Holy Spirit."

As Elise spoke, Annora took her hand and led her to a stool, motioning her to sit. She sank down, unobjecting. Drawing an ivory comb from her sleeve, Annora moved behind her and released her brown hair from its ribbon. The comb tugged through long, snarled curls. After the snarls had given way to smoothness, the comb's rhythmic rise and fall was so soothing to Elise that she let her eyes drift shut and reveled in the reassuring feel of such an everyday thing.

"You do love to have your hair combed," said Annora, in the singsong voice she had used to calm her since Elise was a child. "Part it down the middle, braid it into two plaits, twist the plaits low." She suited words to deft actions, humming snatches of a lullaby between. "Around the back, across the nape, tuck the ends atop. I've even pins to secure it. Clever, am I not?"

When one of the pins nicked Elise's scalp, she opened her eyes. Just then the mouse, or its cousin, made another dash through the rushes.

Her old friend came around to face her. "You couldn't begin a journey with your hair all streaming down your back, could you?"

"Now I look respectable?"

"You're a good and innocent lady, and so you naturally appear." Annora tucked the comb back in her sleeve. "But now it grows late, or early. We ought to make a timely start if we hope to have the whole of the day before us to walk. It's a pity Maelgwyn no longer boasts horse or cart. Still, the hour rushes onward."

Attesting to the truth of that, a song thrush began a brave predawn refrain, very near. Probably it perched on the roof.

Annora cupped her ear. "One more lucky sign," she said. "Now we're certain to be blessed."

"But the thrush sings every morning, every evening."

"Listen keenly, child. It sounds more hopeful now."

By the time they were ready to leave Gray Hill, the sky had grown rosy in the east. The day promised to be clear and dry.

In that easterly direction from where light would soon spill over the edge of Wales, the old Monks' Trackway meandered through marshes and over wet green hills. It ended at ancient Bangor-is-y-Coed, the ruined Monastery under the Wood, on the River Dee. Long ago that place had witnessed the slaughter of a thousand monks, so Father had once told Elise and her wide-eyed brothers. Before a terrible battle, the monks were hacked to bits—while on their knees, beseeching God for peace—by a Saxon king who did not admire their particular style of Christian prayer.

Between Ysbyty Ifan and Bangor-is-y-Coed lay Foel Frech. Traveling that way, one left behind the streams flowing north, into the

Conwy, and from there to the Irish Sea. Streams ahead emptied south, into the Dee. Past Foel Frech were Cerigydrudion, Betws Gwerfyl, Gwyddelwern, and Bryneglwys. All were sites of turf-and-wattle churches, or rather, their lonely husks, built in the dark days after the Romans abandoned Britain. Fervent days they must have been, though, to spawn so many houses for God. Not far beyond was Valle Crucis, a Cistercian abbey. Past the abbey was Offa's Dyke, the great wall raised by a long-dead Mercian king to repel Welsh invaders.

Part of what she knew of the Trackway Elise had learned from her father, of course. But many tales came from Maelgwyn during long evenings in his great hall. How he had loved to parade his knowledge. Had Maelgwyn but known it, Elise's only interest then had been to delay their retiring for as long as possible. So she'd kept him talking with dozens of artless questions he'd been pleased to condescend to answer. She had heard his stories many times and could recite most herself.

Because of Maelgwyn's endless discourse she could walk the Trackway in either direction—in her mind, at least. In truth, except for the marshes, to travel east might be a joy for the devout pilgrim or the student of history. But Annora and Elise were neither.

They would not walk toward the rising sun; that way would be too daunting, too unknown except in story. Though neither of them said it aloud, both understood they would go northwest. Elise knew they would begin their journey on the Trackway. But when the Trackway went on too steadily westward, somewhere near Dolwyddelan, when it led other travelers toward Clynnog Fawr, she and Annora would take the less holy but more necessary route to the north. Eventually, barring misfortune, they would reach Conwy Town.

Perhaps one day when they were safe and settled, they would even cross the Menai Straits, go by ferry on a personal pilgrimage—back to Anglesey. They'd traverse that familiar flat island to Beaumaris and go on to their old home.

How Elise longed for home.

Simple enough in Conwy or Beaumaris, with God's blessing or at least His benign indifference, to hide among the native Welsh and the English, their subjugators since 1282. Conwy and Beaumaris were both places where the fierce English king, Edward I, grandfather of the present monarch, had built great castles. He had peopled them with English settlers to lord over the resentful Welsh. Because of her mixed parentage Elise knew she could pass for either race and smooth their way as translator.

If Annora spoke true, it would be easy enough to find decent work. After all, the world was a place of such grossly diminished population. Though Elise's family had been well moneyed, she was not afraid to work. Both she and Annora were knowledgeable enough about herb lore and healing arts to assist some simpler or apothecary. If the place they finally found themselves boasted no such person, then they could even set up shop themselves. After all, each had been treating family and neighbors for years.

Elise had inherited her skill with medicine and simples from her mother, Katherine, who had been raised with all the trappings of wealth. Katherine had never been compelled by necessity to forgo expensive physicians and their regimes, but from her youth she had showed instinctive love and understanding of natural healing. High or low, no one in the English village where she grew up hesitated to come to her for help, for gentle discernment.

Annora gained her knowledge in a more mundane way; cruel thrift was master at her childhood home on Anglesey. Doctors were never a consideration or even a possibility. But the fields surrounding her family's cottage at Bodgyched, inland from Beaumaris, provided a free and dependable array of green cures. Long before she reached her final modest height, Annora knew all the plants and the healing recipes to which they contributed.

Thus Elise and Annora were both adept at making salves, plasters, flower charms, powders, and the like. Both enjoyed the doing of it too, as pleasure is derived from laboring with confidence and proficiency. Each woman also knew a variety of other ways to soothe a sufferer. They knew a lady might find prayer to Mother Mary beneficial during her monthly troubles. They knew the spleen was the seat of laughter and the liver the seat of honor, and that opening the Holy Bible and reading the first verse to spontaneously attract the forefinger of the right hand could give clues about health or life concerns. But this practice, called sacred lots, was only used by Elise, as Annora could not read.

Elise had been an inquisitive firstborn who was doted upon by her parents. Surprised by their daughter's eagerness for knowledge, but also rather pleased by it, they had hired a priest to teach their bright girl how to read Latin as well as English and Welsh. She was eight when her unconventional lessons began. Neighbors had warned that she was in danger of becoming better educated than most of the men on Anglesey, and woefully overeducated for a female. But her parents let the lessons continue until her fourteenth year, so sincere and obvious was her pleasure in learning.

Sometimes Annora or Elise might tell a patient to eat more vegetables, to offset a preponderance of ale and grains and meat. If caterpillars took too high a toll on a vegetable patch thus prescribed, the patient would be advised to place a bone from a mare's head at the garden's edge to chase the caterpillars away.

The women also had knowledge to share with families of those who could not be saved; when a loved one died, they enjoined relatives to remove from the house all basins of water, all pitchers of drink, for a fortnight. Otherwise the dead soul might see its reflection in the liquid and drown. Another thing Annora and Elise understood: if the left eye of the deceased refused to close properly, another member of the family would also die soon.

They accepted without doubt that the soul of an infant who expires before its baptism becomes a will-o'-the-wisp. Eerie haze over marshland on any given night demonstrated the truth and sad frequency of that occurrence.

With all this portable knowledge, Annora and Elise surely could find decent work here or there. Surely. But whether in an herbalist's cellar, a cloister, or a hovel, Elise wanted only to forget the past two years, the past day, and live out her hours in unmolested peace. She wanted Annora to wear again her onetime glow of contentment.

Still, though she'd endeavor to hide it from her old friend, in her heart she feared a thousand things.

She feared the past, the present, and the future. All three. She feared their journey, and the nights along the way. Would they sleep in a teeming market town, a black wood? On an empty, whispering meadow? Doomed men changed into wolves by Satan sometimes attacked vulnerable travelers, she'd heard. Or ruthless *mortal* men could steal their sacks, break their bones, and leave them bloody in a twilight glade. What of evil lepers, seeing in them an easy target for their infamous and diseased lust?

Then, in Conwy, should they be lucky enough to make it so far, who would give them work? Who, in truth, would not be leery of two unaccompanied women? Would she and Annora ever know a moment of joy or ease, if they reached their journey's end?

Another secret fear: she feared she'd dream of Maelgwyn, see his punctured throat in the river, his dead smile, see those cold blue eyes that would accuse and condemn her until she did not breathe again. As he did not breathe.

But there was even worse. She feared dreaming of her lost family. She feared longing for love without hope, forever.

Finally, in dreadful imitation of Maelgwyn's terror for himself, she feared witnessing in a vision her own damnation.

The sun shone brightly when Annora joined her on the path.

"Done, and mightily convincing," she said. "I used ashes and the juice of beetroot"—she paused to catch her breath—"to mark the doors and color the rags." Her gray tresses and beige wimple were now more ordered and presentable.

In their long cloaks, Annora's tawny, Elise's deep blue, they began to walk. West, over green slopes dotted with middling trees. If the morning went well, the first place they would come to was Bryn Llech, Hill of the Flat Stones. Then Penmachno, a village where they knew no one. But going would be slow, for neither had slept.

Woodsmoke from the hearth of a distant cottage or shepherd's camp rose on the wind, to the southwest, drifting above like the fronds of gray ferns. After the smoke blew away, the women smelled apples and dead fish.

"We're blessed the way is dry," said Annora, when they'd walked in silence a while. "This track is less used than the one that brought us this way before. I feared it might be a quagmire."

"Nor is it so steep as I imagined," Elise said. "But I remember hardly anything of our journey two years ago. It was like a bad dream, always gray, hemmed in by spying trees."

Maelgwyn had dispatched a covered cart to collect his orphaned bride and her servant. The cart was pulled by a horse of dull gray, and the driver wore a pilgrim's hat as gray as the horse's hide. From the hat's brim a small ampule had dangled, not an unusual thing. Eager for diversion by the second day of their dreary trek, Elise had asked the fellow what the ampule held. Holy water? A strand of martyr's hair?

"Thomas à Becket's blood," he'd answered, his eyes fixed on the dark road ahead. "One fat red drop, for mercy."

Though he had not looked a devout sort of man, he'd made a pilgrimage to Becket's shrine at Canterbury, or stolen the ampule from someone who had. The women never knew more than that. For the fellow, one of Maelgwyn's dwindling number of servants, disappeared a week after their arrival at Gray Hill, along with the horse and cart— much to Maelgwyn's fury.

Annora and Elise walked on.

When she sensed Annora's gaze, Elise turned to her.

"Cariad, your cheek has not grown as bruised as I thought it might. But you seem so solemn," Annora said quietly, her face showing its age as it never had before, her manner and gait less certain. "Remember how you used to dance, tell fine stories, and count the stars with your brothers? Remember how your mother called you all in from the hill? 'Angels, angels, to bed,' she'd say. 'The stars will be there tomorrow.'"

"Mother was right, the stars are still there. I suppose they will always be there." It seemed strange to Elise, as she said this, that her voice barely shook.

"Things can never be the same, child. But I'd dearly love to see you dance again, or hear one of your happy tales. You can't be sad forever." She glanced over at the younger woman. "Or be afraid forever."

"Afraid?" Elise ripped a laugh from some hidden cache inside herself, knowing the price for such a pretense of joy was sure to be high. "I'm not afraid. I feel dauntless enough for the pair of us." Lifting the corners of her mouth, she gave what she hoped was a credible smile, to act as crutch for her laugh. "Truly, I'm more excited than afraid."

Annora stumbled on the nub of a tree root. Elise reached out to steady her, but she waved away the offered hand.

In a moment Annora produced her own overbright grin. "Ah, you've always been my dauntless girl. My sweet, dauntless girl. So—as

the Lord is sure to be our guide—I know we will be happy and safe."
She swung an arm skyward and around, blithely, as if to embrace the
morning.

Elise kept her own smile pinned in place but didn't meet her
friend's eyes.

They walked. Behind them, the thrush called. Its song grew fainter
and fainter, until it could not be heard at all.

6

HOSPITALITY

During the third week of his captivity in Paris, two of Gwydion's guards kicked him awake and manacled his wrists together.

"Come on, Welshman," said the guard with the flat face. "You've had enough beauty sleep. It's almost daylight. Rise and shine and stand on your feet like a good boy."

Gwydion struggled up. His bound hands went to his side as if reaching for a weapon.

Watching him, the second guard let out a guffaw. "Look at the fool. He thinks he's going for his sword. Only there's nothing there, Guy, nothing at all."

The guards dragged Gwydion forward until he faced the wall. Then they looped a chain around his manacles and attached the chain to an iron ring pounded shoulder-high into the stone. "Our fine Charles sent word he's coming to visit you today, Welshman," said Guy. "So Yves and me decided we better get you looking a little more fit to be seen. Otherwise he might think we're not paying you sufficient attention."

Yves nodded solemnly. "Otherwise he might think we've been ignoring his special guest. That would get him upset. You surely don't want our Charles upset. He's nobody's darling if he's peeved, I promise."

Guy ripped Gwydion's shirt upward, exposing his back and broad shoulders. "It grieves me to say some of the ladies might not fancy the stripes we're going to decorate you with today, Welshman," he said. "Then again, some might. You never know, with women."

Yves pulled a double-tailed scourge from his belt and cracked its leather thongs through the air a few times for effect. He grinned at the sound. "Ready?" he said. Receiving no reply, he lashed the thongs down across the middle of Gwydion's back.

"Throw your weight into it," said Guy, shaking his head and scowling. "This great fellow's thick-skinned. Christ's sake, I don't think he even felt that. He barely flinched."

Yves took a deep breath, braced himself, and reared back. He struck eight times in quick succession, grunting mightily after each blow.

"Not so wild," said Guy, stepping away. "You nearly had my nose that last time."

"Then move the ugly thing," said Yves. He wiped his mouth with his free hand and replanted his feet in the straw. Then he struck six times more, even harder.

Leaning his forehead against the wall, Gwydion closed his eyes. Beads of sweat formed on his upper lip. He tasted salt.

"What's wrong, Welshman?" said Guy, peering around at him. "My friend Yves didn't hardly start yet and you're flagging already?"

Warm, wet streams coursed down Gwydion's back. He felt his waistband grow sodden with blood.

Yves became impatient and lashed him four times more. The thongs sang through the air, landing higher on his victim's shoulders. "Guy asked you a polite question," he said, breathing hard with his efforts. "Are you flagging already? he asked you. Spanish Charlie told us you were short on manners, and now I can see he was right."

Turning his head slightly, Gwydion did his best to bring Guy's face into focus. "You'll have to make allowances," he said, attempting a smile. "I'm not always at my best before breakfast."

That made Guy chuckle. "You're no gutless, weedy thing, I'll give you that much," he said. He looked to his fellow guard. "Wouldn't you give him that much, Yves?"

"I'll not give him anything. On account of him, I had to leave my warm bed early and come up to this stinking hole to get blood splashed over myself." He looked down at his frayed sleeve and ineffectively flicked his hand at the bright red droplets he found there.

"I think you've been working for Charlie too long, Yves," said Guy. "Next thing, you'll be combing your hair every morning and wearing rings on all your fingers."

"Shut your mouth," said Yves.

The lashing continued. Outside, dawn birds sang. December sun rays slanted through the narrow window and lit the filthy straw on the floor.

The guards exchanged surprised glances when the strains of a French ballad came wafting up from somewhere beneath them. It was a woman's voice, sweet and brave in the morning air.

"Our little friend is in good throat today," said Yves, stilling the whip to listen.

"Aye," replied his confederate. "You know, I think we ought to go see her, long as we're already up."

Yves wrapped the whip's bloody thongs around its wooden handle and tucked it back in his belt. A slow smile exposed his jagged teeth. "We ought. We haven't visited her in four whole days, friend Guy."

"I'm all of a sudden missing her something fearful."

They released Gwydion from his restraints and let him drop to the floor without further ado. Then the guards were gone, locking the door behind them.

Gwydion managed to rise and stagger to his cloak. He lowered himself onto it. If he lay unmoving on his side, he found, the pain was manageable.

The woman's ballad soon stopped.

Gwydion drifted into sleep. He dreamed of diving naked into a warm blue lake, gliding underwater in languorous silence. When he came up for air, he saw on the shore a golden table with three ripe cherries atop it. He gathered the fruit in his hand and pressed them to his mouth.

That image dissolved into fog. He waited, listening to the sighs of the wind, seeing nothing. Then a woman took shape in the emptiness. She approached him and placed her hand over his heart to see if he still breathed. Her hair spilled across his face. She smelled of flowers, and other sweet things he could not name. He wanted to pull her to him, to make her stay, but he couldn't move or speak.

He revived to the sound of men's laughter.

"This is what you do all day, Gwydion ap Gruffydd?" said Charles of La Cerda. "Shameful sloth, I call it."

The Castilian stood in the doorway. Guy and Yves were closer, one near Gwydion's head and the other near his feet.

"Should we haul him up, your lordship?" said Guy.

"Of course," replied Charles. "His indolence begs remedy."

The guards dragged Gwydion to his feet.

"Straighten up, you," said Yves, giving him a hard slap on the back.

Gwydion swayed forward, righted himself, then swung his left arm around as hard as he could. He took Yves unaware. His fist connected with the guard's jaw, making a loud snapping noise.

Yves screamed and dropped to the straw.

Guy drew his sword and held the trembling point against Gwydion's chest. "Should I puncture him?" he said, glancing anxiously at his employer.

"Not yet." Charles rubbed his chin, scrutinizing the prisoner. "No, not just yet. By the pained look on his face I do believe he's too spent to be any more trouble for the nonce. So you may leave me with him. But mind you wait just outside."

Guy sheathed his sword with some relief, then pulled his moaning friend to his feet and helped him out the door.

"My dear Welshman," said Charles, "no more dramatics. You and I will have a small tête-à-tête. Civilized, yes? Now, to begin, would you like me to tell you what's been transpiring lately at court?"

Gwydion only stared.

Charles shook his head. "Still sullen, of course. Well then, never mind. I will only say this—everyone in the world has forgotten your miserable existence, as far as I can tell. The kings certainly have, both my admirable John and your boorish Edward. Your unwashed band of conspirators, as well. If you have a wife, she has likewise not uttered a peep to try to learn your fate." He smiled apologetically. "Perhaps she's already made new arrangements."

"You put yourself to unusual trouble on behalf of my . . . miserable existence."

Charles admired a ruby ring on his middle finger. "The dreadful truth is, I've taken you in dislike. Did you guess? It's because you're not respectful. Since I was a boy, I have reacted badly to insolent behavior from inferiors. To make matters worse, I couldn't help but notice you just broke my guard's jaw with your left fist. Logically, I conclude you are left-handed. I have always, always held left-handed persons in abhorrence. It's so ungodly and unnatural."

Gwydion walked forward, a bit unsteadily, until he stood a few feet from the Castilian. Charles didn't move; his hand had been resting on his sword's hilt since the moment he entered the cell.

Gwydion studied his face. "Take pleasure from your moments of ascendance, Charles of Spain," he said. "I've known other men like you. Whatever they gain in this world, they never hold for long."

Charles sneered. "A left-handed cur, a failed diplomatic minion, and now a soothsayer. How busy you keep yourself, Gwydion ap

Gruffydd. Then pursue your various callings while you may, for I've suddenly decided what I shall give myself for a Christmas gift."

"A conscience?"

"Your dead heart to roast on my Yule fire."

"Why am I not surprised?"

"That's your trouble, Welshman. You're too clever for your own good."

Charles moved to the door.

"Wait," said Gwydion.

"What's this? Have you wisely decided to try a more conciliatory tone?"

"I was merely wondering about the wine. You said I'd have wine with my dinner, now and then, but so far I've not seen a drop."

"My appalling memory." The Spaniard gave a graceful wave of one beringed hand. "You shall have wine this very night. Never let it be said I am a miserly host."

In this, at least, he kept his word. Guy brought Gwydion the usual slop for supper, along with a jug of wine that smelled like spoiled vinegar and scorched the throat as it slid down.

"Beautiful stuff?" said Guy, grinning as he watched Gwydion take his first sip.

Gwydion's eyes watered, but he took another swallow. "The best I've had in weeks."

"Aye?" Guy's grin grew even broader. "By the way, you'll be happy to know poor Yves' face is swelled up twice its normal size. His cheek's so puffy he can barely open one eye. He says when he's better, he'll come up and thank you personal."

Sitting on his cloak on the floor, Gwydion took another drink of wine. "I've a lot to look forward to, it seems."

"I said it before, at least you're not one of those gutless, weedy fellows."

"Thank you." He offered Guy wine, but the guard waved the jug away with a comical grimace. The Welshman nodded understanding. "As we're talking so amiably, Guy," he said, "may I ask why it is your employer hates me so much? That is, if you can guess."

Guy picked a bit of food from between his front teeth. "Oh, our Charlie's just a putrid little bastard," he said, flicking the bit to the straw.

"That's all?"

"You didn't lick his boots pretty enough, I suppose. Don't take it to heart. You're not the first, you won't be the last."

"That's a comfort. Why do you stay in his employ?"

"Well, I had to choose between a life one rung above a slave's, here in Charlie's pile, or being a mollycoddled lover to a panting duchess who has breasts like cushions and fifty stacks of gold. Aye, those were my choices." He winked at his prisoner. "Impetuous boy that I am, I picked this."

After Guy left, Gwydion took off his ruined shirt and poured the remainder of the wine over his shoulders and back as best he could. He bit down on his wrist to muffle the cries that rose in his throat as the liquid trickled over open wounds.

For the next fortnight he had no more beatings and no visitor save Guy. Yves, it seemed, was taking a long time to mend. According to Guy, his temper was as fragile as his jaw.

"There'll be the devil to pay, friend," said Guy, "when poor old Yves finally manages to drag himself up here."

"Find me a sword and let me make a fair fight of it, then," said Gwydion.

That only made Guy laugh. "You're a treasure, you are," he said. "Find me a sword, he says. A fair fight, he says." He went away shaking his head, smiling.

Gwydion's wounds healed well enough, although he was filthy and stinking and often dizzy with hunger. By far his worst problem was the cold. As Christmas approached, Paris found itself in the clutches of a rare spell of white, freezing weather. Snow swirled into the cell through its narrow window. Gwydion spent nights wrapped in his cloak, shivering, drifting in and out of sleep, imagining pliant women in featherbeds, or fillets of roasted beef stuffed with bread crumbs and pepper. Sometimes he dreamed of his father, or his dead mother.

He entertained himself with imagined scenes of the future. For four years he'd been doing the English king's bidding. His sweet mother had been English, and he'd grown up with thrilling tales of her country's honor and pride. Half of him understood that loyalty, embraced it. That was why he put his life in danger in France. But wasn't four years enough? He wanted to go home to Wales and make some sort of reasonable life for himself. Why not? Other men married, sired children, stayed happily on their own lands, in their own firelit halls.

He was the son of devoted parents, devoted to their two children and each other. Unlike many, he believed contentment in marriage was possible. Although he had no particular woman in mind to assist him in this pleasant domestic scheme, he was not averse to searching for one when he returned to Britain. She could be Welsh or English, no matter, as long as she pleased him and he pleased her.

Of course, he'd have to give up his carousing. At least he'd have to curtail it to discreet, occasional incidences.

Every day the water Guy brought froze in its shallow bowl. With raw knuckles, Gwydion broke the ice into pieces to suck.

Yves returned to the cell on a Friday morning just before Christmas. His face was a trifle lopsided. Guy was right behind him, looking resigned and unhappy.

"I've come to cause you damage, Welshman," Yves said. He spoke slowly, out of only one side of his misshapen mouth.

"I tried to tell him it really wasn't your fault, anybody might have done the same," Guy told Gwydion. He spoke as if Yves were not in the cell with them. "It won't do any good. A female in the street laughed at his poor face yesterday, you see."

Guy had grown somewhat fond of his prisoner over the course of the weeks. He admired Gwydion's lack of complaint, his dark humor. Guy also knew, from firsthand observation, the sort of prolonged, gruesome death Charles of La Cerda would soon mete out to him.

Days of cold and hunger had taken their toll on Gwydion. But he made an attempt to fight off the manacles and chain with which Yves and the reluctant Guy now secured him. But he was weak and exhausted, no match for well-fed guards. Soon he hung from the wall as he had before. Soon Yves landed his first furious blow. Spittle flew from his twisted mouth as he swung his arm.

"You oughtn't lash him so hard," said Guy, frowning. "You'll kill him, Yves."

"I hope I do."

"Bold talk. But remember our Charles wants to do the deed himself. He'll not thank you for snatching away his fun."

Horses suddenly pounded into the courtyard. As if the mention of his name had miraculously conjured him, the Castilian's distinct voice could be heard, clear and menacing from below. Guy hurried to the little window and squinted down to make certain he hadn't imagined it.

"Himself. Damn, he's picked a fine time to make a surprise visit." He ran to Gwydion's side and released him. "Put that whip away," he told Yves as he helped the prisoner back to his filthy cloak. He lowered Gwydion to his improvised bed and tried to pull the remnants of his shirt around him to conceal the new crimson marks seeping blood across his back.

Yves went a bit pale and jammed the whip under his belt. Both men headed to the door. Sitting dazed with his head bowed over his bent knees, Gwydion began to laugh quietly.

Guy and Yves stopped and turned around. "What's this?" said Guy. "What's funny?"

Gwydion looked up. "You were only supposed to make me more fit to seen," he said, smiling crookedly.

"He's gone mad," whispered Yves.

"Small wonder," said Guy, as he locked the door behind them.

The guards fled down the stairs and made themselves busy sweeping the mansion's dusty armory.

Charles soon sauntered indoors and found them amongst the swords, knives, and rusty hauberks that had belonged to the mansion's original owner. "How is our rude Welshman, gentlemen?" he said, brushing his gloved fingertips disapprovingly over a grimy tabletop. "Uncomfortable, I trust."

"Aye, my lord," said Guy, setting aside his broom.

"But not dead," said Yves, and he flushed.

Charles didn't seem to find the comment strange. "I'll go pay my respects. I've brought him some more wine." As he was leaving, his eye was caught by an ornate dagger in definite need of repair. "Gaudy old thing," he said, picking it up.

"It wants smithing, my lord," said Guy. "There's a bad chink in the shaft near the tip."

Charles examined it more closely. "Yes, I see it now. A definite chink." He tested the fractured metal, working it incautiously. "But perfection can be so monotonous, after all." He left the armory, taking the dagger with him.

A knowing look passed between the guards before they went back to their work.

When the Castilian entered Gwydion's cell, he sniffed the air and wrinkled his nose. "Heavens, it smells like death in here. But I suppose you've grown accustomed." He placed a corked jug on the floor. "Look, I've brought you more wine."

Gwydion rose with what dignity he could summon. He took in Charles's grandeur, his dark eyes sweeping from the man's thigh-high boots to his enameled buckle, his sable collar and mantle, then his curled raven hair. "You look to be thriving, Charles of La Cerda."

One corner of the Castilian's mouth turned up. "Alas, I can't say the same of you."

Gwydion smiled. "You don't think I'm fit to be seen?" After a moment he once more began to laugh.

"Something about your situation obviously diverts you." Charles held up the ornate dagger. "Does this?"

Gwydion ceased his laughter. He stared at the blade. "My God, you're actually going to kill an unarmed man." He seemed shocked but not alarmed.

Charles came to stand before him. "No, I'll not kill you yet, Welshman," he said. He lowered the dagger, relaxing his stance. "Not yet." His arm shot out. The dagger sank into Gwydion's side just below the ribs. Charles twisted the hilt, then yanked the blade back out. Gwydion gasped and staggered against the wall. Charles followed. "First, I'll be sure you *wish* you were dead. I'm not a man who can tolerate a lack of respect, as you'll learn before you die."

The Castilian glanced down at the weapon he'd just wielded. Its tip had broken away, as he'd hoped. "Oh, my. I fear this old thing has left a souvenir"—he gestured to Gwydion's torso—"in your unfortunate person. Mea culpa."

Charles left the cell, humming.

Gwydion pressed his hand against the new wound and winced when he felt the hardness of the blade tip below his skin. It was too far imbedded to try to dig out, even if he'd had something with which to dig. Gathering what remained of his strength, he lurched across the cell to the jug. Taking shuddering breaths, he pulled the edges of the dagger wound apart. Then he poured wine into the bloody hole. He tried not to cry out. But a hoarse scream escaped him as he sank to the straw.

Halfway up the stone stairway, Guy plied his broom. He froze when he heard the scream. Checking to be sure no one was about, he made the sign of the cross.

Toward evening of that day Guy climbed up to Gwydion's cell to see how he fared. He found him in a grim, feverish state.

The guard hurried away to fetch a blanket and a bowl of broth. When he returned, he tried to get the ailing prisoner to swallow some of the warm liquid. At first his efforts failed. He threw the blanket around Gwydion's shoulders and pulled him away from the window, where he had been leaning into the cold wind, smiling crazily out at the darkening sky.

"Come on now, friend," said Guy. "That demon Charles is gone off to kiss the king's backside, but he'll murder me if you curl up your toes so soon, though it's his own doing. You don't want me murdered, do you? I've been fair to you, haven't I?"

Gwydion nodded uncertainly. His dark eyes rested on Guy's face. "Who are you?"

Guy swore. "Your only friend in the world. I brought you a blanket, and soup. See?" He pretended to take a slurp of broth. "Tasty. Chicken, it is. Try some."

Gwydion's eyes never left Guy's face. He pretended to slurp, just as the guard had.

Eventually Guy did manage to get his prisoner to drink part of the broth. He also made him promise to stay away from the window. "It's freezing cold over there," he said.

Slumped on the floor, wrapped in the blanket, Gwydion looked beyond Guy's shoulder. His face broke into a delighted smile.

Startled, Guy likewise looked over his shoulder, then cursed himself. "What am I lookin' at?" he said aloud. "No need for both of us to go all giddy in the head."

By then Gwydion was happily conversing, in rapid Welsh, with whatever invisible beings he'd spotted.

"Say proper words, man," said Guy, rattled by this new, incomprehensible development. "Who are you talking to, anyway?"

Gwydion raised a haughty eyebrow. "My father's dogs," he said, in French. "They want me to throw them a stick."

"Tell 'em you haven't got a stick. Tell 'em to go away."

Gwydion abruptly slouched to one side and closed his eyes.

"If you die, friend," said Guy, awkwardly tucking the blanket more securely around him, "then so will I, and that fool Yves. So be easy on us all and don't die."

He did not. But his fever grew worse over the next days. He saw other things that weren't there, most not so benign as playful dogs. He had nightmares of battle, of blood-crazed men screaming over mangled foes. But sometimes in the mornings when he was lucid, he heard the woman singing her pretty ballads. It was the only solace he had.

"Is she a prisoner too?" he whispered to Guy one dawn as she sang. Yves had thrown a bucket of cold water on him earlier, to stop his fevered shouting, and anxious Guy had come up to the cell to bring him a dry shirt and another blanket.

"She is. You and her are the only ones in the place right now. But she's way down in the cellar. I hear tell she was caught giving comfort to the enemy. Too bad, eh?"

"Will the Spaniard kill her?"

"Probably."

"That's a sin and a shame."

"Lots of things are that, friend."

It was Christmas.

Two days later Guy informed Gwydion the ballad singer was dead. "Smashed a bowl and cut her wrists open with a sharp piece," he said. "What a sight she was, snowy white in a red pool. Eyes like boiled eggs. I said a prayer for her, though she'll surely be denied Heaven. But at least Spanish Charlie won't care. He forgot about her months ago."

Gwydion stared toward the window. "You truly think she'll go to Hell?"

Guy looked with sudden hard concern at his only remaining prisoner. "Don't get any silly ideas, Welshman. One corpse is more than enough."

Guy soon heard interesting gossip from a servant friend who heard it from another servant friend. It seemed Gwydion's ransom had been paid. At court, the French king had actually relayed that news, days ago, to Charles of La Cerda. But then the distracted king had immediately pushed on with other business; the fate of one British hostage was of minor importance in the royal scheme of things.

Well aware that King John's interest in his insolent prisoner would be fleeting, Charles did nothing. He hoped to play secret host to Gwydion until the end of his days: this was the servants' surmise.

Only when a second request arrived at the court, via an English abbot, for word of Gwydion's whereabouts, did King John publicly remonstrate with his favorite, Charles. "Why have you not yet released this damned fellow? Shall I go release him myself? After all, I have nothing better to do," the monarch said. According to Guy's friend's friend, who had the *on dit* from a palace charwoman, he had said it rather peevishly.

"Charlie will have to let him go now, whether he likes it or not," Guy told Yves, as he shared the story with his colleague. "He won't risk the king's temper just to take his bastardy to its usual nasty ending."

Guy predicted well.

The next afternoon a minion arrived with brief, unexpected orders from Charles of La Cerda. Gwydion was to be released. Someone would come to fetch him that very day.

"How?" asked Gwydion. "Who?" The fever was still upon him. He stood swaying near the mansion's front door as Guy bundled him into his raggedy cloak.

"Don't ask questions, man. Just hurry away before that devil Charles shows up with a better idea. He'll be enkindled and terrible thwarted now for certain, if I know him. Just go get some hot food inside you, take a little rest, and be glad the sun's shining again."

Yves stood at Guy's side. He scowled and massaged his damaged jaw. "Aye, and be grateful I'm the forgiving type."

A loud knock sounded. Yves threw open the door.

There in the winter sunlight stood a lean man with a white scar down his forehead. He blinked. "Gwydion ap Gruffydd?"

Gwydion shuffled forward from the shadows. "William? My friend William. Welcome, and thank you."

William took his arm before he fell over. "Jesus and Mary," he said, gaping. His friend's pallor, his raw knuckles, his straw-specked cloak, and the bloodstained waistband he'd glimpsed when the cloak gaped open—these things shocked William to the core. What had befallen the handsome, immaculate man who had set out for Hôtel de Nesle in November? William swallowed and said, "Are you— You look a bit rough, Gwyd."

Gwydion peered hazily at his friend. "But fit to be seen?"

William nodded, not convincingly.

"May you fare truly well," called Guy as the two men walked slowly away. "I'll say a prayer for you, Welshman."

William glanced back at the guards in the doorway. "Whatever that Frenchie fellow just said," he told Gwydion, "I could have sworn it sounded friendly."

"Guy gave me soup."

"Did he? It looks like he gave you more than soup, if you don't mind my saying so."

"Charles took me in dislike—my host, that is. I didn't show him proper respect, so he stabbed me." He spoke matter-of-factly. "But the dagger tip broke off and now it's"—he gestured with vague apathy to his side—"somewhere. A souvenir."

William stopped to stare at his tall, gaunt friend. "My God, Gwyd. You need a surgeon. We'll find you one soon as can be."

"Good. Then I think we ought to go home, Will. I've been dreaming of home."

"You'll get no argument from me."

As they moved slowly on, Gwydion asked, "How did you know where to find me?"

"I nosed around and found what sum the Frenchies wanted for your ransom. Then I heard the sort of cur La Cerda is. People who go into that house of his have a habit of coming out dead, they say. So I got a scribe to write a letter home, a good while ago. Your sister sent the money. I'm just sorry it took so long."

Gwydion suddenly reached out and gripped his friend's hand. "Thank you, Will."

William flushed. "As if you wouldn't have done the same."

"But you say Elizabeth paid? Why not my father?"

"I don't know." The white scar on Will's forehead puckered as he frowned. He looked down the deserted lane. "The inn's just around the corner now."

Gwydion halted as a wave of vertigo washed over him. He pressed a hand to his side, then resumed his slow pace.

"A doctor will have you fixed up in a twinkling, never fear," said William. "Then we'll sail back across the Channel soon as you're able."

"There's nothing I want more."

"Cob's at the inn, and Jack. And the other two from our sortie. But we have to keep our heads down, still yet, in case these Frenchies turn surly. I have papers to be here to fetch you, but the rest don't. They've been lurking around Paris for weeks, just waiting."

Gwydion looked confused. "That only makes six. We were seven in November."

"Warin's dead. Took an arrow in the back when he tried to get away the day they executed de Brienne."

Later that night a French doctor dug a piece of metal from Gwydion's side. He told his patient, who by then was under the influence of several tankards of strong ale, that he wasn't certain he'd removed every bit. He couldn't probe further, he explained, without the risk of doing more harm than good.

Gwydion's eyes were wild. But he smiled drunkenly and told the man not to fret. "You dug out most of it?"

"Most, monsieur." He held up a small silver triangle. "Certainly most."

Gwydion sank back against a pillow. "*Most* will have to be sufficient."

The next morning he was less fevered and was able to sit up in bed. He even made an attempt at breakfast.

The passing of another few days saw him further improved. He rested near a sunny window and looked out at the world. One afternoon he woke from a brief, dream-filled sleep and saw a good-sized white puppy across the lane. It sat beside the body of another white dog, a larger dog. Gwydion hobbled to the door and went outside.

The puppy wagged its tail when he approached.

"Trouble, my young friend?"

The pup dropped its chin to the other dog's still side. With some difficulty, Gwydion squatted next to the whimpering creature and scooped him up in his arms.

By that evening William had taken away the dead animal. "Appears mama dog just starved to death," he told Gwydion.

The puppy would meet no such fate. He was fed like a king at the inn and soon nestled next to his rescuer. "Vortigern," said Gwydion. "I christen you King Vortigern."

Cob, one of the English soldiers, objected. "This fellow's too puny yet for such a grand moniker, Gwyd," he said. "Call him Vort until he grows into it."

Vortigern stretched his short white legs and rolled to his back. He yawned.

Gwydion smiled. "You're right, Cob. We'll call him Vort and take him safe back to Britain."

Seeing his friend was recovering his strength, William decided it was time to deliver the news he'd been holding back. He told Gwydion why his sister Elizabeth had been the one to pay his ransom. It was because there was no one else to pay it. His father had been murdered.

7

Mud, and Rowanberries

The day ripened.

After walking for half the morning, Elise and Annora rested atop the rock-strewn hill that Elise believed was Bryn Llech. The weather stayed bright and cool. As they took turns sipping from a bladder of ale, they rested in a patch of dappled shadow beneath two leafy ash trees. Moorland and empty pastures ringed them all around, and they had encountered no other travelers.

Elise leaned on her staff, looking to the west. "This is a cheerless enough place."

"We've known worse," said Annora, bending awkwardly to fish a pebble from her shoe.

Though Annora was not a woman to accept any help with grace, Elise knelt beside her all the same, grabbed her ankle, and plucked out the stone.

"I'm not decrepit yet, you know," Annora said, much as Elise had expected. She jammed her foot back into her shoe. "Nor am I a horse."

They went on. After another hour passed, they glimpsed a house amidst trees far ahead. Then another house. The Trackway was rockier now, and hilly. It was also more welcoming than where they had earlier walked, the terrain softer and less bleak.

Distant hammers clanged on metal. Smells of cooking rose on the air. A cow bellowed and unseen children laughed. Soon, both women were sure, they would be among kind, decent people, as they had not been in two years.

"Penmachno's edge, I think," said Annora. "Look up ahead to the right. A church. See the whitewashed roof?"

Yes. It was like a star, gleaming in the forest's firmament.

"There are two old churches in Penmachno, in one churchyard," Annora went on. "So tales go." Ever mindful of her appearance, she paused to arrange her mantle more evenly at her shoulders. "These folks are either very godly or very sinful."

"They could well be both," Elise said, remembering her dead husband.

Walking steadily onward, she grew anxious with the idea that his murder would soon be discovered. The tug of disquiet came as no surprise; Maelgwyn's shadow had floated below the surface of her pretended unconcern all morning.

Maybe he'd already been plucked from the river by some overbusy monk at Ysbyty Ifan, to cajole favor from Heaven. Maybe when that monk prepared the body for burial, he gasped at the signs of violence. "This was no natural death," he might have exclaimed to his fellows, hours ago. "This man has been stabbed. Let's learn his identity soon as may be and rake the hills for his killer." Or so Elise's fancy imagined.

These concerns grew too heavy to bear alone. She spilled them out to Annora as they passed into a tunnel of oak trees whose branches twisted overhead like green and black whipcords. The bit of white roof disappeared as they went forward.

"No one has found the body, cariad. He's still in the river bobbing like rotten fruit," her friend told her. "Your mind is just fretful from lack of sleep. And if you don't need to fill your belly, I swear I surely do. Calm yourself. When the people in Penmachno behold us, they'll see only respectable women. A mother and daughter off to join kin, perhaps. Which of us looks most like a knife-wielding monster?" She touched Elise's arm. "Neither. For neither is."

Nevertheless, a cold prickling danced across Elise's fingertips, raced up her arms, flew to the hollow of her throat. Swallowing, she tried with slight success to dislodge the chill. "Of course," she finally answered. "My mind is merely fretful."

But declaring an understanding of her own fretfulness did little to dispel it. As they walked, she grew more possessed with the notion that Maelgwyn's murder had already been found out. To heighten her unease, she saw again in her mind's eye how his eyelid had seemed to flutter, under the cold moonlight, in the black river.

The spread of *that* apprehension, at least, she was able to check. No, he could not still live. Though he might have survived for a time after they lost sight of him, even for a half dozen turns and meanderings of the Conwy, he could hardly have lived longer than that. He would have been leaving too deadly a trail of red blood in the water of the Conwy to survive.

Being only human, even if monstrous and hateful, he could not endure bloodless. Not even Maelgwyn could endure bloodless.

The path widened to reveal two long rows of wattle-and-daub cottages cheek to jowl with rougher structures whose leaning sides were made of wickerwork filled in with mud. Some dwellings shared walls, some were separated from their neighbors by only an acorn's span. A runnel of mud coursed down the middle of the lane. Tethered chickens scratched and squawked as Annora and Elise passed by. A few flapped russet and black wings and leaped as far in the air as their cords allowed. Hints of burnt pottage swelled the breeze but were soon displaced by the smell of pig droppings. Piles of manure sat perilously close to some thresholds.

It was much like other villages Elise had seen. Or was it more ragged and grim? Did her tired eyes only paint it that way?

Before one house's open door, a barefoot toddler in a rucked-up flax smock sat on his naked rump, examining his filthy fists. On their approach, he raised his little arms, generously offering his hands, palms out, for their edification.

A childless woman who dearly loved children, Annora moved toward the black-haired boy as if he were a lodestone. "What heroic things are you doing with all this fine mud, young man?" she said, beaming. "Such a lot as you've managed to smear across your forehead. What a good, busy fellow."

Elise wanted to share her friend's pleasure at seeing the child but found she could not. A vision of her brothers—eager and merry as in life—rose up just then, to beg a portion of innocent play. Their shades hovered, their eyes beseeched. Then her darlings drifted slowly to the mud. Echoes of their voices whispered her name in plaintive, ghostly protest.

They had not come to foretell or warn, she knew. Nor was their origin unworldly. No, they were creations of her own need, shaped solely by her heart.

As a rush of wind disturbed the looming trees, a shadow fell across the threshold behind the child. A gaunt woman stepped into the sunlight. She carried a small branch laden with leaves and orange-red berries. Rowan, a talisman against evil.

She regarded the two women dispassionately.

"A fetching child," said Annora in a friendly voice.

Apparently sensing approval, the baby chortled and leaned forward to slap his hand into the stream of mud before him. Brown droplets spattered his chin. This delighted him further.

"My son's child," said the woman. Her face lost some of its hardness as she looked down at the boy. "Mine, now."

So the Pestilence had likely found this place too.

Elise took a step closer to the cottage. "My mother and I are on a pilgrimage to the cathedral at Bangor," she said, lying with what she knew was distressing ease, naming the first Welsh city that flew into her head. "Can you point the way to your churches here, say which is suited to wayfarers? We glimpsed a white roof but lost sight of it. We hoped to rest there to break our fast, then pray for a safe journey before we go on."

"Either church will do," said the woman. Then she frowned. "But you would go to Bangor, you two alone?"

"These times are hard and the choice was not ours."

"That's as may be." The woman pulled a berry from the branch. Putting it between her lips, she worked her tongue around it for a moment, then spit it into the mud. It sank.

Annora cleared her throat.

Trailed by a trio of muddy piglets, two girls in frayed dresses passed by, behind Elise and Annora. Elise saw them from the corner of her eye and felt their scrutiny. Hands to mouths, they whispered as they walked on. Piglets followed, squealing.

"We don't see many strangers these days," said the woman, watching the girls go. "Mostly men. Soldiers, monks, or beggars." Her gaze returned to the women, sweeping over their cloaks of fine wool. She sniffed. "Sometimes we do see whores."

Elise raised her chin. "The churches?"

The woman shrugged and pointed to her right. "Follow this path to the Machno River. Just ahead. There's a ford with a stout rope. Have a care when you cross it, for it's high as ever it gets. When you're over, you'll spy a yew tree so tall it tickles the clouds." She turned away to wedge the end of the rowan branch into a jagged hole in the face of her cottage's wall. Secured, the branch swayed limply, its leaves rustling in the breeze. She turned back. "Father Yew marks this place so the angels can see it from Heaven. So no demons can worm their way among us."

"How blessed you are to have such a tree," Elise said. "Would that every village in Christendom was so privileged."

Annora reached down to touch the little boy's black curls. Then they turned to go, to cross the Machno River and rest a while in the sanctuary of a churchyard.

8

A Stone's Throw

No one shared the path with Annora and Elise, except a yellow cat. But the cat soon slunk away. It jumped to the sill of a derelict, lopsided shed. They passed more cottages, and shuttered shops. Prominent was an alehouse whose painted sign creaked in the wind. A worm-eaten plank, that sign bore as enticement to patrons a jaundiced fox lapping at a tankard.

Unseen hammers had stopped clanging. Children were silent. But Elise sensed sharp eyes beyond cottage windows and inside the doorway of the alehouse. Accordingly she straightened her spine so their speculation might roll off unrewarded.

Why did they skulk? Was their veiled curiosity a vestige of the days of the Pestilence when any traveler might breathe death? After all, it had only been two years since the worst of those times. Or perhaps these people, in their hilly village, had been made unnaturally suspicious by the habit of isolation.

A much more fanciful but disquieting choice to account for this furtive interest: some swift, magical messenger—Gray Hill's watchful spider or its song thrush—might have already told the villagers a murderess moved on the Trackway. It might have even whispered the victim's last words to his killer.

Elise knew them. *Satan's bitch*, Maelgwyn had called her.

A large white dog of cheerful demeanor and dubious ancestry loped from between two trees to sniff their shoes. It turned to match their steps, tongue lolling, long ears flapping. It was hardly more than a puppy, with shaggy fur, and huge muddy paws it had not grown into, despite its impressive size.

"Go away, pest," said Annora.

It licked her hand.

An unexpected gurgle of laughter welled up in Elise. She was surprised and warmed by the feel of it in her throat.

"You'll have none of our food," Annora told the dog. "Don't you imagine you will."

Elise halted, still smiling. "The poor thing's probably hungry," she said, slipping the sack off her shoulder.

"Of course it's hungry. It's probably always hungry." Annora scowled at the grinning pup. "You only have to look at the great size of it to see it could likely eat until it burst."

Elise held out a small piece of cheese.

"Child, this is foolish. Put that cheese back before the brute has your fingers with it."

The dog took the offering, very gently, like a prince's pet.

"See," Elise said, giving it another bit. "Docile as a lamb. Aren't you, sweetheart?" She looked at Annora. "And you would let it starve."

Annora walked to its side and peered down. "A male. Well, we'll never be rid of it, now you've fed it."

They walked on and came to the river. A sullen, roiling green, it flowed swiftly past. Shiny black sticks, a web of yellowish foam, and the carcass of a wood pigeon littered the near bank. Perched to their right at the first northerly bend was a mill, partly overhung in willow branches.

"See the rope, there, tied off on either end? A hand bridge," Elise said. "The river's not wide here. You could throw a stone across. Can you manage it, Annora?"

As the dog examined the dead pigeon, fixing it to the mud with a clever paw, Annora glared at the water. "I've been managing since you were a minnow's eyelash, young lady."

They removed their shoes and stockings and knotted their cloaks and skirts as high as modesty allowed. Staff in one hand, Annora grabbed the rope with the other and waded into the river.

Elise bade farewell to the preoccupied dog and followed her friend, shocked at once by the water's coldness. Never had she felt a summer river so icy. "Steady," she called. "I'm just behind you if you fall."

Wavelets lapped at their ankles, their knees. Thighs. No higher. But the current grew vicious as they neared midpoint. Grit washed over Elise's toes, pushed under her arches. Ahead, Annora staggered. She folded over the rope, clutching it to her waist with one hand as if the river had grown too ferocious to let her go forward.

They stayed like that for a nightmare moment. The rope swayed with deceptive gentleness, first bending Elise's arm, then straightening it, and rocking Annora. All the while the river sang like a deranged mother.

A tree trunk the length of a horse shot past, silently, between them. It cleared the bottom of the rope by a hair. Elise swung her head around to look upriver for others.

"Hurry, go on, before another comes," she shouted, teeth chattering. A thought struck her. "Or are you hurt? Have you hurt your foot?"

Annora shook her head a fraction. Elise couldn't see her face. But she saw that her friend's hand on the rope was waxy white, the knuckles rimmed with pink.

Finally Annora straightened, with fearful deliberation, then moved slowly forward. Her cloak's hem dragged behind her, teased by the greedy current.

When Elise reached the spot where Annora had staggered, she understood why. The river pounded her knees. It whipped pebbles against her ankles. She curled her toes around rocks, but the rocks were too slimy for anchor. She reeled. Fear pulsed in her ears and hissed down to the insides of her elbows.

She sent an urgent prayer heavenward, then looked ahead. Two children stood on the bank, a boy and a girl. They watched impassively.

The throbbing in Elise's ears grew louder. It became the only sound she heard. Still, she stumbled forward.

Annora grew taller. She reached the bank—by the mercy of the Maker—and toiled up it, out of the freezing river. Within moments so did Elise.

They collapsed on the Machno's reed-choked edge. Annora sat with her gray head between her knees, struggling for breath.

After her breathing and Elise's became quieter, less tortured, Elise lifted the sack from Annora's shoulders and hugged her fiercely. Then she sat back on her haunches and set about rubbing her friend's icy feet between her warmer hands. The children approached and sat down cross-legged, spitting distance from the women. The boy wiped his nose on his arm.

Reviving, Annora pulled her foot away. "Will you leave my foot alone?" she said, still breathing hard.

"Here, look," said the girl, pointing to the river.

Halfway across was the dog, just alongside the rope. It battled toward them, white head barely above the water.

Elise scrambled up and skidded over the low bank.

"Let it be!" shrieked Annora. "It's God's culling of the brainless."

The boy appeared at Elise's side. "Here, look," he said, echoing the girl. "I'm a doughty swimmer." Without hesitation he launched into the water and shimmied down the horizontal rope like an acrobat on a feast day.

Venturing in more cautiously, Elise instantly slipped on a muddy, half-submerged rock, and fell to her knees. "Boy, don't drown," she gasped, struggling up, water dripping from her sleeves. "Dog. Please don't drown."

In a flash the lad reached the animal and grabbed its scruff. The dog didn't resist. Both came toward Elise in surges. One leg still thrown over the rope, one hand grasping it, the boy was on his stomach—nose in the river, nose out. Nose in, nose out. The dog's method was more startling, his whole head disappearing and reappearing at intervals.

Finally they crawled up the bank.

"You are indeed doughty," Elise told the boy, grasping his wet hand. "Truly, truly doughty."

The dog shook himself nonchalantly, muzzle to tail, then sat down at her bare feet, panting. She wiped his baptism from her face, laughing once more. It felt so good to laugh.

"Just it's a sin to waste a healthy animal," said the boy, wiping his nose on his arm again. Then he scampered off and threw himself down beside the girl.

A shrill whistle sounded. The children rose and raced away without a word.

Tapping the dog's large, damp paws, paws no longer muddy, Elise shook her head. "So, my reckless friend, I suppose you think you've earned more cheese."

White ears twitched.

They walked back up the bank to Annora.

"Look at you, Elise," she said. "Filthy as an eel in a night pot." She turned to the dog, who was watching a jackdaw flit around the branches of a nearby sapling. "Why? For a beast with more fur than sense."

Elise looked past her and up.

Annora labored to her feet. "Whyever are you gaping?"

"I believe 'tis Father Yew, tickling the clouds."

They donned shoes and stockings again and unknotted their skirts. Elise's hems and sleeves were wet, Annora's all but dry. Then they followed the path, traversing a purple-heathered slope. With the dog as companion, they gained the canopy of Penmachno's mighty yew. Partly in its shadow were the two white-roofed churches it guarded, seemingly unoccupied at that midday hour. Wooden grave markers were scattered all around.

Elise suddenly recalled an old tale that claimed yew roots, in graveyards, searched out the mouths of the dead for macabre sustenance. But she willed the tale away, disquieted by such lurid superstition.

"We'll sit in the sunshine," said Annora, "so your clothes can dry, if only a little. I'll scrape the worst dirt off later, though you surely deserve to stay muddy."

The closest church's western wall made a good bolster. They fanned their skirts about their legs, then Elise drew the cheese and a loaf from her sack. Annora fished a knife from hers, and set a bladder of ale on the ground between them.

"Don't dare give a morsel to that idiotic dog," she said, watching Elise slice dense brown bread. "Especially don't give it more cheese. By the size of it, I'm sure some fool has the misfortune to be its owner. It hardly looks to be starving."

Elise sighed and nodded, still sawing at the stubborn loaf.

Finally they ate and drank. Hidden birds gossiped in the yew tree as the distant hammers started up again. The dog lay nearby with his head on his paws, watching them woefully, the very picture of betrayed canine martyr. The dark ribbon of the Machno River was just visible behind him, downslope, a foil for his whiteness.

"I'll steal a nap now," said Annora, when she finished eating. "So should you, or you'll not have strength to go on."

But Elise wrestled with a troubling question. "The sun is past its prime," she said. "Where will we sleep tonight? I suppose I know— forest floor for our bedding, darkness for our cover. But I'll admit now I'm a coward and I'm wretchedly dismayed by the thought of it."

"Child, don't borrow trouble. There's surely some cozy house or inn ahead where we can shelter." Annora leaned her head against the sunny church wall. "With hot stew, and drink."

"And the wherewithal for such a treat?"

"Oh, I've a few coins tucked away. So hush now and rest."

Too tired to question her, just then, about these mysterious funds, Elise curled and uncurled her bruised toes inside their worn shoes. Fishy, less than pleasing, the smell of damp wool wafted up from her cloak. Giving it a shake, she wished she could speed its drying. It was then she noticed the rue bracelet had gone from her wrist. She held up her arm and stared.

Annora watched her. "Well, the river's taken that rue charm you thought I hadn't noticed. Good riddance." Then she yawned and closed her eyes. "Ah, the Lord has an eye out for even the smallest detail."

When she was softly snoring, Elise twisted off another piece of bread and broke off more cheese. The dog sat up.

"You are *not* brainless," she whispered, as he came to accept the food. "You're a lovely boy."

He made short work of his meal, then put his head on her knee. She smoothed his damp ears. Like Annora, he soon slept.

Stretching her arms, Elise looked once more at her bare wrist, then did exactly the same.

9

A SINISTER RIDER

How long Elise slept she could not have said. It seemed to be for-ever.

Through a filter of fears, wishes, and secret riddles, she heard the cries of fantastic birds and sang with them as equal. The kiss of rain — she knew that too. Hundreds of drops lay on her breast, a tiny red heart throbbing in each crystal bead.

The wind took her hair in its gentle grip, as a true lover might, and twisted her to the west. She arched her back and faced rushing rays of sun. Singing, singing gladly. Dripping wet with the beautiful rain. Wet with the beautiful rain . . .

Until two rough hands seized her. Ten coarse fingers. They held her hard and sure. Down. And down. Until green waves replaced golden sky. Until all four directions fused into one, and the wind didn't know where to find her.

Stirring, roused by the weight of some imagined loss, she moved her hand in protest — and met the dog's soft fur.

"It was a dream," she murmured. "Only a lie of the mind."

She opened her eyes. Annora still rested peacefully, as did the dog. Birds still sang. Father Yew was as he had been, marking the place for the angels.

Again her eyes closed. A kinder sleep bore her away then, let her settle into more soothing rest. But that rest too soon grew threadbare. Then the vision came, her first in many weeks.

Unlike any dream, Elise's visions were always more akin to the shape of the waking world, so real she felt she could almost touch what she saw. And always marked by the strangest *sense*, palpable at the onset, of prox-imity to Heaven. Or was it perhaps Hell? She didn't know. But they were also marked without fail by the sound of unseen wings beating. Angels or carrion crows — surely one or the other — they hovered, they witnessed. Sometimes she pictured them above her, patient and unblinking.

This was her vision, that day: A man. His naked back, broad, straight. Shoulders, scarred shoulders. Sinewed arms, streaked red, raised to a crimson sky. It was sunset.

The man threw back his head. He split the dying day with a wild cry. But she could not see his face. A sword was gripped in his left hand. In his right hand was a severed head, held aloft by gory hair.

"Elise, you're safe. You're with your loving Annora, in the churchyard." The worried voice came from leagues away.

"It was a dream, cariad. Open your eyes, you'll see."

As the sound of wings faded, Elise did as the voice bid.

"There, darling," said Annora, peering into her face. "You gave me such a start, dreaming, crying out like that."

"No, not a dream," Elise said, clutching Annora's arm. "It was a vision. A man held a bloody head in his hand. Blood was everywhere. And he was . . . ecstatic."

Annora patted Elise's cheek, trying as ever to ease her anxiety with words. "Then say a prayer to steal the memory, for what could a vision like that mean to a sweet girl? One day in Heaven you can ask why you were burdened with such disturbances."

The dog stood. He looked toward the river, head cocked.

Annora still doled out advice. " 'Holy Father,' you'll say, 'how inscrutable are Your ways.' And I'll ask why—"

Elise raised her hand, halting Annora mid-flow.

They both looked down the slope.

Two great horses, one brown, one black, crossed the Machno at the ford. Each was guided by a man at its bridle. The first horse shied, tossing its head up and down. But it quieted after a moment, and moved forward. Soon both horses were across and being mounted by the men who led them. They followed the Trackway up the slope. Toward Father Yew. Toward the women.

"They've come for me from Ysbyty Ifan," Elise said, surprised at the acceptance in her voice. "I'll ready myself."

"Don't be such a doomsayer, child. I'm certain their business has nothing to do with you." She slapped Elise's hands away from her sack. "Stop your tidying, this instant."

As the horses came closer, the dog began to whimper.

"Quiet that mongrel," Annora said softly. "There's still no need to announce our whereabouts to a pair of utter strangers."

Elise hugged the dog, glad to feel his soft fur against her cheek. "Shhh," she whispered. "Hush."

The riders reined in at the edge of the churchyard to confer in inaudible voices. Annora and Elise sat like statues against the church wall, staffs in easy reach, and surveyed the men through the yew's lowest branches. One, astride the brown horse, was rather young. He wore a short cape in the fashionable color called plunket celestyne—sky blue. Elise had seen costly cloth of that hue at a fair in Beaumaris. His cape was cut up in studded strips. On his head sat a deceptively simple hat of drab cloth, with a blue plume hanging to his shoulder.

The other man was older, perhaps thirty. He sat straight and tall, dark-haired, clean-shaven, unsmiling. Like his horse, his clothes were black. His long, hooded mantle was flung back at the shoulder to reveal a red lining. Sun glinted on his silver spurs, and on the hint of chain mail beneath his mantle.

The dog let out a yelp, struggling against Elise's arms.

Both riders wheeled their mounts in the women's direction. The older man's gaze fixed them unerringly, Elise was sure, even behind their screen of branches. Annora's hand went toward her staff. Elise rose, leaning hard against the wall—as the dog dashed away toward the horses, sparing the females only one backward glance.

"Vortigern," said the dark man, matter-of-factly, when the dog reached his side. The man then inclined his head, courteously, in Elise and Annora's direction.

"Where have you been, young Vort?" said the youth, in English. "Running ahead to cadge food from wayfarers again? There we were, thinking you must have perished."

The riders moved back to the Trackway as the dog gamboled at the black horse's side.

"An ingrate, as I predicted," said Annora, telltale relief in her quiet voice. "Don't you feel foolish now, Elise, thinking they'd come chasing after you? They saw us too, you know, but paid no heed at all. Just to that fool of a dog."

Elise stared after the horsemen, her eyes held by the silver scabbard resting at the right thigh of the black-garbed man. Only left-handed men wore their scabbards on the right, the more readily to unsheathe their swords.

Her friend didn't hear her silence.

"Those were never louts on their dead masters' horses, like we prattled of this morning," Annora said. "That fellow on the black warhorse has *had* no master, or I'll be deloused by a cockerel." She wagged her chin, agreeing with herself. "A nobleman he was, or a knight. Or some other plausible rogue."

The men were now lost to sight. Even as Annora continued full prate, Elise acted on the counsel her friend had offered before the strangers appeared; for reasons she made no attempt to fathom, it seemed a wise thing to do. She shut her eyes and asked God to take the memory of the blood-soaked vision from her heart.

Annora was right, surely. What could such a violent vision mean to Elise? Besides, though some called it a devilish thing to be left-handed, there was more than one swordsman of that persuasion in Britain. More than a hundred, surely. It would be foolish and exhausting to imagine every fellow with a scabbard on his right side might be waiting to lop off a head, Elise's or anyone else's. Without doubt her visions were often devoid of discernible meaning. Some things must remain mysteries. This was just another.

Annora was finishing her discourse. "They were English," she said. "A pox on the whole wicked race." She made the sign of the cross. "Excepting your sainted mother."

"Yes." Elise turned to her and smiled. "Excepting Mother."

After a fervent prayer for safe passage, the women were once more on the Trackway. They traveled in the same direction as the horsemen, and Vort, but Elise thought it probable they would not see them again.

"It's getting cooler. I'll be glad if there's a place by the hearth at this fine inn you've promised," she said, as they walked. "But my cloak is airing well in this wind and might be dry by the time Bwlch-y-Groes is behind us. A few miles more."

Bwlch-y-Groes, Pass of the Cross, was the next notable place they would reach. Once they scaled it, Elise hoped they would have an easier time and make a gentle, quick descent into the valley of the Lledr River, to the village called Dolwyddelan.

The track grew winding. Shadows lengthened, like the lulls between their bouts of conversation. They crossed meadows and ravines and passed through a hollow where a honeysuckle vine embraced a leafless tree. The vine's yellow-pink flowers had released their heavy, sweet scent early; they were hungry perhaps for dusk.

As they crested a stony hillock, Annora broke the silence that had fallen. "You know, I wasn't much enamored of that river," she said.

Elise looked away to hide her smile. "Nor I."

"You'd think that rat-faced woman with the rowan branch could have made more effort to warn us how wicked it was. But will there be other rivers to cross, before Conwy? I pray not. One was more than enough."

"A few others but not nearly as wide. Compared to the Machno they'll be as sun showers are to cloudbursts."

"Poetical, child." Annora raised her staff to rap it idly against an oak branch they stooped to pass under. Giving careful attention to the placement of her feet, she said, "You know that dog?"

"Yes."

"I didn't really mind him so much."

"I know. I liked him too."

The wind still danced through the treetops and whirled in the dust at their ankles. It murmured and it moaned. It gathered itself at their backbones, urging them to the west.

10

HOUSEKEEPING

L ate afternoon was giving way to evening when four riders approached Dolwyddelan from the southeast on the Trackway of the Cross. They reined in their steeds when they saw ahead of them a richly dressed gentleman, alone, standing on the verge of the wide path.

"Careful," said a straight-backed man on a chestnut stallion. He spoke quietly to the other three, in Welsh. "Don't go too near."

The sole woman of the group wore a miniver capelet over a gray mantle and matching riding dress. At the edge of her hood, black curls showed. "What can he be doing here, Eadric," she said, "in the middle of nowhere?"

"It might be prudent to go ask him, my love," said another man, at her side. He had cropped brown hair and strong features and wore a fur collar that was the masculine match to the lady's.

"Let me do the asking, Sir Nevill," said Eadric.

The fourth member of their party was a young giant with a stolid face. He held a flanged truncheon in one gauntleted hand and kept his eyes fixed on the waiting stranger. "Be wary," he said. "That fellow is smiling too wide for my liking. What's he got to be so happy about?"

The woman threw the giant a fond but slightly impatient look. "Perhaps he's just friendly, Herv. Perhaps he took a tumble and lost his horse and wishes our help. It would hardly be sensible for him to scowl and glower, if that's the case."

"Maybe not, Lady Elizabeth. But yea or nay, you can be sure he's not Welsh."

"Why?"

"Look at his cloak, ma'am. Purple. With green swirls. What Welsh-man would wear a thing like that? No, he's bound to be English."

Sir Nevill reached out and patted the woman's hand. "Do you hear that, Elizabeth? English. Whatever is the world coming to?"

She smiled. "Whatever indeed, my love."

Herv's broad face went ruddy pink. "No affront intended, sir," he said. "I just meant, well, we've come back to Wales now, so you might suppose we'd meet up with decent Welshmen rather than fancy-dressed foreigners. That is, I mean—"

"Calm yourself, Herv," said Sir Nevill. "I know exactly what you mean."

"No point in wasting time," said Eadric, dismounting. "Herv, keep good watch while I go hear his tale." With that, he walked toward the stranger.

The man in the purple cloak came forward. Up close, he was youngish, dark-haired, and handsome. "Hello," he said as Eadric approached. "Do you speak English? I'm afraid I have no Welsh."

"Aye, we speak English."

"Oh, good. Might I tell you my dilemma? A few moments ago my horse was panicked by a pair of wild pigs. He's run off altogether. Meanwhile I was knocked out of the saddle by a low branch." He gestured to his head, evidently to some resultant but unapparent injury.

"It's not far now to Dolwyddelan, my party's destination," said Eadric. "Your horse has likely already fled there on the path, sir."

The man gazed around him at the high trees that bordered the way. "But it's nearly dusk. As I beheld the approach of your company, it occurred to me perhaps I might beg the courtesy of a place with you for the rest of the ramble to the village. These grim woods feel so unwelcoming to a solitary man."

Eadric regarded him without answering.

The man met his scrutiny with a pleasant, confident smile.

"Let me ask my master and mistress and see what they would do," Eadric finally said, turning away.

The stranger held out a hand. "Wait," he said. "Are they honest Christians, your lord and lady? Who are their people?"

"I beg pardon?"

The man lowered his voice. "I have not the previous pleasure of their acquaintance, you see, and wouldn't like to accidentally fall in with a heathenish set."

Eadric stood even more erect. "Lord Nevill is of the House of Weston in Cornwall. His family's been fixed at Weston Hall since before men ate apples. My lady's good father . . . was likewise well placed. They're the most respectable people you'll ever have luck to encounter."

"Are they? What a relief, for I've a dislike of heathens. I come from a family of archbishops and the like. A deterrent to normalcy, sometimes, my kin's inborn piety."

In Eadric's long experience, a fair percentage of rich folk—and this person appeared to be rich—was exceedingly odd, prey to many queer notions and anxieties. So he merely inclined his head but made no reply.

The man didn't notice. "Tell them I am Sir Ivo Frowick of Pont-Albion near London. They may have heard of me." Around his neck hung a jeweled crucifix on a golden chain. He raised it to his lips and gave it a quick kiss. "I've come to Wales to visit my uncle Benedict, an abbot who guided my footsteps as a youth."

Eadric nodded. "I'll go tell them."

He paced back to the other three.

"Well?" said Sir Nevill. "Who is he, Eadric?"

"Sir Ivo Frowick of Pont-Albion, my lord. From near London, he says, and he says you might have heard of him."

The lord and his lady pondered that possibility but decided they had not.

"Says he comes from a family high up in the Church," Eadric continued, sounding unimpressed. "Wild pigs made his horse bolt and he wants to know if he can join us the rest of the way to Dolwyddelan."

Lady Elizabeth shrugged. "Why not? He looks harmless enough from here."

"I don't like it." Herv cocked his head and gazed stonily toward the stranger. "Purple. Churchly types don't wear such peacocky stuff as that."

"You obviously haven't been to Canterbury or Westminster lately," said Sir Nevill.

"He's just one man, Herv," said Eadric. "Unsuited to mayhem, by the cut of him. You could swallow him whole for dinner if need be."

Herv wasn't appeased. "If he's so high connected and so fearful of being on his own, what's he done with his servants?"

Eadric frowned. "I didn't think to ask, but I should have."

"They probably went on to Dolwyddelan to advise the innkeeper of their master's arrival and don't know he's been unseated," said Elizabeth. "A hot meal and a bed may be awaiting him even now. Fortunate man, if that's the case."

"I'll admit to fatigue and peckishness, myself," said her husband. "But I suppose the best way to remedy that is to hurry to this promised village and let the poor man go with us."

His decision made, he urged his horse forward. The others followed his lead.

As they came nearer, Sir Ivo's face broke into a relieved smile.

After some discussion, it was decided Herv should surrender his horse.

"I didn't intend to inconvenience anyone, not even a servant," Sir Ivo said, as he settled into the saddle Herv had just vacated, arranging his purple cloak around him.

"It's no bother," said Sir Nevill. "Herv enjoys walking."

Herv's face suggested otherwise.

Lady Elizabeth smiled. "I don't think it's far now to Dolwyddelan. Did your men go ahead to advise the innkeeper of your arrival?"

"They did, dear lady. My servants are always so solicitous of my comfort. If only my horse were as unswerving in his duty."

At the head of the group, Eadric kept his eyes fixed on the path and his face straight. But Herv, plodding behind the four riders, curled his lip.

"As I told your man," Ivo continued, "I've come to Wales to visit my uncle Benedict, an abbot. Rather aged and infirm, I fear."

"An abbot? From where, Sir Ivo?" Elizabeth asked. "Aberconwy or Penmon? Perhaps Llandrillo?"

"I'm lost without my servants," replied Ivo, raising a hand to his aristocratic forehead. "The truth is, I can't name my uncle's place of residence. Not even if you held my feet to a fire. I leave such minutiae to my people, as an excess of information always makes my head ache."

Eadric leaned forward to pat his horse's neck and thereby disguised his grin. Then he straightened and went stoically on. But Sir Nevill did not appear to be amused.

Elizabeth looked nonplussed by Ivo's answer but soon recovered her manners. "I do sympathize," she said. "Welsh names can be daunting if one is unaccustomed. I grew up in North Wales, but my husband is English. Fortunately my mother was also English, so I have the advantage of both languages."

"Give credit where it is due, Elizabeth," said Sir Nevill. "Have I not learned to converse in laudable Welsh under your patient tutelage?"

"You have, my lord, and are to be commended. What about Herv and Eadric? Stubborn Welshmen, yet they now speak tolerable English. It merely requires resolve."

"However do they, mere servants, manage to keep dozens of strange new words from tangling up inside their heads?" said Ivo. "I could never manage."

Sir Nevill made some bland reply, and they rode on in silence.

"You've heard my humdrum tale," said Sir Ivo, after a while. "But what brings *you* gentlefolk out to the wild world? Your man mentioned you've journeyed from Cornwall."

Nevill threw his wife a warning look. "Like you, we go to call on relatives," he said. "Nothing wonderfully interesting."

"A funeral, perhaps?"

A slight crease marred the smooth expanse of Elizabeth's brow. "Why do you ask that?"

"Speculation, dear lady. Aren't births or deaths often the only reasons we busy folk make time to leave our usual duties?"

Meanwhile Herv slowed his pace and glanced behind. He looked right and left to the trees crowding the path. Able through habit to sense Herv's lack of ease, Eadric drew back on his reins.

"What is it?" said Sir Nevill, bringing his horse to a standstill.

Sir Ivo and Lady Elizabeth also halted.

"I thought I heard something," replied Herv, "in the woods."

Ivo's brown eyes widened. "Thank God I'm not on my own. Is it lepers? I pray not."

"Calm yourself, sir," said Nevill. "It's probably more wild pigs, or birds returning to their nests for the night."

"Birds? Not rooks," said Ivo, now gawking upward. "I'm not equal to dealing with rooks."

Sir Nevill exchanged a look with his wife. "Not rooks, I'm sure," he said. "More likely a flock of clumsy pigeons."

"Thanks be." Ivo ceased scanning the sky. "I'm not at all frightened of pigeons."

"Let's go on, Eadric," said Elizabeth, as her horse swished its tail and whinnied. "If we stop for every little noise, we'll never get to Dolwyddelan."

"Herv," Eadric called, raising up in his stirrups and looking over the other three riders' heads, "is all well? Can we move on?"

Two buff-colored hares just then shot across the path between the riders.

Sir Nevill's horse reared, but he quickly brought it under control. "There go your noisy culprits," he said, watching the rabbits bound into the darkening woods. "Sprinting away to supper, as we ought now to do."

"Aye," said Herv, allowing himself a grin. "We can go on."

Everyone moved forward down the path.

An instant later the young giant gave a strangled cry. Sir Nevill swung around in time to see him pitch to the dirt on his face. The hilt of a dagger protruded from the base of his neck. His arm twitched once and his fingers clawed at the earth. Then he lay still.

Eadric turned and saw his fallen friend. He paled. Sliding from his horse, he rushed to Elizabeth's side. "Fly to Dolwyddelan." He spoke to her in rapid Welsh. "Trample anyone who tries to stop you."

Eadric drew his sword as she fled.

Sir Nevill dismounted and likewise drew his sword. He cast a grim look ahead toward the place where his wife galloped into the dusk.

"What happened? What shall I do? Oh, we're doomed," cried Ivo. "I think I may be ill."

"Have you no weapon?" said Nevill.

Ivo pushed aside his cloak and fumbled with his embroidered belt. "Wait, yes, I think I do." He produced a knife with a long blade and lifted it to the weakening daylight. Then he swung one leg over the pommel and jumped to the ground as his cloak floated out behind him. He stood just out of arm's length of the other two men.

Eadric's brows drew together as he watched Ivo's deft dismount.

Nevill also stared. Surely no helpless fop had need for such a knife as that. Terrible suspicion dawned in his eyes.

"You're looking at my toy, Sir Nevill," Ivo said. His voice had altered, grown deeper and not at all fearful. "It came from Madrid, actually. Pretty, isn't it?"

Eadric launched himself forward. Ivo hurled his knife. It struck the servant hard between the eyes and lodged firmly there. The hilt quivered. A drop of blood escaped from the wound and ran across the bridge of his nose. He dropped.

Nevill looked down at the man who had been his wife's servant since childhood.

Ivo said, "At least he didn't suffer," and crossed himself.

A tall, bald brute crashed from the woods. He ran straight for Nevill, knocked him to the ground, and straddled him. Then he slit his throat with a dagger.

Sir Nevill thrashed. The man plied his dagger again.

"That's enough, Percy," said Ivo, stepping back. "Must you be so theatrical? Look"—he lifted a foot from the ground and pointed his toes—"you splashed a drop of blood on my boot."

The shiny-headed man clambered up. "Sorry, your lordship." He grinned, raised nonexistent eyebrows, and didn't look at all sorry. "But he was flopping 'round like a fish."

Ivo inspected Sir Nevill's motionless form. "Not anymore."

Percy barked out a laugh and began to go corpse to corpse, hunting booty.

Ivo observed him with tepid interest. "That's rather a vulgar thing to do, Percy, isn't it?"

"Aye. But a man does what he can, sir." He considered Sir Nevill's bloody fur capelet, then left it where it was. "I ever mention I got a toddling son up toward Chester? Eats like a horse. Little Percy, they call him."

"You never mentioned Little Percy, nor did I ask. But where is our tardy Dexter? It's getting dark and I'm fatigued."

A short, wiry fellow emerged from the mist that began to obscure the Trackway. "Here, sir," he said. "Oh, she's a precious bitch, this one." He dragged Lady Elizabeth behind him by a rope bound to her wrists.

A gag kept her from screaming when she saw the bodies of her two servants and her husband.

Ivo watched her blanch.

"Should I fix her?" asked Dexter.

The nobleman shook his head. "Not yet. But Dex, I swear you'd have been amused. I told them my name is Ivo Frowick of Pont-Albion, a creature entirely of my own creation. From a fine Church family. You know, it's rather a shame I haven't more time to devote to acting."

Dexter's close-set eyes gleamed with unfeigned admiration. "When the Maker fashioned you, Sir Nicolas, the mold was surely broke."

Elizabeth stared at Sir Ivo, who had suddenly become Sir Nicolas. She made a strange sound in her throat.

Sir Nicolas looked back at her. "I know. You're angry with me. But if *you* had inadequate funds to lead a noble sort of life, you'd be more sympathetic. As my friend Percy says, a man does what he can."

Percy chuckled and dropped gracelessly to the ground to sort through the contents of Sir Nevill's money pouch.

Dexter looked from his master to Elizabeth and back. "Think she's dibbled who you are, my lord?"

"I do. But remove her gag and let's hear."

When Dexter did as he was told, Elizabeth spit in his face. He slapped her so hard, she fell to the dirt.

"Desist, you two," said Nicolas. He squatted at Elizabeth's side while Dexter stood beside them, watching, brandishing a knife. "So then, dear, I believe your late father was the justiciar of North Wales. *N'est-ce pas?* And don't spit at *me*, if you please, or I'll let Percy have his way with you this instant. He'd be no dream of love, I'm confident."

She looked toward her husband's corpse. Her eyes filled with tears, but she wiped them angrily away.

"Yes, you're very fetching and plucky, Elizabeth," said Nicolas. "I can see that. But if you want to save yourself, you'll answer my questions."

She raised her head and looked at him squarely. "Yes, Sir Nicolas de Breauté" — she pronounced his full name as if it were the lowest, most hideous curse — "my father was justiciar. But you killed him. I know. Nevill knows —"

"He knew. Poor Nevill knew. But go on."

A lone tear rolled down her cheek. "He knew people in London. They told us a man wanted Father dead so that he could be justiciar. That man hired a common assassin."

"Common? No, he hired me. But there's more. You also have a brother. A shadowy kind of character, they say. A spy for England."

She went even whiter. "No. Gwydion's dead. He was killed in France."

Nicolas reached out to touch her cheek, but she drew violently away. "Now you're lying, Elizabeth," he said, in tones of mild reproach. "Your brother's not dead. You know that because you paid his ransom so he could leave France. When he returned to England, he killed the man who hired me. So you must have told him, in a letter, I suspect, where to find that man. In that same letter you must have also told him about me—unless he happened to learn it from his victim in London."

Her eyes were wide.

He nodded. "He must be headstrong, your Gwydion. In any event, I was promised in good faith by the man who hired me that I could have your father's manor, and I intend to have it. Really, who in London is ever much bothered by what transpires in wild Wales? But if your brother is lurking about, as angry as you but more able to strike, what are my chances of keeping my new house? In fact, your brother probably assumes *he* ought to have it."

"You're insane," she said, her voice breaking.

Behind her, Dexter growled.

"Hush, fair Dexter," said Nicolas. "Insane, Elizabeth? Oh, no. I'm eccentric, intriguing, passionate. But not insane. So now tell me, finally—where is your mysterious brother? I really do think you know."

She put her head in her hands and choked back a sob. "I *don't* know. I thought he was still in France. I've been waiting to hear from him."

"Then why did you leave Cornwall? Weren't you intending to meet him somewhere outside Conwy near my new house? Didn't you plan to shed a few tears over your wretched pater, then make arrangements to catch the fiend who made you both orphans?"

"No! I'm only going to Conwy to see to my father's affairs. I have no plan to meet Gwydion. How could I? There's not been one word from him since I sent ransom money to Paris." She raised her head and spoke in a voice thick with loathing. "But if—*when*—he finds you, you'll wish you had never been born."

Nicolas peered into her face. "You know, I believe you. I do. However, that might only mean you're a desperate, convincing liar sacrificing herself for her sibling. But lying or not, I fear you can't help me further. At this point, you're disposable." He stood and nodded at his henchman. "Go on, Dexter. But don't dawdle."

Dexter dragged her up.

She scratched and writhed in his arms. "My father, my husband, my servants," she gasped, "you'd murder us all?"

Nicolas rose and brushed bits of grass from his cloak. "And your brother, eventually. When you put it like that, it does sound a bit unfair."

She went still in Dexter's grip and fixed her frightened gaze on the jeweled crucifix. "But what of your eternal soul, Nicolas de Breauté?"

He looked vaguely troubled, then sighed. "I'm always conscientious about confessing. Don't fret."

Dexter reached up—for Lady Elizabeth was tall and he was not—and yanked back her hood. He gawked at her shining black hair. "My lord, first can I, you know—"

"If you must. Just do it and be quick."

Percy guffawed. "As if he could be aught but quick." Then he scowled. "What about me? Don't I get a turn?"

"No, you don't," said Nicolas. "Your reward is all those nice coins to buy pies for Little Percy. Don't be greedy."

Elizabeth wrenched away from Dexter and ran toward the forest. He swore and dashed after.

Sir Nicolas wandered to the other side of the Trackway and admired a view of distant shadowy hills just visible through the trees. He plucked a yellow flower, sniffed the bloom, then tucked it behind his ear.

After a few moments a long scream sounded.

"He'll be back now in two shakes of a lamb's tail," said Percy.

Another piercing cry came. This one stopped abruptly.

"Told you so," said Percy.

"You're an absolute oracle," said Sir Nicolas.

Dexter returned, smirking.

"Gentlemen," said Nicolas, "we've had a long day. But there's still more to accomplish. Percy, I'd like you to hurry to my new manor and be sure all is in preparation for my arrival."

"Now? But we're miles away and it's nearly dark."

"You'll be fine, Percy. Who would molest such a great handsome fellow as you?"

Percy grumbled but was soon gone.

"Dexter, fetch our horses from the thicket," Sir Nicolas said. "Then you'll arrange Elizabeth and her husband nicely on the path so they may be readily found. When her brother gets wind of it, he'll likely rush to my new house for revenge. I'm hoping he'll be too stricken and angry to use sensible caution."

"Then we'll give him a rare reception, eh, my lord?"

"We will. But perhaps we won't even need to trouble ourselves."

He looked thoughtful. "What is the name of that man I sent out last week to hunt for poor Elizabeth's brother?"

"Harold Munceny."

"Yes. Perhaps Harold Munceny will find him first and kill him while he sleeps. For all we know he may have already done the deed."

"That'd be tidy, sir. But what about this other pair? What should I do with them?"

"These?" Sir Nicolas considered the dead servants. "We're taking them with us."

Dexter's mouth fell open.

"Fasten your lips," said his master. "You know four is an unlucky number. I've told you often enough. We can't leave four corpses here or we'll meet with no end of bad luck. No, we'll have to deposit these fellows elsewhere."

Dexter complained but to no avail. Sir Nicolas could rarely be dissuaded from a plan once he had decided on it. If superstition came into play, logic was especially futile.

Herv and Eadric were draped over their horses and led away by the nobleman and his lackey.

Night fell. Except for the occasional rustlings of busy, innocent creatures, the woods grew silent. The sweet scent of honeysuckle filled the air, luring moths from far and wide.

Side by side on the path, Lady Elizabeth and Sir Nevill lay, hands placed thoughtfully together. Matching gashes decorated their throats.

11

Doubtful Accommodations

The path climbed toward Bwlch-y-Groes. Annora's pace flagged, accelerated, flagged again. Elise tried to match her uneven progress but stumbled more than once with the effort.

"My body wasn't built for this kind of speed," Annora finally admitted when she stopped to catch her breath along a particularly steep bit of path.

Then on they went, and upward, until they stood on a massive gray rock. Here it was as if they were held in a hard, smooth palm, offered by the hills to the sky. They surveyed the green lands below, before and behind, as their skirts billowed around their ankles. Annora shivered in the ever chillier wind. Teased from her wimple, a few curling strands of gray hair blew about her face like a living frame.

"May God give us succor, child," she whispered, "but I have the sudden notion this place may be peopled by ghosts. Don't you hear that tapping, like dead fingers on a drum? It's drifting on the wind all around. Listen."

Elise stood still and closed her eyes. She smelled the sap of fir trees. But she heard only the sound her own blue mantle made as it whipped in the stronger gusts. That and leaves rustling.

But soon indeed there came a faint tapping. It grew louder. Then it receded.

"You've surely heard it," Annora said, moving a step closer to her companion.

The tapping sounded again, more clearly. Tapping, or clacking. It arose from the direction they had just walked. Along with it, even as they listened, there came chanting. It was a dirge, with words too low and distant to comprehend.

Maelgwyn, thought Elise, with a choir of satanic angels to avenge him.

"It isn't Maelgwyn," said Annora, as if she had read Elise's mind. "So don't you dare to think so."

The singing faded. But the clacking became more distinct, like the striking of hollow wood on hollow wood, or bone on bone.

Elise turned fully in the direction of the sound and stood rooted to the spot. Her eyes grew wide. "Lepers," she said. "Lepers with hand clackers to warn the world they approach."

"Merciful God, then rush away. Hurry, before the unclean devils are accidentally upon us. We have to reach Dolwyddelan, for they'll stay well away from any village."

Without another word, they abandoned the gray rock of Bwlch-y-Groes and hurried forward into the Lledr Valley.

Of course Annora and Elise had seen many lepers, but only from a distance. Gossip, however, had told them how one might appear if encountered at close range. Dressed in brown or white, he or she would have thin hair or none, no eyelashes or brows, enlarged nostrils, swollen lips, and polluted breath. He would lack toes or fingers, even an ear or nose. He might possess the evil eye. But if he didn't, one would always find the fixed stare that marked their kind, the horrible leer of the satyr.

Everyone knew it was a satyr's lustful habits that made a leper a leper to begin with. Lepers, it was said, liked to usher the vulnerable into their own ranks so they might have even more rotting brethren. Because of that wish to seduce the unwary, they hated their own betraying clackers, hated the warning sound the things made. But they were bound under dire penalty of law to use them, always, to alert the innocent populace of their loathsome whereabouts.

Still, they were rumored to subvert the king's edict from time to time, to secretly leave their clackers behind—if they believed they could do so with impunity. They were said to then sneak into brothels or bathhouses late at night when fires burned low, when prostitutes and their patrons might be too drunk to discern the danger making its way into their domain. Once inside, the lepers would delight for hours in diseased intercourse in the shadows with oblivious wantons, thereby spreading their malady. For that reason the current English king, the third Edward, issued an order banning all lepers, the unclean, from London.

"Which cottage shall we try first, Elise? Why is no one about? I hope they're not all indoors, gulping my meal."

"There's a stake fixed over that door ahead, with an ivy wreath tacked on. A public house, Annora, giving notice they have ale. There will be a drink for us, and with luck a bed."

"In a pig's whisper there will be when they see the coins I clink beneath their noses."

Elise gave her a curious look. "We must talk about this lucre. We will, soon."

"Soon. But not before our supper."

As they approached the wide door beneath the ale stake, they heard a woman's voice on the other side, and men laughing. Two frowning peasants in green cottes, brown hosen, and brown hoods with short liripipes at their ends came out through the door. Off they strode toward a nearby cottage.

"They seemed vexed," said Elise, watching them go.

"Let's hope it wasn't by the victuals or drink they had."

The public house's sole front window was covered by a lime-washed shutter and allowed no view inside. Only guessing at the kind of establishment they might find, and hoping it might be reputable and safe, the women smoothed their skirts and cloaks and tucked strands of hair back in place.

"Am I respectable?" asked Annora.

"An apostle's dream of worthiness. And I?"

"You are. Even that mark on your cheek has disappeared."

"Oh." Elise raised a hand to her face. "I'd forgotten."

"Good."

"Yes, I suppose it is." Then Elise's voice dropped and grew earnest. "But now you must heed me before we go in, Annora. It's vital that you do. Our story is sad. You see, only urgent straits push us to this journey, without benefit of any man's protection. We are widows from Brecon, mother and daughter, on our way to join your brother, my uncle Ifor, at . . . at Rhuddlan."

"Brecon to Rhuddlan? If I walked all the way from Brecon, my feet would be worn to pegs. It's miles and miles. And why Rhuddlan? You told the rowan woman we were for Bangor."

"Does it matter? I didn't say we journeyed this far from Brecon in one day. We've been on the road a while. Anyway, Rhuddlan and Brecon make a better tale, I think. Rhuddlan is north of here, Brecon well south. There's a good chance no one will have much knowledge of either, to confound us with awkward questions."

"Why didn't my brother Ifor come to us? A man would be safer on the roads than two defenseless women."

"You're right. Well, I fear . . . I fear Uncle Ifor is afflicted with the falling sickness and only waits for a glimpse of our faces before he gives up the ghost altogether. We are his last living relatives. He believes he won't enjoy an easy passing if he fails to look upon us one last time."

"How do we know all this?"

"How? Oh, from a messenger Ifor recently dispatched."

"How strange my brother is. And what a wily girl you are."

"Too wily. Father and Mother are probably looking down this instant, shaking their heads at my way with deceit."

"More likely they're cheering your ingenuity. I'm sure your brothers are. Besides, this tale will hurt no one and may dampen unwanted interest. But do let us go in now, for that roast chicken is clucking my name through the door."

"Remember then, from Brecon to Rhuddlan to comfort Uncle Ifor. Are you ready?"

"Surely I am, except we have never been in such a place as this before without a man to lend us respectability."

"Then we must rely on our own demeanor to lend it."

Elise pushed open the door. Immediately the tantalizing scent of roasting fowl and onions wafted out to greet them. Peering into the long, smoky room, they saw that a fire blazed at one end. It lit the faces of a quartet of men who turned and went mute as soon as the new arrivals appeared in the doorway.

One of the four was a young man in undyed robes that proclaimed him Cistercian, a White Monk. His countenance was unlined and his brown hair perfectly tonsured; firelight reflected on his bald dome. Captured in that unguarded moment, however, his expression may have been fairly described as beleaguered. A glance at his fellows, in their dun tunies, did much to explain this. Each of his companions bore shaved into the back of short, stubbly hair an imprecise crucifix. Two of the fellows, both young and thin, grinned foolishly. The oldest, the third, looked back down after a moment and used his thumb to draw invisible pictures on the table.

Annora nudged Elise. "We did so well to outstrip the lepers," she whispered. "But now we've fallen into a nest of lunatics."

Bustling forward from some nether region came a tall, squinting woman in a grease-spotted blue apron, a dress of the same hue, and a lopsided gray wimple. Lines were etched beside her wide mouth, but a stiffness in her manner suggested she had not earned them laughing. She wiped her hands on a limp rag, then tucked the rag under her apron's string.

"Good ladies, welcome to Dolwyddelan," she said. "Will you shut the door, if you please, to keep out the mist?" She left no pause for reply but went on in a rush as Elise closed the door. "Have you traveled far? Our accommodations are the finest to be had. Four or five to a bed, never more. Even less, tonight. We've a stable for your horses—if your men have horses, of course." She smiled ingratiatingly. "You've stumbled into good luck for supper, for there is chicken stuffed with herbed onions, and a minced beef mock hedgehog fashioned from a pig's belly, roasted on a spit"—she gestured to the fire—"bristling with glazed almonds."

From the corner of her eye Elise saw Annora swallow.

The woman's eyes narrowed tighter into the squint. She smiled more broadly, apparently seeing her speech was having good effect. "Stewed crab apples, if you're partial," she continued, brushing at a clump of lank brown hair plastered to her cheek. "And ale like an angel's kiss, so gladdening it is. Sweet wine from Gascony too. But I judge it sickly stuff, myself."

She peered from Elise to Annora, then back.

Annora leaned toward her and spoke softly. "What of these, with the monk? If they pass the night here, can you swear they will be kept well away from decent women?"

The landlady made an ineffectual attempt to straighten her wimple. She frowned. "They are harmless, blithering madmen, I'll witness. God's light shining through those shaved crosses onto their fevered brains has had good result, as Brother Gerald there assures me. He shepherds them to the hospice at Ysbyty Ifan for a course of fasting to finish routing their demons."

Annora persisted. "Are you certain they're harmless?"

The woman pursed her lips. "Your own menfolk will be your best guard, after all. But these fools are not robust and could be knocked on their ears by any healthy man."

"Madness imparts strange strength," said Annora, still concerned but looking longingly toward the chicken and mock hedgehog a red-haired boy turned on a long spit over the fire.

A brief silence fell.

"Likely it can impart strength," the woman then said. During the span of the silence she seemed to have arrived at a mean conclusion, for her voice had grown less friendly. "But now I'm asking myself where your men have got to. It's a long time to be tying up horses."

Elise drew herself to her full height. Annora could only stare, for she was all at once reminded forcibly of Elise's dead father, of his occasional imperious manner when some subordinate did not jump quick enough to do his bidding. Annora had never before seen this trait in the girl but was not sorry to see it now.

"My mother and I are widows, traveling alone out of sad necessity," Elise said. Disdain cooled her words. "We go to Rhuddlan to give comfort to my dying uncle."

"A dying uncle, is it? Oh, I'm sure it is. Well, well, I suppose the truth is some scoundrel has given you to believe the house of Ieuan ap Morgan Goch is a house of toleration. But he misled you badly. We'll harbor no easy women here."

Monk and lunatics strained blatantly to listen, as the yawning boy turned the spit. Another woman, younger than the landlady and all in gray, entered the room from an interior door in the back. She leaned against the wall, head tilted, unspeaking, as a black and white cat cleaned its paws by the fire.

"You seem conversant with the slang of worldly sin, ma'am," said Elise. "However, my mother and I are not. Perhaps you would do well to accompany the good brother and his patients, to try to cast out your own demons."

A hurriedly stifled laugh rang out from the gray-clad woman.

The landlady spun around to her, further disarranging her wimple. "Since when are you paid to squawk like a magpie, girl? I told you to fetch the ale."

The girl hurried out, but not before Elise saw by the glow of the fire that she possessed no upper lip; her teeth showed in a permanent grin. It was a common punishment in some cities for a female found thrice guilty of whoring to have her lip cut off so she could no longer pleasure men with her mouth.

Maelgwyn had told Elise this with vicious satisfaction, one night in their chamber. "But if it is a crime, is it not also the man's crime?" she had foolishly asked. Maelgwyn slammed her against the wall and took her like a dog. "Is this my fault, Elise?" he said, over and over. "Or this? Or this? No, the blame of enticement, Elise, is yours. The blame is entirely yours."

The landlady turned back to her would-be guests and folded her arms across her chest.

"Well, never mind," said Annora to Elise. She held out her cupped hand, shaking the coins she had now produced. They made a jangly sound. "We'll call at some other house for lodging. It wouldn't surprise me if another place in Dolwyddelan didn't prove more hospitable than this." She looked at the woman in blue. "Less likely to be infested with vermin."

"Vermin," said the lunatic sitting closest to the monk. He slapped his own face lightly. "Maggots and red worms on snow."

The young man next to him had a scar down his cheek. "Stingy udders," he said. "Yon innkeeper's all bile, no milk."

"Quiet, I implore you," said the monk, Brother Gerald.

But the landlady paid no heed anyway. The coins held her gaze.

"Yes, Mother, let us depart," said Elise. "The cottage with the leeks growing on the turf of the roof looked welcoming. Those leeks have surely kept evil away as well."

They turned toward the door.

"Don't go," said the landlady, reaching out. "An uncle, ill in Rhuddlan? Then please, rest here. Eat and rest. You see, sometimes the aches in my bones make me hasty, and my knees are throbbing so today, with the mist creeping in." She wagged her head. "I sensed right away you were respectable by your fine cloaks. Both widows, with two dear husbands cold in the ground?"

The third lunatic, a gray-haired, haggard man, raised his eyes from his large hands. "*De mortuis nil nisi bonum*," he said. Then he stared down once more.

Everyone looked to the monk for enlightenment.

"It's Latin. Of the dead say nothing except good," he told them. "He was a butcher at Machynlleth, where a doctor taught him Latin as a diversion. But the doctor died in the Mortality. After, youths broke down this man's door and stole his cleavers and his two books."

"Tragedy and sackcloth," said the man who slapped himself. "My tale is ten times worse."

Brother Gerald gave his unsympathetic charge a reproachful look and continued. "Now he speaks only Latin—when he speaks. Sometimes the whites of his eyes go bloodred for no evident reason. Often he is smitten with melancholia."

"Bake cuttlefish bones until they turn to powder," Annora said. "Make a wash of the powder and put it in his eye."

"Cuttlefish?" said the monk.

"To rid the eye of bloody webs. It works wondrous well."

"Fish and bones, who cares?" said the slapper. "They found *me* in a river, bobbing with a dead ox. Like the dog that guards the gates of Hades, that ox spoke to me. It spoke to me"—he looked at the faces around him and grinned—"in Latin."

"*Crepitus infinitum,*" said the butcher, rousing.

The Cistercian sighed. "A discharge of wind from the bowels, without end."

The slapper banged his fist on the table. "How can you have wind from the bowels if you have no end? It would pop right out of your navel."

"You've been duped, Brother Gerald," the landlady said, her lip curling. "These fellows aren't lunatics. They're asses, feigning madness to avoid honest work."

"Hee-haw," said the slapper, baring crooked teeth.

The other lunatic spoke, he of "all bile, no milk." "I had a comely, untrue woman once," he said. His tone had grown somber. "All green beads and fingertips she was. She watched me craft bows from yew branches. Her beads tapped together when she stood behind me, and her breasts brushed my arm."

Slapper's hands rested on his chest like sleeping gulls as he regarded the bow maker with unwholesome interest. "Did you stop her beads from tapping, friend," he said, "and end her untruths with your bow?"

"No, ended mine." The fellow plucked something from his ear and placed it on the table. It glinted in the fire's light—a shiny green bead.

Slapper stared down at the bead, then up at the bow maker.

The boy stopped turning the spit to tiptoe toward the men at the table.

"Hie you back there before everything is burnt black, Alun," snapped the landlady. "It's only a stupid bead."

The boy kicked at a chair and stalked back to the spit.

Then a rooster crowed just outside the front door.

"Your rooster is confused," said Annora, eager to talk of something wholesome. "Perhaps it's as thirsty as I am."

It crowed again.

The landlady frowned. "It's an ill portent for it to be so off its proper time. But I'll go out in a trice and anoint its crest with oil. That always stops it from crowing at sunset."

The bow maker scooped the bead from the table and wrapped it in his fist.

Slapper sat down, sighing. "Rub my cock with oil and I'll stop crowing too," he said.

"Brother," said the landlady, now red-faced, "curb these fellows' tongues or sleep outdoors."

The monk scrambled up. "I beseech you, no, for there may be lepers in the woods. But I vow I will strap angelica leaves to my poor lambs' heads after supper and dose them with ground goat's horn and syrup of poppies. They will sleep like the dead, I promise."

"We'll see. After my husband returns from settling the other two guests in their private quarters, our fine cottage next door, I'll ask his opinion. Distinguished gentlemen *those* are, at least."

"One has a silver sword," said Slapper to Elise and Annora. "And a dog."

"Whose manners are better than yours," said the landlady.

"I believe I would like to sit down," said Elise.

12

SUCCUBUS

A philosopher's idle question, perhaps: the beams that dance so nimbly before my inner eyes, and this easy flowing forward into the seduction of the dark—will these two things ever tell me how I came to be here, wherever I am? Or does it even matter?

This is what the man asked the all-encompassing silence. He asked without words, without apprehension. He felt no worry. He was quite content to feel nothing at all.

Then an alchemist's question: is it possible for a man to turn to marble, cool marble, spinning the tale of Pygmalion's statue in reverse? Or does it even matter?

The man blinked.

So he was not made of marble, not quite, not yet. For he could blink. His eyelids moved. A sweet sensation—wasn't it?—the caress of the lid on the eye.

Gradually there was more. He began to hear. He heard—he believed he heard—a low pleasant murmuring, all around him. Serene and undemanding. How good to simply allow oneself to be borne along with the murmuring, satisfied with any destination it chose. Or with no destination at all.

Still more. He saw—he believed he saw—the moon. There. No, there. He commanded his eyes to see sensibly. Yes, there. The moon, perfect and round and complete in its uncaring. First here, now there, constant above him in a most inconstant way.

But wait. What was that? A swift hint of a thing that was surely unwanted—pure sensation, vanishing as suddenly as a breath. A hint of . . . pain?

No, not pain. Impossible. Unthinkable.

It was too late. He couldn't disown the thought once he had given it life. Now he was unable to sink back exactly into the pleasure of his previous lack of feeling.

Again the hint of pain. Stronger, radiating from everywhere, every part of him.

Likewise the pleasant murmuring took on new, unwelcome life, became more than sound, became an entity. Hurrying, burbling. Worse—it was impure, filled with tiny dirty things, the man was sure. This murmuring surged beneath him and beside him. Finally it took hold of him and carried him to a soft wall, where it held him without effort.

The moon appeared again, just overhead, and stayed inflexibly in that one place.

Soon the pain ebbed. For that the man was glad. Time passed and he grew accustomed to the wall that constrained him.

More time passed. Again his small world grew manageable . . .

Until he took a deeper breath. As he did, a dark, bent shape blotted out the moon. He gasped. Trembling racked him. Above, the dark shape wobbled as if in sympathy or scorn. Watching the shape as he fought to control his shivering, he commanded his mind to think sensibly. But what was this thing, this silhouette so warped and silent, so impossibly near?

It was his own arm; he understood, after a moment. And he almost laughed. Then he reproached himself for a fool. What else could it be but his arm? True, it was not as he remembered. It was crooked now, strangely arranged at the elbow or where the elbow had been. This new limb jutted up, then hung down at an odd angle, useless, naked, dripping—

Dripping. So he was in water. Somehow he was in water.

A woman all at once appeared directly before him, a ghost or an angel. Composed, grave, intent, she hovered above the black water that he now saw surrounded him entirely. She shimmered in the pale path of the moonlight. Her long dark hair nearly brushed his face and her fine gray eyes were clear and knowing. Their disdain burned through his skin.

She offered him a shard of bloody, glowing glass.

A strangled cry welled from deep inside the man. Starting as a wordless roar, it surged from his belly to his chest. But it could rise no higher than that. Furious, futile, the cry was only able to imbed itself like a toothed hook, a messenger of agony at the base of his ruptured throat.

"Elise," the man finally strained to hiss. The name was so low and frenzied that no creature save a lone song thrush, just waking in a nearby tree, was able to hear it.

The song thrush flew away, and the dream image of the woman disappeared.

There was a splash. Captured by wrappings and water, the man could not turn to see what caused it. Anxious some unspeakable danger approached him in the night, his breathing grew rapid. Each of his own treacherous breaths cut into his throat. In this wretched state he was seized by an excruciating fear of spirits, demons, water monsters. Succubi.

The river rose and fell a fraction. The water's motion lifted him a little, then let him fall. The movement caused the cord that bound his wrappings to snag on a sinewy overhanging branch. He felt himself unwind, felt his nose and mouth submerge. His good arm, then his legs were loosed. He floated, came face up, again beheld the moon, and blinked one more time. He was naked now. No cloth or cord held him. No demon arrived to assail him.

But so cold. The moon turned blue above him. His numb fingers flexed in wavelets of his own making, plucking convulsively at the soft, crumbling matter of the bank. No use. He sank. His undamaged arm tore at the water. Sucking in a great mouthful of river and grit, he tried to scream but only produced a bestial rasp. Bending, writhing, he surfaced again. Fresh pain shot through him below his waist.

Once more he sank. His heart pounded. He knew now he would die in the river, dissolve into tiny dirty pieces, become a puzzle of pebbles, become a broken ghost.

Oh, but then he'd fly straight to Heaven—wouldn't he, wouldn't he?—like the living motes of a dust storm. God would reconstruct him with love and celestial ease. Surely, surely God would reward such a righteous believer as he.

Underwater he opened his eyes slowly as if from a deep sleep. He beheld his dead mother swimming beside him. She was naked and indecently fair. "Procreatrix," he said, "you are just as I remember." She raised thin, arched brows but didn't answer. Rather she whirled in a circle, in the river, underwater. She undertook a mad, abandoned spinning. Faster, faster. She spun with her hair drifting all about her, unrestrained by any natural law.

When at last she came to rest, fair strands settled on her shoulders and coiled around her pale breasts, framing her nipples. The man couldn't look away.

The night current distorted her gray eyes, eyes so like Elise's, and showed them vibrant and full of strange promise. Raising a languid arm, she gestured to the man's middle. He peered down. A curling ribbon of blood escaped from an untidy slit between his navel and his manhood. The wound did not gape. But it was edged with the color of the human tongue, a flat and wicked hue against the whiteness of his groin. Around him, the river was suddenly dyed a thin pink. He smelled decay, rotting bodies, excrement. His mother closed her eyes and clapped her hands without a sound. She laughed, again soundlessly, and glided backward to the farthest limit of his vision. Then she disappeared.

He screamed—this time he truly screamed—as he flew up out of the river.

"Well, you don't look like Baby Moses, and there's nary a bulrush about," said a bemused voice. "But I'm a good Christian fellow. So as I see no sign of the Pestilence on your sodden hide, I suspect I ought not let you drown."

Lying icy and bleeding on the river's bank, the man blinked up at his gangly, white-haired rescuer.

"You confess to any name, old ram?" The tall Samaritan took off his ragged cloak and flung it over the naked man.

The man tried to say "Maelgwyn" but could only croak.

"No name? Then I'll call you Gryg. Some hound snap your arm and rob you, Gryg? Throw you in the river? Fie, I see the hole they put in your neck. And the other down by your cock."

Maelgwyn raised his head and spit up as much water as his gut could have possibly held. It soaked his rescuer's cloak.

Sheep appeared out of the dark. Pale cautious heads, gray-white bodies crowded behind the Samaritan's legs. They brought a greasy, musty scent and muted bleating.

"My old flock's what saved you. One of my clumsy fools slid down the bank and landed in the river. Elsewise I wouldn't have tottered over and caught you floating. Now they've come back to see what the excitement's about. Didn't you, stinky beggars?"

Maelgwyn raised his hand to his throat. The shepherd turned away from his animals in time to see this halting motion.

"Softly, old ram. I'll heave you home and knead unguent into those slashes, and I'll truss that arm. Put some clothes on you too, so you don't look like a half-drowned Adam."

Maelgwyn let his hand fall. For one splendid moment he contemplated the wonder of the Resurrection. He considered Lazarus. He imagined his own haloed image woven on ten thousand silk banners, carried by ten thousand holy knights. Then he smiled.

The shepherd scratched his chin. "It's bitter as Judas's heart tonight. But likely the coldness of the river stopped you bleeding to death. Your juices must have gone too thick to pour out." He bent and lifted Maelgwyn easily into his arms. "I waddled into a millpond when I was a babby," he went on conversationally, unfazed by his exertion. "The day of the Asses' Feast. Mother swore it was sprites kept me alive, for I was underwater till vespers. But see, old ram, I'm right as a stallion now."

Maelgwyn closed his eyes. He would live. He would find the stinking rose who thought she had killed him and surprise her with a special kiss, as a loving husband might be wont to do. Then he would dispatch her to her master, Satan.

13

SWEET ALE AND
DISMEMBERED CHICKENS

"You'll stay?" said the landlady, snatching the cloak from Elise's back, then Annora's. She led them to a table, one of four in the room. "You won't be sorry. Drop your sacks on the floor, lean your staffs on the wall. My servant will fetch water for your feet to keep away chilblains, then you'll have ale." She turned toward the side door and called out, "Marged, useless slattern, where have you disappeared with the ale?"

Away she bustled.

The rooster crowed again, much to the jollity of Brother Gerald's two youngest companions.

"What if they see us, those men?" asked Elise, under cover of the lunatics' laughter and the monk's scolding.

"The horsemen? They saw us well enough in Penmachno and went on their merry way. Didn't give a fig." Annora's forehead creased. "Why are you still so bothered?"

"It's nonsensical, but I can't help it. I told you about the bloody head in the man's right hand, in my vision. Annora, that man on the black horse had his scabbard on the right, so—"

"So you've put it all together and come up with a left-winged prince of darkness? You're right, it's nonsensical. Two of my brothers were left-handed, and my uncle, and none of them carried bloody heads around. Although I do recall Uncle once knocked three teeth out of a tanner's jaw for saying my aunt looked like a stoat."

"Am I a fool, Annora?"

"In this matter, yes. An exhausted, hungry fool."

The maidservant tottered in with two wooden buckets of water. She set the buckets on the straw-strewn floor and handed Annora a square of old linen.

"Mistress says she added twelve drops of milk from a spotted cow to the water, and lavender, and a sprinkling of oatmeal." She smiled, or tried to. "To soothe your aches."

Because she lacked an upper lip, some of her soft words were hard to understand.

The room was quiet, except for the occasional hiss of fat dropping into the fire. Elise tried not to stare at the young woman, but found it impossible; her exposed gums were so mottled and pink, her teeth so yellow, and her lower lip so chapped. Her figure, however, was lush, and her eyes gentian blue. It was easy to see she might have once been lovely.

As the silence grew awkward, the maid lowered her gaze and brought a hand to her mutilated mouth.

"Forgive me," Elise said. "But who did this to you?"

The girl spoke through her calloused fingers. "The sheriff in Harlech. Three years ago last Easter, miss. After, the mistress bought me from my aunt, as I had too many respectable cousins to be welcome there."

"Men like to pluck pretty flowers," called the eavesdropping bow maker. "But your rose was plucked once too often, eh?"

"*Ubi mel, ibi apes,*" said the butcher.

Brother Gerald's eyebrows rose. "Ah, yes. Where there is honey, there are bees," he translated, as the maid scurried from the room.

Annora gestured to the red-haired boy to face the wall and proceed with his spit-turning. Then she and Elise turned their backs on the men and slipped out of their shoes and stockings. They eased their feet into the buckets as only the cat watched.

"There must be such footbaths as this in Heaven," said Elise, leaning over her lavender-scented bucket, watching her toes wiggle in the cloudy water.

"Alongside a mountain of roast chicken. And never any worry," said Annora. "Not a whisker of worry."

After a few minutes of blissful soaking, the women took turns drying their feet on the linen, then put their stockings and shoes back on. Soon the maid came back with the promised ambrosial ale and polished bone cups. The monk offered a prayer as six cups were filled.

Ambrosial the ale certainly was.

Annora quickly served herself a second cupful. "How does such a sour-tongued woman manage to brew so sweet an ale?"

The landlady bustled into the room, unaware aspersions had been cast upon her temperament. Wielding a notched paddle, she slid the chickens and the mock hedgehog from their spit and piled them on a plank. When almonds fell to the floor, the cat sidled over to sniff.

"Off, off," said the landlady, flicking her skirt at the little creature. She bent to retrieve the nuts and tossed them back onto the plank. Meanwhile the maid returned with a knife and handed it to her mistress.

Soon the plank held eight dismembered chickens, heaps of herb-flecked onions, and the mock hedgehog carved in slices. The maid brought out an earthenware bowl filled with stewed crab apples, then small loaves of brown bread, and a whole cold salmon—"smoked over peat four days yesterday," as the maid shyly informed Elise. She also slipped a radish into Elise's hand and another into Annora's. "Nibble these," she whispered, "to protect yourselves from harmful gossip while you journey."

Mistress and maid filled wooden plates for the six diners. They then watched from the back of the room as the lunatics tore bare-handed into their suppers, even the hot stewed fruit, all before Brother Gerald could finish his second prayer of thanks. Three pewter spoons went unused on their table.

"They've not eaten a bite since yesterday," said Brother Gerald, quailing at the lines of disapproval that deepened on both sides of the landlady's mouth.

The fruit was so hot it caused the men to yelp even as they continued to dip their fingers into it.

"If they blister their greedy paws, don't come to me for balm," said the mistress of the house.

The front door opened to admit a portly, pink-nosed man. "Wife, why do you loiter?" he said to the landlady. "The two gentlemen will be here as soon as one of them finishes a letter he is scribbling. Pour ale, fetch meat, for they are hungry and thirsty and openhanded. Hurry."

His gaze fell upon the lunatics, and his mouth snapped shut. Audible ale-gulping, along with yelping, lip-smacking, and marrow-sucking filled the void his silence left.

The landlord looped his thumbs under his snug leather belt. "These slavering cretins are a disgrace," he said.

"We're not deaf. And we are not cretins," said Slapper through a mouthful of food. "We're lunatics."

A youth in a sky-blue cape and a feathered hat joined the landlord in the doorway. "Lead me to your famous ale and roast chicken, innkeeper," he said, rubbing his hands together.

Only the landlord and Elise understood exactly what his words meant. But everyone knew what language he spoke.

The bow maker swiveled to inspect the newcomer and ran a finger down the scar on his cheek. "*Saesneg*," he said. English. "Strut up, capon, and I'll squirt piss up your beak."

Apparently not fluent in Welsh, the youth looked puzzled but unmoved by the antipathy in the bow maker's manner.

The landlord's cheeks puffed out and his nose went even pinker. "Shut your mouth, brainless fool," he told the bow maker.

Another man entered the room. His height drew all eyes as he came to stand beside Brother Gerald's table. When he lowered his hood, firelight played across the chain mail at his shoulders and his wrists; it caught the intricately worked silver of the scabbard that was revealed when he pushed his cloak aside to rest his left hand on his sword's hilt.

He smiled, but the smile didn't reach his dark eyes. "I'd make a better target than my cousin, friend," he said to the bow maker. His voice was deep, almost friendly, and he spoke in perfect Welsh.

The landlord's alarmed attention went back and forth between the two men, while Brother Gerald tugged at the small wooden cross dangling from a leather cord at his throat. Slapper and the butcher went on eating.

"By Cadwaladr's manhood, you'd more likely make a piss-awful target," the bow maker replied. He used a chicken leg to gesture to the silver scabbard. "You'd give my guts an airing."

"I'll toss them out this instant," said the landlord.

"You should have never let them in," called his wife from the back of the room.

"Please," said Brother Gerald, "I swear they'll be no further trouble."

The fair-haired Englishman sat down at an empty table and leaned against the wall, watching.

"I hope so, monk," said the tall man, taking his hand from his sword hilt. "Patience is not among my virtues."

"Sir, you needn't worry, not a pip," said Brother Gerald. "We'll go straight to our room and each say ten prayers for mercy."

At the monk's signal the lunatics shuffled to their feet, grumbling. When he saw that the butcher clutched half a loaf of bread to his chest, the landlord tried to wrest it away.

"Let him be," said the tall man.

The landlord released the loaf, bobbing his head like an overfed goose. Monk and madmen headed for the back of the room.

Slapper, last out, paused at the door. "Have you beheld the whore from Harlech, O mighty warlord?" he said to the dark man. "She slipped off to the buttery, I think. Her mouth will do you no good but the rest might suffice. Then there's this one." He jerked his head in Elise's direction. "She might be a fallen angel too and still has both her lips." When the landlady marched toward him brandishing an empty pitcher, his eyes widened. "Good night, old cow," he cried.

"That was regrettable," said the dark man to Elise after they'd gone. His tone was polite but perfunctory, like the look that went with his words. He gave no sign of recognizing her as one of the women he'd seen through the branches of Penmachno's great yew tree.

He went on—somewhat wearily, she thought. "I would happily defend your honor, but cannot in good conscience do battle with a madman. Forgive my inaction."

Elise stared at him, at a loss for reply.

As for the lunatic's lewd advice, she was more embarrassed than offended. She knew the man who slapped himself was a fool, if not a madman. But she wondered how a virtuous woman, as she represented herself to be, might be expected to respond. Discarding notions of pretending to sob, or quitting the room in a huff, she turned away with dignity and made no reply.

Her effort was wasted, however, for the man paid no heed. He was already engrossed in conversation with his cousin. From the serious looks on both men's faces, it might have been supposed neither would notice if the inn caught fire.

14

THE SLEEP OF THE DEAD

Elise swallowed a few bites of supper and did her best not to stare at the man with the sword. Annora kicked her under the table. "Eat," she said, mouthing the word. To appease her, Elise took a spoonful of fruit.

The landlord hovered near the men. "Noble sirs, my apologies for that fool's insults," he said in bruised English.

"Did he insult me?" said the younger man, stretching his arms above his head. "Well, I'm certain my fierce cousin offered to teach him some manners."

"Bring ale," said the dark man. It was a command. He unstrapped the belt supporting his scabbard and shrugged himself out of his cloak. The flustered landlord spun around and rushed off, shooing his wife before him.

Elise thought the dark man winced when he turned to throw his cloak over a bench.

His cousin also appeared to notice. He frowned. "You've done too much, Gwydion. Ridden too far in one day."

"Yes, Thomas. Tomorrow I'll lounge in a cart pulled by five plumed ponies. It will be a treat."

"I'm serious. You're not doing yourself any good by acting as if you're indestructible."

"Show me I have another choice, Tom, and I'll cosset myself like a lapdog. In the meantime I'll go on as I think best."

"If you wake up one morning and find yourself dead, don't blame me."

Gwydion sat down. "If I wake up and find myself dead and blame you, it will be a strange morning for us both. But Tom, you're too pessimistic. How came you to be this anxious?"

Thomas shook his head with fond exasperation. "Merely from spending these last weeks with you. You're a never-ending source of worry, cousin."

"My apologies," said Gwydion lightly. Elise noticed he glanced toward the inn's front door from time to time, as if from force of habit. He spoke again. "But you really needn't waste a scrap of your worrying on me."

"Someone ought to."

"Perhaps." The dark man smiled, a touch ironically, it seemed to Elise. "But it's not a perfect world."

Annora was on her first serving of mock hedgehog, her second piece of chicken, and her third cup of ale. She had little attention to spare for else. Besides, the men spoke English. Her knowledge of that language was rudimentary at best, since Elise's mother had taken pains to learn Welsh and had tried always to speak it to her servants, if not her three children.

But Elise listened intently even as she pushed food around her plate with her spoon.

"Has anyone ever told you you're a bloody-minded bastard?" said Thomas to his cousin, after a brief silence.

"A score or so heroes, but I ripped the arms off half of them and disemboweled the rest." Gwydion smiled again, this time genuinely. Elise was surprised at how his face changed, how his mouth went from grim to generous. She was further surprised when he looked up and found her eyes upon him. His smile remained, but his regard challenged her to go on with her inspection. His was the sort of mocking look a worldly man might bestow on a squire's easy daughter.

She swung her gaze to her plate and thought she heard him laugh.

"You're not eating, child," Annora said softly. "You have to eat. And you can stop watching those two, fascinating as you obviously find them. Even an idiot can see whatever business they have on the Trackway, it isn't with us."

Elise adjusted her focus to regard her friend. "Yes. You're right," she said. Finally she believed it. These men had no interest in her. They weren't hunting for Maelgwyn's murderer. The look she just received told her that to the dark man she was merely another presumptuous female. Fatigue and guilt, aligned with her meaningless vision, caused her to worry so. "Enough of my foolishness," she went on. "You're a saint to bear with me so well."

Annora nodded, then took another sip of ale.

Elise commenced to dine with appetite. She turned a haughty

shoulder to the men's table and ate chicken, onions, and bread. On hearing a plaintive mew, she tossed bits of fish to the cat.

The landlady brought ale and large tankards for the men as the girl from Harlech carried in more food. The younger man stared openly at her mutilated face, but his interest seemed curious rather than unkind. His cousin, however, ignored the landlady and her servant altogether. He filled his tankard to the top and drank it down at once.

Then the two men dined heartily and in silence. The women did likewise. Wisps of smoke from the languishing fire hung on the air, making Elise's eyes tear.

Later the landlord returned. Finding the red-haired boy asleep near the hearth, he nudged the lad awake and sent him to the buttery. The child staggered out, rubbing his eyes.

The landlord approached the women's table. "Ladies, a belated welcome to the house of Ieuan ap Morgan Goch," he said, with a flourish of his hand. "My wife says you are on a mission of mercy to Rhuddlan. But how perilous for two females. I'm just sorry you also had to bear the boorish behavior of those so-called lunatics. Ah, there are too many madmen on the roads these days, false and true alike."

Holding her cup in one hand, Annora waved dismissively. "We will say a prayer for their souls," she said rather grandly.

The landlord threw Elise a curious glance as she spooned crab apples onto her plate. When she looked up, he produced a moist-lipped smile. "Forgive me," he said, "but you are young to be widowed. Was it the Mortality?"

"A fire," said Elise.

"Drowning," said Annora at the same moment.

The landlord looked from one to the other.

"I thought you meant me," Annora said, hand to wrinkled cheek. "My husband was swept into a river and drowned, long ago. But my daughter's man died in a fire last year."

Elise stared aghast at her friend.

"Yes, a fire in a church," Annora went on. "He died rescuing holy relics."

"How brave," said the landlord, pink nose quivering.

It was Elise's turn to kick her companion under the table. "Mother, this gentleman can't spare time to hear our whole dreary history."

"She still can't bear to speak of it," said Annora, moving her shins from harm's way. "But I fear your ale has loosened my tongue."

"Perhaps it will tighten up again if you leave your cup on the table, Mother."

Annora drained her ale, then put the cup down so quickly it tipped to its side. It rolled across the table, coming to rest against the clay salt pot. "Oh dear, am I babbling?"

"You are, darling. But now would you show us where we may sleep, sir? We've been traveling since early morning."

As the women followed the landlord from the common room with their sacks and staffs, Thomas did not glance up. He was too involved in relating some tale to his cousin. But Gwydion watched them go. Elise kept her posture rigid as she swept out of the room.

Soon the women were inspecting an unadorned chamber at the front of the inn, up a narrow flight of stairs. Neither was unhappy with the accommodation; even with limited experience of such things, they knew it was as fine as most such rooms. Besides, they had been given the luxury of a fire-warmed rock wrapped in a rabbit pelt, to make their bed more snug.

"My wife put Brother Gerald and his burdens in a room down by the buttery. I hope that calms your fears. Luckily, we are one night past the full moon, when lunatics are at their worst." Ieuan ap Morgan Goch's tallow candle smoked as he hesitated in the doorway. Its wavering light made his round face appear oblong and shadowy, his nose sharp. "Of course, I will check to see they're all asleep before I go to my bed."

When he left, Annora wedged a bit of wood under the door.

Before their host went off with his candle, the women saw that their room boasted a window without glass, small as two hands side by side. It was fitted with oiled parchment tacked down at the top but not the bottom. The room's mattress, stuffed with straw and feathers, was wide enough for four or five people, a usual size for an inn, and covered with a pea-green blanket. Elise was glad she didn't have to share the bed with any woman but Annora, for one night at least. She was also pleased to know there was a jordan in the room's corner; the thought of faltering outside to the privy was not pleasant. It would have been a dark walk. They'd been given no candle, as candles were forbidden in the bedchambers of inns for fear of fires caused by drunken or careless guests.

For Elise, the idea of stumbling downstairs conjured images of the other patrons of the house of Ieuan ap Morgan Goch. What if one of the madmen, mad or not, only pretended to drink the syrup of poppies Brother Gerald gave him?

Or what if the man with the silver sword, Gwydion, woke early from a lusty dream and decided to make the dream real? Everyone knew that sometimes wealthy men lived by different rules. What if he came to their room and—

"What are you thinking, cariad? You're quiet. It makes me nervous when you're too quiet."

"About the lunatics."

"Sleeping like the dead, the monk promised."

Elise went cautiously to the window, raised an edge of the oiled parchment, and looked out at the misty night. "Those other two," she said. "Who do you think they might be?"

"Now I've had a closer look and heard him speak properly, I don't doubt the dark one is Welsh, though he's tall for one of ours. Did the sprig call him Gwydion? A proud Welsh name. Maybe he's part English, like you. Maybe he's a wild bastard son of a great family. He has that sort of bearing."

"A bastard's sort of bearing?"

"I'm just supposing. But he can claim the wild part, I'll wager. A man with secrets. He has a certain reckless way about him."

Elise dropped the parchment and turned toward her friend's voice. "You've leaped to definite conclusions for a woman so thoroughly engrossed in making chicken and ale vanish."

"Unfair, cariad. You know I'm always a keen observer, even at table."

"True. But talk enough of the Welshman, I think. What of the fair-haired fellow?"

Annora gave a dismissive sniff but did not deign to answer.

"I think the dark one has some injury," said Elise, forgetting she'd decided they'd speculated sufficiently upon him.

"If he does, he probably earned it."

"Do you suppose they might be dangerous?"

"All men are dangerous. Bearing that in mind, it would be wise to sleep with our knives close at hand—and you with your knees tight together."

Each woman fumbled in her sack, in the dark, to find a knife. Then they took off their wimples, undressed to their shifts, and climbed into the bed.

Elise looked toward the window. There was not a glimmer of light. Full only yesterday, the moon was probably now lost above the mist and unable to shine through. Across the meadow the river sang. She listened to its thin, lonely music. It had sounded so merry in the daylight, careering over pebbles, teasing green shoals.

She shut her eyes and warded off the thought that began to whisper and hum with the nighttime flow of the river. But the thought whispered more boldly, just at the edge of her mind.

The thought had followed her from Gray Hill, she knew. She knew it had been her shadow ever since she left.

Now it gained strength in the darkness. It abandoned the river and moved across the meadow, then slinked to the wall of the inn. Up, up. It slithered under the parchment, flitted across the dark chamber, and climbed onto the bed.

It was only a thought, a disconnected notion. But having worked so hard to find her, it would not be repulsed.

"Satan's bitch," it whispered in her ear.

"I'm sorry if I drank too much," said Annora, unknowingly chasing the dead man's message back to the night. "And if I talked like a fool at the table. I promise I won't again."

Elise sat up, breathing hard.

"Cariad, are you ill? Is it another vision?"

Elise put her hand to her throat, thankful her friend couldn't see in the dark. "No. It's only a cramp in my leg."

Annora sighed. "I'm not surprised. We've come so far today, I don't know how either of us managed."

Elise sank down once more.

Someone sneezed, downstairs. A door slammed. The river went on singing.

"Annora," said Elise, after a while, "I'm so tired. I've never been so tired. But I'm afraid to fall asleep. What will happen if I can never sleep again without nightmares?"

The only response she received was rhythmic breathing, interspersed with tiny snorts.

15

THE BLOOD OF STRANGERS

In spite of her fears, Elise slept. But it was a restless sleep, and Maelgwyn's ghost haunted her dreams. Yellow-white and naked, he
rowed a boat that was a coffin and wore a red cloth around his neck.
She stood on the shore pretending not to see him, but he sneered as
he went by, dropping the oars to fondle his manhood. "Thomas
Aquinas tells me you are defective and misbegotten, wife," he called
to her. "He says I should cut off your lip."

Noises woke her before dawn. They came from outside the inn.
She heard them with weary relief, for they were not threatening or un-
earthly, as her dream had been. There was the crunch of gravel, and
low words. Then nothing.

She crept to the window while Annora slumbered on.

Lifting the bottom edge of the parchment, Elise peered out. At
first she saw no one. Still without sun, the world was shapeless,
wrapped in the far end of night. Squatting barefoot and chilled, she
waited, idly hoping to be comforted by the homey sight of farmers on
their way to tend sheep, or perhaps the innkeeper's wife or her servant
seeing to some early chore. Or maybe Brother Gerald had decided to
start early on the Trackway with his challenging flock. Their departure could make for a more peaceful breakfast.

Soon the mist had nearly vanished. All that was left was a pearly
cloud lying low on the ground. Elise leaned her cheek on the cool
stone wall, watching the world grow less dim. Beyond the gradual
brightening there was nothing much to see. But she didn't mind. This
gray world was better than her dreams.

Then two figures emerged from the mist. Like specters, they
moved away from the inn and headed for the meadow. By their strides
she knew they were men, though only a hint of morning touched
their silhouettes.

They stopped just before they were out of Elise's line of vision. A murmur of voices floated to her window, but she couldn't make out words or guess the language they spoke.

The voices stilled. For a moment the only sound Elise heard was the singing of the river.

Then both shadows lunged forward and merged. Metal hissed on metal. They drew apart. They lunged again. One tripped and nearly fell, but immediately straightened again.

A dog growled near the inn. The less sure-footed man scurried toward the dark shape of a tree. A horse waited there, Elise could just discern. The man mounted, and his opponent made no move to stop him.

Horse and rider fled north. As they raced across the meadow, the pounding of the horse's hooves was muted by the thick morning air.

The day had grown steadily brighter. Vort, for it could be no other, bounded to the remaining man and ran around him in a circle. Man and dog walked back toward the cottage beside the inn. When they were nearly there, the dog dashed forward and stopped near the inn wall. He looked straight at Elise's window and gave a yip. His master, Gwydion, stopped to see what attracted his pet's attention. Gazing up, he found Elise watching him. His mouth lifted in a crooked smile, more mocking than the one he had directed at her hours before.

"Do I see a fallen angel?" he called softly, in Welsh. "If sunrise finds the bed too cold for your liking, sweet girl, slip down and let me warm you."

She let the parchment drop.

Annora mumbled something unintelligible and rolled to her stomach.

Returning to bed, Elise pulled the blanket to her chin.

Gradually, snuggled into the blanket, she coaxed herself to indifference. What did it matter if an ill-mannered, disreputable traveler insulted her? His conduct was only a fleeting aggravation.

Then she considered the confrontation she'd witnessed. Who was the other combatant? Why did they fight?

But she was drowsy and unable to make sense of it, so drifted back into a doze.

The sound of liquid splashing on hard ground woke her again. The hint of an unpleasant smell told her someone emptied jordans far out in the yard. It was still early, but sunlight shone into the chamber through the window, at the parchment's edge.

One moment more in this warm, safe bed, she told herself. One moment more to delay the inevitable morning.

When she opened her eyes again, a large black spider sat inches from her face, motionless on her breast.

She flung the blanket off and kicked it to the floor. Her knife clattered with it.

"What in the world?" said Annora.

"A spider."

"A spider? Is that all? Oh well, I suppose it's time to get up anyway."

Both women looked about for the spider while they dressed, Elise with more concern than Annora. But there was no trace.

Before they went downstairs, Elise described for her friend the clash she had seen out the window at sunrise. She didn't mention the indecent proposition she'd received.

"I wager it was just some lawless rival on the outs with him," said Annora as she straightened her brown dress. "Live by the sword, die by the sword."

In the common room they found Brother Gerald and his charges, along with the innkeeper's wife. She wore a fresh apron, but her face was still sour and pinched. The room smelled of the previous night's onions.

Slapper greeted them too familiarly and with news. "It's an odd old day, make no mistake. Soldiers were in here hoisting tankards, and there's a constable from Caernarfon. Now they're all outside." He lowered his voice. "And by the knob at the back of my throat, the food tastes like offal this morning."

"Be grateful for what you are given," said Brother Gerald.

"Millet mashed in cold oil? I'd rather eat dung."

Elise turned to the landlady. She tried to speak nonchalantly. "Soldiers and a constable?"

"Aye. My husband is with them now, but they'll likely be leaving soon. It's appalling; there's been a murder off toward Penmachno, a rich man left for dead."

Elise saw Annora blanch. Strangely calm herself, she wondered if the two of them might be able to sneak out through the back of the inn, steal across the meadow, and hide in the forest—forever. Might such a thing be possible? Then she remembered the lepers. Well, perhaps she and Annora could live in the shell of the castle on the ridge and take their chances with rain and wind and the uneasy ghosts of princes.

The bow maker interrupted her thoughts. "*Two* murders. A lord and lady, in mantles of miniver." He drew a line across his throat with his thumb and let his eyes roll up in his head.

The monk crossed himself.

"Millet in oil sounds lovely to me," said Annora, sinking into a chair, her face less white.

The innkeeper entered the common room from the back door, bulging pink with news. "You never heard anything so dreadful, wife," he said. "Seems the dead lord and lady were friends, relatives even, of our guest, the tall one."

"Then they'll be wanting more ale," his wife replied. "And those berry tartlets I made yesterday. Oh, I've a brilliant idea, Ieuan: think of our takings if you can persuade them to arrange a funeral party here at the inn."

Landlord and mate departed to the buttery, looking excited.

Gwydion came through the front door. Elise watched him but couldn't read his face. Wrapped in his cape, he walked to the hearth and stared down at the fire. There was little about him to suggest the disrespectful libertine she'd seen earlier. He had an air of desolation. Was there rage as well? She observed the rigid set of his jaw as he stared down at the fire. Slowly his left hand reached across to his sword hilt.

Thomas came in, with a subdued Vort at his heels. He approached his cousin and spoke in English. "I'm truly, truly sorry, Gwyd. But what will we do now?"

Gwydion didn't look up. "Find the ones who did it," he said. "And repay them in kind."

16

Gnawing on Bones

Brother Gerald and his companions departed the inn not long after. In the quiet that followed, Elise watched Gwydion stare incredulously at the landlord when that fellow sidled up beside him at the hearth to unctuously suggest a gathering of mourners.

"If your lordship's friends had other dear ones in this region, as they might have, would not my establishment provide a fine spot for you to console each other?" He spoke rapidly, in Welsh.

Still staring, Gwydion said nothing. He seemed fascinated. So were Elise and Annora. Feigning deafness, the women sat at their table in a corner, each pretending to be engrossed in sorting through the contents of her sack.

The landlord rushed on, taking his guest's silence for encouragement. He went so far as to reach up and place a plump hand on Gwydion's arm. "You've seen our standard of service," he said. "My wife and I would do our all to be a credit to your generosity."

The tall man didn't answer but let his gaze drop to Ieuan's hand on his forearm. He peered at it as if it were a steaming, five-pronged mound of rodent viscera that had inexplicably appeared there.

His look could hardly be misinterpreted. Ieuan snatched away his extremity.

Gwydion moved from the hearth. As he did, he met Elise's sympathetic regard. She thought to convey a word of condolence, as any feeling person might, whatever the sorrower's manners or lack of them. But though his dark eyes flickered as they rested briefly on her, they invited no pity. He turned away to address his cousin, who sprawled glumly in a chair near the window. "Pay Master Carrion Crow his reckoning, Thomas," he said, in calm English. "I doubt I am able, without carnage."

From his place near Thomas's feet, Vort had been observing the cat with restrained interest. But when Gwydion strode past him out the inn's front door, he rose, stretched his front legs long, and trotted after.

The landlord looked beseechingly to Thomas. "Sir, he mistakes my motives. Merely I proposed a gathering of your friends, here at the inn. Can there be anything amiss in that? I meant only to be of respectful service."

"Respectful service," said Thomas, nodding. "Not greed. Then it must merely be your bad sense of timing to blame." He stood and tossed a few coins toward the innkeeper. One skidded across an empty tabletop, stopping short of the edge. The others fell to the straw.

"Will that suffice to pay for our food and our beds?" said Thomas.

The innkeeper dropped heavily to his knees to search for the money. Then he lumbered to his feet again, red-faced, breathing hard. The belt slung low around his belly was too tight to encourage exertion. "So generous, sir," he said when he had breath. It was true; the money was treble what was owed. He leaned forward to sweep the last coin from the table into the gaping pouch that hung from his belt.

Thomas bowed perfunctorily in Annora and Elise's direction, then went through the door.

"You are eternally welcome to tarry with us again," the innkeeper called after him. "Please speak of us to your friends."

"Vort didn't bother to visit before he went off," said Elise to Annora. She spoke quietly.

"He probably already ate, so why would he bother to visit? On the other hand, I'm famished."

The landlady stalked into the common room from the rear door. "I heard everything," she told Ieuan. "What a great notion of himself that fellow must have. Hah. Too proud to answer a courteous offer with even a show of manners."

"Well, they're off now," said Ieuan. "Be content they paid nicely and with no ado. Not like some of the rabble we get here."

Husband and wife seemed to have forgotten they had other guests, guests with ears.

The landlady went on. "Lordship, you called him. To be sure. He could be a common thief on a stolen horse for all we know. Mayhap he killed his own people for rings and riches."

"Wife, you didn't see his face when the constable told him of the deaths."

She sniffed. "Easy enough to school your features to shock if you're a creature of perdition."

"I tell you no, woman."

They both started when Annora gave a cough behind them. "My daughter and I are waiting for something to eat before we go on our way," she said. "Did you mention tartlets?"

The landlady made no effort to hide her irritation. "Millet in oil, that's all there is. Honest enough food to break the fast of any good Christian."

"I was sure you said tartlets."

"No, no, only millet." The landlady departed, tugging at her wimple.

"Who were the two people murdered?" Elise asked Ieuan as he began, without enthusiasm, to make the room tidy.

He craned his neck, peering toward the rear door as if to assure himself his wife didn't lurk there. He looked back at Elise. "Highborn strangers, killed on the Trackway toward Penmachno." He made a motion with his arm in that general direction. "Whatever servants they had were gone, but two horses wandered nearby. Monstrous. But only a typical kind of robbery, in all likelihood." He picked up empty bowls and stacked them against his ample stomach. "Aren't there always knaves who'll cut your heart out for a penny and a pair of old shoes?"

Annora glanced down at her worn goatskin slippers. When she first bought them in Ysbyty Ifan, two years before, they had been a buttery tan. Fine enough, and soft. Now they were so scuffed and shabby that they'd gone a grayish black. She'd need a new pair and soon. Raising both feet off the floor, she flexed her ankles. She said to Ieuan, "We all agree there are depraved men. But my daughter and I would prefer not to hear of such things so near our time to venture back on the road."

"My pardon," said Ieuan. "I know it's unpleasant to imagine the slaughtered pair, what they must have endured. It's just a happy thing wolves didn't get to them afterwards."

"Exceedingly happy," said Annora.

"But wolves are always far worse in the winter, and it's still summer. Even with that, I've heard the red-fanged beasts are leaving these parts. They're going north to gnaw on Scotsmen's bones a while, praise God, so it's unlikely you'll see any today. One less worry, eh?"

Annora pursed her lips.

As he seemed keen to gossip, Elise asked another question. "Who were your guests, those men who knew the victims?"

"A highborn Welshman and his English cousin, that's all I can tell you for certain. The constable knew them, and knew right away to seek them here and inform them of the murders."

"Why do you say that?"

"I heard them speak of a recent meeting in Caernarfon—not that I meant to eavesdrop. But they must have given the constable a notion of their direction, so mayhap they expected trouble. Some people lead more drastic lives than others, don't they?"

Annora tapped a foot and looked toward the door, hungrier for food than hearsay.

The landlord aimed his chatter toward Elise. "All in all, I smelled intrigue." He looked pleased by this, as a gossip might well be. "But no one saw fit to offer me any details, though my good inn could well have been in harm's way." He shrugged. "Of course, I boast no lofty connections."

Elise nodded, encouraging him to continue.

He obliged. "The tall one did have a grand, military sort of bearing. Maybe he's just returned from the troubles in France, because late last night his cousin asked for clean linen and nettle roots, and butter."

"To make ointment for a wound," said Elise, glancing at Annora as if to say, There, it's just as I supposed.

"My wife thought so. But she figures he's a man of bad fame, belonging to no churchly tithing in the land. Still, he has an air." He scratched the side of his nose. "In truth, my missus shares one trait at least with our priest, as she makes few errors on the sweet side of judgment."

"What does it matter if the man's a rascal knight or King Nebuchadnezzar? He's off and gone," said Annora. "But what of us? Will we ever have our food this morning?"

Happily for Annora, the disfigured maidservant came in just then bearing ale, along with millet in oil. As she left, she dropped two more radishes into Elise's lap without a word. With the arrival of the food, the chatter session ended.

The ale was fresh and fine and the radishes crisp, but the greasy pap did not go down so nicely. When the two women were alone in the common room, Elise said, "Our landlady must have exhausted her talents on last night's supper."

"But I suppose the monk was right, cariad, and we ought to be thankful for what we are given. Didn't we sleep unmolested, and aren't our bellies full?"

As soon as Annora paid the innkeeper and collected their brushed cloaks, she and Elise once more began their journey toward Conwy. Both were still secretly troubled by the memory of Maelgwyn's violent end and their parts in it, but now there was also the newer fear that throat-slitting murderers might be nearby on the road. Neither woman gave voice to her concern, however, thinking she might infect the other with it.

The red-haired boy chased them across the meadow while they were still within shouting distance of the inn, for they had forgotten their staffs. The lad ran comically, a staff's neck clutched in each hand, with the bottom end dragging on the path behind him on either side.

He blushed when they thanked him for his trouble, then skipped back toward the inn.

"That maid was so sweet, wasn't she? She must not often meet with kindness, so I slipped a coin into her palm," said Annora when they reached the mouth of the trail. "But we ought to be miffed our hostess saw fit to give us no farewell. She didn't even show her face."

It was a blue-skied morning, warmer than the day before. The wind was less persistent.

"Don't let her bad manners vex you. We rabble are too pea-witted to take affront anyway," said Elise.

Just as on the previous day, she felt the desire to speak openly of her worries. But when she did, a bit later, she tried her best to make light of them. "Our only concerns today are stray murderers, wolves, lepers, righteous men come from Ysbyty Ifan bent on justice—"

"None of it is so dire as that. The wolves are all chewing on Scotsmen, remember, and we'll meet with no lepers or vengeful men."

"Only murderers?"

"No, no. We aren't worthy targets, not being draped in miniver and jewels." Annora laughed, almost convincingly, then made the sign of the cross. "Still, those two poor souls. May God have mercy on them—and on that man you found so fascinating you had to quiz the innkeeper."

Elise held out a hand to force a halt. "What are you saying? If I was curious, it was because of the vision, because he wore his sword on the right."

"That might be. He was a fine-looking man, nevertheless. Tall, wide-shouldered, if lacking somewhat in courtly charm. My eyes are not so ancient they'd misjudge such a thing."

"But they would misjudge me. Do you suppose I can kill a man one day, then calmly sniff out another the next? I have no interest in any man, wide-shouldered, hunchbacked, or honey-lipped. One was sufficient until the day I die. No, one was too many. I'd have more use for . . . a wolf."

"To gnaw your bones?"

Elise recoiled as if she'd been struck. "You offend me sorely, and your timing is distasteful," she said, and stalked down the path.

Annora hurried after. "I only meant that your body, anyone's body, might wrestle with matters the head won't admit. That's no sin, if you're human." She nearly tripped as she tried to catch up. "Must you rush so?"

Elise slowed her pace. Her cheeks blazed pink against the blue of the sky. "And forgive my asking, but what can a maiden lady know of such things?"

If Elise's cheeks were pink, Annora's grew more so. "Now who is offensive? You think my days have always been so dry? You think I've never known warm, moist nights? Do you really suppose no man ever turned a neat phrase for me, or swore he would die if I did not lie beneath him?"

They kept walking, but slowly. Neither met the other's eye, for this was not a kind of conversation they had ever endured before.

Finally Elise spoke. "Forgive me. But as you've never married, I thought—"

"Wrongly. And though you were called a wife for two years, you're still a greater innocent than I have ever been. There is more to such things than a few solemn words, miss, though you do not yet comprehend it."

"I am no innocent, but I wish with all my heart I were." Elise brought a hand to her cheek. "Maelgwyn forced me to such perverse things as Lucifer would blush to witness."

"Maelgwyn was filth stitched up in skin to resemble a man, it's true. But believe me, there are no tricks between men and women, satanic or sweet, forced or given, that have not been undertaken ten thousand times before."

"Then I won't be condemned for his unclean lust?"

"Of course not. Did you truly think you would be?"

They walked on.

Elise said, "Risking another jibe, I would mention one thing more about that man. Gwydion. If he interested me, it truly was because of my vision. Then, this morning, because of the murders. I'm sure what I saw earlier in the mist has something to do with it all."

"Yes, child. I believe you."

"I was only curious. But now I suppose the story is finished—at least for us. We'll never know the ending."

"Then I won't tease you further. Only know that in my clumsy way I was saying your *life* is not finished. The wretchedness you've been through is ended, and there are still so many fine tomorrows. Don't let Maelgwyn take the tomorrows too. He's dead. Gone. Like a bad dream, like a bout of illness."

They came to the ghostly castle, far above them on their right. In lost grandeur it sat on a bed of rocks, forbidding and sad even in the glory of the morning. A vertical shadow like a knife's blade split one high wall, cutting across two blank windows that stared down on the path.

"Our way converges with the Roman Road soon," said Elise, as if to break the spell of the ruin. The castle's melancholy aura seemed to hang on their cloaks even when they could no longer see it if they glanced behind.

"The Romans built fine solid roads," said Annora, "even if they were debauched heathens who worshipped naked gods."

Swallows soared overhead, unerring in their sky dance. The women both paused to admire the graceful birds, then walked on.

"Annora?"

"Child?"

"There's another prickly subject to delve into now, since our morning seems bent toward confession and deep talk. So at last, tell me how came you by that bulging purse of yours."

"The money? I'll tell you about the money, cariad. But I'm afraid you may not be pleased."

17

Not Ghosts, but Men

The color faded from Elise's cheeks, leaving her as pale as she had before been flushed.

"Why did you do it, Annora?"

The path had by then joined with the remote part of the old Roman Road that was called Sarn Elen by the Welsh. The sarn, that is, the causeway, was said by many to be named for Empress Helena, mother of Constantine the Great, first Christian emperor of Rome. Others claimed it was named to recall a British noblewoman, Elen, gone long ago to judgment. She was the beautiful wife of a warrior, Macsen, Magnus Maximus, Scourge of the Picts.

No one could be certain which story was fact, which fiction— Helena's or Elen's. Even Maelgwyn, in the course of his nightly lessons to Elise, hadn't offered an opinion. Since the matter concerned nothing more than a road and a female's name, he hadn't considered it of any import.

Perhaps the truth blended fragments of both dead women. But the rutted road could not answer the riddle for itself. In places its sturdy pavement had been torn apart from beneath by gorse roots starving for sun. For short distances the sarn disappeared altogether, its white or gray stones washed down ravines by floods or carried off by herdsmen to build sheep or cattle pens.

Nevertheless much of what remained of Sarn Elen was sound and worthy. A thousand years old and more, it bore mute witness to Roman ingenuity and tenacity.

Walking upon it, Annora did not entertain secret terrors of wolves or killers. Nor did Elise. Neither listened for the sound of lepers' castanets borne on the breeze. For now, the matter of stolen coins erased all other worries.

"Will you tell me why you did it?" said Elise again.

"Aye, if you'll say what Maelgwyn might have bought in the place he's surely gone. Does Satan run a marketplace?"

"I asked you to take nothing. Everything in his house was tainted. You heard me ask you, yet you did this shameful thing."

"Deliver chastisements until your throat dries up, cariad. But understand this: I'd pilfer Maelgwyn's cache again in the blink of an eye. Part of this money belongs to you, girl. You know your father spent a fortune on charlatans' cures for your brothers and your mother when they fell ill. But the rest went for your dowry. What did Maelgwyn do to deserve your parents' honest money? Nothing, and far less. Providing us with funds is the only useful thing he ever did for you."

"He didn't provide the funds. You stole them."

"What if I did? I chanced upon him fiddling with his trove one morning, smirking in that way of his, digging his fingers into the coins. Under the floor of his chamber, the box was hid. The fool was too rapt to guess I spied him, but I did. That's that."

"Can't you see you've made us into thieves?"

"Don't be stupid. Any night wanderer or malefactor could have sauntered in and had it if I had not. The door was open. Probably it still is. Isn't the money better ours than some shiftless stranger's? Maelgwyn had no heir but you. Didn't you earn the money with your pain? Where do you suppose we would have slept last night without coins?"

The trail wound through an alder copse. The light wind sped westward, weaving between tree trunks that grew alongside the path. The wind bore acrid hints of marshy ponds somewhere nearby but unseen. Also there arose tantalizing whispers of the perfumes of flowering herbs. There was sweet, hay-scented woodruff, persisting past its usual season in these hilly woods. And tansy, pungent and piney.

Gazing up at her former nursling, Annora's brown eyes were uncommonly stern and the lines on her round face more deeply etched than ever by the play of sunlight and shadow.

Returning her regard, Elise observed with a shock that her friend's old beige wimple was beginning to fray in spots. Also, new fatigue was imperfectly disguised by the brave but rigid set of her shoulders. The younger woman felt a rush of tenderness and concern.

They followed the sarn for a while, each conscious of the other's silence.

Picking up her pace, Annora began to hum a tune. Meanwhile the summer sun grew warmer, less like its raw spring sister.

Elise said, "You're humming, even though your feet hurt. You always hummed, before we went to Gray Hill."

"You always sang and danced. So you will again."

Elise smiled. "You're wiser than I."

"Aye, and older." Annora's tone lightened, for their quarrel had ended. "And fatter. That oily mess we ate this morning has made me windy as well." She shrugged her sack higher on her shoulder and tucked a thumb under its cord. "Well, noble guide, where next will we land?"

"If my memory isn't tangled, by midday we'll pass near the Foaming Falls on the Llugwy River. They've a reputation for rare beauty. But the gullible say they hide trolls and undines and doomed mortals held captive."

"I hope you don't expect me to hop over a waterfall or leap across holding a magic vine, as I suppose undines and trolls may do. I doubt I could manage."

"We're already on the right side of the falls. We'll only admire them and go on."

"Good. I'm not partial to cavorting with trolls. We've had enough of that on dry land. Besides, there are two coin-stuffed leather pouches tied under my skirts for safekeeping, not just one, and they aren't quite light as feathers. They banged against my thighs something fierce when we crossed that river yesterday."

"If they're too heavy, I'll carry them."

"No, Elise. Ill-doers are a hundred times more likely to look under your skirts than mine."

They had reached a thicker woodland. This place had a different character than the forest of the day before. Here was no menacing army of ancient trees like the one they'd rushed through between Bwlch-y-Groes and Dolwyddelan. Here were elegant rowan and beech and ash, sessile oak with leaves of delicate green. Among these trees small brown birds darted, singing as if their hearts might burst with gladness.

Underfoot grew tiny white or violet flowers, shivering in the gentle wind. At one place near the path, plump mushrooms clung like misshapen balls to the corpse of a lightning-blasted tree, decorating its death.

Golden yellow, a pair of brimstone butterflies alighted on Elise's shoulder, on the blue wool of her mantle, as she paused to gaze around her. She stood quite still, for it was a sign of good fortune to be visited by these capricious things. They closed their wings, as one, then slowly opened them. Then they floated off toward the deeper woods. When frosts came in autumn they would likely find a bed of ivy leaves to dream in. In spring they'd wake again, strangers to the winter.

"This is a lovely place," said Annora.

"As if nothing untoward could ever happen here."

They continued on their way, temporarily unmindful of aches and worries. But things changed. At first subtle, then more insistent, there came a roar of tumbling water. The ground grew damp. Legions of mushrooms now sprouted everywhere. Peeking from under fallen leaves and sloughed bark, they were creamy tan or brown. Some were banded with purple.

The roar became so deafening it carried away all other sounds. The path was slippery with wet earth and half-buried rocks.

The women arrived at a clearing and stood transfixed, clinging together. Ahead towered a high cataract of liquid silver, fierce with spume and spray. This ravenous thing, this maelstrom, had eaten deep into the shale sides of the luckless ravine that contained it. A down-swooping avalanche of thunder and force, it cascaded over boulders and whole trees that were torn out by their roots and dangling by their branches, before it screamed into a chain of pools and ponds below.

Elise cried, "Mortals held captive here would indeed be doomed."

Annora did not hear her, for the fury of the cataract snatched the words away.

Around them broken miniature rainbows born from tiny watery beads appeared and disappeared on the floor of the forest. Veils of mist gave a sheen to the women's cheeks.

Elise gestured to Annora to go forward, away from Rhaiadr Ewynol, the Foaming Falls. Their cloaks had already grown damp, and their shoes. She halfway feared one of them might slip off the pathway and drop through the deadly ravine to meet the water spirits and trolls below.

When they reached a place where a voice might be heard, Annora said, "Beautiful and terrible. That should be its name."

"A proper dwelling for magical folk. Doomed mortals too. No wonder there are no houses in this wood."

"None our eyes saw. But I don't feel so safe here now as I did. Do you, child?"

"No. We'll keep walking."

They continued upvalley. Their likely resting place that night would be Llanrhychwyn, Elise believed and hoped.

"Can we stop for food soon?" said Annora, as they passed a tranquil pond. "It's a while since we downed that greasy millet and my stomach is still complaining. Besides, our bread and cheese need eating."

"There should be a place ahead, a deserted farm. Castell-y-Gwynt it's called, if I remember aright." Castle of the Winds.

Since they would arrive and depart in daylight, Elise didn't think it crucial to tell Annora that Castell-y-Gwynt, on the upland hills, was said to be nightly haunted by legionnaires. A cohort of Roman soldiers—four hundred ghosts clutching spears and curved shields—marched silently past the Castle of the Winds under moonlight or cloud. Travelers caught there after dark swore they saw them pass by on the ancient road, moving in formation, disciplined even without hearts that still beat. Accounts were in eerie accordance; every ghost was legless from the knee down. No living person could say why that should be.

As it happened, two dead men lay before the gaping doorway of Castell-y-Gwynt—a sad, crumbling ruin—when Annora and Elise arrived there. But the men were not apparitions.

One was very tall and young, the other less so. Each still possessed a pair of feet; each stared unblinking at the sky. The older man had a small wound between his eyes.

Gaping at the bodies, Annora said, between suddenly rapid breaths, "I can't, I can't," and immediately vomited onto her scuffed shoes. Then she fainted in a heap with her tawny cloak bunched around her.

It was the first time ever that such a thing had happened.

Elise cried out and sank down near her friend, throwing a protective arm across her back. She felt light-headed and queasy herself but in no danger of losing her senses. Closing her eyes, she tried to think of nothing at all, at least until she could hit upon some action to take. What ought a sensible person do upon encountering corpses in the wilderness?

She mouthed the Paternoster but kept a firm grip on her staff. Dazedly, illogically, she willed any lurking killers to believe she and Annora were dead. Didn't canny animals feign death to thwart attackers? But she realized things were now grim in a new and appalling way, for Annora had fainted—unyielding Annora. Anything was possible now.

A twig snapped. A robin stopped its song mid-chirrup.

"Come feast your close-set eyes on this, Dexter," said a man, quite near, in haughty English. He sounded somewhat youthful. "Come observe the lassitude of rustics."

18

AN UNLIKELY MEMBER OF THE FLOCK

Miles east of Castell-y-Gwynt, a deceptively domestic drama unfolded.

A white-haired shepherd wiped muck from the bottoms of his bare feet with handfuls of yellow grass, then pushed a gnarled finger between his toes for a more comprehensive cleaning. After, he rubbed his hands on the dirt floor. He then dropped to his backside on a pile of stiff sheepskins near the low, open doorway to coax his brown boots back on. One boot bore a hole large enough to expose an entire big toe.

His hut stank of muck and sweat, greasy smoke, mead, and of beetroot and suet pottage bubbling in a black pot over the fire. Invisible just above the earthen floor, there also hung the elusive stench of butchering. It was a scent composed of terror, surrender, and sickly sweetness; the shepherd had slaughtered a lame ewe earlier that morning and suspended pieces of her carcass from the woven reed ceiling of his summer hut. The ewe's last lamb could be heard bleating just outside the door, though the shepherd heeded its cries not at all.

"I've an inkling my stew will be a fearsome treat, Gryg," the shepherd said.

Across the short length of the hut, Maelgwyn, supine, responded with a grunt. It was a sort of peevish acknowledgment.

The shepherd continued. "I had that beetroot off a farmer down by the moor's edge. He didn't know I had it, selfish hound. You fond of beetroot, Gryg?"

"No."

This reply was harsh and low. One word was sufficient to hear that the man's throat was painfully sore. In fact that's why the shepherd called him Gryg. It was a Welsh word. An Englishman would have said instead, hoarse.

"But beetroot it is, or naught. Now, if ever we go east to London to parley with the Saesneg king, we'll feast on whale tongue and milk from

Holy Land almonds. But I doubt it." The shepherd laughed without re-
straint; the noise filled his low-ceilinged hut. Then he shook his head.
"True, you're not too apt a parleyer, though I'll say you're a shade improved. But mayhap you yammer like a jaybird when you scrape jowls
with fancier folk than me."

Maelgwyn tried to sit up and failed. "Help. Help me," he said, a
little indistinctly.

"To piss?"

The shepherd went to help his guest relieve himself into a cracked
pottery bowl. The effort of this task seemed to exhaust the invalid.

"No matter the piss and all, it's a fine thing for one fool to have another fool to talk to," said the shepherd, tossing the contents of the
bowl out the door. Then he went to the fire to stir the pottage with a
long, thin stick.

The next day Maelgwyn sat up when the shepherd returned from
seeing to his flock.

"Ho, here's a change. You're not so whitish as you were." He tossed
a hunk of brown bread toward Maelgwyn and winked. "Another little
gift from a farmer down the hill. You know, if I had a handsome house
and a plump wife, I'd be more openhanded to those that are lacking,
that's no lie."

"You . . . like women?" asked Maelgwyn, grimacing as he spoke.

"You're more inclined to blab today," said the shepherd, raising a
raggedy eyebrow. "But for what? Do I like women for what?"

Swallowing a small bite of bread, Maelgwyn grimaced again. "No,
no." He closed his eyes, seemingly unequal to the task of explaining.

A dirty black and white lamb rushed through the open door into
the hut. It butted its head against the shepherd's knees. Calmly, he
pushed it back outside.

"Well, I suppose I like women pretty well, Gryg, if they're not too
bony-rumped. I heard of a gentleman over by Oswestry had a scrawny
rich wife. Someone asked him if he married her for love, and he said,
'Aye, for love of her cattle.'"

Maelgwyn didn't smile.

The shepherd dragged a three-legged stool to his visitor's side and
sat. "You want more stew? It takes good food in the gut to make an
honest man feel like laughing." He offered the other a bowl.

Holding the wooden bowl for himself with one hand, Maelgwyn took sips of beetroot pottage. He shuddered after each sip. Meanwhile the shepherd regaled him with jokes he'd picked up here and there and with tales he'd heard from his mother.

"You know what God's first words were, Gryg?" he asked. He didn't wait for an answer. "*Fiat lux.* Let there be light, that is, except that's the tongue they twitter in Heaven."

Maelgwyn sat up straighter and nodded.

"You like that, old ram? Then you know who put down the first words in a book? A giant called Mercurius. Mother told me when I was a three-winter lad, yet I remember still. He came in a golden ship and had a beard he wrapped around himself forty times. Carried a larch rune rod for scribbling letters in the dirt and kept ten tame seabirds."

Maelgwyn's brows nearly met over his nose. "Never was there such a man," he said.

"Aye? My mother lied, I suppose." The shepherd kicked at the dirt floor, then rose, dragging his stool back across the hut. "But my mother never lied once in her sweet life, hound." He sat once again. "Pretty tasty talk, while you wolf down my beetroot and bread and wallow like a pet pig in my bedding."

Maelgwyn clutched his bowl. "No, no."

"No, no," said the shepherd, mocking the other's rasp. "You think you know so much, hound. Did I ever insult *your* mother?"

"My mother was a whore." This was said in a surer voice than Maelgwyn had used since he came to the hut.

The shepherd gave him a disgusted glare. "That makes you a whoreson by your own confession, and more's the pity. I'm no blue-bell-scented earl, but I don't need any wheezing whoreson in my place to make slurs against dead kith. Maybe you ought to crawl back to the bank where I snagged you."

"No, no," said Maelgwyn, again. He clambered unsteadily to his knees. "Forgive me, as we are fellow Christians."

"God-loving folk don't insult their friends." Without warning the shepherd stood, knocking his stool backward. Hunched over in the low, one-room hut, he shambled toward his guest. "Out you go, old ram."

Maelgwyn shrank back. "Wait. I have money. You can take one quarter for your kindheartedness. One full quarter."

The shepherd stopped. "What's that, one quarter of a penny?"

"By Paul's preachings, no. I have stacks of coins, and four jewels set in gold."

"Where's this treasure? I never saw it. You cram it up your backside?"

"Hidden at my house, a high stone house. Not far, I think. We'll go get it, you and I."

The shepherd rubbed his forehead.

"Your sheep can shelter in my barn," Maelgwyn said.

Retiring to the stool he'd righted, the shepherd cogitated. He tilted his head toward one shoulder, then the other, as if listening to two inner voices giving their opinions. Finally he rubbed his forehead again and nodded. "We'll set off soon as you're more upright, when your arm's less bungy. But if you're lying, Gryg, I'll slice you up hot and sticky while your miserable eyes are still wide open." He pointed to the meat hanging above. "Like I did poor Blanche."

"Dear Samaritan, I swear on the Scriptures it's true."

"You'll never speak ill of my mother again."

"I swear."

"Be sure you don't." The white-haired man smacked his hands together. "All right, I bear no grudges. You gobble that provender now. Get fitter so we can sniff out your trove before the world ends, for riches won't be a snoutful of use to me then."

Cradling one arm with the other, Maelgwyn moved back to his blankets and sank down.

The shepherd spit toward the fire. "Meantime I'll tell you about when Lucifer fell," he said. "How he took a choir of rat-hearted angels with him and that's why only nine choirs sing the Virgin to sleep these days. Besides them, there's a fairy harpist who boasts three quivering breasts, like a milky Trinity. Her name is Daege Angelus, the Dough-Kneader." He leaned back, crossing mud-crusted ankles. "Unless you think my mother lied about that too."

"Oh, no." Maelgwyn flinched as he touched the stained cloth around his neck. A sudden look of wild, searing wrath lit his blue eyes from within like a flare on winter's deepest midnight. But as the room was dim and smoky and the look quickly gone, the shepherd didn't see. "For an ignorant wretch like myself," Maelgwyn then said, producing an anemic smile, "it will be a privilege to hear such learned history. As we are friends now, I would be honored if you'd call me Maelgwyn."

"Had a ram once name of Maelgwyn. Sank his teeth into my thigh."

"Why?"

"Some rams can be piss-spiteful. But he never did it again, I can tell you." The shepherd's mouth curved up in a sour grin. "Anyway, I'll carry on calling you Gryg."

19

THE CASTLE OF THE WINDS

Beneath Elise's arm Annora stirred. But she did not revive. Elise stayed sitting on the ground, leaning against her unconscious friend. She smelled Annora's vomit and heard the buzzing of flies a few feet away, nearer the two dead men.

The haughty Englishman spoke again. "Come, you harebrained females. Do you think your impersonations of statues will persuade us you are dead? Of course, it *has* worked for these two fellows over here."

Another man guffawed, then gave his opinion in coarser accents. "Likely they're just drabs from some farm across the valley, Sir Nicolas."

"Thank you, Dexter. I'd supposed they might be a disguised duchess and her daughter out for a ramble."

Unfazed by mockery, or unequipped to perceive it, Dexter ventured another opinion. "No such thing, sir. And mayhap they didn't understand proper language when they heard it spake and were wazzled out of their wits straight down into a swoon."

"If I comprehend you, Dex, your reasoning is that these are Welshwomen and so most *im*proper. In fact I have heard that Welshwomen sprout fur from their necks to their knees, owing to nocturnal couplings with beasts. I've heard they're plagued with fleas."

"You flees from fleas, Sir Nicolas." Dexter guffawed again.

"Unlike you, fool. Now be quiet and unwrap the younger female so I may judge this matter of furriness for myself." He gave a cold laugh. "Then go play at passion with the hag. I'm sure she'll be thankful for any little morsel of attention."

Dexter disregarded his superior's command and spoke again. "I sported with one of this kind once, but she didn't take to my attention. In the end I had to shut her face for her."

"Tales of your adventures are always diverting, but you are still speaking when I bade you cease. Worse, you've not undraped that female." There was a warning in the drawl. "Do you think it is acceptable to pay my wishes no heed?"

Elise couldn't see the men's faces but found their talk ghastly and perverse. With her eyes shut, her only view was inward. She was shaken and amazed, however, to find it an extraordinarily illuminating view and providential in its timeliness—for strength and resolve she didn't know she possessed instantly crowded forward to astound her introspection. She beheld the core of her spirit and saw it was bold and strong. The victim whom Maelgwyn, and the Pestilence, had made of her—or she of herself—retreated to the shadows as she watched. It backed into the darkness, sniveling.

There was something even more important to see: she saw the time had come to act.

Elise swore at that moment to protect Annora, with her life if need be. She felt fury, boiling and barely contained. How could these men speak so lightly of rape and murder? They undoubtedly killed the two men who lay on the path, and probably others. Why didn't God strike them dead?

Or could it be that God meant to work His will through *her*?

Well, had she not felled Maelgwyn?

She fixed upon a plan. If she could deliver a fierce blow with her staff, preferably to the head, she might daze her assailant for long enough to take his knife. Surely he had a knife to subdue her, or a sword. She could plunge the blade into his chest. In the blink of an eye she would then turn it against the other, the sneering Sir Nicolas, who so blithely gave his blessing to his underling to defile Annora.

After this *Sir* Nicolas lay leaking blood from the hole she would put in him, she'd tell him his final tale. She would say, in English, "Cur, you have been bested by a female, and half Welsh at that. When your bone-case commences to crumble, soon, a thousand maggots will torment you. After they chew away your face and your bowels and your inconsequential manhood, your heavy sin-bonds will pull you down to Hell. Do you hear me? Then know that this is who I am—Elise, only daughter of Dafydd ap Rhys ap Rhiwallon of Bronhaul, and of Katherine, born the Lady of Ambrespring, who was called Katherine the Gentle. It is I, a not-so-gentle Elise, you must thank for your deliverance to Satan."

Yes, she would silence these men. Just as Maelgwyn had deserved to die, so did they. The world would be better off without such monsters. Annora knew, and now Elise understood. So she would remove them from the world or be lost in the attempt. If she succeeded, she would feel no remorse. She and Annora would laugh and dance. They would claim Sir Nicolas's purse, probably a fat one by his rich man's speech. They'd canter down Sarn Elen on his horses; certainly he'd have sleek horses. She herself would gladly twist the rings from his cooling fingers, snatch the chains from his neck, and have no use ever again for rue bracelets.

Footsteps approached. She shifted her legs a fraction to ready herself to spring and held her staff rigid against her side in a manner she imagined some warrior queen might have once employed. She said another swift Paternoster.

And was yanked upward and back by her hood. Thrown off balance—her flawed assumption had led her to imagine that the underling would grab her by the arm—she sprawled gracelessly on her back. Her skirts billowed all about her, revealing her legs to the thighs.

She barely managed to keep hold of her staff. But quick and hard she struck. The blow landed with a *thwack*.

She hit the man's ear as he leaned over her.

Dexter swore as Elise dragged her skirts back over her legs. Glaring down to examine the bloody hand he had raised to his injured ear, he said with surprise, "That bitch has smacked me."

He brandished no knife or sword, Elise saw. She guessed he had not expected to need them.

Sir Nicolas laughed. "Dexter, you've no finesse with women. Stand aside. I'll see if I can persuade her to behave."

"First just let me wallop her once, sir. Easy-peasy."

"Leave her, I said. Drag the crone to the woods and wallop *her*. Only do it in the thicket, as I've no wish to behold your grapplings. Go, before I smack you too."

Dexter moved away from Elise. But first he bent to deliver a swift blow between her shoulder blades with his fist. Her head snapped back. She bit her lip and tasted blood, but raised her staff again to strike. No use. He was out of reach, scowling down at Annora's form with his beautiless felon's face.

The lackey sniffed the air, then pinched his nose. "The old one's cast up her bubblings," he said, his voice necessarily nasal. "She stinks like a gong raker with it."

"Since when are you so nice in your requirements? Just pretend she's your sweet old mother," replied Sir Nicolas.

Bitterness flooded Elise. She had failed, she'd saved no one. Bloodlust and pride had inflamed her into supposing herself capable of executing God's will. But she and Annora would still be raped and murdered, for these men would surely tolerate no witnesses to their crimes.

Sir Nicolas approached Elise as she sat with slumped shoulders. Of average height and somewhat lean, he captured her chin in his white hand and forced her to look up. Instinctively, she straightened her spine.

"You know, you are actually rather pleasing, in an unkempt sort of way," he said. "I wish you knew a proper tongue so we might banter. Such speaking gray eyes. Look how brilliantly they hate me. Such pretty legs to wrap around my waist. Almost I could allow myself to admire you, Welshwoman."

A phrase came back to Elise, something Annora had recently said. She resolved to speak it in English, and to say more, as a parting gift to the creature before her. As revenge, it wasn't much. But with luck, maybe it would haunt him.

She said, "You are merely filth stitched up in skin to resemble a man. But one day Lucifer will find you winsome. Exchange your banter with him and he might see fit to reward you with a horde of fiery partners, below, in his domain."

Sir Nicolas's brown eyes widened. Elise studied his lush black lashes and straight nose. Arrayed in a purple cloak of costly kerseymere embroidered with pale green spirals, he couldn't have claimed more than twenty-five years. But his face was too jaded for such a middling number. She wondered if he had always been evil, for he must have been a pretty child. Indeed, he was a handsome man.

"You speak English," he said. He reached for the jeweled cross on a chain around his neck and clutched it. "Who are you?"

20

WHERE THE DEVIL
HANGED HIS MOTHER

With bleak curiosity Elise wondered at his response to her words. How tightly he gripped his crucifix. It was large as an August oak leaf and flashing with red and yellow stones.

After a hesitation she answered him. "Who am I? Once a man called me Satan's bitch. But he was wrong."

Still in a heap on the path beside Elise, Annora moaned. Dexter wiped his bleeding ear with his sleeve but made no move to drag her to the thicket.

Silence fell, except for the buzzing of flies.

At that hushed moment scores of large dark birds suddenly rose overhead like a cloud. They flew up from a stand of tall trees behind Castell-y-Gwynt, beating their wings at the air. Elise wondered if she had fallen into a vision. Wasn't this the familiar sound of wings she always heard in visions, so world-swelling and thunderous?

But this was no vision. These birds didn't hover like the unseen birds in her visions always seemed to do. These swung away. Darkening the sky, they screamed out frantic *caws*. The sound was so loud she covered her ears.

Finally the birds wheeled higher and farther away. They flew as if one to the south. Sunlight striking their wings picked out purple-blue glints in the undulating sea of black.

"Rooks, Dexter," said Sir Nicolas in a suddenly altered tone. "Wicked cousins to the raven." His voice sounded odd and flat. With the hand not clutching the cross, he shaded his eyes to watch the birds' departure. "All fleeing their rookery. I ask myself, why do they flee?"

Dexter replied with unwarranted cheer but also a hint of unease.

"Nothing to fret for, sir. They're only off for a feeding of grubs or some such."

"No," said Sir Nicolas. Elise saw that the hand that held the cross had begun to tremble.

"They'll be back," said Dexter soothingly. He seemed well practiced in this mode. "Back to the last bird."

Elise wondered at this peculiar exchange. Why would the vile nobleman grow distraught over birds? She couldn't guess, but at least he was distracted from his attentions to her.

"They won't return. I know it," said Sir Nicolas, still trembling, still watching the vanishing flock. "If a rookery is suddenly abandoned, it's a desperate omen. A thousand times I've told you it's so. It means someone will soon die."

Dexter snorted and pulled out a curved dagger that had been concealed under his wide belt. "Then let me make quick work of these useless females, and the omen will come true."

"You can't force the outcome, fool. The birds already know exactly who will die. Christ's teeth, there shouldn't even be a rookery in this place. Rooks like open fields, but these are all overgrown. Why else are they here but to foretell?" Sir Nicolas walked to the men's corpses and looked down. He chewed his lower lip. "The rooks saw everything. They know—"

"They don't, sir. They're only poxy birds."

His master paid no heed. "Just this morning we passed a wild cherry tree," he said, "and I congratulated myself on my composure for saying nothing of it."

Dexter stroked his injured ear. He shrugged, with a touch of resignation. "Aye, and we've seen scores of cherry trees before, sir, with no hard result. Can you say we've ever had one bit of sorry luck only on account of going past some little wicked tree?"

The noble's face now twisted with an emotion that looked like fear but with something more obscure laced in it. "A wild cherry tree is where the devil hanged his mother. I've told you *that* a thousand times too."

"Aye, you have. But recall, my lord, the devil had no mother. You remember. The priest promised you, last winter. He showed you words in a painted book. You said a prayer at the altar, lit five candles, and were mightily content."

Sir Nicolas closed his eyes, breathing deeply in and out, in and out. Finally he said, "Why . . . why yes. Yes, I was." He allowed his hand to release the crucifix. It swung back and forth on its chain and came to rest just below his heart. He opened his eyes. When he spoke again his voice was as assured as it had earlier been. "What I need is wine, Dexter. Wine."

"That's it, my lord. Or ale."

"Then we must hasten to rejoin the rest of the men at my new manor. We can be there tomorrow unless I'm constantly obliged to press you not to loiter."

Looking relieved, Dexter wedged his dagger back under his belt. He walked to Sir Nicolas's side. "I could do with a drink meself, sir."

"You might have it soon enough. Just throw those men on a horse in case the rooks come back to spy. Then we'll go."

The grin disappeared. "We have to drag these stinking carcasses? Still? Is that—"

"Question my orders again and *you'll* be a stinking carcass."

His face darkening, the lackey stepped away from his master. "Aye, my lord, as you say. What of this pair of females?"

Annora chose that instant to revive, and she gave a small cry. As Sir Nicolas turned casually toward the two women, his well-formed lips turned upward. "Dear ladies," he said, shaking his head with sham contrition, "I wish I had better news."

Although she didn't understand his words, Annora read the meaning on his face. She put a hand to her mouth. But Elise only regarded him with fearless appraisal.

Amused, Sir Nicolas met her stare. Suddenly he sucked in his breath with a sharp hiss.

Dexter leaned toward him. "My lord, you're unwell?"

Nicolas clutched the lackey's sleeve. "Her eyes," he whispered.

Dexter glanced at Elise. "What of 'em?"

Sir Nicolas continued to whisper. "Look, look, fool. Her eyes *see* things. They know things. They're the deepest, deepest shade of gray and full of night."

Dexter pulled out his dagger again. "Then I can fix 'em so they'll not bother another soul after today."

"No! This woman is one of the chosen. I know it."

"Who chose her then? She's just like any other poxy female, far as

I can tell. She speaks English, which is not altogether a good thing neither."

"You, Dexter, are a dolt. But I am cursed, or blessed, with a comprehension of mysteries. And I tell you she's one of the chosen."

"Then *I* choose to send her to Hell and let Satan sort her."

"Put that stupid dagger away or I'll use it to dig a spigot in your neck. Just go and deal with the corpses as I asked and stop interfering in the affairs of your betters. Meanwhile I'll try to make everything right with this special woman."

"I tell you, sir, if we leave 'em alive, they'll yap of us to the first person they meet."

"You tell *me?* How dare you? I said go—now. Anyway, they will never tell a soul." The nobleman turned to Elise. He all at once smiled sweetly. "Will you tell a soul?"

She hesitated only a moment, then said quietly, "No."

Dexter gawked. "She's lying. Whyever would she not tell?"

"You can't possibly understand, Dexter, but somehow I know *she* does. I see it in her face. In her pure gray eyes. She understands about the rooks and the wild cherry trees too. You do understand, my dear, don't you?"

Dexter looked from Elise to his master. "But Sir Nicol—"

"Be silent, fool, and go."

The incomprehensible conversation above her head became too much for Annora. She started to sob quietly. Elise hugged and shushed her like a child, as the lackey swore with innovation before striding away.

Sir Nicolas watched Elise console her friend. Then, reaching down, he placed his hand on the younger woman's shoulder. She flinched and tried to draw away.

"Don't be afraid, I won't harm you. Just tell me how you came to know so many things. For you do know things, I'm certain. Even more than I, and I know so much. Speak freely. Was the caul fixed over your eyes at birth to proclaim the gift of mystical seeing? Or was there another sign?" His fingers bit into her flesh. "Won't you tell me, as a kindness?"

What words did this dangerous man want to hear? Elise couldn't guess. Her brain was not fevered, as his clearly was. What dealings did *she* have with bloody corpses, soothsaying rooks, or cursed cherry trees? She *did* know she wanted him to go, to ride away with his lackey and his corpses and never be heard from again.

Was it possible that a truth marking her as a kind of fellow misfit would soothe him? Without doubt, he was a misfit. She turned to look up at him. Yes, such an offering might be enough to appease. So she said, meeting his eager gaze, "There was no caul, but I have long been prone to visions."

He jumped back like a scalded cat.

Annora stopped whimpering and sat up. Her face was pink.

Farther down the path, Dexter, after terrific effort, had heaved the corpses over one horse and was holding the reins of another. Scowling, panting, he waited for his master.

"Visions. Of the future?" Sir Nicolas edged away from Elise and moved toward his henchman. "But you'll never have a vision of me, will you? For I've only been noble and kind to you and your vomitous companion. You'll have no visions of me, I'm certain." He stopped, stood quite still. "No, I believe you ought to swear it. Swear you'll have no visions of me."

This was ludicrous. How could she make such a promise? She had no control over her visions. It was an absurd thing to ask.

She caught sight of Annora's weary, bewildered face.

"I swear I'll have no vision," Elise said in a rush.

The nobleman smiled broadly once more. "I'm glad. Otherwise I might have to kill you, and that would be tragic because I'm sure we could be friends, even if you're Welsh or . . . or Babylonian." He walked to his glossy sorrel and swung into the saddle.

Dexter looked up at his master, bafflement stamped plainly across his ugly face. "Sir Nicolas, I honestly think—"

"You? Honestly?" Nicolas reached down in one fluid motion and rapped his knuckles against his minion's forehead. "You never do anything honestly, especially think. It's dizzying to contemplate such a thing. Scuttle along now and we'll relish good wine with the sunset, maybe even the company of fellow Englishmen. Perhaps obliging doxies, eh? But be quick, for we need to dispose of those cadavers in the woods, where the rooks won't spot them."

He turned his mount to the west and trotted down Sarn Elen without looking back. The henchman stayed a moment longer. Holding his horse's reins, he advanced toward the women. Flies circled and buzzed around the corpses.

Dexter spat on a rock near Elise's foot, then wiped his mouth. "Nobody saw me and Sir Nicolas here but you two," he said. "So say one word, I'll sniff you out. Oh, and I will. I'll truss you to one of his bedamned cherry trees. Then I'll grind raw onions and spiders' legs into your eyes, and sew the lids shut. You'll scream in the woods till you rot."

He walked off but turned back after a few steps. "I'll sew 'em shut, Mistress Vision. Ask the rooks if I won't. For a prune I'd do it now, but Master's a fair wizard at snagging me in falsehoods."

Then he and his horse and the two corpses were gone.

Annora made the sign of the cross. She had quickly regained her usual color and self-possession. "I don't know what that unlovely man just told you, but I didn't care for how he told it," she observed, as if she had not seen a pair of bleeding corpses, or fainted for the first time in her life. "I never beheld eyes so close together. Who was he, child?"

Elise lied. "A harmless fool."

"The other?"

"A madman."

"Another madman."

"This one was different. This one was truly mad."

Annora leaned against her friend. "Meanwhile there's me, collapsing like a princess weaned on melted butter, leaving you to cope. Lately all I do is say I'm sorry. But cariad, those dead men, the flies, that millet sloshing around my belly like greasy gravel—"

Elise took her friend's hand. It disconcerted her to hear Annora acknowledge her fainting spell. In the past she would have been dragged backward through a field of boars' bristles before admitting to "weakness." But in the past she wouldn't have fainted. It seemed their days were all blending alike into startling oddness now.

She raised Annora's worn hand to her cheek. "You know you wouldn't have understood their English anyway. Besides, I did manage to give that fool a gash on his ear with my staff when he was . . . rude. You would have been proud."

"I am. But we're managing to meet more than our proper share of bad characters, aren't we?" With her free hand Annora played with the drawstrings of her sack. "Such things would likely never happen if we traveled with a man."

"Well, we could have tried to cajole Maelgwyn to come with us, but he was looking so poorly when we left," said Elise. Then she clasped her hand over her mouth.

Annora only laughed. "Don't you dare go puley. It does my brittle bones good to hear you make jest of that hell-spawn. You sound like my old Elise. But forget that now and tell me: did the madman and his knave kill those two men? I couldn't make out one word in ten. I suppose they must have done it."

Elise decided it would be best to tell her friend a reassuring un-truth. "Sir Nicolas, in the fine cloak, said they found them already dead. Robbers' victims, he thought. They took the bodies just now to give them a decent burial."

Annora accepted this readily enough, as if she wanted to believe the least disturbing thing. "Sir Nicolas? What *sir* would have a horrid underling like that? Still, a civilized burial's a small kindness at least. So they can't be all bad, in spite of that fellow's mean eyes and spit-ting. But I'd surely be surprised if those dead men didn't have some-thing to do with the troubles back at the inn. And with that Gwydion."

Elise would have been surprised too.

Annora sighed. "I'd love to meet with some decent folk for a change."

Elise was glad her friend understood scant English, or she might appreciate how indecent Nicolas and his lackey really were. She rose. "I don't mean to hurry you, but can we go on soon? We've lost an hour and would be far better off reaching Llanrhychwyn by dusk. Or am I being heartless?"

Annora looked dismayed but quickly schooled her features to brightness. "Don't be a goose. I'm a new woman after unswallowing that slop. I understand we can't idle the day away and expect to get anywhere." She held out her hand to be hauled up. Once on her feet she slapped dust from her cloak and glanced down. "Only let me swab the sick off these shoes before we set out. At Conwy I'll buy a fresh pair. Then I'll fling these into a midden."

Elise felt contrite for rushing her. Annora was hardly a young woman, though she was a plucky one. She had already been through a deal of upset and upheaval, even real danger, without a word of serious complaint. She wondered if it might be a good idea to tell her of the possible appearance, at moonrise, of spectral legionnaires; they might help enlist her enthusiasm for a rapid departure. In truth the legionnaires were only one reason Elise wanted to be quickly gone from the place.

21

DREAMS OF NECTAR,
DRIPPING AND GOLDEN

The track to Llanrhychwyn was downhill, sometimes steep, and lush with trees. When the trees gave way to naked hills, the women caught tantalizing views across the Conwy Valley to the Denbigh Moor, and beyond, to the cobalt promise of the coastline. A miscellany of floral scents was now borne on the breeze.

After eating crumbled handfuls of bread and cheese, they walked without conversation. The air grew warmer. Annora was intent on making progress downhill without taking a tumble. Her head ached, her feet throbbed, and her stomach had still not fully recovered from the oily millet's visit. But she was too stubborn to ask her companion to shorten her stride.

For once Elise was insensible to her friend's struggle and her effort to conceal it. She had her own troubles to consider.

First there was Maelgwyn. As she moved forward, putting one foot before the other, she became defenseless against a battering of memories. She remembered his skewed history and geography lectures, his homilies. Again she suffered the malice in his blue eyes as he stared down at her in their bed. She saw how his neck muscles knotted. She remembered his perversity, and the times he grew vicious without warning.

Oh, how easily the jagged glass had pierced the skin of his throat.

His death seemed so long ago. Examining her own emotions, she was suddenly surprised at how little guilt she felt. Testing every curve and corner of her mind, she was quite unable to locate any remnant of sorrow or regret for Maelgwyn's demise and her part in it. But her lack of remorse gave rise to a tremor of dismay. Shouldn't she feel more racked with guilt? Or did some innate sinfulness, something deep inside her, prevent her from knowing proper Christian anguish for more than a few paltry hours?

No. She abandoned that notion with a tiny shake of her head. No one but a saint could feel grief for Maelgwyn, no matter how shocking his end. Any woman would have defended herself against his rage, his grotesque piety.

So glad did she all at once feel that she raised her face to the sky. How sweetly God scented the day, she thought. How good it felt to breathe deeply, to be free.

Thus Maelgwyn was temporarily banished from her thoughts.

Unfortunately her mind soon leaped to other ominous characters and events. None of her unspoken worries could be called trifling.

Who was the nobleman who feared rooks and cherry trees, and why had he and his toady killed the men at Castell-y-Gwynt? Why were they in Wales, and who had their two victims been? How many of the "fellow Englishmen" he mentioned gave the nobleman their fealty, and where were those Englishmen now? It could hardly be a coincidence that another pair of bodies had been found, the lord and lady in miniver. If Sir Nicolas had committed four murders, she and Annora were fortunate not to have become numbers five and six. But their jeopardy hadn't yet ended.

Corpses, unanswered questions: intuition and logic told her Sir Nicolas and Gwydion were at the center of it all. There was surely some lethal link between them.

The thing that disturbed Elise most was that the wave of blood and violence surrounding the men seemed to be sweeping Annora and her along with it. She wished she had elected another route to Conwy, but the Trackway of the Cross and now this well-traveled path were the only sure ways she knew. She hadn't anticipated they would be littered with bodies.

Fighting fresh anxiety, she tried to ward off jumbled thoughts of spiders, sentient trees, missing lips, and missing feet. There was a further host of frightful unconnected images, chaotic pieces she commanded her mind to repulse. Taken singly, none of these items was pleasant to ruminate upon. Considered together, they formed an even more disturbing whole.

She did her utmost not to think of them at all.

Most especially she tried not to think of death. However, that proved nearly impossible, as it seemed to be all around them. But she made a valiant effort to turn her mind from carnage, from murder, and tried to envision instead a new home for Annora and herself.

As they continued their journey toward Llanrhychwyn, she conjured an imaginary cottage with a garden of herbs outside its door. Goldfinches sang nearby and happily gathered seeds from burdock and thistle heads. Roses twined up to the eaves. Inside, sunlight streamed through a window. An oak table sat by that window, and on it rested three copper bowls and a homely brown pot. One bowl held walnuts, another bilberries, and the last, dried peas. The brown pot contained honeycomb, dripping and golden; she imagined it had been fetched from the Conwy Honey Fair and was sweet as the blossoms growing on neighboring hills, sweet as any honey could ever be.

Over everything lay a silent blessing. In every corner rested serenity.

Elise tried to hold this enchanted picture in her mind. For a time she was successful. "Annora and I will have all this," she told herself. It was a secret oath. "We will plant lavender and hyssop and drizzle nectar on our bread. Each night we'll rest in soft blankets and dream gentle, untroubled dreams."

But soon the cottage and the goldfinches, copper bowls, honey all faded away. She reluctantly admitted to herself that the time was not ripe for such happy imaginings. She and her dear old friend still had too far to go.

For now they'd walk as quickly as they could to the village of Llanrhychwyn and spend an uneventful night at the most respectable place they could find. If by cruel chance they spied Sir Nicolas and his man, they'd hide, take refuge at a church.

Then onward. They'd trek to Llanbedr-y-cennin. If all went well, they might stop to pray at Ffynnon-bedr, Saint Peter's Well. Annora often mentioned a wish to visit there, and it was not out of the way. Then through Caer Rhun, Tyn-y-Groes, Gyffin. To Conwy.

Elise didn't want to think of traveling beyond Conwy to Beaumaris. For now, Conwy would be enough.

And if they encountered Gwydion again? The thought confounded her. Who was Gwydion? Was he as dangerous as Sir Nicolas?

Without conscious volition she remembered her vision at Penmachno. The man in that vision was wild and streaked with blood. He'd raised a severed head in his right hand. He'd gripped a sword in his left. His shoulders were broad and scarred, and his elation primitive.

"Gwydion *is* that fierce man. And he *is* dangerous," an inner voice whispered.

If Elise believed Annora was unaware of the anxieties besetting her mind, she erred. Annora fretted about the same grim things her friend did but was equally loath to give their dark forms more power by describing them aloud. She too felt threats multiplying all around. They would need a miracle to reach even the dubious haven of Conwy unscathed, she feared.

An ancient story told of a warrior who calmly accepted his impending execution by fire. He said, "I have long been eager for rest." Annora understood this well. She knew she was no heroine, but some mornings she felt decidedly ancient. Although strong and sound in the main, she was no longer a young woman. But Elise was. She couldn't abandon Elise. As a constant friend, almost as a daughter, she loved Elise with all her heart. The girl had inherited her father's courage; it was just now beginning to declare itself after two nightmarish years. The gifts of her mother Katherine's sweet nature, and her delicate beauty, were also Elise's by birthright. A discriminating observer might note her subtle grace of countenance and form, might note those clear gray eyes that saw so much and yet revealed so little.

More than anything Annora wanted Elise to have a chance at joy, though the prospects were admittedly slender. God knew the girl's passage to adulthood had been unspeakable. First the Pestilence. Then Maelgwyn. It was his well-deserved death that had forced them to this flight. Annora realized full well that a person as sensitive as Elise couldn't end a man's life, even an evil man's, and suffer no pangs as a result. But Annora had to at least try to protect her from other evil men and from further grief.

In spite of their separate, unspoken burdens of worry, the women made quick progress toward Llanrhychwyn.

Sarn Elen and the regular path no longer ran together. Just past Castell-y-Gwynt, Sarn Elen branched off alone to wander windswept hills. Its cohort of legless legionnaires wandered with it, according to travelers' reports.

"Are we getting closer?" said Annora, when she feared her feet might drop off entirely.

"It can't be far. Are you weary?"

"I was only asking."

Elise smiled. "You've the stamina of a horse."

"That's sweet, child."

They came to the Llugwy River and crossed it, gingerly and with nervous jokes, by way of solid stepping-stones. Luckily the water was peaceable and clear. It only rippled softly. Minnows flashed downstream, gleaming silver in the current.

"It's warmer today," said Elise. "I'd love to take off this cloak, but it would probably be even worse to carry it."

"I suspect you're right. But I think we may be cooled by a proper storm before evening. I think I smell rain. If it comes, I'll hang this rank frock of mine outside for a cleaning. Not to forget the small-clothes beneath." She didn't say it aloud but knew sweat rivulets ran between her breasts, dampening the front of her dress and under her arms. The afternoon was so warm, the air so thick. She felt like a fuller's apprentice who hadn't bathed in half a year. She suspected she stank like one too.

22

A STORM, AND THE TALE OF
AN ADULTEROUS PRINCESS

At last they came to a clearing on a ridge, with timber-framed houses scattered all about. Most were one-story. All had lime-washed walls and thatched roofs. From atop a nearby rocky eminence, a small stone church guarded its handsome and seemingly tranquil parish.

This was the village of Llanrhychwyn. The travelers arrived there just as muddy clouds began to swirl and swell at the horizon.

"I was right," said Annora. "A proper tempest brews from the south. The wind is already bad-tempered."

Elise regarded the sky with misgiving. "We need to find an inn, or at least a cottager who will let us stay the night for a coin or two."

Just then a woman came plodding toward them, up the path from the village. Her ample skirts fluttered and billowed in a sudden gust. A piece of linen covered her hair, and atop it sat a broad-brimmed hat made of fine straw; both of these she held in place with one hand. As for the rest of her—and there was rather a lot—it was draped in respectable brown.

Stopping when she reached Elise and Annora, she looked south and indicated they should do likewise. "The good Lord's angry with someone today," she said. Her gaze then took in their dusty clothing, their sacks and staffs. She peered beyond them and saw they were not accompanied. "Aye, someone," she said again. Her tone suggested she had her suspicions about the specific culprits incurring divine displeasure. But then she shrugged. "If it isn't someone, it's someone else. Unless it's the Devil's work."

"The Devil?" said Annora.

The woman looked surprised. "Surely. When he's not in his palace in Hell, he dwells in the north. This storm comes from the south, so it might be Old Sin fleeing back to the north."

"But are you going up the track, alone, with foul weather nearly on us?" said Elise, concerned for the well-padded stranger.

"Bless you for asking, but no. I watched you toil down the slope and ventured out to see if you've need of a night's lodging. Elsewise Mistress Lowri might waylay you by her abode just there." She gestured disdainfully behind her to an imposing three-bay house. "She'd make you pay through the nose for foul food and a bracken bed full of crawly creatures that arrived days ago. What's more, I'll declare without pleasure she's no better than she ought to be."

"Whereas you'll give us a lovely supper and a perfectly tidy and respectable bower to rest in," said Annora. "All for practically nothing."

The woman's face broke out in a smile. "I will, indeed."

Soon all three were ensconced in a one-room cottage about twenty-five-feet square. This cottage sat quite near the larger dwelling belonging to disreputable Mistress Lowri. The place was as clean as promised and filled with the scents of fresh floor rushes and wax. This latter fragrance was explained by the many candles, unlit, lined atop the house's narrow trestle table.

Their landlady told them her name was Efa. A childless widow, she made these tapers to supplement her income from overnight lodgers who periodically came through Llanrhychwyn. She only took in honest pilgrims or virtuous families, no unvouched-for men. *Those* types, she said, with a telling waggle of her brows, were more the preferred clientele of her degenerate neighbor, Lowri.

Efa said she sold her candles to the monks at Maenan Abbey and sometimes at Trefriw's twice-weekly market. "I don't often waste the best ones on myself," she said. "But as it's growing dark so early today, and as I see you are upright ladies who might appreciate the steadiness of their burning, I'll make an exception and light one or two tonight."

After a while the women enjoyed a meal on clean earthenware plates. The widow served eggs mixed with bits of chewy pork. Alongside there were salted leeks and freshly picked Good King Henry that came from a secret spot next to a pond in the nearby woods. It, the Good King Henry, tasted like a mix of spinach and chestnuts. There was also a coarse barley loaf and diluted ale. If the ale was not as ambrosial as that served at Ieuan ap Morgan Goch's establishment, at least the hostess was more amiable than Ieuan's wife.

After dining, Annora reclined on a feather-filled cushion near the central hearth.

"That feels better," she said, rubbing her round stomach. "As soon as I can make myself get up, I'll change into my clean dress and put this one out in the rain for a good soaking."

"I'll do the same," said Elise. "And thank you, Efa, for the meal. It was lovely."

"No need to thank me. I appreciate the company, dear, especially on a night such as this promises to be."

Indeed the light shining through the cottage's single window grew steadily weaker, and the room took on an eerie yellowish green cast. Efa opened the door and gazed at the sky.

"I say it again—the good Lord is angry at someone," she said. "The birds have gone quiet and the clouds are a strange color. Look, lightning tails lash the south."

Thunder rumbled. It was a menacing, drawn-out growl that stirred unremembered echoes behind Elise's eyes and down the long bones of her arms and legs. As the sound rolled away across the southern distance like an omen, the landlady closed the door with an unequivocal thud and immediately lit two thick candles with a piece of straw she held to the fire. The pair of flames glowed upright, then bowed back and forth in skittish drafts that squeezed past the shutters and around the doorjamb.

"We were lucky to arrive when we did," said Elise, dreamily watching the flames' shadowy twins dance on the room's rear wall.

Widow Efa agreed as she knelt to pull blankets from a wooden chest. "God watched over you, and that's a mercy. Last June a maiden from Gyffin wasn't so blessed. She came up here to see her sister's family. But a storm broke from the south, like this one, just as she arrived. They say she was but a hiccough from her sister's door when there came a white flash. Then there rose up a smell like Hell's cellar. Her nephew swore he saw her raise her hand"—Efa raised her own, to show how it might have been—"then she froze. The boy blinked and she fell dead. Shriveled and smoking on her sister's threshold she lay, hair burned all away."

Annora gazed through a gap where the shutters didn't quite meet in the middle. "Poor thing. But I suppose she felt no pain."

The widow spread a tan blanket on one of the cottage's two mis-shapen mattresses. "We found out later she'd been dallying in the woods with her sister's husband. Her own sister she was betraying, the one she'd come to visit. So you see, she was no maiden at all."

"She raised her hand to Heaven and she died," said Elise, in a far-away voice.

Annora turned her head to cast her friend an uneasy look.

"But it was only the wages of sin, after all," said the widow, smoothing the blanket.

Church bells started to clamor. There were three quick tolls, a halt, then three tolls more. Ten times the chiming followed this pattern.

Efa looked approving. "Father Sefyl is pushing away the storm," she said. "Three chimes is once for every day William the Bastard wore his crown in any year. Easter, Pentecost, and Christmas. And ten rounds of that, one for each commandment."

"William the Bastard?" said Annora. "Why a grasping Frenchman?"

Efa shrugged. "Father Sefyl says he was a pious king, despite being wrathful and foreign."

"At Hastings one of William's soldiers separated Harold Godwinson from his manhood as he lay dying on the field," said Elise, her eyes now closed.

The widow frowned and wrinkled her nose. "Odd bit of history for a young female to be speaking of, isn't it?"

Annora forced an unconvincing laugh. "Pay no heed to my daughter, Widow Efa." She then decided to modify their story to make it closer to the truth and thus simpler to remember. "That is, she's just like my daughter, as I've been looking after her for years and her own mother is gone. But as I was saying, her deceased husband fancied himself an authority on history and filled her head with outlandish stories. I was forever begging him to stop. Now, when she's fatigued, Elise forgets herself and recites them again." That tale, at least, had a core of truth in it.

"Is that right? Well, youth is susceptible, I always think," the widow said, her face relaxing into good cheer.

As thunder sounded again, a child in some nearby house wailed. A dog barked, then yelped and went quiet.

"The storm will be here soon," Efa said, leaning on her windowsill, pushing the shutters open a bit to look out at the evening. She turned around and gave Annora a conspirator's nod. Her voice had gone discreetly low. "I'll entertain you with another tale while we wait, unless you fear you might find it impious."

"Tell away, friend. Elise is too spent to pay much attention, I think. For myself, I savor an impious tale—for the sake of moral instruction."

Efa grinned. "Let me instruct. So, friend Annora, our village has suffered its share of wayward women. Besides Lowri, I mean. The most famous was a hundred years ago. She was a princess, daughter of a king, consort of a loving ruler."

"A princess?"

"Joan, wife of Llewelyn Fawr, our greatest Welsh prince. They were happily wed twenty years and more when Llewelyn took a hostage in battle and left him at his court at Aber, near Conwy, to be courteously watched. Then our prince went back out to fight—the fool. The hostage he left was a handsome English lord from the south, William de Briouze."

"Courteously watched, you say. Tell me she didn't."

"She did." Efa glanced over at Elise and lowered her voice further. She needn't have bothered, as Elise only gazed at the shadows on the wall and didn't seem to hear a word. "Our princess and the handsome lord were even observed in Trefriw, for Llewelyn had a house there as well. They were often seen here in Llanrhychwyn, in the dell by Minnow Pond. They weren't picking mushrooms, I'm sorry to say. Likewise they sneaked to Lowri's house to tryst. Of course it was her mother's mother's mother's house back then. The pair fornicated gleefully in a bed Lowri keeps to this day. Wanton in the moonlight they were, if you can credit such carryings-on."

Annora hugged herself. "Satan must have done a jig. But how did it end? Don't tell me Joan was burnt up by lightning too."

"No. But Prince Llewelyn found out the truth, since people delight in spreading gossip. He must have been heartsore, but he put de Briouze properly on trial for indecency. Truth being truth, the wretch was found guilty and hanged. Joan was put in a tower for a year."

"No victors on that field."

"Not at first. But Llewelyn eventually forgave Joan, if stories are true. They regained much of what she almost threw away for the joy of a stranger's lips."

"Not just his lips, I'll warrant," said Annora, causing her hostess to chortle.

Wind blew the door open. Efa lumbered over and secured it with a wooden bar. Lightning illuminated the interior of the cottage even through its single window. Thunder crashed. A plate fell to the floor.

Elise covered her ears.

"Cariad," said Annora, rising with effort and going to her friend's side, "the storm won't last forever. Come, we'll stay busy changing our dresses and hanging them out in the rain. There's bound to be a deluge soon."

Elise didn't answer.

There began a rhythmic pounding close by. It came closer but didn't sound like raindrops.

The widow stared out her window. "Hold me fast. Men on horseback, in this weather. A half dozen or more. And worse."

"Worse?"

"Three women they've got with them. Not decent women. They're riding lolled back against the men's chests, like overgrown babies. Dressed in a fashion you'd be more liable to see in some godless city. Like Sodom."

Annora joined her at the window. "Perdition," she said, gawking. "You'd think they'd perish with shame, with their bosoms on show that way."

Efa nodded. "Straight into Lowri's den they go. And the horses in her shed. What did I say about that creature I call neighbor? Oh, they'll be a dreadful mob of sinners tonight."

At the back of the room Elise swayed. She dropped to the rushes.

Annora hurried to her side. "Child, what's wrong?"

Elise stared at the wall. "Noise," she said. "The noise."

"It's just the rain beginning," said Efa. "Listen how hard it drums."

She was right. Fat drops hit the walls and beat against the door. The widow rushed to secure the shutters fully, fussing and exclaiming as she did.

Regaining her senses somewhat, Elise clutched her friend's arm and said in a soft, distraught voice, "I heard wings. Then Maelgwyn was there, with a scar on his throat. We were in a room with a tapestry and pink light, but I couldn't speak. His breath was hot on my face, Annora. So hot. He lifted my skirt. Then he said we both love the sight of blood—and he choked me."

Glancing at her hostess, seeing she still wrestled with the shutters,

Annora turned back to Elise. "He's dead, child. Dead. Nothing like that can happen to you ever again."

When Elise's nails dug into Annora's tender wrist, the older woman flinched. "It was real," Elise said.

Annora released herself from the girl's grip. "It wasn't. Collect your wits and remember: it was only a dream, a dream, the spawn of exhaustion. He can't hurt you anymore."

Efa finished her task, swung around, and beheld the anxiety on her guests' faces. She propped her wide derriere against the stone windowsill. "What's amiss?"

Annora pushed a strand of hair from Elise's ashen face. "Weariness," she said. "And she's never fond of storms."

There was a shout of feminine laughter, outside, in the storm. A man swore. A door slammed. Then all that could be heard was the pounding of the rain.

After a moment Elise sat up slowly, eyes bleak.

Thunder crashed. Fingers of rainwater crept under the door and darkened the rushes.

Annora gathered Elise back into her arms. "Remember, he's snug in Hell," she whispered. "You've had a glimpse of old fears, that's all. Compose yourself now for the sake of appearances, child."

Elise pressed her face against her friend's warm shoulder, then straightened and gave Efa a weak smile. "Forgive my foolishness," she said, in a more lucid manner. "Dreams have always plagued me, though they grow less frequent. I'll not disturb you again."

Efa shrugged. "Don't apologize. Once when I was a maiden, I dreamed an eel long as a jouster's lance took me for his bride. To this day I prefer cockles."

23

THE PRICE OF DREAMS

The storm raged outside Efa's house. Wind tore limbs from trees and lashed them against Llanrhychwyn's houses and against the whitewashed sides of the church. A vicious gust sucked two ancient limestone crosses from churchyard soil and flung them down the ridge like whirligigs. Tall and wide as men, they smashed together midway and broke into dozens of pieces. Strange symbols carved into their flanks disappeared forever, along with the legend that claimed they'd been erected by King Arthur to celebrate his defeat of Saxons on a nearby hill. Within a generation of the storm, the tale of Arthur's triumph at Llanrhychwyn would be as forgotten as if it had never been. Fragments of the symbol-etched crosses would wash down the valley to the river or come to rest against the roots of gnarled oak trees. Some would scatter across the forest floor. In the dark places where they settled, they would eventually grow to be indistinguishable from pebbles, squirrel bones, or the teeth of long-dead children.

The rain was too intense and wind-driven to allow Elise or Annora to hang their clothes out on the trees.

"Soak them in my pail," said Efa, "then drape them near the fire."

Annora frowned. "They'll still be wet in the morning."

"Probably. If you want my opinion, you ought to stay one more night at least. The path will be a swamp tomorrow and make for hopeless going—wherever it is you're going." After waiting a moment for some response to this sally, and receiving none, Efa took a red shawl from a peg near the door and threw it around her shoulders. "Why not give your clothes a chance to dry? The day after a storm is often fine, good for drying clothes."

Annora sat on a bed beside Elise. The younger woman had fallen into a fitful doze, leaning against her friend. Released from its wimple, her brown hair hung in tangles and wild curls all around her. Dark lashes brushed her cheeks.

Annora watched her, her own face pinched. Meanwhile Efa swept rainwater and wet rushes toward the threshold with a determined arm and a sturdy broom.

Flashes of lightning grew less frequent. Thunder rolled farther away.

Resting on her broom handle, Efa gazed thoughtfully at Elise. "Stay one more night," she said again to Annora. Her voice was soft and serious. "I know there's more to your journey than you're saying, but stay. That girl's in no state to be on the road. Any fool could see she's bone-weary. Any fool could say the same of you."

Unshed tears glistened in Annora's brown eyes.

As if to punctuate the storm's retreat with a last show of defiance, a great lightning flash turned the inside of the cottage stark blue-white. Finding its way through the shutters' gap, the flash lit the candles on the table, and the copper handle of a pot by the fire, and haphazardly picked out shining strands of Elise's unbound hair. After that flash, there was no more thunder.

Efa persisted. "If you're in trouble, or her, it's plain as a wafer it's not your own doing."

"We're strangers," said Annora, voice tremulous.

Efa began to sweep again, more briskly, although water no longer pooled. "I may indulge in a morsel of gossip sometimes," she said, "but I know decent women when I see them. After all, I've lived next door to an indecent one for years."

So it was agreed. When Elise awoke a while later—after gasping once and staring wildly around the room—Annora told her they'd be Efa's guests for two nights instead of one.

"No one will make progress on the roads tomorrow, child," she said. "We might as well rest, wash our dresses and let the sun dry them, and eat Efa's good food."

"The rivers are all likely in flood anyway, impossible to cross," said Efa.

Looking down at her hands where they rested in her lap, Elise sighed and nodded. "I am content to stay, then. Content and thankful."

The travelers rinsed their dresses in Efa's large pail. She gave them nuggets of green soap to stir into the water. "I've a barrel of that stuff from a merchant in Trefriw, an old bachelor with too keen a colt's tooth," the widow said, blushing. "He thinks to win me as wife so I can trim his toenails and shell his green peas for him."

Annora grinned. "Are you inclined to shell his peas?"

"No, I'll stick to Good King Henry for my dinner. Even so, it's fine soap. Came on a Spanish ship, Master Colt's Tooth boasted. Mixed of herbs, rose petals, and oil squeezed from olives. You'll smell like a pair of flowers."

"A nice change," said Annora. "But have you a bit more of the stuff so we might dab at ourselves with it too? We're needy as our clothing, I fear."

"Plenty, and extra."

Elise and Annora were soon in their spare dresses, cleaner than they'd been in months. Maelgwyn had not encouraged bathing. He believed it caused illness and often lectured Elise on the insidious way water and soap encouraged bodily humors—blood, phlegm, choler, and black bile—to become unbalanced. Catarrh, lung lesions, and pus-filled ears were some of the illnesses resulting from overzealous cleanliness. Further, he hinted bathing was a sly form of vanity, that dreadful vice.

It was the middle of the night by the time the clothes had been sufficiently sloshed about in the pail and churned with a paddle to be declared clean. By then the rain had stopped entirely. The three women ventured out of doors to hang the laundry from the branches of a tree near the cottage. Remaining clouds were fleeing north, and the moon shone overhead.

"Mercy," said Efa, gazing at her moonlit village. "The thatch has blown off poor Maredudd's place. And Elen and Gwilym's stout door is gone. See them there, confounded?" She turned, then sucked in her breath. "Moses. Scorch marks down Lowri's wall. Lightning struck it, then rain must have put the fire out. It must be true the Devil protects his own. I'm only glad it wasn't my place hit. Still it was too near for my liking."

Other villagers stood about, assessing damage.

"But Mistress Lowri and her customers won't be up until midday," predicted Efa. "She'll be ale-potted as a harvest fairy by now, if I know her. Mind you, it's probably hard to crawl out of bed when there's an unbreeched lecher weighing you down."

Elise didn't hear, but Annora chuckled with scandalized delight. New streams ran everywhere. They cascaded down the ridge near the church and gurgled in the unseen distance in the forest. Cool night wind held a pungent trace of smoke.

"More lightning strikes somewhere," said Annora, sniffing.

Efa nodded. "A nasty storm."

After picking up branches that had fallen on the patch of land around her cottage, Efa grew restive. She decided to visit Father Sefyl to see how the church had fared in the tempest, and to call in at the houses of some of her friends. "I'm just nosy, if you want the truth," she said, laughing at herself. Off she marched toward the rocky ridge, clutching a flickering rush.

Annora and Elise stood near the doorway and looked out at the night. Not a creak or mumble could be heard from Mistress Lowri's, though her house sat near Efa's cottage. However, faint light showed under the door and in an upper window.

"Some soul has risen to observe matins," whispered Annora. "You suppose one of Lowri's lodgers is an admirer of Saint Benedict?" The Benedictines were well known to rise in the middle of the night to pray.

Elise guessed her friend's foolery was put forward to deflect other discussion. But she felt obliged to speak of certain things. "Let's go inside," she said, moving to the door.

Annora sighed and followed.

They stood on either side of the widow's table, regarding each other over unlit candles. "Cariad, you want to talk about your dream. But if you're after my opinion, the shock of everything that's happened has shaken you more than you suppose."

"Shaken me?"

"Your emotions are tangled. So your dreams or visions may not mean a thing for a long while—not in any way you can make sense of. Which isn't entirely bad."

"My emotions are tangled?" Elise picked up a cream-colored candle and ran her fingertips absentmindedly down its length. "You might be right. Truly, this dream, or vision, was different than any I remember. Not that the visions have ever been much alike, except for the noise of the wings and how I feel when I come to my senses."

"You heard the wings?"

"Yes. But I didn't *feel* as I usually do. I felt more . . . tied to the earth."

"See? It wasn't a vision, just a stew of fear."

Elise replaced the candle on the table. "I know Maelgwyn is dead, Annora. I finally believe it. But I wish I'd never have to see him again, even in a dream."

A horse whinnied somewhere in the valley. Another answered from higher on the ridge. Their noise distracted Annora.

"The animals are restless after the storm," she said. "They must be having trouble settling down."

Elise turned toward the closed door. Her face was half in shadows, for Efa's two candles still burned at the end of the table. "Horses. Might it—"

"It might not. Even if Maelgwyn's body has been found, no one would come out on a night like this to mete out justice. Anyway, how would they know where to look?"

"You're right. It's so hard to think sensibly." Elise looked down at the table.

"There's still more you want to say, isn't there?"

"There was something else—in the dream."

"Tell me and forget it."

"He called me a whore. He said he'd kill my lover."

Annora licked her lips, wondering what it must be like to dream such awful things. "Lover?"

Elise gave a bitter laugh. "That was the best part, that he should imagine I have a lover. I've never had a lover. All I've had was Maelgwyn."

Annora raised her hand over the table, but let it fall when Elise turned away. "Cariad," she said quietly, "you can't be hurt by a dead man. You can only be hurt by dwelling in the past and thinking there's nothing left for the future."

Crossing the room, Elise took the knife from her sack. "I never will have a lover, will I? I'll never know peace."

"Don't talk like that. You'll have both."

Elise tested her knife's blade on her thumb. "I'll tell you another sorry thing," she said, half smiling. "I *have* dreamed of a lover. An honorable, handsome man. Ridiculous, isn't it?"

"Don't let your hopes die, Elise. Hold them close."

Annora's words had no impact. "What prudent man would want me, knowing I'm a murderess?"

"You're not! And why would you ever need to tell a soul, even if you were? Some things are best forgotten."

Just then Efa returned with a flourish, stamping her shoes on the threshold. "The king's crosses are both blown down the ridge and smashed," she said. "After standing for who knows how many years."

Silence greeted this news. Efa looked from Elise to Annora, then extinguished her torch in the pail. "Mayhap we could do with a splash of oak beer before settling in our beds at long last," she said. "A bracing brew, is oak beer. Mixed with honey and a sprinkle of mistletoe." She was chattering to divert them, and all three knew it. But she went on cheerily. "You both look like you could use a drop of something bracing." She bustled over to a shelf.

The women drank generous portions of oak beer while Efa expounded on the virtues of mistletoe as a safeguard against poison, magic, and lightning.

Annora drained her cup and graciously accepted another. "On Anglesey mistletoe means good fortune and long life."

"Amen," said Efa, pouring more beer for herself and Elise.

Not long after, Elise fell into a heavy sleep. Her knife rested at her side. Next to her, Annora lay on her back, frowning at the ceiling.

When Efa slipped another knife beneath the edge of the cushion Elise's head rested on, Annora raised up on her elbow to watch. She looked a question at her hostess.

Gently Efa withdrew the knife from under the cushion. She held it out to Annora, who squinted to see the tiny words etched up and down the blade. Annora was unable to read them but knew what they were—Anaxeimeys, Malchus, Denys, Marsianus, Thon, Serapion, and Constantynn.

"The Seven Sleepers," Efa whispered. "You know the charm?"

Annora nodded and rested her head once more. She knew the old charm and had sometimes witnessed good outcome from its use. Her grandmother had been its proponent, though the identity of the Sleepers remained a mystery to that good woman. As an adult Annora learned from a priest they were men who lived a thousand years ago in a place called Ephesus. They fell asleep in a cave during the days when Romans slew Christians, then awakened two hundred years later, miraculously hale and young. Although the story could not be proved, the spell of the Seven was undoubtedly potent, sometimes.

Deftly the widow replaced the knife. "The Sleepers will bless her. Now she's sure to rest well and have only untroubled dreams," she said, before blowing out the candles. Then she climbed into her own bed.

Embers from the hearth gave the only light.

Gazing once more toward the ceiling in the nearly darkened cottage, Annora wished she could share her new friend's innocent confidence. She rolled to her side, considering the mystery of God's design for man, and for woman.

A stray heretical thought drifted across her mind—that the Maker could sometimes be capricious, even cruel. But she pushed the thought angrily away, recognizing it for the Devil's sin trap it clearly was.

Two yawns later she slept.

24

THICKENED CHERRY JUICE

A noise startled Elise out of sleep. Knife firmly in hand, she lay listening. But now all she heard was Annora's dainty snores. The interior of the cottage blushed with the faint pink glow that sometimes precedes sunrise on clear, bright days. Turning her head, she detected Efa's plump silhouette at the window. The shutters gaped, but less than halfway.

When Elise rose, the charm-inscribed knife dropped to the floor with a soft thud. She peered down at it. Efa glanced over her shoulder. She came to retrieve her knife, frowning, as if its appearance there mystified her too. Then she put a finger to her lips. She and Elise crept to the window while Annora's snores continued without pause.

They looked through the opening between the shutters, Elise with a cold feeling in the pit of her stomach. At first she saw nothing except the black outlines of tree trunks and bushes and the hulking shape of Mistress Lowri's house almost straight ahead.

She touched Efa's hand. "What do you see?" she whispered.

"Be patient." Efa's voice was as low as she could make it.

As they waited, Elise fought the urge to tremble. Her bare feet grew chilled on the damp rushes. She lifted one foot, then the other, trying to warm them on her calves.

From across the village wafted the smell of baking bread.

"Meurig the baker," whispered Efa. "Someone's brought their dough to his oven earlier than usual."

The morning air was also redolent of mint, earthworms, and wild hops.

Then came the slightest *ting*, a striking of metal on metal.

"There," said Efa, gesturing toward the phantom sound. "Between the trees where the path begins."

In the thick opalescence that marked night's departure, a shape revealed itself to Elise. Gray against the hint of morning, there appeared the outline of a horse, with a rider. They stood at the edge of a copse, still as stone.

"More," said Efa. "Four or five, to the right."

Elise discerned them too, though they were as silent and unmoving as the first.

Efa touched Elise's arm. "I doubt they're ghosts, child. Is their business with you?"

Elise's heart pounded. It beat so loudly she thought its thudding might spill out of the cottage. "I fear so," she said, surprised to hear that her voice, at least, sounded almost normal.

Efa must have felt otherwise. She took off her shawl and draped it around her guest.

Hooves struck the ground near the cottage, startling both women. A horse whickered. Stirrups and spurs chinked.

The noises ceased just between Efa's dwelling and Mistress Lowri's.

A man spoke. His voice was flinty and uncompromising in the darkness. "Send out the murderer."

Far in the woods a song thrush called.

Efa jerked away from the window. She leaned on the wall with her back and shoulders pressed against it. "Murderer?" she breathed. "You, child?"

Annora woke with a soft cry, as if from a bad dream. She assessed the state of affairs with laudable speed, then scrambled into her dress like a veteran of surprise attacks. Stumbling to the window, she stood beside Elise.

Again Efa peeked outside.

"What do you want?" said a woman, further shocking the three who listened in the widow's cottage. This woman's voice was slurred and unrefined.

"What in the world?" said Efa. "That's Mistress Lowri, drunk as she can be."

"Send out the murderer," the man repeated.

Efa gave Elise a relieved but appraising look. "Well, child, it seems their issue is not with you."

Mistress Lowri spoke again. "We have no murderers here, only plain folk whose rest you disrupt."

As Elise nudged the shutter open wider, her heart commenced a more manageable pace. She commanded herself to think sensibly.

These horsemen had not come to Llanrhychwyn for her and were not Maelgwyn's minions. Then who lurked in Mistress Lowri's house?

Annora squinted out at the brightening world. She rubbed her eyes. "Your neighbor leads a colorful life," she said.

The man spoke again, more loudly, but not in Welsh as before. This time his words were in clear, if accented, English. They were also full of scorn. "It ill becomes a man to hide behind a woman's skirt, Sir Nicolas."

"Saesneg?" said Efa.

"Nicolas?" said Annora. "Cariad, wasn't that the name of that man, the Englishman you told me was mad?"

Efa gaped at her guests. "My neighbor isn't the only one who leads a colorful life, I think. What sort of journey have you two been enduring?"

Her guests did not reply.

By barely noticeable degrees dawn's light revealed more of the scene. It revealed three men with soldierly bearing, on good horses. Likewise it showed fair-haired Thomas, also mounted. There was another man, on foot, standing nearer Lowri's house. Judging by his impatient stance, this last fellow was the one who had called out with disdain to Sir Nicolas.

Wringing her hands some slight distance from her own doorway stood Mistress Lowri, swaying, seeming much the worse for drink. Sir Nicolas, his purple cloak slung around his shoulders, was just sauntering out of her house.

Finally, at the far edge of this tableau, was Gwydion. He sat astride his black warhorse, his face partly in shadows.

For a few moments no further dialogue sounded.

"It's like a pageant, isn't it?" whispered Efa.

"It may end more untidily than most," said Annora.

Sir Nicolas finally spoke, in disdainful English. "What churl wrests me from my nest?"

"Saesneg," Efa repeated. "Here? Why?"

"Hush," said Annora. "Let Elise listen so she can tell us later what's been discussed."

Efa's eyes widened. She was acquainted with few folk who could utter or understood more than a dozen words of English. But she nodded and went still.

Sir Nicolas spoke again. "Well, who are you? Plainly you've come to the wrong house. But this drunken doxy"—he gestured to Lowri—"was just showing me a trick she does with her mouth. Though she comprehends no jot of the king's English, I was rapt. So I'd like to go back inside and let her continue." He made a mocking bow. "If you've no objection."

Gwydion spoke. "I have an objection." He had not raised his voice, but his words carried on the morning air.

Sir Nicolas had already spun on his heel, but he turned back. "Have you?"

Gwydion dismounted without reply. Merely he drew his sword from its silver scabbard—it gave a metallic sigh—and let its point rest on the ground. The blade flashed in the light of the sun just rising above the eastern treetops.

Thomas called out, "No man can mock the law. Not even you, Sir Nicolas."

"Oho, a real Englishman," said Nicolas, swinging his gaze to Thomas. "Whereas a hint of primitive cadence tells me this terse fellow with the sword is . . . not. So be it. I'll converse with my countryman instead."

"Ought I to feel honored?" said Thomas. Sarcasm did not mask his youthful uneasiness.

Nicolas smiled gently. "Of course you ought. But what concern is this of yours, young man? Please don't tell me you have distressing Welsh kin who dance naked in oak groves."

Thomas blinked, too taken aback to formulate a quick response.

Sir Nicolas waited, but not long, before he continued. "Not much of an orator either, bantling? I'm disappointed." Once more he turned toward Gwydion. "So, largest and grimmest disturber of my peace, I'm forced to confer with you. And you're remarkably hostile for so early in the morning. Or do you simply enjoy abusing English nobles?"

Rediscovering his tongue, Thomas rose up in his stirrups. "Noble? You make me ashamed to call myself an English noble."

"How unfortunate." Nicolas rubbed his hands together. "Hold a moment, and I'll try to unknot these skeins. I'm certain it's a misunderstanding. I'm also sure you don't seriously mean to insult me." He then called out toward Mistress Lowri's open door. "Dexter, drag on your rags. A man with a sword importunes me."

Dexter appeared before Nicolas finished speaking. He came out straightening his tunic.

"By God, you're a gruesome sight," said his master.

Dexter only glared across at Gwydion.

Sir Nicolas heaved an extravagant sigh. "Gruesome or not, Dex, I believe this fellow with the unsheathed blade is a scion of this backward land. Should his rancor mean anything to us?"

Dexter shrugged, then spit. "It might, my lord."

"It might? Most enlightening, Dexter." Nicolas again looked to Gwydion. "My man is being evasive this morning. So pray tell me more to aid me in my unknotting, son of Wales."

"We're here to assert that murder has been committed," said Thomas, boldly. He sounded more assured than he had only moments before. "Does that goad your memory?"

"Someone has been murdered, you say." Nicolas shook his head. "Tragic. My own father was murdered. He was a duke, you know, very wealthy. But he preferred my older brothers to me. He once told me he should have had me drowned at birth."

Thomas ignored this speech. He swung down off his horse. "Furthermore, the victim's hall near the town of Conwy has been seized by his killer or killers," he said.

Sir Nicolas caught Dexter's eye and gave him a look of mock alarm. Then he smiled cordially at Gwydion. "But I still don't know where all this is heading, Lord Blade . . . ap Cur ap Swine—and so on. Ap, ap, ap, *ad infinitum.*"

Gwydion returned his smile.

In her cottage Efa shivered. "That fine Englishman seems odd, but I wouldn't want the tall one for an enemy," she said. Elise took off the borrowed red shawl and draped it over its owner's shoulders.

Mid-smirk Nicolas's mouth turned sharply downward. "By Saint Sebastian's wounds, I don't care for your smile, Lord Blade. Your smile is insincere." He looked down at his crucifix. With a trace of consternation, he flipped it so its jewels faced outward. "But steady," he said, after a moment, "I've something that may thaw you." He spoke low words to his servant, and Dexter nipped back into Lowri's house.

He reappeared at the threshold in an instant. In tow he had an exotic woman; he whispered pressingly in her ear. She nodded. He released her and sent her out the door. Blinking in the morning light, she stood in front and to one side of Sir Nicolas. With a hand shielding her eyes, she searched the faces of the men confronting the noble. Her gaze settled on Gwydion.

"Morning to you, handsome sir," she said to him in English. A dimpled smile accompanied her greeting.

Efa gawked. "Mercy, she must be chilled."

"She'll warm up fast the day she dips her toes into Satan's boiling lake," said Annora.

Their remarks were in response to the woman's enormous breasts, for she wore a blue-and-white striped dress whose cutaway bodice revealed the pair completely. Further, her nipples were obviously painted with crimson coloring—boiled cherry juice, if rumors concerning such females could be believed.

The voluptuous woman propped a hand on a hip. "Morning, sir," she said again, tossing her head. "I'm called Rose from Bordeaux."

Nicolas slapped his thigh. "Bordeaux? Rose, you liar. Rose from Southwark, *je pense.*"

Gwydion spared Rose one impassive glance, then let his eyes return to Nicolas.

The prostitute rolled her shoulders. "Wherever I hail from, he's naughty to ignore me," she said. Bending, she inched her skirts to her thighs. "Aren't my legs pretty? Walk to the woods with me and I'll show you something else. I'll show you a moist field you can furrow all day with your mighty plow." She giggled and looked over her shoulder at Sir Nicolas.

The nobleman reached around her and tweaked a painted nipple. "Wouldn't you like to suckle these red teats, my sour friend?" he asked Gwydion. "Play at mother and son?"

Inside Efa's cottage Annora's hands flew to her cheeks. "Wicked, wicked woman. And that disgusting man."

Elise only took a deep breath and went on watching. But as she leaned forward for a better view, she observed Dexter conferring with unseen confederates just inside Lowri's door.

Lowri herself stood well apart from Sir Nicolas and Rose. Mouth rouge had smeared over half her chin, and her restless fingers worried the creased skirt of her green dress. It was a frock with a relatively modest bodice—that is, her breasts were only partially revealed. Lowri looked from Sir Nicolas to Gwydion over and over again, as if she wished she might be anywhere in the world but in the midst of this "pageant."

"Don't care for ladies, Lord Blade?" Sir Nicolas was asking. "If you'd prefer, I'll fetch Dexter again to . . . bend to your will. He'll grouse, but he's biddable, albeit a trifle fetid."

The first man who spoke, the man who demanded the murderer, stepped forward. "We've wasted enough time," he said. "I'm officially charged to inform you, Sir Nicolas de Breauté, that you stand accused of the murder of Gruffydd ap Anarawd of Llys Garanhir and of the criminal seizure of his hall and chattel and lands."

If Sir Nicolas was surprised or concerned by this pronouncement, he gave no sign. Rather he requested his servant to cease loitering in the doorway and come answer a question. When Dexter sidled out, his master asked, "Have we killed some dog of a Welshman called Griffith—I believe it's Griffith, or something that sounds like Griffith—and appropriated his house? Have we really been behaving so badly?"

Dexter grinned and rubbed his ear, the ear Elise had damaged. "We might have, sir."

25

ALL'S FAIR

Raised voices could now be heard inside Mistress Lowri's house. Dexter edged back toward the door and slipped in. The voices stopped and all grew still.

Gwydion's other companions dismounted. Each drew his sword.

In a damp thicket not far off, a crowd of villagers gathered behind the trunks of two fallen oaks while others approached from their cottages. A pair of fuzz-chinned teens gawked like lack-wits at Rose, while wives and mothers whispered. Meanwhile a little girl with auburn braids waved to Mistress Lowri, then danced in a circle with her braids flying—until a woman grabbed the child's arm and pulled her against her side.

In Efa's cottage Elise took her spare dress from the peg it had hung on in the night. She dragged it over her head and secured its little hooks from her throat to just below her waist. Then she put on her stockings and shoes.

"What's this?" asked Annora. "You're not thinking of going outside. This is none of our affair, thank goodness. Besides, a fool can see it all will turn ugly soon."

Drawing a white kerchief from her sack and tying it around her uncombed hair, Elise said, "I don't intend to go out. But I doubt any of us will be going back to bed either."

Once again the three women watched through the window. They had no further need to keep their voices low, for there was a growing confusion of noise outside.

Sir Nicolas moved behind Rose and wrapped his arms around her waist. He rested his chin on her shoulder and gazed over it at Gwydion. "So, my surly friend, I can't persuade you to wander to the buttercups with this bit of English delight? It might benefit your constitution. You seem so tense."

Gwydion shrugged off his cape and tossed it over his saddle. He was not dressed for a pageant. He wore black hosen, tall boots, and a thigh-length black jupon, quilted body armor made of thick, hardy cloth. The jupon was edged with golden dagges and laced at the sides with leather cords. Chain mail showed at his throat and on the cuffs of his black gloves.

He slapped his horse on the rump. It wandered away to graze in a patch of grass. Facing Nicolas again, he resumed his stance, with his sword's point resting on the ground.

"You're admirably turned out, Sir Blade," the English lord said begrudgingly. He reached around Rose and pointed at his adversary's boots. "Those are handsome. From London?" He lifted his eyes to Gwydion's face. "York? You surely never bought them in this benighted realm."

"Let the woman go," said Gwydion.

Sir Nicolas's brows shot up. "I ask about your boots and you respond by issuing orders as if I were a peasant? Well, I will not heed your orders." He tightened his arms unexpectedly and hard around the prostitute so that she gave a squeal.

"My lord," she cried, turning her head as far as his embrace allowed in order to see his face, "you're hurting me."

"I suppose I am. But if you had a brain bigger than a pea, you would know by now I'm using you as a shield. Endure it. You fancied me well enough in this position last night."

Rose kicked backward. She landed a solid hit to Sir Nicolas's knee with her heel. He swore and dropped his arms. She ran to one side but he caught her by her curls and she fell against him. He grabbed her again, this time with a hand on the back of her neck. His other hand he used to twist her arm up between her shoulder blades.

Twenty or so feet away, Mistress Lowri screamed and dropped to the mud. She covered her bowed head with her arms.

"Now, what game shall we play?" said Sir Nicolas. "Knucklebones? Handy-dandy?"

Dexter appeared at Lowri's threshold. He too restrained a woman—a girl, really—with a short snare 'round her neck. By her bosom-revealing dress, she was one of Rose's colleagues. Her young face was white.

Lowri's shutters burst open from the inside. Through them, three men vaulted to the ground, one after another. A fourth exited less dramatically, stepping out the door. Like Sir Nicolas and Dexter, this last fellow used a woman as a shield. A fleshy female, she looked to be the eldest of her unchaste lot and was definitely the most improbably arrayed. Bare-breasted, she wore only ankle bracelets and a strip of blue cloth wrapped around her waist and between her legs.

Six men and three reluctant women stood facing Gwydion and his companions.

The youngest prostitute cried in English for release. But she stopped when Dexter jerked his snare. Rose whimpered only once, but her chest heaved. All the while the fleshy woman swore ferociously in English and fractured Welsh, until the fellow who held her advised her to "shut her brainless birdcage" or he'd crack her skull like a nut.

"An impasse. Six against six in the new-risen sun," said Sir Nicolas when all was quiet.

The man who had first bade Lowri to send out the murderer spoke again. "Sir Nicolas, come quietly to Conwy. I think we'd all prefer not to shed blood."

Nicolas sneered. "And who precisely are you, other than a Welsh toad who mauls England's tongue as if his mouth were stuffed with shite?"

"Constable for Edward the King in this—this part of Caernarfonshire," the man said, now self-consciously hesitating over English words. "I have a proper warrant."

Sir Nicolas's mouth curled. "A stuttering constable with a proper warrant. I'm overwhelmed."

"You won't be mistreated."

"A herd of Welsh swine and an ass of a young traitor won't mistreat an innocent English lord? Would I could believe you."

Thomas took an angry step forward.

"Hold, consorter with pigs," said Sir Nicolas, "or I'll snap poor Rose's neck."

Thomas stopped, as Rose sniveled.

"I'm curious, Lord Blade," said Nicolas, shifting his sharp gaze to Gwydion. "You seem convinced I murdered some Welsh fellow. Your clothes and demeanor suggest you are what passes for nobility in this wretched realm. Then why cower behind this paltry lot? Wouldn't it be more *noble* to deal with me yourself?"

Gwydion examined his sword's silver hilt, turning it in his gloved hands; he seemed engrossed in the intricacies of its workmanship. Finally he raised his eyes to Sir Nicolas and replied in a serious voice, "It's a selfish wish, de Breauté. You see, I want to watch cake sellers weave through the crowd the day your legs dangle at Conwy. A bright, blue day, perfect for a public, shameful death. Afterwards I want to watch herring gulls rip out your eyes."

Dexter's mouth worked without producing any words. His hostage clawed at the rope around her neck as he unintentionally tightened it.

His master admonished him in an amused voice. "Cease, Dexter. You'll leave nasty bruises on that girl." Still seeming entertained, he looked across at Gwydion. "What you really mean, Sir Blade, is that you're afraid. A poltroon. Or shall I say, a poulard?" Then he raised his foot to the base of Rose's spine and kicked her away.

She landed facedown and stayed there briefly before laboring up again. Her dress and her breasts were shiny with mud. Brown droplets fell from her forehead. Just as soon as she'd wiped her eyes, she bolted toward the trees.

A pockmarked minion tossed a sword to Sir Nicolas. He caught it deftly and made straight for Gwydion, whipping the weapon in an arc. Gwydion stepped easily aside. He raised his own sword and waited for Nicolas to turn and lunge again.

One of Sir Nicolas's companions hung back—the man restraining the ankle-braceleted prostitute. Perhaps not fully committed to his lord's cause, he hovered with his hostage near Mistress Lowri's door. Meanwhile the others fell with guttural cries on Thomas, the constable, and their three compatriots.

The pockmarked Englishman was quickly dispatched by the constable; the unlucky fellow slumped backward with a wound to his middle. Then another of Sir Nicolas's men fell, this one with a severed hand. Dropping to the mud, he gaped at his detached extremity. With solemn concentration, he leaned forward and picked it up with its intact mate. The Welshman who maimed him dragged him to a tree and propped him against it.

Thomas, more formidable than his youth and stylish clothes might suggest, bore a gash across his cheek and a rip down the back of his blue cape, but he fought on with zeal. For his part Dexter pressed and parried around his hostage. Afraid to hurt the girl, no opponent came too near. Their chivalry allowed Dexter to thrust and scurry away. In this sorry manner, he slightly wounded two foes. But he grew impatient with the limitations of this mode of fighting. Suddenly he barked out an oath, then bashed his fist against his hostage's head and shoved her away. She staggered to the woods and folded over a red currant bush. A pair of village women crept to her aid.

Numbers evened. Two Welshmen now lay bloody and still.

When Dexter edged toward his master to join him against Gwydion, Sir Nicolas waved him away. Thwarted, the lackey turned on the constable instead. The pair circled each other like mud-spattered gamecocks.

Adroit, and taller than his opponent by more than a handbreadth, Gwydion kept Nicolas at arm's length. The Englishman tried to attack, with less and less effect. Although he struggled visibly to maintain self-possession, agitation began to show in his demeanor.

Changing strategy, he danced back and strove to imitate Gwydion's cool smile. "You fight well enough," he said, a drop of betraying sweat suspended from his chin, "for a peasant."

Gwydion followed him relentlessly. "My father was an exacting teacher." He feinted one way, then thrust the other. When he stepped back, a diagonal slit ventilated the front of Sir Nicolas's mantle.

After a glance at the rend, Nicolas skipped backward again and gave a strained laugh. "Ah, but I think I know who your father was. Exacting or not, I'm grieved to say he died like a squealing pig. Now tell me, Sir Blade, do you have siblings? Perhaps a comely sister?"

Gwydion was on him in a stride. He wrenched him up until they were eye to eye. "Don't try so hard to enrage me, de Breauté. I swore I'd watch you dance in the wind at Conwy." He thrust him away. "It's a pleasure I won't forgo."

Nicolas sprawled in the mud.

One more Welshman lay curled silently on the ground. Thomas battled on against a barrel-shaped brute with an overgrown red mustache, as the uncommitted Englishman disappeared with his hostage into Lowri's house.

Glancing up from his own battle, Dexter had beheld his master's ignominious fall to the mud. Reacting to the sight with manic anger, he sent the constable to oblivion by slamming him into a tree trunk. The lackey then scanned his surroundings. Detecting no witnesses but a knot of villagers quailing behind foliage, his eyes narrowed. He slipped into the woods.

The villagers were not the only ones to see him go.

"Look at that villain scurry away," said Annora, following his form as it merged into shadows.

Efa nodded. "Aye, a fine coward. May he run until he falls into the sea."

26

Long-Lost Kin

Sir Nicolas regained his feet. But as he did, Mistress Lowri likewise staggered up. She reeled toward him with arms outstretched.

"My God, he'll kill her," said Efa, leaning out her window. "What in the world is she doing?"

Lowri hiccoughed and sobbed as she wobbled to de Breauté.

"She's lost her mind," said Annora.

"It's the ale," gasped Efa. "I always told her it would be her downfall."

Lowri reached de Breauté's side. "Steffan, Steffan," she blubbered. "Mother wants you home."

"Idiot," said Efa. "She thinks he's her brother."

"Her brother's dead?" asked Elise.

"No, he lives near Bangor. What a fool she is."

Lowri reached for Sir Nicolas's arm. "Come inside, Steffan. It's too early to—"

Nicolas scowled, unable to understand a word. "Get away," he said and knocked her to the ground.

When Lowri grabbed at his legs to pull herself up, Efa darted to the door.

"You're not going," said Annora, barring the way. "He surely won't harm a defenseless woman, not with so many witnesses. And remember, you called her immoral."

"So she is, but I used to dandle her on my knee. Who else will help her?"

"Efa's right, we can't just leave her," said Elise. "I'll go. At least I speak English."

"Are you mad too?" cried Annora.

While they argued, Efa thrust Annora aside and escaped from her own cottage. Elise tried to follow, but Annora caught her at the threshold. "One fool is enough." But she was too slow; Elise ducked under her arm and went after the widow.

Although Thomas and the barrel-shaped man were at first too intent on swordplay to notice newcomers to the field, Gwydion saw the women. He raised his head and frowned. Meanwhile Sir Nicolas retrieved his weapon and shoved Lowri aside. She sat in the mud looking flummoxed.

When a shocked stare appeared on his enemy's face, Nicolas followed Gwydion's gaze to see why.

Elise and Efa stood at a safe distance from the two men, well out of reach of either.

"Are you insane, woman? Why are you here?" demanded Gwydion in quiet, angry Welsh. "Did the company of lunatics at Dolwyddelan do injury to your brain? This is no place for females."

Recognizing her, Sir Nicolas lowered his weapon. "My interesting friend," he exclaimed. "You, here?" Then he scowled and reached for his jeweled crucifix. "Why?"

Why? Elise cudgeled her brain. She might tell him the truth—that she couldn't allow a brave old lady to venture out alone in aid of a delirious prostitute. But he'd likely be unmoved. He'd already shown he wasn't overnice in his notions of how females should be treated.

"Well, why are you here?" de Breauté repeated, less politely. Suspicion and agitation already clouded his face.

Not the truth, then. No, not with this man. Then what would be the best way to get Efa, Lowri, and herself off the field without harm?

Elise all at once had her answer: superstition and flattery, of course.

So she ignored Gwydion's incredulous stare and looked into de Breauté's long-lashed brown eyes. "This morning I woke from a terrifying vision, my lord," she said.

Gwydion raised an eyebrow, listening with obvious surprise to her flawless English.

"A vision? You swore you'd have none of me. Just yesterday." Sir Nicolas raised the golden cross to his cheek and held it there like a talisman.

As they spoke, Efa pulled Lowri up and helped her totter toward her cottage. Annora stood there by the door, wringing her hands. By this time Thomas and his opponent had become aware of Elise. They suspended their quarrel to listen.

"But it wasn't a vision of you," she was saying. "It was of this man." She nodded toward Gwydion. "And when I looked out the window, just now, there he was."

Sir Nicolas gave the crucifix three quick kisses and let it fall back to his chest. "How strange. Of course I'm relieved. But tell me, what was your vision? A hellish one, I hope."

Elise again searched her mind. Could her pretense of a vision somehow also serve to rid the village of de Breauté and his men, and quickly? Perhaps. She said, "I saw rooks."

He watched her closely. "Rooks, dear friend?"

"Thousands. I believe it's why they were amassing yesterday. They'll fly here soon to find this man—"

"He's marked to die?"

"Yes, and all who linger with him, friend or foe. As you were so kind to me, I felt obliged to warn you."

Gwydion stared at Elise. "Your brain *is* injured."

"What is he saying?" demanded Nicolas. "He's speaking that uncouth tongue."

Elise hung her head. "He hopes you share his fate."

Sir Nicolas's lips stretched into a smile. "But I will not." He turned to Gwydion. "I shall ride away and let the rooks have you, Sir Blade. You want birds to rip out my eyes, but it's not *my* eyes that will be forfeit."

"You'll go nowhere except the gallows," said Gwydion.

Nicolas paid him no heed. "Thank you," he told Elise. "Someday I'll try to repay your kindness."

"Cousin, in the woods behind you," shouted Thomas, suddenly racing toward his kinsman, past his surprised opponent.

Dexter reached his destination first. He burst from the cover of the trees to press his dagger against Gwydion's side. "Toss down that pricker," he said to Thomas, who slid to a halt a few feet away, "lest I do damage to your man here."

Elise forced herself not to cry out. Her plan to assist Efa had worked well, but had it given the lackey a chance to put his own plan into action?

However, the unpredictable Sir Nicolas was as dismayed as Elise by his rescue at Dexter's hands. "Fool, get away from Sir Blade," he told his bewildered lackey.

"My lord—"

"Did you not hear my friend's vision? The rooks want him. Do you not see my friend's white scarf, see how uncannily she resembles a saint?"

Dexter didn't budge. "Saint?" he said, and spat. "A poxy liar. Sir, can you still not see she's a liar?"

Once more Sir Nicolas had recourse to his crucifix. He said, as if to a slow-witted child, "We can't kill the rooks' chosen prey, Dexter. If we do, we will take his place. Would you like to be devoured by satanic rooks? No. So sheath your dagger and hurry to the horses. Poor ass, have you absorbed so little of my wisdom?"

Dexter looked across at Elise. "All I know is she's lying. Why else would she show up here so convenient?" He grabbed his crotch and gave himself a lewd squeeze. "Likely she's this tall one's whore."

"So blind," said Sir Nicolas, shaking his head. Then to Elise, "Disregard him as if he were a flea."

She nodded eagerly. "I will. Only go, before it's too late."

Sir Nicolas looked troubled. "But you—"

"Oh, the rooks won't harm me."

"Discerning rooks." He bowed with a flourish, then moved toward the shed where the horses waited.

The red-mustached man looked perplexed. But he gave Thomas an apologetic shrug and limped off after his master.

The Englishman holding the last hostage appeared in Lowri's doorway as his master passed. The fellow's color was heightened. "Are we leaving, my lord?" he asked, still gripping the wrist of the struggling, half-nude prostitute. "I thought we could take this handy piece with us."

Sir Nicolas regarded him with mild curiosity. "Ah, Gilbert," he said at last. "Yes, we're leaving." Without warning he shook a misericorde from his sleeve and flipped it blade out. "But not you. You may stay to nourish the rooks." He plunged the blade into Gilbert's belly. Gilbert made a single gurgling sound, then toppled, yielding his hold on the prostitute. Erupting with imprecations, she dashed away toward the trees. Golden charms on her ankle bracelets jangled, and her breasts slapped against her midriff as she ran.

Nicolas wiped his blade on Gilbert's twitching shoulder. "If that disgusted you, I'm not surprised," he called to Elise. "But I detest poltroonery."

She kept her gaze averted from the corpse and took a breath. "You must act as you think best."

He bowed again. "We'll see each other soon, at my hall. You'll be my guest. Bring the woman who vomits."

Collecting herself to give the answer he wanted, she said, "We would be honored."

"Ask in Conwy and someone will direct you." He all at once strode straight back to her side and raised her hand to his lips. "My, your fingers are cold. But thank you so much, truly, for your timely warning today. We're fated to be friends, you and I. Both of us are so clearly among the chosen."

"Sir, you must hurry. Please."

"Yes, but wait." He placed the tip of his index finger between his eyes and frowned mightily. "My friend, inner lightning has just now struck me. Can you feel it?"

Would he never go? "Lightning?"

"It showed me, in a blaze, that you and I are more than friends. Indeed, we are siblings of the soul."

"This is incredible," said Gwydion.

Elise hurriedly said, "I think I understand what you mean, Sir Nicolas."

"You feel it too. Do you see why you *must* come to my hall?"

"I do."

"No one else in my family will visit me. But now I don't need them because I have a new family. I have you. Oh, this is so lovely, because if you visit, I'll be able to make sure you aren't having any visions of me. You solemnly swear you'll come?"

"Yes, I swear it." But she gave the horizon fearful scrutiny as if expecting to see rooks swarming there.

Sir Nicolas followed her gaze. "I must go, mustn't I? You don't want to lose your new brother as soon as you've found him." He turned to Gwydion. "I'd like to say I'll pray for you, Sir Blade, but that would be a lie. Come, Dexter."

Surprising Elise with his docility, Dexter stepped out from behind Gwydion—who watched him with bemusement. Elise was certain Dexter would argue further, but he followed Sir Nicolas like a chastised dog.

Sir Nicolas was already astride his sorrel. "I'll see you without fail at my manor, very soon," he told Elise. "Remember, *sister*, you swore it." Then to Dexter, "Why are you so slow?" Off he raced with his other remaining servant close behind.

Dexter too was quickly gone.

The constable came stumbling forward. Blood streamed from his forehead, where a great lump had already formed.

"What happened?" he said, swaying, blinking in the sunshine.

Thomas picked up his sword, but tossed it back to the ground again in disgust. His cheek still bled a little, and the feather had disappeared from his hat. "I'm wondering too. Why did we just let that maniac walk out of here? They were ours, cousin. We had them. You should have grabbed the lackey when he crept from behind you. Why didn't you?"

Gwydion shook his head as if the strange turn of events had also taken him by surprise. He put his hand to his side and looked down at his long fingers. He said, "I seem to have had an unexpected parting gift from the lackey." His fingers dripped blood.

Sliding on the damp ground, Thomas sped to his side. "Damn you, Gwydion, for letting me rattle on." He took his cousin's arm and draped it around his shoulders. "That bastard, did he reopen the other wound? I'll pull his liver through his teeth when next we meet, I swear it."

Gwydion looked fondly down at his kinsman, but his gaze was becoming unfocused. "You were always a great one for rattling, Tom. Remember—"

"Hush," Thomas said. "Remember later." He blanched when he saw the blood seeping over the laces at the side of Gwydion's jupon.

Elise took Gwydion's other arm and did her best to help keep him upright. She gestured to Thomas and they moved slowly toward Efa's cottage.

Peering vaguely down at Elise, Gwydion spoke in Welsh. "I'm certain, madwoman, you couldn't truly be kin to de Breauté. But do you have visions of the future?"

Then his eyes closed and he slipped away from them, to the ground.

Father Sefyl came striding down the ridge from the church. He carried a pole with a golden cross atop it and wore a long-suffering face.

The sun coaxed steam from the mud as villagers surged into the clearing. Llanrhychwyn shimmered in the green and gold morning, its air rich with the aroma of baking bread and the sweet stink of congealing blood.

27

SIXES AND SEVENS

Maelgwyn rapidly regained his strength, though his voice was not as strong as it once had been. He stood outside the shepherd's hut and looked at the world with new wonder. Elise would have stolen all this from me, he thought. He touched the throbbing wound on his throat. If the Maker did not love me as fiercely as He does, she likely would have succeeded.

The shepherd voiced surprise at Maelgwyn's swift recovery. "Sell your soul to Satan, old ram? That why you're on the mend so quick?"

Maelgwyn knew it was wise to stay in the shepherd's good graces but couldn't bring himself to chuckle at this jibe. He said, "All I know of Satan is that he often hides in the deepest folds of women and waits there to strike at innocent men who claim their husbandly rights. He strikes through the core of the female, clawing at her husband's manhood, and tries to suck the man into the woman's void to feast on his soul."

The shepherd rubbed his chin. "Not had a happy kind of life, have you, Gryg?"

Maelgwyn didn't deign to reply.

It was dusk. The men stood outside the hut, staring up at a pair of sparrow hawks that flew in low, stiff-winged circles. The hen was dull brown, the cock gray and rust red.

"Wily bastards," said the shepherd, pointing upward. "Kill off the thrushes and finches."

"Hawks are God's creatures too. They must eat."

"Leave it to you to take their side."

Maelgwyn disliked his rescuer, and the feeling was reciprocal. The old herder was surprised how quickly one man could grow to despise another, but he found his guest pious and sly. Next time he saw a body bobbling in the river, he vowed inwardly, he'd let it sink.

The shepherd cracked his knuckles. Then he pulled his hosen to his knees and scratched his bare white backside.

Maelgwyn turned away. "Please," he said.

"Please what? Please pretend nobody has an ass?"

Maelgwyn bit back angry words. He knew they would only amuse his host, for the fool adored vulgar jinks. He'd recently given his guest sheep piss to drink; Maelgwyn took one unknowing sip and spit it out in a spray, much to the prankster's delight. And he'd waved an impressive erection in Maelgwyn's face one dawn, declaring, "I should be called Old Ram, eh?"

On this occasion the shepherd looked disappointed when his victim refused to quarrel. He pulled his hosen back up, saying, "Poor sour Gryg."

Later, wrapped in his filthy blanket, Maelgwyn passed the time before sleep by considering ways to silence his host. He could strangle him, but the old man was strong as a bear. It might be better to slit his belly open as he slept or slam a rock down on his skull.

Examining these possibilities was only a diversion, Maelgwyn understood. It would be wrong to actually harm the man.

"Thinking of ways to finish me, Gryg?" said the shepherd, in the darkness.

Maelgwyn sat straight up in bed. Was the man a visionary like Elise? Was he doomed to be hounded by such creatures?

The shepherd laughed. "Lucky guess? But you ought to take into account that I'm a fitful sleeper, like my mother. She used to wake if a bird's egg fell from a nest in the next valley. And naturally it wouldn't be Christian to harm the selfsame fellow who plucked you from a river. That sort of sixes and sevens dealing is what sends old rams to Hell."

Maelgwyn gasped, for this allusion to sixes and sevens was a way of invoking the malevolent number thirteen without naming it. Thirteen, the number of guests at the Last Supper when Judas betrayed Christ. Thirteen knots made up a hangman's noose. Thirteen deranged harpies oversaw Satan's pantry. In effect he, Maelgwyn, was being called malevolent. *He.*

But he also suspected he was being toyed with. So he swallowed his rage. "Thou shalt not kill," he said. "The Commandments are my creed."

"Except in self-defense, Gryg. To kill in self-defense is no sin."

"You've no need to defend yourself from me." Perhaps the old thief was really worried. That possibility pleased Maelgwyn so much his ire subsided. "I'm certainly too grateful to dream of harming you, despite our contrary views on petty things."

Thunder rumbled in the distance and a few sheep fretted, out in their rough pen.

Several moments had passed when the shepherd said, in a friendlier tone, "Gryg, did you ever know that fairies live seven years on earth, seven in the air, and seven underground? They can't ring a bell more than ten times. One peal for each finger. Mother told me."

Maelgwyn rolled his eyes in the dark. But he said, "Your mother must have been a fine teacher."

"Aye, I miss her. Especially I miss her on Easter Sunday when she baked us a fat goose. And talking of the Resurrection, did you know the sun always dances with joy on Easter morn?"

The shepherd carried on in this vein, occasionally sipping at the jug of mead he kept beside his bracken bed. Eventually his voice grew slurred. His closing utterance was "Praise the day when it is over." Then he began to snore.

Maelgwyn wrapped his arms around himself. He tried to picture Christ's sweet, tortured face in his mind, to help him sleep. But the image was elusive. So he considered the wiles of sundry demons. He knew that when they assume human shape, they can't be seen from behind. They're hollow, have no backs, and withdraw by walking backward. He had seen the shepherd's back, so knew he was no demon. Anyway, the fool was simply too obtuse to be even the lowest sort of demon.

Before a nightmare-ridden sleep overtook him, Maelgwyn's unwilling thoughts flew to Elise. He reached down to appraise the familiar stirring below his waist. As he'd feared, his body was betraying him yet again with its usual swelling, and shameful need, in spite of his healing wound. Would he never be free of his unwholesome aching for the slattern he'd married?

Why was he so helplessly wild for the witch?

There were rituals he'd heard of that might explain his sick lust-fever, certain enslaving tricks a woman could employ to guarantee a man's lust. Yes. Perhaps Elise had baked her monthly flow into a loaf of his bread to inflame him, as he'd heard females sometimes did. Perhaps she had served him a baked fish she'd secretly suffocated in her womb; that was another trick practiced by the daughters of Eve. He'd overheard his own mother whisper of its efficacy to a scandalized— and receptive—lady friend. But then his mother caught him at his eavesdropping and punished him in an unforgettable way. That, God knew, was a memory Maelgwyn did not wish to examine closely.

Besides, his mother was dead and gone.

Elise was not. God would deal cruelly with her, he was sure. He, Maelgwyn, would be a willing assistant. Hadn't he assisted Him before, with Matilda, the whimpering parasite who'd been his first bride?

At least he didn't fear those two harpies, his wife and her hag servant, would still be skulking at his home, defiling it with their sinfulness. Even a fool like Elise would know enough to leave the scene of her wrongdoing. Hell-bent to avoid retribution, she and the crone had probably run off like crazed mongrel bitches as soon as Elise had accomplished the heinous deed. But the hag had surely helped roll him into the Conwy; Elise couldn't have managed on her own. They definitely must have believed he was dead. Stabbed twice, then thrown unconscious into the river—by all rights he *ought* to be dead. But God had saved him.

Before he could deal with Elise, he had to find her. Then justice could be served.

When the two men rose in the morning, mist hid the hills.

"A sunrise not fit for beggars or beauties," said the shepherd, peering out his door. As usual his liking for strong drink didn't trouble him much the day after. "What say we rumble down to a farm I know, with apple trees at its side. That farmer called me a dirty skint last Michaelmas, and I've a mind to snatch some apples to repay him. Eggs too."

"I'll not steal from an unsuspecting farmer."

"There are worse things than stealing, old ram. Anyway, I'd say you're fit enough to walk now. Apples or not, tomorrow we'll go find that fine house you boast of and get me my reward. My reward for kindheartedness. Remember, Gryg?"

Maelgwyn inwardly cursed the woman who had left him weak enough to make such a rash promise. But he turned to the shepherd and gripped that startled fellow's bony elbow in a gesture of accord. "You'll have everything you deserve, friend."

The shepherd jerked away. "I don't want what I deserve or your double words. All I want is what you promised." He patted the knife strapped to his thigh. "My friend wants it too."

The younger man sucked in his breath. "What have I done to deserve such enmity?"

"Nothing I can name. But I've been asking myself how you got in the river. Who liked you enough to toss you in?"

"That's unjust. I told you I was beset by thieves. Just recall what criminals did to Nectaran the Blessed."

"I can't recall what I never knew to start with."

"In the days of Beuno and Cadoc and Dewi, our Welsh saints, Nectaran was a holy man of this realm. Robbers beheaded him."

The shepherd gave a smile, but it was not pleasant. "You claim likeness to a martyred saint?"

"You twist my words."

"Why should I twist 'em when you do it so handily yourself? No matter. Just gird your loins for a journey tomorrow, like I said. I'll even loan you some boots. Meantime I'm off for eggs and apples. Scrape out a bit of Blanche's cheek if you're peckish."

The shepherd gave a mocking salute and strode across the damp, verdant slope. Soon he was swallowed by mist.

28

LIKE A PRAYER

Propped against an oak tree, the maimed Englishman bled peacefully to death. His severed hand sat curled and dripping on his thigh, until a child knocked it to the ground with one well-aimed rock.

Four other fellows cooled in the mud—de Breauté's pockmarked subordinate, Gilbert the poltroon, and two of the constable's men. Another Welshman was injured but not gravely and had been carried off to a cottage to have his wounds dressed.

The church bell tolled, three times three times five. Striding from corpse to corpse, Father Sefyl waved his cross-topped pole and recited death prayers, while village men dug graves at the far western edge of the churchyard.

Dozens of villagers filed past the corpses after the priest muttered his benedictions. Men, women, and children grazed a thumb across each dead man's forehead, though the priest exuded disapproval. The villagers braved his annoyance. They hoped their precaution would afford them supernatural protection from all nightmares featuring those who met violent ends.

In Efa's house Gwydion lay insensible under a clean blanket, stripped of boots, clothing, and weapons. Annora was surprised at the maze of scars across his back and shoulders. She examined his other wounds, the fresh one below his ribs and another just under it, weeks or months old. This second injury appeared to have been badly healed right from its infliction and was now partially reopened by Dexter's blade.

Efa stood in her doorway arguing with Elise, who hovered outside. Thomas sat on a nearby tree stump, head in his hands.

"I'm as skillful a healer as Annora, or better," said Elise, with an unusual lack of diffidence. "Let me go in and assist her. I've seen any number of naked men before."

"Then why put yourself to the bother of seeing another?" replied the widow, not budging. "In any case, she says no. She says you're fatigued—though you look more fidgety than fatigued. She wants you to go find flax and sheep's cream and honey."

Elise tried and failed to see past Efa's solid form into the one-room cottage. "Annora," she called, "Efa knows where to find what's needed better than I. Why not send her?"

"Keep her out, Efa," was all Annora replied.

"Do as she tells you," said the widow, folding her arms across her chest. "The poor man may not live to see the stars rise tonight anyway. If he dies, you can busy yourself weaving a cross of flowers for his coffin."

"Is he so bad? He surely won't die."

"Those aren't pretty scratches. Now go fetch what you've been told, child. My neighbors will help, if you ask."

Vort just then returned from wherever he had been. He approached the tree stump and allowed Thomas to hug him. But he soon pulled away to stand beside Elise. He looked up at Efa and nudged her wrist with his nose.

"Whose horse of a hound is this?" said Efa. "If you've come to beg, scoundrel, you've picked a bad time. Off you go."

Elise placed her hand on Vort's broad head. His tail thumped the ground. "He belongs to the man inside."

"Fine. But I won't have a dog in the house mucking up my rushes."

"He's well behaved."

Vort gave up on diplomacy and lunged forward. He wedged his head between the doorjamb and Efa's leg. "Stay out," she sputtered, but he squeezed past.

"Well behaved," sniffed the widow. She tried to take hold of Vort's plume of a tail, but he'd reached Gwydion's side. He sniffed the bowl of bloody water Annora held, then hunkered down far enough to squirm under the bed.

Efa took up her broom to chivvy him out.

"Let him stay," said Annora. "Love is never wasted."

So Vort kept his vigil.

Seeing she had no choice, Elise hurried away to find wild flax, cream, and honey. Thomas emerged from his reverie and followed her to the woods.

"Who are you?" he said, in no congenial way. "You speak English, and it's obvious you're a friend to de Breauté. Now you're helping us. What game is this?"

Pausing in her hunt for the seedpods of blue-flowered flax, Elise spun around. "I'm no friend of de Breauté. He and his servant attacked my mother and me only yesterday."

"Then why did you speak to him kindly this morning? And what was that nonsense about visions, about being siblings?"

She didn't respond. On a sun-bathed hillock she knelt by a tall plant and raised her face to the sun. "Blessed Father," she said in English, so Thomas could know her words and not mistrust them, "I beg You charge these seeds with the grace of the healers' triad—homage to goodness, love of the herbs of the field, and knowledge of the course of the stars. Amen. With God's help, even so let it be." She made the sign of the cross and rose.

Thomas looked at her oddly. "Why did you say all that? It sounded like a prayer."

Elise cradled the flax in the crook of her arm. "The words give the plant more power to heal and fight evil."

She walked back toward the village with the frowning young Englishman at her side.

"You still haven't explained why you spoke agreeably to de Breauté, especially since you say he attacked you," he said. "Didn't your interference give his man a chance to sneak behind my cousin?"

She stopped to look at him intently. "You can believe me or not, but Sir Nicolas let us go yesterday because of superstition. He decided I'm a kindred spirit. Not very flattering, but that's what he decided."

"Where was he? Who was with him?"

"The one who stabbed your kinsman was with him, at a deserted house on the path between here and Dolwyddelan."

"Why were you there?"

She bridled at his questions but lamented her need to lie. "My mother and I are on our way to visit my uncle. An innocent journey, but we've had no peace along the way."

They'd come full circle, returning to the edge of Llanrhychwyn. From that distance they saw people tidying their properties after the storm, bustling to and fro.

Evidently the three strumpets had regained their equanimity, for they were gathered at Mistress Lowri's door asking for admittance. A transformed Lowri stood foursquare at her threshold, dressed head to toe in black, like an abbess. She refused to allow her sisters in sin back inside. Her dawn misadventures with violent men had sobered her, apparently, and disenchanted her with the business of professional love. So they argued, in a babel of demands and refusals.

Watching this drama, Thomas shrugged and Elise shook her head.

"What now?" he asked, with a shade more warmth.

"Sheep's cream and honey."

"What are these things for, exactly?"

"Mixed with egg white, they make a potent medicine for wounds."

Outside a low timber house a half-deaf crone gave Elise a pot of honey. "They say your patient is from an old family near Conwy," the crone said. "A good Welshman." Her tone invited gossip. She cupped a hand behind one ear and waited to be informed.

"I don't know who he is, mother," said Elise. "But I thank you kindly for the honey."

The old lady scowled, cast a suspicious glance at Thomas, then looked back at Elise. "Saesneg?"

"Yes, but kin to the Welshman by marriage."

The crone let her cupped hand fall. "That so? Well, it's a strange world we live in. And it wouldn't have happened in my day." With this declaration, she closed her door. But she opened it again. "Tell that jaw-jabber Efa to bring me back my pot soon as the honey's gone."

As they turned away, Thomas said, "I heard her say *Saesneg*. That means English. Do these folk think Englishmen are all like Sir Nicolas and his mongrels?"

"They've probably heard unpleasant stories, since those are the kind most likely to be told. It's natural to be leery."

He considered this. "Fairly said. People trust what they know, what they hear every day. Then how is it *you* speak English so well? How have you managed to be worldly when others are not? You're Welsh, aren't you?"

"And half English. But not worldly, I promise."

"Gwydion, my cousin, is half Welsh, half English. His mother was my mother's sister."

They hurried on, more companionable than before. At the village well they stopped for a dipper of water. A few curious folk watched. When one rude man asked Elise why she allowed a treacherous for-

eigner to walk with her, she explained that Thomas's family claimed
the benefits of Welsh blood by marriage. That quieted the fellow.

Though Thomas understood little Welsh, he knew he was being
observed with resentment. "I'm still not sure why some of the Welsh
despise us," he said as they left the well.

"If Welshmen overran England and killed the king, then built castles all around the country to sneer down on the English people and
guard the land they'd stolen, would you be disposed to be grateful?"

"Well, no."

"You're surely not ignorant of the past. You and your cousin must
speak of our countries' histories now and again."

"He has his own dilemmas. But loyalty to both countries does sometimes grieve him."

"I understand." She scanned nearby houses to guess which might
harbor generous folk. "Should we discuss these things at length later?
For now we need sheep's cream from some kindly housewife.
Annor—my mother will wonder why I'm so long."

Thomas matched her pace as she moved toward a cottage. Before
they reached it, he grabbed her arm. "Will he die?" It was clear the
question had spilled out of its own accord.

She answered as truthfully as she could. "His wounds are dangerous, but he seems strong. I've faith he will live."

He now hesitated and grew flushed. "Tell me, please, do you really
have visions? I wouldn't normally consider such contrivances—not
that I mean to imply you're contriving—but can't you consult a vision
and say for sure that he'll recover?"

She wasn't eager to comply with his request, even if she'd been
able. And she couldn't tell him she'd already had a bloody vision of
Gwydion. Besides, her visions were not a safe subject to broach with a
stranger, for he might decide one day that she was a heretic or worse.

So she merely smiled. "I only told Sir Nicolas I had a vision because he's wildly superstitious. I thought he might listen to me long
enough to let Efa help her neighbor from the field. I'm sure that
sounds absurd, but it worked. Unfortunately, it also gave his lackey a
chance to harm your cousin, and *that* was never my intention."

She turned away to knock on the door of the cottage, hoping he
would accept her tale. Apparently he did, for he made no further mention of visions.

They were soon on the path back to Efa's with the things Annora requested. Elise had also picked some violets.

But it seemed Thomas still had one or two doubts about her part in the day's events. "You could have stayed safely inside," he said as they walked.

"A woman who gave us shelter and food ran bravely outside to help her neighbor." She searched the young man's face. "Would you let her go alone?"

Thomas unexpectedly turned to her and bowed. "Then I can only salute you for your courage."

She was touched and amused by his self-conscious gallantry. "I'm not courageous. Rash, yes, and afraid to be harshly judged by Heaven for cowardice."

"That's the strangest excuse for daring I have ever heard."

"If you want to call it daring, I won't argue. But sir, perhaps when there's an idle moment, you'll tell me the rest of *your* tale, and your cousin's."

"The rest, good lady?"

Good lady. It almost made her smile, the innocent way he said it. "Yes, the rest. The constable's warrant, the trouble at Conwy, and the dead lord and lady near Dolwyddelan."

His brows furrowed. "Perhaps. If there's an idle moment."

29

THE COURSE OF THE STARS

Annora waited at Efa's door. "You were a long time," she said as Elise handed over flax, cream, and honey. Thomas just stood nearby watching.

"Is he the same?" asked Elise.

"Worse. Thrashing. The dog's under the bed and poor Efa's run off to the church to pray, since she gets queasy in sickrooms. You probably caught on to the notion that I didn't want you involved, but now I'm afraid you'll have to be. He'll need constant watching tonight and longer, or else he may decide it's easier to just float up to Heaven."

"What is she saying?" asked Thomas, leaning forward to peer into the cottage.

Elise chose to offer a translation somewhat short of precise. "Your cousin is resting comfortably." She didn't want to worry Thomas before he truly needed to be worried.

Her version of Annora's words soothed the young man. He nodded, then walked back over to the tree stump to spend some time cleaning mud from his boots.

Annora noticed the violets tucked into Elise's belt. "You've your own plan to guess the patient's fate?"

"Mother believed in violets."

"A lot of good they did her."

Annora knew Elise intended to brush her flowers across Gwydion's forehead sometime in the evening. If a patient slept deeply after being touched with violets, it was alleged to mean he would live. But if he didn't sleep, he would die. The origin of the practice was as lost in ancient lore as the identity of the Seven Sleepers scrawled on Efa's blade.

Annora stood in the doorway, plucking seedpods from the flax. "Don't put too much weight on his survival, Elise, handsome or not."

"There's no harm in trying violets. I'd do the same for any man."

"I don't believe you. I think you like the look of him, rogue or not. That's the stuff of troubadours, child. Besides, he probably already has a wife to make into a widow."

"Don't be silly. It's only the vision in Penmach—"

"It is *not* only the vision. But he's not for you."

The imaginary shadow of Maelgwyn rose between them. Out in the world, his corpse waited to tell its tale. Or already had. Of course, the body might have drifted to the bottom of the river or been eaten by wild creatures. But what if it had not?

Elise stared down at the violets.

Annora sighed. "Anyway, I'll allow you to tend him. Let me bathe his wounds again and mix this plaster, then we'll see how he fares. Meanwhile stir up apples and spring water, in case we can get him to drink." She handed her a beaker.

As Elise passed Thomas, he rose and gave a tentative smile. "Off again? But you never told me your name. I'm Thomas Fulk, from Ipswich." He blushed. "Youngest son of the Earl of Athelcarr."

Grateful for his courtesy, she returned his smile. "A pleasure, Sir Thomas Fulk."

"You needn't fear I'm like de Breauté. I've been taught to revere ladies."

Elise liked the young man more and more, so told him her name, her name before her life was blighted by Maelgwyn. "I'm Elise, daughter of Dafydd ap Rhys ap Rhiwallon of Bron-haul, and of Katherine, Lady of Ambrespring."

He looked confused. "Isn't the lady tending Gwydion your mother? She's Welsh, surely. And your father's name is Welsh, but you said you were half English and—"

"Forgive me." She wished she could manage her stable of falsehoods more adroitly. "Annora, in the cottage, has been a mother to me since my own mother died. I often call her Mother, from affection."

They turned around as the ongoing disagreement at Mistress Lowri's briefly escalated into a shouting match. But as they watched, the reformed Lowri unexpectedly relented and let the others pass inside to reclaim their belongings. The three prostitutes afterward left Llanrhychwyn, this time by foot.

Thomas sat back down as Elise went off on her mission.

Glad to share information with an interesting stranger, and to tell the tale to his friends, a boy guided her to a tree where she picked two small red apples. Then she collected water from the spring to which the boy next led her; the cool liquid bubbled up amidst a mound of black rocks.

Back on the village path, she pared off pieces of the apples' flesh and stirred them into the water. This drink she bore carefully to Efa's.

"He stopped thrashing," said Annora. "Now he's gone still."

Approaching the bed, Elise was startled by Gwydion's pallor. She touched his cheek. "Was he so warm before?"

"I'm guessing he's been fevered for days and was willing it away. Men are often fools." She held up a piece of metal the size of a flattened pea. "The older wound had this in it. Part of a blade, no doubt. Whoever tended him made a poor job of it. But we've work to do now, so keep your mind clear." She pulled the blanket to Gwydion's waist to expose his wounds. Both were wicked crimson under a coating of new medicine.

Elise nodded, then went to the table to prepare more herbs.

Morning stretched into afternoon, then evening. By dusk the patient's fever raged. Efa came back, took a look, then freely admitted she simply couldn't abide the sights and smells of the sickroom. She left again and tarried late at a friend's. But she reappeared as darkness encroached.

"He'll die tonight," she said, beholding the patient. "Broad and well made as he is, he'll die. Mind you, he'll make an exceptional corpse."

A retort sprang to Elise's tongue. But she bit it back, for Efa had only given voice to the thing she feared herself.

30

COLD CLAY AND DEAD FLOWERS

Maelgwyn and the shepherd set off for Bryn-llwyd. They walked slowly to accommodate the less nimble of the shepherd's fifty-one sheep. The animals couldn't be left alone in one of their usual pens to fend for themselves, even for one night. Wolves, pixies, or elves might descend from the Migneint Moor to do them mischief. So said the shepherd.

"Elves live up on the moor," he told Maelgwyn. "You can smell their hair and their secret parts when the wind rises. Smells like cold clay and dead flowers."

Maelgwyn had to beg for an occasional stop to catch his breath. It galled him to ask but was necessary. The wound on his groin was healing satisfactorily, but the one on his neck sometimes ached if his heart beat quickly.

As he placed his hand across his throat, the half-healed gash pulsated beneath his fingers. "Elves smell like clay and flowers?" Every word brought a sting.

The shepherd slowed to give answer, as Maelgwyn had hoped. "Aye. Bryn yr Ellyllon, their hamlet is called, and no human can find the entrance twice. There's a sign posted at the gate, with a doodle of a dead man daubed on it, a tinker told me. 'Let bramble be your sepulcher,' that sign says."

Bryn yr Ellyllon, Hill of the Elves. At least it was a change for an idiotic tale to originate from someone besides the shepherd's cretin of a mother, Maelgwyn thought. He gave his best approximation of an enthralled smile. "I thought I knew the legends of the moor, but I've never heard of hostile elves dwelling there."

"Might be lots of things you don't know, Gryg. You ever hear tales of Llyn y Wrach?" Lake of the Witch.

Maelgwyn denied it.

"It's in the vale down the meadow from my hut. Oh, you'd love to lower your backside into those warm waves. Like floating on mother's milk or diving into a woman's secret fountain."

"What do you mean, or should I bother to ask?"

"I mean the waters of Llyn y Wrach are warm as the inside of a woman's thighs. They smell like peat smoke and good fish and they snake around a man's—"

"I take your meaning."

They went on. Maelgwyn supported his left arm with his right. He assumed he'd smashed the left on a rock when he was dumped into the river. It usually didn't pain him much, but if he stretched it too straight or bent it abruptly, it ached. Also, it had to be held at an awkward angle. He hoped the handicap was temporary. But temporary or permanent, he'd more cause to hate Elise.

"Old ram?"

Maelgwyn left his vengeful dream. He left Elise naked and bleeding, moaning with terror and desire in some hidden bed.

"Ever have a cozy wife to warm your bones?" The shepherd's questions were too often of this salacious ilk. "Or she'd run off with some fellow with a stiffer cock? That why you hate women?"

Maelgwyn refused to rise to this bait, though the effort to be civil was great. "I had a wife, but she died of an oppressed liver." He'd never admit he'd been bested by a woman.

"Bad liver? No. You killed her, didn't you?"

"Don't be a fool."

The sheep crowded around the two men where they had stopped at the edge of a field. The morning was gray with a cool breeze.

The shepherd shrugged and twisted at the waist to count the portion of his flock that stood docilely behind him. "*Yan, tan, tethera, pethera, pimp, sethera, lethera, hovera, covera, dik,*" he said—one to ten, then beyond, in an ancient language of old tribes mixed with syllables from the Roman tongue. The numbers had been taught him by a humpbacked shepherd run out of Yorkshire. "Fifty-one, all here. Let's be off again."

They walked on in silence that could hardly be called companionable. As the path took them slightly downhill, Maelgwyn passed the time by continuing to imagine the brutal punishment he'd wreak on Elise when he found her. Once, he thought of his mother.

As for the shepherd, he fretted about an ache in his toe.

After a while he said, "How far off now you think your palace might be, Gryg? Doesn't any of this countryside look homey to you?"

"I can't understand why *you* don't know my house. Everyone who lives near Ysbyty Ifan has heard of Gray Hill."

"If I was born and bred hereabouts, maybe I'd know. But I wasn't. I came here from farther south just last year."

"Steal too many eggs and apples over in the south?"

"At least no one stabbed me and threw me in the river."

The sun peeped from behind a cloud. A rainbow appeared. It began its misty curve behind a copse of trees and ended at a far hill. But as quickly as the rainbow appeared, it vanished. Mizzle commenced to fall, though the watery sun still shone.

The shepherd looked askance at the indecisive sky. "Satan's beating his wife."

"What?"

"If the sun shines and it rains at the same time, it means the Devil's beating his wife. Everybody knows that. It's an ill omen when Satan gets his temper up."

Maelgwyn swallowed his vexation. It wasn't the time to be quarrelsome. There would be an opportune moment later, at his house, when he could tell the oaf at his side what he really thought of him and his idiotic tales.

How he wished he didn't have to part with a quarter of his riches. It was unjust. The jewels had been in his family for years. The coins too amounted to quite a fortune, a fortune his barely remembered father bequeathed him. Yes, some of the coins had come from Elise's dowry. But he'd earned them double, treble—no, a thousand times over.

When they crested the next rolling hill, a line of oaks came into view.

"I know those trees," said Maelgwyn, stopping to stare. "We're near. We'll see the Conwy River again soon." They'd had brief glimpses of its gleaming water all morning.

"By God, I believe you're happy," said the shepherd, studying his companion. "Your face isn't half so twisted."

Maelgwyn began to walk again, faster.

"Not so sprightly, old ram. Think of my woolly fools."

Maelgwyn didn't heed him. He hurried on. "There's the river," he called over his shoulder, after he'd gone ahead to the next hill. "My house is just there, beside it."

The shepherd caught up. A few of the senior animals were vocal in their disapproval of the haste to which they'd been put.

Ahead the Conwy shone in the paltry sunshine. The shepherd stood beside Maelgwyn, gazing toward Gray Hill, and he whistled through his remaining teeth. "You didn't lie," he said in wonder. "It's really a high stone manor. And a barn, and I don't know what else. You really didn't lie."

Men and sheep made their way up a final rise. Here no grass grew. It was a gray hill, indeed. Bryn-llwyd. As they passed the limb-stripped oak tree that had sacrificed its vigor for the triptych that held his glass panes—or what might still remain of his glass panes—Maelgwyn reached out to caress its tortured bark.

Home.

The shepherd let his flock amble to the river while he gazed at Gray Hill's fine outbuildings. From the Conwy's banks the main house was not visible.

When the sheep had lapped their fill, the party moved on. They came to the empty barn.

"There's breadth in here for a hundred beasts," the shepherd said, eyes wide. "Yet you keep no livestock, Gryg? Or did they cede to bad livers too, like your wife?"

Maelgwyn scowled. He considered the sarcasm an affront, even though his story of the lethal liver was a fabrication, like the tale he now offered. "I lost my servants to the Pestilence and was forced to sell my stock since I couldn't maintain them alone. I'm pleased it amuses you."

"All your servants? How many was that?"

"Five men, and three females for house chores." This much was true. He had once had eight servants.

"Did you bravely see them through their pains?"

"I paid a village woman to nurse them. In the end she herself succumbed." More lies.

The shepherd suddenly squatted and wrapped his arms around the neck of a large, shaggy ram. The creature balked, but he restrained it easily. "Well, Puw, will you trot into this fine barn and have a snooze? The other fools will shadow you, if they see this place is to your liking."

Puw's yellow and black eyes remained unreadable. But when the shepherd released him, he strolled into the barn. As the other sheep followed without hesitation, Maelgwyn only stared.

The shepherd closed the door. "That's them sorted," he said. "Now lead these old bones to their prize."

The men passed the unused brewhouse and bakehouse as the river babbled behind them.

"Not keen on tidiness, eh?" said the shepherd, taking in the unkempt condition of the place, the weeds and mounds of rubbish he hadn't seen from a distance.

To Maelgwyn, nothing seemed out of order. Gray Hill had been in this same disarray at least since the advent of the Pestilence more than two years earlier, when a pair of his servants died and all the others gradually deserted him.

But Elise, Maelgwyn recalled, had certainly done nothing to improve the state of his property, as a decent wife ought. She had only sighed far too often over the niggling amount of work she'd been requested to do. No matter that her sighs had been barely audible, he had sensed her resistance to his authority. Her old servant had even had the impudence to sometimes direct disgruntled looks his way.

Oh, how he wanted to avenge himself on Elise. But not yet. For now he would enjoy his homecoming. For now he only wanted the comfort of his own house, his own things. Most especially he yearned to lift his fortune from its hiding place and let the coins and jewels run through his fingers. True, he'd be forced to give his rescuer one-quarter. But he'd still be a wealthy man, by any worldly standard.

Then, when he felt fully recovered, he'd set off after his spouse.

Maelgwyn's pace slowed and he shut his eyes for an instant. Again he pictured Elise's face—pinched, white, pleading.

Unexpectedly the shepherd swooped forward and ran a finger across the wound on Maelgwyn's throat.

"What are you doing?" said Maelgwyn, recoiling so swiftly he nearly fell backward. "Don't touch me."

The shepherd tilted his head without umbrage and regarded the wound. "Settle down. I only wanted to feel the thing. It's like a pink caterpillar. It wobbles, like it's trying to crawl right off you."

Raising a hand to the scar, Maelgwyn again counseled himself to restrain his anger. Under his fingers the wound pulsated.

Something about the lesion's faint quivering called back to Maelgwyn's mind a memory from his childhood. As a boy, he saw a cruel nobleman, his mother's acquaintance, slice open a downed bull.

Known in the neighborhood for its temper, the bull had shown such
faulty judgment as to chase the haughty nobleman across a paddock
one cold afternoon. To its misfortune the beast stumbled on a rabbit's
hole and broke its leg. Hearing its cries, the noble checked his flight.
Sauntering back across the paddock, he went down on one knee and
plunged a knife into the bull's neck. Five times he stabbed it. Still the
animal bellowed. The man began a casual but efficient disembowel-
ment, even as the beast's legs slowed their flailing. Viscera and blood
spilled everywhere. Some of the innards, and the beating heart, clung
to the depth of the creature's chest cavity as its cries faded.

Watching that scene as a child of perhaps eight winters, Maelgwyn
had longed to turn away. The sights and smells made his stomach
churn. But his mother held his head between her hands to compel
him to watch. He recalled her skin's coolness even through her gloves'
supple leather. "Maelgwyn, you see how thin is the cord that anchors
life?" she whispered. "You see, my dearest boy?"

But what he remembered most vividly was this: he remembered
the animal's heart swinging inside its body like a seed suspended by a
thread in a squash. That was what it had looked like to his young eyes.
Earlier the same year he had handled one of those foreign fruits. The
squash had been a gift to Gray Hill's cook, brought from Spain by a
cousin who had gone on a pilgrimage to the shrine of Saint James at
Compostela. With the cook's permission, Maelgwyn had cut a hole in
the side of the squash. He had peered in and beheld dozens of pale
seeds shaped liked teardrops.

He shook off the memory. What did it have to do with his wound?
He was no gutted beast. His scar didn't dangle like the bull's heart.
And if the shepherd was reminded of a caterpillar, it was only more
proof of the man's idiocy.

"Too bad you can't see your own neck, Gryg," the unfazed shepherd said, with a wink. "That poor gash of yours surely does look like a
caterpillar. It'll be a curiosity the rest of your days. A conversation
starter."

Unable to find an appropriately scathing response, Maelgwyn
stalked toward his home. His grinning companion followed.

They reached the house's wide steps. Something on the path
caught the shepherd's eye and his amusement vanished. He nudged a
stained rag with his boot. Maelgwyn stood staring at his stone steps,

his gaping door. The beetroot cross Annora had painted was partly washed away by rain, but it was still visible, and shocking. Another red-daubed rag had snagged on the rue bush beside the steps, and yet another lay across the threshold.

"Pestilence," breathed the shepherd, coming to Maelgwyn's side. He too had seen the faded cross on the door.

"Who would have been here to suffer pestilence, fool?" Maelgwyn stared at the rag in the rue. He reached down to untangle it from stems and leaves and held it between his hands.

The other man backed away. "Someone must have been here, Gryg. Maybe they're here yet, inside, oozing and weeping, or stiff as sticks. Joseph's holy donkey, it must be their blood on that rag. For God's sake, throw it down."

Maelgwyn just stared at the cloth. "No. It's too red." Then he raised it to his nose.

The shepherd shrieked and bolted behind a tree.

"Come out, you ass," said Maelgwyn. "It smells of nothing worse than beetroot."

Peeking around the trunk, the shepherd said, "Beetroot?"

"Try it yourself."

Maelgwyn threw down the cloth and hurried up the stairs.

The other man followed. Inside, the two gazed around the great hall.

The shepherd hitched up his hosen and rubbed the back of his neck. "This is a fine house for certain, old ram. But why would anyone paint a cross on your door and rub beetroot on rags? What would be the game?"

"Think, man. It was surely the robbers who accosted me who did it. They must have heard tales of my house and came here to ransack it after they threw me in the river."

The shepherd's brow puckered. "Then why bother to make a false show of pestilence? They could steal what they wanted anyway, with you gone safely floating."

Maelgwyn could think of no reasonable answer. Of course he understood who had actually painted the cross. The hoaxer certainly hadn't been any imaginary thief.

Shrugging, the shepherd assessed the room's luxury. He saw the faded wall tapestries and thought them handsome. Across the hall was a dais, and a long table, also impressive. Wooden screens graced the other side of the room, and a hearth sat in the midst of it all. A pair of bronze tripods perched on opposite sides of the circular hearth. Each tripod was used to hold one end of a removable roasting skewer, he rightly supposed. Then stairs led his gaze to the next level of Gray Hill, but there the house's mysteries were lost in shadows.

"You know, Gryg," he said, still gazing all around, "if robbers had been here, they would have stolen your tapestry and screens and more. But this looks tidy enough to me."

"Maybe they were interrupted."

Maelgwyn started up the stairs. The sick feeling in the pit of his stomach grew as he went higher, and the wound on his throat thudded. The shepherd followed close at his heels.

The solar Maelgwyn and Elise had shared for two years was not as neat as the great hall. Female clothing was strewn about, and the fox coverlet lay in a heap in a corner. Wind hissed through the jagged remnants of the center windowpane.

But a more dire sight greeted Maelgwyn when he squatted down. On the floor at the foot of the bed a plank had been pried up. The resulting hole yawned, holding nothing. On the planking beside the hole sat a metal casket. It too yawned and held nothing. A web decorated its hinged lid.

How had the bitch known where to look? How?

The shepherd wandered about the room. Picking up a lady's torn shift by its hem, he let it dangle from his fingers. Then he let it fall and rushed to peer out through the window, to marvel at the semi-translucence of the glass, the first he'd ever been near enough to touch. He contemplated the saw-toothed edge of the broken middle pane while sucking on his bottom lip. Next he went to the corner and picked up the fur coverlet. He smelled it and rubbed it against his face.

But he soon became aware of the other man's rigid kneeling posture by the bed. Dropping the fur, he strode to Maelgwyn's side. As he looked down at the metal box, his face grew grim. "Is that what I think, old ram?"

Maelgwyn rose. "I fear my house has indeed been robbed."

"That's where your treasure was and now there's none left?"

"None." Maelgwyn edged to the door. "All stolen."

The shepherd's voice became silky. "Yet you swore I'd get my money."

"I'm the victim, not you. You haven't lost a penny you possessed before, but I've lost everything. In the snap of a thief's fingers I've been transformed into a pauper."

The shepherd didn't seem to be listening. "Remember what I told you? I told you I'd slice you up like I did old Blanche."

Maelgwyn didn't wait to hear more. He spun around and fairly flew down the stairs. Near the bottom he tripped and went sprawling facefirst into the rushes. His nose bore the brunt of his fall.

Behind him loomed the shepherd. Maelgwyn scrambled to his feet. His bad arm ached, and blood dripped from the tip of his nose. "Because of my catastrophe I've no money left to reward you," he mumbled, walking backward, cautiously, across the hall. "But wait. I know. What about that fur coverlet upstairs? It's worth a fine sum, if you sell it. Take it. Take anything you want."

"What I want is my money."

Maelgwyn swallowed blood. He gagged, then pivoted and ran.

Near the screens the shepherd caught him. "Come along now, Gryg. This has to be. Take your ending like a man." He clasped his hands around Maelgwyn's throat. "Let's say a prayer together for your soul, then I'll send you nicely on your way."

"You can't kill me." Maelgwyn choked out the words. "You'll suffer the torments of Hell."

"I won't. God will give me a mansion for ridding the world of such a nasty ram as you." Taking one hand from Maelgwyn's throat, he reached down and pulled the knife from its sheath on his leg. "Here's a fine sharp tool. It will do its work easy, unless you make a struggle."

A warm stream trickled down Maelgwyn's thigh, to his knee, to his ankle. Some drained through a hole in his borrowed boot, then soaked into the rushes. As the wound on his throat throbbed out a wild rhythm, he heard Elise's taunting voice deep inside his head. "How rotten your soul must be. How endless your fear."

Rage washed over him. His body shook and his teeth snapped together. Breaking suddenly from the shepherd's grip, he hurled himself away and searched for a weapon.

Luck smiled. He spied the roasting skewer, leaning upright in the alcove.

The shepherd's smile died. "Steady. I was only joking. You know I like my jokes."

Maelgwyn seized the long rod and brandished it like a spear. "So do I, friend."

He lunged forward and drove the sharp end of the skewer into the other man's gut. The shepherd made a sound like a puffball mushroom being squashed and tried to clutch at the rod. But Maelgwyn growled and drove it in farther.

The white-haired man fell to his knees. "Mercy," he whispered.

Maelgwyn bent forward until they were face to face. "Your mother was a fool and a whore. You're a fool too, so don't ask me for mercy." Bracing a foot against the shepherd's shoulder, he wrenched the skewer from his body. The surrounding rushes turned dull red as blood pumped from the wound. "No, you'll get no mercy."

The shepherd crumpled. His eyes closed and he went still.

Maelgwyn dragged the corpse all the way down to the river and heaved it in, too exultant to heed the aching of his arm. As he stood on the Conwy's bank watching the body drift away, the wind blew harder. He felt its coolness where urine dampened his clothes, and shivered. His nose began to throb. As euphoria subsided further, the pain in his arm reasserted itself.

In spite of these complaints he was proud of his renewed strength and resourcefulness. This time he was not the one to be tossed into the river.

Hurrying to his barn, he flung open the door. Bleating sheep surged toward him. "Get out," he said. "Get out, get out." He waved his good arm and kicked at their rumps. The terrified animals scampered off toward the Migneint Moor. Maelgwyn laughed as he watched them run. "Be supper for wolves and elves," he called.

Standing at the barn's threshold, he noticed fresh blood on the front of his hosen. Whose was it—the shepherd's or his own? Alarmed, he pulled the hosen down to check the wound on his groin and gasped when he saw that it bled from a fresh tear at its edge. He had toiled too recklessly, he realized, while dragging the shepherd to the river. Then he touched his throat. Had it also suffered new damage? Yes, his fingers found stickiness there.

Well, what was done was done. He took a cautious breath and resolved to be optimistic. At least neither wound gushed like a fountain.

Yes, yes, this setback to healing would be minor, he thought, with some slight care. If he rested, and cleaned both injuries, no further harm would ensue. But he'd certainly have to be more careful in the future. After all, less than a week had passed since the original trauma. He was strong and well blessed, but his body at least was mortal. Happily his soul was not.

But then he remembered two less pleasant things: he remembered he was a pauper, and he remembered that this, like his other misfortunes, was the fault of Elise.

31

THE MOUTH OF THE NIGHT

Thomas and the constable trudged away to make beds on the floor of the priest's house. Gregarious Efa decided she absolutely couldn't bear the gloom of her cottage turned hospice and so took herself off to sleep at the home of an amenable neighbor.

"I'm sorry we've chased you from your place," said Elise, as Efa left.

"It's my own choice. I'm no nurse, and you two are. But everyone in Llanrhychwyn will be clamoring for my company anyway. I'll have free suppers for days, as they're all eager to hear news of the doings in here."

Annora walked outside with her.

"You may not have much news to share, Efa," she said. "If the fever doesn't break soon, his heart will burn up. Then it will be over."

"I hope he doesn't die," said Efa. She lowered her voice to a confidential murmur. "Elise seems taken with him, though he's a stranger. I couldn't help but remark on it."

Annora shook her head and sat down on the stump Thomas had occupied earlier.

"Who can blame the girl?" Efa continued, probing gently. "A widow, at her age. She must miss the comfort of a man's arms."

Annora looked at Efa as if she'd sprouted a second nose. "Comfort? Her dead husband beat her regularly just to demonstrate his superiority."

Efa shrugged. "Some men do."

"Do they quote Scripture while they do it? And he was worse, for he used her to slake his foul lusts, used her harder than the lowest whore."

"That poor girl. I only wonder why she'd consider another man."

"She's young. And she comes from good blood, on both sides. No snivelers."

"It's true she has an air of quality. But I imagine it might not be easy to forget the past and go on with her life."

"Harder than you know."

"I'll pray for her, and your patient as well. Have you learned anything much about him?"

"Only his name. Gwydion. The name of a great wizard and warrior from ancient days."

This crumb of history pleased Efa. "Wizard and warrior?"

"This Gwydion will need to be both to survive."

Elise sat on a stool next to the patient's bed while Annora and Efa talked outside. Only a sweet-smelling candle lit the room.

Gwydion's most recent wound began to bleed more than she thought it ought, so she softly recited the healer's prayer to restrain bleeding. "Stay, thou blood, in the Father's name. Amen. Stay in the Son's name. Amen. Stay in the name of the Holy Ghost. Amen. Rest, blood, in the name of the blessed Trinity. Bleed not. Amen, amen, amen. So be it." She made the sign of the cross three times.

Vort appeared from beneath the bed. He sniffed the edge of the blanket that covered his master, then padded outside to attend to canine business as Elise closed the shutters to discourage night vapors and intrusive eyes.

Soon the healer's prayer proved effective. This crisis past, Elise applied more salve. Gwydion did not react to her touch or make any sound. Lifting his hand from the blanket, she placed three fingers on his wrist to feel the beat of his blood. But the deep music of his pulse revealed no auspicious secrets. It only told her he lived. She glanced toward the door. There was no sign of Annora's return. With no attempt to make sense of her own behavior, Elise measured Gwydion's hand against her own, palm to palm. The difference in the length of their fingers surprised her. She smiled. But when his hand slipped away from hers, her smile vanished.

Soon Annora came back inside, and the two women shared a meal of bread and cheese from their sacks. Their charge began to utter strange words, not quite Welsh, not quite English, but a fevered blending. Annora squeezed a cloth soaked with water and apple juice over his lips. Drops slid down his chin and pooled at the base of his throat.

Earlier in the evening Efa had given the nurses a bottle of Celestial Water, another gift from her merchant swain. It was famous, costly stuff from an Irish monastery, distilled from angelica roots and reputed to protect against poison and spells. Annora had voiced skepticism of these claims. But even if it didn't help, Efa had said, what harm could it do? After all, angelica was an herb endorsed by Saint Michael the Archangel. Could any mortal hope for better sanction?

Now Elise said, "I'll try to give him the Celestial Water."

Annora agreed but expected no successful outcome.

After dipping her hand into Saint Michael's drink, Elise ran her wet fingertips over Gwydion's lips. Droplets coursed down his jaw. She tried again. "You're thirsty, so thirsty," she said, her voice soft and persuasive. "And this is so cool and clear. Part your lips to taste it."

Watching her, Annora suddenly wished the ordeal would end. The outcome would probably be the same, however long it dragged on. The patient was so still.

As Elise continued her efforts, Annora leaned forward to feel his cheek. She drew her hand back, for his skin was like fire. Surely his heart was ablaze inside his chest.

"Cool and sweet," Elise said, over and over. "Only part your lips." But her voice had grown less sure.

"It's clear the fever has won," Annora said, after more time passed. "He can't hear you. One of us should fetch the priest."

Elise shook her head. Once again she raised her fingers to his lips. "Sweet water, Gwydion. Water from the angels."

As she bent over him, a draft crept in beneath the shutters. It brought with it a hint of evergreen. Then Gwydion's lips parted. A drop of water rolled into his mouth. Annora stared, certain that weariness had caused her to imagine it. But Elise quickly offered him more. He took it with growing energy. Then more. Now he swallowed frantically. She made a cup from her hand, filled it with Celestial Water, and held it against his lips. He opened his eyes and drank. But it wasn't enough. He reached up, seized her wrist, and pressed her hand hard against his mouth. His strength made her gasp, but she didn't pull away.

Suddenly he went still and looked past her. His face became composed.

The bottle of Celestial Water slipped from Elise's fingers and fell to the floor, but there was nothing left to spill. She turned to the place where his eyes had fixed, prepared to see an angel or a demon. But she saw neither.

Gwydion's fingers went slack. His eyes closed.

Elise reached out and touched his eyelids, first one, then the other.

Annora nearly sobbed but stopped herself. It would be foolish to waste tears on a stranger. Instead she recited aloud an emotionless prayer for the dead. Whatever else needed to be said, the priest could say it later.

32

FEVER AND FAITH

Annora's prayer was premature, for Gwydion was not dead. His heart still beat. Even so, the fever worked harder and harder to conquer him that night, as stars danced across the sky.

Certain he would not revive again, Annora fell into an exhausted sleep on the second bed. But Elise sat, wide awake, keeping vigil.

When Vort scratched at the door, she roused herself to admit him. Fur smelling of some benefactor's viand, he went to his master's side and sat patiently for a while. But like Annora, he soon slumbered, curled in a mound beside the bed.

Elise was glad the others slept.

She watched Gwydion's face. Then she brushed the violets across his brow, as her mother had done to her brothers just before they died. "They're only sleeping," Mother had said.

Gwydion gave a soft cry around the time the moon set. Elise touched his cheek, then his brow.

She turned her face skyward, imagining a place beyond the moon, beyond the blanket of stars. She thanked God and Saint Michael. Heaven, it seemed, had been kind.

Gwydion spoke. His hoarse English words were bemused and strange. "The saddest tales are told in the mouth of the night." He opened his eyes and tried to sit up but could not. He seemed far away.

Elise willed him to return. "But not always. Not this night."

His gaze became clearer. Less lost. "Gray eyes. The madwoman," he said. He knew her. "Have you come to hear my confession—or share my bed?"

These were not the words of a man at the brink of the grave, and she smiled. "I've come to be sure you don't die."

"Will I, madwoman?"

"No, not this night."

33

A PRIVATE CONVERSATION

Two days went by. Naturally Annora and Elise frequently discussed their need to depart Llanrhychwyn. They fretted. As they chopped herbs or ate hurried meals, they whispered their concerns.

But both soon agreed that the need to flee seemed to grow less dire with each hour. Efa told them that every traveler now coming through the village talked only of the rich couple killed near Dolwyddelan. Some travelers also asked about the conflict rumored to have taken place right there in Llanrhychwyn between agents of the Crown and an anonymous gang of criminals—several of them still at large. But that story was cast far in the shade by the more lurid and horrible tale of the Dolwyddelan throat slashings, especially since word had leaked out that the female victim had been viciously molested.

One thing was agreed on by all the pilgrims and wayfarers: a band of cutthroats was loose in the region. Even if another body *had* been found near Ysbyty Ifan, it might well be widely supposed these same villains were responsible for that crime, just as they were responsible for the others. But no one had news at all of any murder in the vicinity of Ysbyty Ifan. There was no word of a body found in or near the Conwy River. So Maelgwyn's corpse must have truly found its way to oblivion.

This belief found a welcome foothold in Elise's mind and in Annora's and made it much easier for them to stay on and tend their patient. In any case neither would have felt it right to withdraw their good care of Gwydion so soon. He was much better but still in need.

The third evening of his recovery, a cooler evening than usual, Thomas wandered off to the home of a good-tempered couple who brewed drinkable ale and bartered or sold the surplus. A gathering of men was promised at the couple's house. It was a traditional Llanrhychwyn diversion, the male counterpart to a simultaneous assembly of the village's women.

Annora went as Efa's guest to the ladies' gathering, near the village well. Efa assured her she'd be entertained. Just be on guard, Efa advised, against the beverage brewed by the tall and wide Nela, wife of the blacksmith. More than a swallow would guarantee a throbbing head all the next day.

At Efa's cottage Elise remained to watch over the patient. Gwydion did little but sleep from late afternoon until sunrise—"like a useless, cosseted babe," he had complained just that morning to his cousin. So by the time Annora, Efa, and Thomas departed for their outings, he was certain to be too worn from the day to require much attention. In fact he was already quietly sleeping when the three socializers left.

Annora wasn't concerned that leaving Elise and Gwydion alone would present a problem. The patient had improved but was still too weak to attempt any masculine mischief. Besides, she had decided he was too worldly and sensible to trifle with a decent girl, even if the decent girl admired him more than she ought.

She knew very well Elise and Gwydion spent many daytime hours conversing on such things as history, politics, philosophy, and other subjects she could not pretend to grasp. The two switched blithely from English to Welsh without warning and seemed to trade obscure quips.

The older woman wondered sometimes at their rapport. But she decided it was innocent enough, unalarming enough. It likely had its roots in their bilingual ease, in their seemingly similar interests. The simple fact of their unexpected sequestering in a one-room cottage surely also contributed to their amity.

Still, she realized that was not *quite* all of it.

Unbeknownst to Gwydion, Annora had seen his eyes alight on Elise with revealing speculation several times. He was a man, after all, and Elise an attractive young woman. But reasonable men—he was surely reasonable—solicited women of a different stamp to assuage their lower needs. For purposes more legal, such as marriage, highborn men required another sort of female. Elise fell somewhere between these two categories of women. She was too respectable to be lightly seduced by a reasonable man and too seemingly obscure to be considered as a wife. She would be safe alone for one evening.

By then the two caregivers had actually moved out of Efa's cottage, and Thomas had moved in. The patient still needed daytime watching, but they felt confident in leaving his kinsman with him during the night. They were close by, staying at Mistress Lowri's with Efa.

The new, righteous Lowri had dismantled Princess Joan's infamous bed of adultery and stowed it in a cupboard. Nightly she entertained her three lady guests with stories of her former wicked life, told in a properly remorseful manner, followed by parables she claimed illustrated the miracle of her salvation. Of these, Elise's favorite was the tale of the saintly blind woman and the libidinous lion who falls in love with her. At the story's end the lion emasculates himself with a magical ruby-encrusted spoon and settles down to a life of asexual ecstasy at the dainty feet of his lady. The mismatched pair while away their remaining days whittling rosaries from the bones of the lion's earlier victims.

This was Efa's favorite story too. She howled with laughter every time Lowri reached the part about the ruby spoon. But Annora called it the silliest thing she ever heard. Lowri didn't mind; she was just happy to have reputable guests.

On the night of Llanrhychwyn's traditional gatherings, after the others departed, Elise dropped the bar across Efa's door. Then she sat on a stool near the window. As evening light filtered between the shutters, she busied herself by rubbing stems of lemon balm into the fabric of her two spare dresses. The scent of lemon balm had the power to make the heart grow merry, she knew.

Light waned. She added wood to the modest fire as the first star appeared in the sky. Setting aside the dresses and frayed herbs, she folded her hands in her lap and considered the future.

Its inhospitable territory had grown all too familiar. She almost wished she had never come to Llanrhychwyn. Despair had been easier to endure, somehow, when she'd had nothing with which to compare it.

"Can there be so much sadness in the world, madwoman?"

At this soft question she turned her head. "You should be asleep," she said, going to Gwydion's bedside. It surprised her to see him sitting up, very much awake. She should have been paying better heed to her surroundings.

"I've been trying to read your eyes," he said.

"Then you must be bored indeed."

"They're filled with secret things. Lonely, secret things."

"Of course they are," she said lightly. She picked up his hand and recorded the rhythm of his blood with her fingertips. Then she touched his forehead. "You're making good progress, I think, even if you *do* talk a deal of nonsense."

"Perhaps I'm delusional."

She gave him a smile but in the manner of a mother indulging a child who's recovering from some tiresome illness. "Would you like something to eat or drink? Are you in any pain?"

His smile changed to something more difficult to interpret. "Pain is such a strange word."

Alert to an unsettling undercurrent in his tone, she pulled the cottage's newest chair farther from the bed and sat. The oak chair had been made by Thomas, to ease her back and Annora's. It was a sturdy enough piece of furniture, if imperfectly constructed, and an improvement on Efa's backless seating.

"Feel safer now?" he said.

"You *are* nonsensical."

Feminine laughter sounded in the distance.

"You're missing out on all the merriment, Elise."

"Alas. And my life is usually an endless whirl of fêtes."

"Then I can only thank you for taking the time to care for a stranger. But why have you?"

"Annora and I know something of healing. We couldn't just leave you here to die."

"But your journey has been delayed for longer than you supposed it might be, I'm sure."

She thought of their headlong flight before arriving at Llanrhychwyn. "Yes. But we both needed to rest anyway."

"You've not rested much. So again, thank you." Looking toward the closed window, he initiated a new subject. "Thomas told me of your previous encounter with de Breauté."

"Did he?"

"He said de Breauté set you free because you told him you have visions."

"Yes. He's quite mad, I think."

"Not altogether mad."

She thought of the scene she witnessed at Dolwyddelan and decided to ask about it, since Gwydion had spoken of personal things.

"Can you soothe *my* curiosity? That dawn, at the inn where the mad-men stayed, why were you fighting? Who was your opponent?" She belatedly recalled his proposition that morning and felt her face grow warm.

"Another of de Breauté's hirelings, probably," he answered, watch-ing her with an expression that suggested he hadn't forgotten his proposition either. "When I surprised him lurking outside our door, he told me his name was Harold and claimed acquaintance with my father. He said he'd come to pay tardy condolences—at sunrise. Then he tried to kill me. Luckily he was as bad a swordsman as he was an actor. But I was in no fit state to make chase when he rode off, and I haven't seen him since."

"He wasn't one of the men who fought here in Llanrhychwyn?"

"No. A cadre is entrenched at my father's manor, so it's likely he's there. De Breauté attracts thieves and outcasts and pays them well to obey."

"Your father, did he, was he—"

"Was he killed by de Breauté? Yes."

"But why?"

A muscle worked in Gwydion's jaw before he answered. "It's a sor-did tale. De Breauté was hired by a man in London, another noble-man. My father was an obstacle to that man's ambitions. You see, Father was justiciar of North Wales. The vice-regent, effectively."

"A position of great importance."

"And only the second Welshman to hold it. Now, not surprisingly, I hear another Englishman has been given the honor. That new fel-low chooses to make his home farther east, in Flint." He shrugged. "But these details can't be of much interest."

"But they are. I'd like to know more." Thomas hadn't told her much, even though he'd said he might, on that bloody morning three days before.

"Would you really like to know, Elise? All right. Then I'll tell you." His face was grim. "I was in France . . . on the king's business. I might have been able to stop de Breauté otherwise." Then he smiled, as a wolf might. "At least the man in London didn't live to profit from the crime. As it turned out, that man was actually doing the bidding of *my* enemy, a coward who wanted to harm me through my father. As I said, the Londoner saw no profit."

Elise wished to hear no particulars of that man's demise but blurted out another question that had yet to be answered. "And the lord and lady near Dolwyddelan?"

Gwydion opened his left hand and frowned down at his palm.

Watching him, Elise was once again taken aback by the pain that crossed his face. It was the same naked grief she'd beheld when he'd stared into the fire at Dolwyddelan.

"Forgive me," she said, rising. "I have no right to pry. I'll go outside now to let you have some peace and—"

"You think I'll find peace if I'm alone, with only my thoughts for company? No, Elise, don't go. You have a remarkably calming effect on me, in some ways."

She felt color rise in her face but sat down again.

"Those two people were Elizabeth, my only sibling, and her husband. We arranged by letter that she would journey from Cornwall to meet me near Conwy. We hadn't seen each other in five years, and I'd never met her husband. But apparently de Breauté feels it will be easier to entrench himself at Llys Garanhir, my father's house, if no one in my family is left alive to oppose him. And because Father was Welsh, the authorities at Conwy aren't overly concerned by his murder, so far, or by Elizabeth's, or by de Breauté's seizure of the manor. So it seems."

Silence fell as Elise considered this tragic tale. But then she thought of a detail that might at least help Gwydion understand another bit of it.

"I didn't think to tell your cousin," she said, "but Sir Nicolas was minding two corpses at Castell-y-Gwynt when Annora and I arrived there. Two men. He took them away when he left. One was young and tall, taller even than you."

"Tall?" He frowned, then crossed himself. "Ah. Liz's servants. They went with her to Cornwall when she married. Good and loyal men. That explains why she and her husband were found alone on the path. Nicolas must have disposed of Herv and Eadric's bodies somewhere else later. I wish I knew why or where. I doubt he gave them a decent burial."

"He told his lackey they'd drop the bodies in the woods where rooks wouldn't see them."

"Rooks, again?"

"He's bedeviled by superstition."

"He left Elizabeth and Nevill on the Trackway. Wasn't he worried *they'd* be seen by rooks?"

"Perhaps it's more proof of his madness."

"Unless he wanted to draw me out and put an end to it."

"But the law will deal with him, surely. What of the Welsh constable who was here? He had a warrant."

"Nicolas de Breauté doesn't recognize Welsh law, even in Wales. And he thinks Englishmen won't bother to arrest him, especially outside England."

"They will, won't they?"

"I'll see they do. I want a thousand people to cheer his execution in Conwy."

She instinctively understood he was not a man to willingly reveal his vulnerability. But she thought how lonely it must be to bear so much heartache with no word of comfort, as he seemed intent to try to do. She could imagine him rebuffing any well-meaning attempt at solace his cousin Thomas might have made.

Without thinking she leaned forward and took his hand. His long fingers immediately closed around hers.

A door slammed at some cottage nearby. Pulling quickly away, she hurried over to the shelf near the window, where she searched recklessly among the tableware. Choosing a random pewter cup, she filled it with water from the bucket on the floor.

"I'm not a very efficient nurse, am I?" she said, cursing her voice for the quaver it had developed. "You must be parched by now."

He watched her but didn't answer.

"You've had nothing to drink for hours, have you?" Regarding a point just above his naked shoulder, she presented the water.

He drank quickly, then offered her the cup back. When she reached for it, he took her hand again. Once more she tried to pull away, but he held her fast. The cup fell to the bed. Ceasing to struggle, she looked into his eyes. What she saw made her draw in her breath sharply.

"Don't be afraid of me, Elise."

She had no will to resist as he drew her down on the bed and eased the kerchief from her hair. A mass of brown curls tumbled to her shoulders. "Tell me your secrets, madwoman," he said, pulling her nearer. "Your secrets are safe with me."

She felt heat rise from his skin, and of their own volition her hands went to his shoulders. She closed her eyes. The air was hushed and scented with herbs. Languor enveloped her as his muscles tensed beneath her fingertips. He groaned and buried his face in her hair.

When she opened her eyes, a distorted face looked back at her from the side of the polished pewter cup that had fallen next to them on the bed. It was her own face—conniving, iniquitous. Her mirrored brows had a devilish slant.

As a sob swelled in her throat, Gwydion pulled back. His gaze followed hers to the cup.

"What is it?"

"My eyes. My reflection on the cup."

He seemed surprised but trapped the vessel and calmly tossed it to the floor. Smiling, he brushed a tendril of hair from her cheek. "Undone by your own lovely face? Strange girl. But let me ease your worries. We are both of us too long alone, I think."

She couldn't bring herself to look into his eyes. Instead she gazed beyond him, toward the door. "We can't do this," she said abruptly. To her own ears, the words sounded hard and cold as they left her lips. They were a stranger's words. No, not a stranger: they were the words of a secret murderess, a murderess whose sins were revealed in her unholy gray eyes. They were the words of a woman who deserved no ease, no passion.

"Yes, we can." His hands moved to her waist and held her tightly, as if he feared she might slip from him and melt into the air. "Tell me what troubles you."

But she was unable to say more.

His eyes were nearly black. But he had already withdrawn from her, if only a little. "Why shouldn't we comfort each other? I only want to hold you for a little while," he said, shaking her gently. "Look at me, and tell me how it could be wrong. I know you're a widow, Elise. Or does some other man claim you? Is that it?"

How simple it would be to deceive him and caress away his doubts, to feel her hands on his skin, and his on hers. It would be so completely new, so glorious, the perfect opposite of the horror she had known from Maelgwyn.

Her body wanted it, and more than her body. She longed, simply, to be one with him.

But she understood with her next breath that though Maelgwyn was dead, his shadow still lingered, whispering that she was a murderess without any right to draw an unsuspecting man into her web of guilt. Her reflection on the cup only confirmed it.

She said, "I'm a widow, it's true. But it would still be wrong."

In an instant his eyes grew completely cool again. They changed from deep, welcoming black to a remote, unfathomable brown. He took his hands from her waist. "If you tell me it's wrong, then of course it must be. Accept my apologies."

"I wasn't thinking properly, I'm afraid," she said, rising, standing very erect. "And perhaps grief and an excess of solitude have made *you* warm for entanglements that wouldn't normally tempt you."

"I'm surprised you know me so well."

His cool mockery made her wince, but she kept her voice emotionless. "I think it might be best if I go outside now to look at the stars."

As he leaned against the cushions, his dark brows drew together. "Take a shawl, madwoman. It grows colder."

She left him. Wrapped in Efa's red shawl, she sat on Tom's favorite stump. A gentle night breeze cooled her face as laughter and songs drifted by on the air. Gazing upward, she wondered, How can the stars be so fixed and so lovely? They ought to come crashing to the ground, blue-white and fading, to mark all the places where unfulfilled yearnings die their sorry little deaths.

Later Annora and Efa wove toward her on the path, warbling an improper refrain. Elise heard the same song echoing across the village.

Efa stopped singing and began to laugh. "My dear friends, Annora and Elise, tonight someone told me that only lovers have soft hearts *and* hard cocks. Not husbands. Can that possibly be true?"

Annora regarded her drunken companion with shock. "You've had Nela's ale."

"Well, and so have you."

"I drank the giantess's ale?"

Efa peered into her friend's face. "You have. A cupful."

Annora grimaced. "Then we're both fools, for we'll be sick as pregnant sheep come morning."

"Mayhap." A look of cunning came over Efa's round face. "But it isn't morning yet."

Annora seemed impressed with her companion's astuteness. "And if we stay up all night, we'll never get sick at all."

Ten minutes later Elise tucked them into their beds at Mistress Lowri's. Both snored mightily.

"That's what drink does to a woman," said Lowri, clutching their shoes to her chest. "How well I remember." She looked at Elise. "Would you like me to tell you a parable now?"

"Another time. I have to go make sure Thomas returns, so Gwydion isn't left alone. But I'll be back. And Lowri, I'll look after these two if they need anything in the night. They shouldn't be your responsibility."

Mistress Lowri's mouth became mulish. "Once I found pleasure being skewered on the staff of a man. No more does such sin tempt me." She pointed a finger heavenward. "So saying, are you and I not God's handmaidens equally?"

"Yes. Of course. In that case look after them if you wish it."

Elise went back outside and waited, listening to the village settle for the night. Before another hour passed Vort and Thomas came home from their revels. Vort sat at Elise's feet and looked up at her in a most winsome way. He pushed his cold nose under her hand to be stroked.

"His head's been turned by the fussing he's had," said Thomas, swaying as he spoke. "Scamp."

She regarded the young man with concern. "Are you sober enough to see to your cousin if he needs you?"

When he took a tottering step toward her, she was engulfed by the smell of ale. "He won't need me," he said. "He doesn't need anyone. Fierce as a lion is my cousin, damn him."

"What *you* need is sleep."

"No, what I need is you. Walk with me to the woods, Elise. Let me count the stars in your eyes."

"Go inside, Tom. You're drunk."

He smiled. "You called me Tom. Say it again."

She led him toward Efa's door. He stopped at the threshold and refused to budge.

"Go to bed," said Elise. "Now."

He reached out and touched her cheek. "I'm as good a man as my cousin, you know. Let me prove it."

"In." Pushing the door open, she urged him forward. "Before you say something more embarrassing."

He drew back. "Offering myself to you is an embarrassment?"

"If you chance to recall this conversation in the morning, you may find it so." She turned and walked away.

He called to her, in a slightly more rational voice. "I'm sorry, Elise. Above all women in the world, I would never offend you."

She looked over her shoulder. "Of course you wouldn't. Now go to bed. But first see if your cousin is well. Then have a drink of water to dilute all that ale you've downed."

Efa's door closed behind him and behind Vort. Elise heard the bar drop into place. For a while longer she lingered outside, standing in the dark, watching the indifferent stars.

34

INFLAMMATION

A bulbous bottle flew out Efa's door and smashed on the ground. From his perch on the stump Thomas regarded its glittering wreckage without surprise. He looked toward the widow's cottage. Standing beside him, Elise and Annora did the same.

Clashing in English, angry male voices sounded from inside.

"Do you know medicine better than I?" said one.

"Could I know it worse?" This second voice was full of exasperation and contempt. It belonged to Gwydion.

There followed a short silence. Then . . .

"I tell you, sir, the care you've received so far may have placed you in danger. It is always so with these herb-pounding females. But if you expect proper assessment of your condition, you must provide me a sample. Why quarrel with such an unexceptional request?"

"Make your own sample, piss-prophet. Bathe in it, wear it for perfume. But let me be."

Gwydion was proving an increasingly recalcitrant convalescent.

A corpulent man of middle years came storming out Efa's door but turned back to deliver a last riposte. "Only a fool has a woman for physician, sir."

"Better a fool than a corpse," came the reply.

The stout man hitched the strap of his medical case across his chest and plodded toward Thomas, straightening his crimson robe as he came. "The man's a demon," he said, worrying the squirrel trim at his collar. He looked uncomfortable. This wasn't surprising, as it was a warm day. The medico spoke exclusively to Thomas, not acknowledging Annora's or Elise's presence. Apparently he didn't feel the need to communicate with females, especially Welsh females.

"Sir, forgive my cousin," Tom said. "Days of idleness vex him."

"I've never been spoken to in such a manner. You heard? Why, I took my training in Montpellier and attend great personages from

Chester to Coventry." He coughed, then spit out the gnat that had flown between his lips.

Thomas slipped a purse into the physician's hand. "You've been sorely put upon."

"Well, yes. Yes." The doctor tucked the purse into his cloak. "But then, I suppose it must be rather frustrating for men of certain dispositions to be too long confined."

"Your generous view is . . . generous."

The men's foreign words meant little to Annora, but she thought she recognized the tenor of twaddle when it whizzed past her ears. It hadn't rained for two days and some of Llanrhychwyn's ample mud had dried; she tapped her foot on the path.

The fashionable physician, brought in by Thomas at impressive expense from Beeston in England, had not finished blustering. "I advise he be unreservedly bled. You must endeavor to render him calm, perhaps convince him to take wine with daisy petals in it, and I'll cup him. The moon is in a propitious phase for cupping, and I much fear his blood volume waxes high. All four humors are likely unbalanced, in fact."

Elise forced herself not to smile. But a mental picture of Gwydion finding daisy petals in his wine tested her resolve.

"Let's consider that, shall we?" The doctor cleared his throat. "Ah, but it has been a trying afternoon. Dry and trying. Wales, when I must be in it, affects my esophagus adversely."

No dullard, Thomas took the man's arm and led him toward the home of the good-natured couple who brewed tasty ale. He looked at Elise and Annora over his shoulder as they went, and grinned.

"I could try theriac," Elise heard the doctor say in his booming voice. Theriac was a costly paste made in Rome from vipers' meat and sixty-three spices. It took twelve years to mature. Rich men and women took it to combat everything from dropsy to pestilence. "I've a dose in my bag. Gold particles in oil might also be effective. Neither is for paupers, but your kinsman surely deserves no remedy that reeks of the half measure."

"What did that Saesneg wind-worm say?" Annora asked Elise as the men's shapes receded.

"He wants to bleed Gwydion and put daisies in his wine."

Annora's eyes gleamed. "I'd give a gem to see him try."

Elise glanced toward Efa's door. The widow was not in her cottage. She'd gone to Trefriw to sell candles and to beguile her smitten merchant. Only Gwydion was inside, fretting and fuming, no doubt. Or eradicating nicks from his sword's fine blade with honestone. Or shining the blade with wax he'd cajoled from Efa. This was how he spent his time now. But he was mending well, in her opinion and Annora's. He needed only a few more days of rest to be recovered. Whether he would take their advice and allow himself those extra days, Elise didn't know. She expected he would not, for he grew hourly more impatient.

"Why did Thomas haul that doctor here anyway?" said Annora. "Wasn't our care good enough? Or maybe he'd prefer it if we handed him a fat reckoning for our services."

"Tom probably wanted an official male blessing. It's what he's used to. After all we're only a pair of unknown women."

"Unknown women who saved his cousin's life. You did, for certain. I bet that doctor wouldn't bless anything unless he got paid a fortune to do it."

"I think Thomas has surmised that."

Annora straightened her apron. Then she made as if to speak but stopped.

"Oh, don't strangle yourself," said Elise, watching her. "Whatever you're dying to say, say it. I can see you won't be happy until you do."

"You're right, I won't be. Well then, child, it's Thomas. Every maiden in the village could be a toad for all he notices. He stays glued to your side more than he ought. The only time he leaves you is to see to the horses."

"Oh, Annora, your imagination is running wild. I'm the only other English speaker in the village except Gwydion, since the constable's gone back to Caernarfon with that other man who was injured."

"Maybe."

"You prefer to suppose my irresistible beauty ensnares every man I meet? That isn't likely."

"Just don't tease him. English or not, Tom seems like a right-thinking boy. You're much of an age, and it wouldn't be strange for him to take a fancy to a likely female."

"I'm hardly a likely female. But I agree Tom's a sweet boy. And rest easy: I go out of my way not to tease him."

The women walked toward the woodland spring. They'd been headed there earlier when the doctor's flying bottle distracted them.

Clear water bubbled over the black stones, as always. Elise held one leather beaker beneath the cascade, then the other. The water smelled of roses and iron, a heady combination.

"We've been in Llanrhychwyn five days now," Annora mused. She carried a bedraggled bouquet of daisies she'd picked along the way— to aggravate Gwydion, she said.

Elise concentrated on her task. When she finished, she set the beakers aside and passed her hands through the spring to let scented water play over her wrists. "Has it been so long?"

"You know it has. But now I do truly believe we can stop looking over our shoulders."

Elise glanced up, her face hopeful. "Do you?"

"If Maelgwyn's body had been discovered, and we were suspects, I'm certain someone would have come after us by now."

"What if his body was discovered only yesterday or the day before? It could take a while to mount a search."

"But I've been considering the whole thing more sensibly. Didn't Maelgwyn say Ysbyty Ifan was full of fools who hated him? Even if he *has* been found, who'd care? And if it's strangers who find him, down-river, they won't have any idea who he is. I'm sure they'd suppose he was another victim of that band of criminals everyone is gossiping about."

"Maybe." Elise rose and shook out her skirt. "But I'll still feel better if we go on, especially now that our patient is better. Haven't we been here long enough?"

The older woman frowned. "Caution may be the best course. But I'm surprised. I was under the impression you were in no rush to go, whether we were being hunted or not."

Elise gave a little laugh. "No. There's no reason for us to linger. Except Efa, of course. She's so sweet."

"Yes, she's a jewel."

They tarried a while near the spring, then strolled back to the village. Each woman carried a beaker, and Annora held the sad daisies. Annora looked down at the flowers and made another attempt to pry loose a confidence. "I've begun to like Gwydion, you know, in spite of his efforts to keep his distance. And really, that's only sensible."

Elise didn't respond.

"Don't you think he's sensible to keep his distance, cariad?"

But by then they had reached Llanrhychwyn's main path and Thomas approached.

"Do I behold two wood nymphs?" he said. His eyes were bright from ale, and he prattled on in a rush. "You'll never guess what happened while you wove spells in the glade. Gwydion threw cold stew over the doctor's robe." He smiled. "I think he's nearly himself again."

"And we weren't there to see it," said Elise. "Did the doctor like his dousing?"

"Not much. He bolted back to Beeston, ripe with broth."

Elise related the story to Annora.

"Ask him why Gwydion threw it," she said, entertained.

When this question was put to Thomas, he grinned. "The good doctor drank too much ale; he's unaccustomed to Welsh brew. He started banging on the table, bragging. I'd had enough of the old sot by then, but he decided he wanted to visit Gwydion again, to cure him."

"Cure him?" said Elise. "He's healing perfectly well."

"The fellow's an idiot. He said doctoring done by females is an abomination—begging your pardon. Said it was his duty to save Gwydion."

"Did you make any effort to stop him from saving Gwydion?"

"No, I urged him on. So off we marched to Efa's. When we got there, he rolled up his sleeves, opened his case, and pulled out potions and pincers. He told Gwydion to strip." Thomas was overcome by hilarity. When he could speak again, he said, "His plan was to dose him with theriac, bleed him, then finish off with an enema of comfrey and goat butter. He had a pig's bladder and tube in readiness."

"Surely not, Tom."

"Yes, and you should have seen Gwydion's face. *Then* you should have seen Vort licking broth off the quack's boots."

When Annora was regaled with this part of the tale, she laughed so hard she had to hand Thomas her beaker for fear she'd slosh out the water.

"But I came to find you, Elise," Thomas said after Annora's laughter subsided, "to fetch you to Gwyd. He says the older wound pains him since he threw the pot. I don't know; he seems fine to me." A shadow passed over the young man's face. "He says he wants you, the madwoman."

Elise reported to Annora they were needed by their patient. To Tom, she made light of Gwydion's request. "He probably wants someone to straighten his cushions. You know how he can be."

Thomas frowned. "I suppose. But why does he call you madwoman?"

"Your cousin has a strange sense of humor."

They arrived at Efa's cottage to find Mistress Lowri outside, standing straight as a plank beside the closed door. A puddle of stew congealed at her feet. She was praying aloud, very aloud, with her eyes shut. As was her habit now, she wore her all-enveloping black dress.

"Here, Lowri," said Annora, "what ails you?"

She opened her eyes. "It's the swearing coming from Efa's cottage. From your patient. It was monstrously wicked, so I'm praying for his soul."

"He appreciates your efforts, I'm sure. But you need to scamper off now, because Father Sefyl wants you at the church right away." Annora uttered this spontaneous untruth without a flicker of her gray lashes.

Lowri hurried away.

Inside the cottage Gwydion sat on the bed, propped against two cushions. It seemed he'd grown tired of cursing, for he was quiet and subdued, even if a glint in his eyes suggested he had not quite drawn the curtain on his episode of temper. He wore a clean dun tunic and black hosen, and he was barefoot. Across his knees lay his sword. His hair was neat, tied back with a cord. He had apparently just shaved off the growth of beard he'd developed since his injury. Only a scratch beside his mouth testified to his impatience or the dullness of his knife.

As Elise despised herself for hungering to minister to that new wound, Annora arranged her daisies on the windowsill, spread out flat like a fan.

Elise looked at Gwydion's sword. "What's this, sir?"

"A sword. Do they not have swords where you come from?"

"I meant, why are you holding it?"

He directed a challenging look at her and lowered his voice. "An excess of solitude tempts me to hold all sorts of cold, unresponsive things."

"Perhaps you should encourage Vort to stay indoors more. He could sleep on your bed, if you like."

"I'll choose my own partners. Not that my choices are always wise."

Elise smiled lightly. She was aware of Tom across the room trying his best to eavesdrop on this hushed English conversation. "Poor Gwydion. This isn't quite what you're used to, is it?" she said. "Don't worry. After you leave Llanrhychwyn you'll once again have a vast array of choices. You'll surely find solace in that."

His reply held no hint of mockery. "The damnable thing, mad-woman, is I fear you may be wrong."

Annora stalked up and took the sword. She handed it to Thomas, and Gwydion didn't object. "I hear you've been making a fool of your-self," she said, returning to the bedside. She drew back the hem of his tunic. With only a drawing together of his dark brows, he allowed this. Her practiced fingers pulled away the cloth that covered both wounds. "At least you didn't do any damage with your tantrum. This looks fine. We can try a looser bandage after tonight, I think."

"Thank you," he said without enthusiasm.

"You're welcome. But now, because you've been such a good pa-tient—for the most part—I want you to drink a cup of that ale your cousin is so fond of. One cup. It will help fortify the blood that idiot doctor wanted to drain out of you."

"That's the most reasonable thing you've said since we met."

Annora crossed to the table and set to work chopping herbs she'd collected earlier that morning. "Elise," she said, "ask Thomas to get a pitcher of ale from his new friends, if they've any left. Enough for a cup each for the four of us."

After Elise translated the request, Thomas departed with some re-luctance. Annora then had another command. "Clean the wound, child. Put on a fresh cloth. If he starts cursing again, bandage his mouth too."

Perching on the edge of the bed, Elise took a concoction made of honey, water, and powdered valerian, and spread it lightly across the injuries. She gave absolute concentration to her chore, refusing to look at his face.

"We're using mostly honey now, because the lesions are healing well," she told him in businesslike fashion. "You don't need the stronger medicine anymore."

He watched her hands. "I know you'll do what's best."

"We try to."

"But an ache is still with me," he said quietly. Then he suddenly switched back to English. "It hasn't faded."

Her hands stilled. "Wounds often ache when they're healing. That's usually a good sign."

"This ache is fierce, Elise. It wakes me in the night."

She upset the pot of watery honey on the blanket, and hurried to right it before more than a few drops spilled.

Annora ceased her chopping. "What are you two saying? It's rude, when you know I can't understand you."

Elise hurriedly resumed her medical chore. "I'm sure there are unguents we can make to help," she said, in brisk Welsh.

He answered, still in English, and still softly. "Don't you ache too, madwoman? No, don't lie: your eyes tell me you do."

Annora tossed her knife to the table. It landed with a clatter. She crossed the room to the bed. "I heard you say unguent, Elise," she said, hands on hips. "Our patient expresses need for an unguent?"

"I think he—"

"Then go find chamomile, herb Robert, strawberry leaves, and agrimony. And borrow a bit of lard."

"It's—"

"Mind your elders, Elise. Go."

The younger woman had no graceful choice, so fled with burning cheeks.

Annora and Gwydion were alone. She took over the task of dressing his wound, without appreciable gentleness.

"I can offer you a bit of advice," she said, when she finished. "An unguent may do some slight good. But in your particular case, it grieves me to say I believe 'tis a kind of low inflammation that is the real culprit."

35

A Man's Needs

Gwydion understood her. "Is it really your responsibility to advise me? She isn't your daughter."

Annora was glad they'd arrived at this juncture. Yes, she'd told Elise she admired the good sense he showed in keeping his distance. But she hadn't mentioned the growing disquiet she felt when she beheld, more and more often now, the way his gaze followed the girl— and the way Elise tried to pretend she was unaware of it. Just that morning she'd caught them with their eyes locked, apparently unaware there was anyone else in the cottage.

Prepared for battle, she stood. "So you've decided she's fair game for your grand attentions."

"Your assumptions about my character are not flattering."

"Forgive me. She may not be my daughter, but I love her as if she were. Whatever your intentions, you would do well to leave her be."

"Your concern is understandable, but she's not a child. She told me herself she's a widow."

"It's true. But that doesn't mean she has the experience to deal with a man's needs."

"I would have assumed otherwise."

His detached conjecture about Elise's likely proficiency as an intimate partner took her aback. Could he be so cold, and so unconcerned about the opinion of a respectable older woman?

Yes, as the world was such a wanton place and most rich men such selfish creatures, she supposed he could be.

She seized the honey bowl and the old bandage. "It's odd you consider yourself entitled to speak candidly about such things. Who are you to speculate? We know virtually nothing about you and have only aided you because it was the Christian thing to do. Is this our repayment?"

"I never asked you to help me. You chose to do so."

She paid him no heed. "And tell me, sir—if the subject isn't awkward—would your wife be pleased to learn of any attempt you might make to seduce a vulnerable girl?" He obviously came from a privileged background and was well of an age. Such men were obliged to marry and beget sons, so he *must* have a wife. "How flexible is your union?"

"My wife." He looked suddenly vexed. "I suppose she would be disconsolate."

Annora pursed her lips.

He sung his legs over the side of the bed and came slowly to his feet. "If I had a wife."

Annora's discomfiture at being duped into unkind judgment was superceded by concern. She tried to take his arm. "Where are you going?"

He shook off her help and walked toward the open window. "To Hell soon enough, if your reading of my character is accurate."

"I'm sorry." She stood on the other side of Efa's table, watching him. "But don't commence tearing around the room to prove your pique."

"This sorry hobbling could hardly be called tearing." As he picked up a daisy and plucked a petal, his tone changed abruptly. "As we seem to be talking of sorry things, these are the sorriest excuse for flowers I've ever seen."

"That doctor wanted to put petals in your wine to calm you." She attempted a conciliatory smile. "I thought they'd make a good joke later."

He gave her a sapient look.

Outside, a woman's undulating voice could all at once be heard close to the cottage. Mistress Lowri had returned. Annora pulled open the door and ordered her to go home, as she was driving the patient wild with her caterwauling. With a contrite apology, Lowri sped off. Her skirts flared behind her like sails on a funeral barge.

"That woman surely made a better doxy than saint," Annora said as she shut the door. "Now, let us understand each other, sir, and let us be frank." She wanted to settle the issue. "While I admit I've no cause to judge you unkindly, that still doesn't mean it's proper of you to speak glibly of a young widow's personal concerns."

He leaned against the sill and smiled. "Madam, go on. I am at your temporary disposal to be spoken to with as much frankness as you deem merited."

It was unprecedented in her experience with him to be offered candor. Who was he, really? He gave vague replies when asked specifically, claiming he was merely a hapless adventurer. She had doubts about that. She *did* know he was somewhat reserved, well mannered if a trifle imperious, and cooperative, usually. Also she'd discovered he was possessed of a devilish sort of humor that lit his eyes at unexpected, often inconvenient moments. She saw too that his young cousin idolized him, was even a bit jealous. Lastly she knew his back and shoulders bore cruel scars that were certainly less than a year old.

The only other clue to troubles from his past or worries for his future surfaced without his knowledge, in the involuntary discourse of his dreams. On the nights she and Elise stayed by his side when he was so feverish, before they went to Lowri's, he cried out as he slept. He shouted warnings in Welsh. Twice he whispered in English; Elise identified his words as prayers. He even spoke in a third language; Elise said it was French, the tongue British nobility often employed.

Beyond that, Annora had learned nothing definitive about their interesting patient.

She now looked at him warily. He was not an easy man to assess. "Frankness. All right," she said. "How is it you have no wife? Was she taken by the Pestilence?"

He nodded to himself, as if she had asked a reasonable question. "A month before our marriage, three years ago, my betrothed did indeed succumb to the Pestilence. But perhaps it was a relief to her."

"Why do you say that?"

"She was in the throes of . . . extravagant love with a nobleman who reportedly encouraged her in scandalous behavior. I would have proven an obstacle to their rapture. I was unknown to her, wealthy enough, but not prominent in the London world to which she aspired. I'm despicably half foreign as well."

His tone did not seem to Annora to mask secret regret for the loss. But she said, "Were you grieved?"

"I'd been told she was wonderfully pretty. A dewy rose. An heiress besides. Also unfortunately given to public and athletic displays of affection with her paramour." He shrugged. "As I never met her, I can't say I was grieved."

"You never met?"

"It was a practical arrangement, signed and sealed while I was in France. Not one of my mother's more successful ideas, I'm afraid. Mother was English. Before she died, she decided she didn't want her only son to fall entirely into wild Welshness. She thought an English wife might be just the thing to secure me a civilized future."

His tone provoked Annora to smile.

"So," he said. "I have been exceedingly frank and even made you smile."

"You have." But she was still fully aware she'd learned nothing critically important.

"And we have grown civil again, madam. So indulge *my* curiosity and tell me about Elise. Pretend for a moment my interest is actually less sordid than you know it is."

She bristled. "Maybe it is less sordid. Maybe you're not just bored and overheated and filled with a sense of your own entitlement."

"Pray, don't be too generous. You'll turn my vain, empty head."

She made a dismissive gesture. "Either way, it doesn't matter. If you must have the truth, it is this: Elise's husband was so cruel and twisted that she can never recover from the union. She's terrified of men. For her sake, let her be." This was a partial version of the truth and enough for him to be told.

He'd been denuding daisies, creating a mound of petals on the sill. Now he looked up. His dark eyes were unreadable, but the intensity of their gaze unsettled her. "Why did her parents marry her to such a man?"

"They didn't know. They were dead of the Mortality."

He responded without obvious emotion. "It's as well her husband is likewise dead. If he were not, someone might make him into such a gory puzzle of pieces even Heaven couldn't put him aright." Then his calm voice grew abruptly fierce. "How could any man think to cause her pain?"

Watching his face, Annora was struck. Perhaps he actually cared for Elise and wanted to help her. What if she told him the truth, told him Elise had stabbed Maelgwyn with a piece of glass, and that together they had put his body in the river? How would he react? Of course, he had never had the misfortune to meet Maelgwyn and so couldn't possibly imagine how truly he had earned his fate.

And what if the worst happened? What if sometime since that awful night, Maelgwyn's body had been fished out of the river? What if in the future Elise was sought for his murder because the criminals currently being blamed for every monstrous thing were somehow proved in this instance to be innocent?

Yes, it was possible.

Would Gwydion want the burden of an association with a woman the world might someday proclaim a murderess? For herself Annora doubted his interest could support such a potential responsibility. Didn't he already have a glut of his own problems?

He wanted to bed Elise, without doubt. But no reasonable man would pay too high a price for pleasure he could get elsewhere without complication.

She leaned against the table. No, she ought not tell him the truth.

Gwydion still stood at the window in reverie. But after a moment he said, "Alas, you and I may once again grow uncivil, Annora, for I am now compelled to ask you an impertinent question." He swept the petals into his hand and scrutinized them as if they held the key to an obscure riddle. "Is it possible you've unwittingly encouraged Elise in her terror of love? Do you fear you might be cast aside if she goes off with some man?"

She made an angry, hurried cross on her chest. "May God strike me dead if I've ever done a thing not fully meant to further her happiness."

"What if, for argument's sake, a man could make her happy?"

"I wish that might be possible. But it is not."

He became engrossed in the view out the window. "She's actually told you she finds the idea distasteful?"

Annora took a deep breath. God forgive me for this adjustment in the truth, she thought, but it's for Elise's own good. For Gwydion's too, if he only knew it. But next she thought, And God forgive me if my judgment is at fault. She said, "Yes, she's told me so. That is, she likes you, of course, if I don't presume too much upon your question. But she has told me quite recently that she couldn't bear for any man to touch her."

He lifted his hand and blew into his palm. Daisy petals fluttered out the window. A few were caught by the breeze and whirled away, but most drifted downward.

"She can't be blamed for the way she feels," said Annora, unable to guess anything from his demeanor.

"Of course not."

"You've hardly known her long enough to be too cast down, after all."

"No. And my fancies are notoriously erratic. I suppose your woman's intuition alerted you to that, madam."

She searched his face for sarcasm but found none.

Thomas came elbowing his way in the door with a pitcher of ale in one hand and a loaf of bread under his arm. Vort followed. "They nearly wouldn't sell me any, thanks to that fool doctor. But I charmed my way back into their graces." He set the pitcher on the table and held out the bread. "They even gave me this."

"What do you think, Tom?" said Gwydion, with a cool smile. "Our nurses decree I'll be well enough to travel by tomorrow. Happy news, isn't it?"

If Thomas found the news happy, he hid it well. He looked around the room. "Where's Elise?"

"Collecting herbs," said Gwydion, watching his cousin try unsuccessfully to hide his thoughts.

"These women have done a lot for you," said Thomas, growing a bit agitated.

"Have I denied it?"

"It seems rash to leave so soon."

Gwydion's response was composed, a little weary. "Did you think we'd stay forever?"

As the men spoke their English words, Annora busied herself pouring ale. She suddenly felt fatigued.

"But such endless chores as plucking herbs on my behalf have nearly ended," said Gwydion, breaking into Welsh, inclining his head in Annora's direction. "Tomorrow your selfless care of me will be only a tedious memory."

She looked up. "Tomorrow? What foolishness is this? You should rest a few days more, at least. That old infection had you in its grip too long to be treated lightly."

"It isn't foolishness, madam, but necessity. Life proceeds, and we all have our little tasks to accomplish. We'll leave here in the morning." He moved to the table, took a cup of ale, and switched back to

English to make himself understood by his cousin. "My apologies for my unceasing demands, Thomas, but is my mail prepared?"

Thomas regarded him with some bewilderment. "It glistens like the sun. The smith mended the tear that jackal's dagger made too. But are you well enough to travel? You seem a trifle . . . not yourself. Didn't you tell me just a while ago that your wound was troubling you?"

"Did I? Blame that old demon boredom, Tom, for I feel perfectly sound now." He reached down to stroke Vort's head. "In truth, I feel like I'm already leagues away."

36

A SENSIBLE WOMAN

Thomas went hunting for Elise. He found her in the woods near a patch of wild berries, staring into space.

"Gwydion has just informed me we depart tomorrow morning," he said without preamble. "I came to tell you."

She dropped the strawberry leaves she had collected, for now no unguent would be needed. "Then I must wish you a safe journey and a wonderfully happy life, Tom."

They picked their way through tall grass and wildflowers until regaining the path that led back to the village. The usual afternoon noises of Llanrhychwyn filtered through a thousand leaves and branches.

His face was solemn as he walked at her side. "If you want me to have a happy life, Elise, take me as your protector."

"What?" She stopped walking.

"I intended to wait for the right time to broach the subject, but there's no time left."

"How much ale have you had?"

He turned so he could see her face. "I'm sober and wholly sincere."

She shook her head.

"Come with me, Elise." He reached for her hand. "I don't know what plans you have for the future, but my offer isn't paltry. Live with me in England and you'll have everything you want and more. Bring Annora. I wouldn't expect you to go alone. I'll come back and escort you home after I help my cousin deal with de Breauté."

She pulled her hand away. "I'm afraid you've misjudged me badly."

"You're surprised."

"Surprised? No, I'm stunned."

"When I approached you before, I was drunk, and you probably think I don't remember how stupid I must have sounded. But I was in earnest. I *am* in earnest."

"I don't want to hear any more."

He moved to block the path. "I'm not a boy. I'm twenty-one and know exactly what I want. I want to protect you forever."

"You've known me less than a week."

"But you're wise and kind, and lovely—I know that. I don't need to know anything else."

"You misjudge me," she repeated. "This is just a silly notion brought about by our odd circumstances, and nothing more." She sidestepped him. "We'll speak no more of it."

"You talk as if I were a child." He grabbed her wrist as she passed him. "You won't take me seriously because of Gwydion. Isn't that it?"

She looked down at her arm.

He released her instantly but then tried to take her hand again. He finally desisted when she drew back. "Forgive me, please, Elise. But time is short and I have to make you understand. Gwydion is the best of cousins, the most honorable of men. But his liaisons with women are temporary, always. He—"

"You've arrived at some dismaying conclusions, sir. In respect to your cousin, I've done nothing to make me blush for my behavior. How can you say such things to me?"

"I didn't mean you were lovers." He waved away her words with youthful disregard for prudence. "I only meant I've seen how he looks at you. And how you look at him."

"Then you've been a great deal too busy exercising improper flights of fancy."

"I didn't just imagine his interest. I've seen it directed at other women often enough. But you're not listening to me at all, are you?"

"Say something not calculated to offend, and perhaps I'll listen."

"My only excuse is ardor." He paused as if to reorder his thoughts, then raced on. "Gwydion came back from France when my uncle was killed. But he didn't mourn. He shut himself up in a room at our house for a week and drank wine, but he didn't utter a word of sorrow that I ever heard. It was the same with Cousin Elizabeth. Did he tell you about her murder? He'll accept no word of sympathy for her death either."

"Everyone grieves differently. How can you judge?"

"I'm not judging him harshly. He can't help how he is. But there's more. When he found out the girl he was betrothed to died of the Mortality, he just shrugged. Then he went out and found a whore. He said a whore would be less complicated than a wife anyway."

She clasped her hands together in an effort to curb a sudden ferocious urge to slap his ardent face.

"Isn't that what *you* think about me, that I can be your whore?" she said. Feeling a little sick, she turned and tried to escape down the path. "I don't want to be told any more about these private matters," she called back. "You have no right to tell me."

He came after her. "But don't you see? I admire my cousin with all my heart and would aid him in any endeavor. But he's not capable of loving you as I do, or of loving any woman with his whole heart—if your thoughts take you in that direction. He doesn't *need* anyone. Not like I need you."

"Tom! Enough, for pity's sake."

"You surely understand why I can't offer marriage. Father is an earl and I have to marry from my own ranks. But it will mean nothing, I swear. I'll devote myself to making you happy."

"Leave me alone."

"I have to make you understand."

She kept walking. "Thank you. I'm afraid I do understand."

Llanrhychwyn's first cottages came into view. Hidden from curious eyes by trees that grew where the forest path joined the village path, Elise and Thomas stood side by side without a trace of their former mutual ease. Her face was pale, his flushed.

"Will you at least consider what I've said, Elise?"

"No." Looking into his anxious face, her embarrassment and indignation softened slightly. They were nearly the same age, but he seemed a boy, a boy smitten with his first callow love. He probably didn't intend to hurt or offend her. She continued with more composure. "My parents were endowed with only modest wealth. But my mother was an English lady of good birth, and my father a noble Welshman. Do you imagine they would have been pleased to see their daughter a rich man's mistress, Tom?"

"It's not as dreadful as you make it sound. A well-loved mistress must fare ten times better than a despised wife."

"Yet I will be neither. Honor my words, and let us part as friends."

"Can we at least agree to meet again later? We can discuss this in the future, at some other place, wherever you'd like in Wales or in England. You've only to send word and I'll come. When you've had time to ponder everything, I'm certain you'll say yes."

"I promise you I won't."

His voice grew more agitated. "It doesn't matter if you don't love me now. That will come later."

"In the future, Tom, try to think of me with the respect my refusal may eventually engender. In return I'll endeavor not to think badly of you."

She went on toward Efa's cottage. Thomas stayed where he was, staring after her.

The night passed without any sort of cordiality to mark it as out of the ordinary. When Efa returned from her visit to Trefriw, she was too exhausted to do anything but fall into her borrowed bed. Meanwhile Mistress Lowri went late to the church to annoy Father Sefyl with detailed confessions of past sins.

Thomas and Gwydion readied their belongings and their horses for the morning's departure. As they worked, they conversed in desultory fashion about the forthcoming conflict with de Breauté and his men. Neither spoke of anything of a more personal nature. Each drank one uncelebratory cup of ale.

Vort joined a pair of village pups for an evening's escapade. Eventually he returned, filthy and disreputable, to Efa's cottage. Annora, on the other hand, was in no fit state for a romp. She complained of a persistent headache and went to bed early.

Elise sat in the dark next to Lowri's front window. As night closed in, she watched what she could of Gwydion's and Tom's preparations. She watched them groom their horses, inspect harnesses and gear, and make a joint attempt to improve Vort's appearance by pulling burrs and clods of mud from his fur by torchlight. Neither man said much. Then Gwydion brought out the blankets he had lain beneath during his convalescence, stretched them over a branch, and beat at them with Efa's broom. This domesticity caused Elise to smile as she secretly observed him. Without doubt he was unaccustomed to the chore he undertook. But he soon began to use more force than was needed. If he didn't stop, she thought, the blankets would be cleaned so thoroughly there would be nothing left but shreds. She worried he would harm himself with the zeal of his attack.

He stopped suddenly and went to lean against Efa's wall with his head bowed and a hand held to his side.

Elise wanted to run out and upbraid him for his recklessness. He wasn't sufficiently recovered for the sort of physical punishment he would be encountering, even encouraging. He was unthinking and a fool. But she knew he wouldn't listen.

Thomas gave his cousin an unsympathetic look. "Shall I fetch your nurse?" Elise heard him say. "Maybe she could relieve you." The hostility in his voice took her aback.

Gwydion straightened and returned his kinsman's look. Throwing down the currycomb, Thomas stalked away.

Elise waited and watched.

Tom soon returned. Both men behaved as if nothing untoward had been said. They led their horses to the shed, then returned to Efa's cottage and went inside.

Elise undressed and stretched out on her bed. Though the room was dark, she placed her hands over her eyes.

When Lowri came home, she perched at Elise's side.

Elise sat up. "What's wrong?" she whispered.

"Nothing's wrong. I just wanted to ask you a question."

"Then ask, and let us both retire."

"All right, then. Elise, when you were with your husband, before he died, did you like it? I mean, lying with him."

Reluctantly Elise thought of Maelgwyn. Already it was growing difficult to remember his face, and for that she was grateful. "He wasn't an amiable kind of man, I'm afraid."

"That must have been unpleasant."

"It was. Why do you ask?"

"No reason, really. Father Sefyl says I dwell too much on matters of the flesh, and I suppose he's right."

"Try to think of other things. You could help Efa. She says she has more candle orders than she can manage, and it would be a good way to earn an honest living."

"Oh, I still have plenty of money—from before. But it's a fine idea, Elise. You're a sensible woman." She heaved a sigh. "Would I were half so sensible."

"The sensible thing to do now would be to go to sleep."

"Wait. I wanted to ask you something else, and please don't take offense. But you like that Gwydion, don't you?"

Elise rubbed her temples. Had Annora's headache transferred itself to her? Was she really so disreputable-seeming that everyone in Llanrhychwyn felt free to speculate on her desires? "I like him well enough," she said. "He seems a pleasant man."

"I mean *like*, the other kind of like."

"Father Sefyl is right, Lowri. You dwell too much on foolish things."

"Well, *I* like Gwydion. In the old days I'd have been eager to lure him to my bed."

"Lowri."

"It's the truth. Telling the truth is never a sin. But I'll stop, since I can tell the subject doesn't sit well with you."

"You're right. Now go to bed, please."

For a long time Elise couldn't rest. She was filled with thoughts of farewells, heartaches, everything sad and soon forgotten. Lost faces drifted past her in the dark. She thought of her parents, her brothers, dozens of friends from Anglesey, even the doomed monks at Penmon Priory, who had prayed beside their holy well for mercy that never came.

Then she remembered Gray Hill and its cold, echoing rooms. She thought of Maelgwyn, how he used his last breath to curse her.

Next came a procession of the living—Annora, Efa, Thomas, Sir Nicolas, Dexter, the lipless maid from Dolwyddelan. Gwydion.

Without meaning to, she thought of his mouth. He had pressed her hand against his mouth to drink Saint Michael's water.

He said he ached for her. But Thomas said he needed no one. It was possible, after all, for a man to ache for a woman without truly needing her in the least.

That was another sensible idea—to need no one.

In the future, Elise vowed, she would make herself as invulnerable to need as Gwydion. She'd harden herself until her heart was merely an efficient red stone buried inside her chest. She'd train herself to hope for nothing more than obscurity and peace. And she'd fear nothing—not memory, death, or loneliness.

37

FAREWELLS

Sleep deserted Elise long before dawn, when the usual morning smell of baking bread wafted through Lowri's window. The other three women slumbered on. For a time Elise lay rapt and dreamy, shaping impossible hopes into scenes to believe in. But every image slid away.

She stood before Lowri's copper basin to wash her face and hands, dragged a comb through her hair with harsh efficiency, then donned her clothing. All this she did with preoccupied deliberation. The most presentable of her frocks had been pressed beneath her mattress through the night; it now hung to the floor without too many creases. The dress was of green worsted, with sleeves to the knuckle, and laced with a tan cord from its modest neckline to its waist. To this ensemble she added her silver crucifix and chain, then tied the white kerchief over her disciplined hair.

It was time to say good-bye to Gwydion, to wish him luck, as any diligent caregiver might reasonably be expected to do. If he had not yet quit Efa's cottage, she would wait nearby and keep to the shadows. She didn't wish the burden of making conversation with other early risers.

Silently she stole out Lowri's door.

Perhaps peace had also eluded the man she sought, for he stood near a tall oak tree, readying his great destrier. She saw him adjust the bit and bridle, test the triangular stirrups. The horse tossed its black mane and pawed the ground.

Grand and intimidating, Gwydion wore a gray jupon that ended mid-thigh and gray hosen. Chain mail showed at the collar and cuffs, and at his side his sword hung. His only ornament was a hip-belt of interlocking silver knots.

To Elise he seemed imposing and unfamiliar. His dark eyes told her nothing.

"Good morning," she said as she reached him. She did not look into his face but stroked the horse's sleek flank.

"Elise. I'm glad you're awake. We're leaving soon and I didn't want to go without thanking you."

His distant manner told her he wished to conduct their farewell in the same sensible way she did. Grateful for the lead, she imitated his light tone. "Annora and I are so relieved you've mended well. I fervently hope you won't tax your strength too far or too soon. But if your wounds trouble you, please seek out a physician wherever you may find one." She attempted a joking smile. "Don't be foolish and wait until you're nearly dead with fever."

He returned the smile. "Good advice."

It was again her turn to speak, to say something light and meaningless. But the civil words she had rehearsed in the night suddenly made themselves unavailable. She had meant to offer him luck in his struggle against Sir Nicolas and give the usual hopes for long life and health. She had meant perhaps to shake his hand. But her intentions disappeared.

Their eyes met. She tried to look away but could not.

"Madwoman." His voice had grown less distant.

Taking her hand, he gently uncurled her clinched fingers. She watched him and could not resist. As he pressed her palm to his mouth, a cry escaped her.

He folded her into his arms. Slipping his hand beneath her kerchief, he caressed the soft skin at the back of her neck. His thumb made tiny circles behind her ear. She shivered. A delicious ache made her almost light-headed.

"Forgive me," he said.

Forgive him—for what? "I don't understand."

"For my behavior. Forgive me."

When she pulled away, he made no effort to gather her back into his embrace. She gave a little shake of her head. "There's nothing to forgive."

But his lapse into intensity ended as quickly as it began. "My advances upset you, when you've already had too much to bear from men." He spoke with marked detachment.

What could Annora have told him? Elise couldn't bear to imagine.

But obviously it was for the best, whatever Annora had said, for he struck her now as quite composed. Clearly his heart was not engaged.

Nevertheless he seemed so kind, there in the morning light. How honestly his eyes gazed into hers. She had forgotten her husband's face in only a matter of days, but knew she would never forget Gwydion's.

Her pride bade her deliver parting words that might at least help dispel the misapprehension he seemed to be laboring under—that she was a fragile, damaged thing. She said, "Acquit yourself of upsetting me, sir, for I'm unscathed by our acquaintance. On the contrary, it has been pleasant." She formed her lips into the semblance of a bemused smile. "I've never expected to be treated as if I were made of glass, no matter what Annora may have told you."

He didn't return her smile. "You are generous. So I thank you and wish you the best of good fortune. And Elise, I will always fondly recall our many stimulating talks."

She nodded, then went slowly back to Lowri's. At the door she turned to give him a conciliatory wave—a final touch. But he'd already gone to attend to something else. Her hand fell. Without an audience her empty smile vanished.

It was borne in on her then, as she stood in the silence, that the business of transforming her heart into a stone would be more difficult than she had hoped. The weight of that understanding was hardly a revelation; deep down she had supposed it would be so.

Not long after, the men were ready to leave. Father Sefyl came to bid them farewell. Efa, Lowri, and Annora rose from their beds to add their Godspeeds. Elise hugged Vort while Annora gave him a nugget of cheese as a parting gift. Throughout these proceedings Thomas maintained a stiff dignity, only throwing Elise one scalding look.

Then the two men were gone. The sound of their horses' hooves grew fainter.

Except for the few children who had gathered to watch the departure, life in Llanrhychwyn went on, unaffected.

Then Mistress Lowri made an unexpected announcement. "I'm going back to my old ways," she said, raising her chin. "I decided last night."

The other women turned to stare.

"Back to whoring?" said Efa. "Why?"

"I tried to be good. But praying bores me to distraction and that's the bald-headed truth. Anyway I must not be very clever at it, because people are always telling me to hush. But besides that I miss a man's touch. That's the truth too, proper or not."

"Why not just find some fool to marry?"

"Someday I will. For now, I'll do what I'm best at. I'll just be more careful to stay clear of men like Sir Nicolas and all will be well." She gave her listeners a defiant look. "I'm going inside this instant to haul Princess Joan's bed out again."

It was later discovered Gwydion had left a letter, written in English, atop Efa's table. He'd also left three stacks of coins. One was for Efa, for the use of her cottage. The second was for Father Sefyl, in the event he might see fit to pray for their good fortune. The last was for Elise and Annora, for their nursing efforts. The task of reading the letter naturally fell to Elise, as she was the only one able. Of course Gwydion had been aware that would be the case.

"Thoughtful and proper," said Efa, counting coins. "Generous as well."

Annora took charge of their new money when she saw Elise would not touch it. The letter was another matter. After she read it aloud, Elise secretly tucked it in her bodice.

She took it out later, when she was alone, and reread it several times before burying it among her other belongings. The letter's first lines gave simple instructions for the disposition of the money Gwydion had left. Then came formal words of gratitude, then his bold signature. But a final scribbled line, the only one Elise had not shared, was quite a different thing.

"Madwoman, I wanted so badly to chase the shadows from your eyes."

38

LUCK OR LACK

After Thomas and Gwydion left Llanrhychwyn, Efa confided to Annora that she had finally succumbed to her persistent suitor's entreaties to make him the happiest of men. Before year's end she'd marry Bleddyn, the affluent merchant of Trefriw.

Annora said, "I'm happy for you," and meant it. "You'll have no more need to drag innocent travelers off the path to earn a paltry tariff."

"True, but I may actually miss that little business." She squeezed Annora's hand. "I've met the best people that way."

Annora smiled. "But you'll really have to explain your change of heart. If I recall rightly, you told us you weren't much interested in shelling Bleddyn's peas."

"Wretch." Efa's giggle turned into a snort. "I suppose I just didn't realize right away how partial I am to peas."

The two women stood near the stump where Thomas had sat so often when Gwydion was fevered.

Beset by sisterly feeling, Annora decided to divulge more truth about her own plans than she had so far considered discreet. "I don't remember, Efa, if I told you that Elise and I mean to go on to Rhudd-lan after this."

"As far as Rhuddlan? You never mentioned that. But I had an idea you didn't want to speak about particulars."

"Well, it doesn't matter anyway, because we're not really going anywhere near Rhuddlan. We never were. It was a yarn we agreed to tell if anyone asked, as women alone can't be too careful about un-known characters knowing their course. In truth we're heading to Conwy."

"You're wise to be wary of strangers. I'm only glad you don't con-sider me one anymore."

"How could we, when you've been so kind?"

The widow waved her hand, making light of the gratitude. "Just think, I can come visit you. I mean, if you'll be in Conwy for a bit."

"Oh, yes. We'd like that."

"On market day, of course. We're not welcome otherwise, we Welsh, so I haven't been to Conwy for years. It's still a grossly English town, from what everyone says."

"Aye, I've heard it's still Englishy."

"How will *you* cope, in a town where they call us foreigners?"

In the settlements of conquered Wales, where Edward I had built castles or fortified existing ones late in the thirteenth century, English law still took a harsh line against the Welsh. Official documents called them "foreigners"—in their own country. The colonists who came from England to inhabit the Welsh castle towns were disinclined to have resentful natives too near them or too involved in the new lives they were forging.

So how would Annora cope in an Englishy place like Conwy? She shrugged. "I'll let Elise manage our public dealings. No one will know she's only half English unless she tells them, which she won't. Her accent is perfect. Whatever happens, I'll just stand by like a witless dearie and keep my mouth shut tight."

"I don't envy you. You'll have to stay mute whenever any Saesneg is nearby."

"True, but Conwy is the best place for us to find work, Efa. We'll trade in herbal ointments, medicines, and the like, if there's sufficient demand."

"You won't lack customers, I've a feeling."

"With the sum Gwydion left and another . . . bequest I recently had, it shouldn't be long before we can buy a snug cottage and settle down with no more worry."

Efa wondered why Annora's face grew flushed when she mentioned her recent bequest, but she didn't voice her curiosity for fear of being thought too prying. Knowing Annora could turn closemouthed in the blink of an eye, she only said, "That would be a relief. You took on Gwydion's healing out of good-heartedness, and look what good came of it—a windfall of money. You surely deserve it, for I was certain he'd die."

"Elise thinks Saint Michael's elixir saved him."

"Maybe so. But tell me, where will you find your snug cottage?"

"Perhaps Anglesey. We're not decided yet."

"You really think Elise will never remarry?"

"Who can guess the future? I doubt it, truly."

"Poor thing. But you know, you might come across your patient at Conwy. How will Elise feel about that? It was sad to watch her pretend not to care when he rode off today."

"She could never have had him, so don't waste the grief."

"You suppose he requested to be had?"

"She didn't say so, but he may have. Though not in any honorable way, I fear. She isn't well connected or rich enough to tempt such a lordly fellow to offer any honorable tie."

Efa raised her eyebrows. "You think he cares for the world's opinion? I did suppose at first he might be overproud, but now I'm inclined to doubt it. Either way, with a little effort she might have turned his fancy to the better side of honor. Why did she just let him go?"

"She had to, that's why." Annora scowled at the stump. "I told you about her dead husband, how he beat her and used her in foul ways. So for now she doesn't want another man, on either side of honor. Maybe she never will. Besides, a woman can survive perfectly well without a man to weigh her down like a millstone. I've done it."

"She didn't look at Gwydion like she figured him for a millstone. She—"

"For mercy's sake, Efa, desist."

The widow gazed searchingly at her friend. "This blather of Elise and Gwydion makes your tongue uncommon sharp. Why is that, I wonder."

"Because . . . because it conjures memories of her days with her husband. You don't know how many times I heard her crying in the night. Besides, Gwydion has problems of his own. I'd hardly consider him the best solution to any female's plight."

This exchange truly did make Annora uncomfortable; Efa discerned that rightly. It added to her burgeoning guilt, her suspicion she may have been wrong not to confide Elise's real history to Gwydion. She began to wonder also if she had taken too much on herself by telling him Elise couldn't bear to be touched by any man. Acting with the best possible motives, had she done them both a miserable disservice?

Because Efa still eyed her astutely, Annora nearly barked at her friend. But good sense and fondness for the widow kept her from outright rudeness. She merely said, albeit tetchily, "Why are you staring? What's so fascinating?"

"You. You're squirming like a dry eel, but I'm not sure I understand why."

"We leave tomorrow to set up house in Conwy, a Saesneg town where I won't know a soul. Wouldn't you be uneasy?"

Neither woman noticed Lowri approaching from behind.

"You're going to Conwy?" she said loudly, causing them both to jump.

"Great God," said Efa, whirling around, "has no one ever told you not to sneak up on decent people?" She took in the younger woman's costume. "And what nasty thing are you wearing? I swear, I can nearly see parts of you I've got no interest at all in seeing. Where's your black dress?"

"I gave it to the fuller's widow, poor thing." Having been hidden beneath sober dark cloth for several days, Lowri's bosom was once again on partial display. "I told you I was bored with praying and parables. Didn't you believe me? But you haven't answered, Annora. Will you really be living in Conwy?"

Annora looked to Efa for aid but received none. "Yes," she finally snapped, "we're going to Conwy. But that's a tale I don't want bandied about. Do you hear?"

Lowri raised her hands in joking defense. "I hear. But why are you so angry?"

Annora smoothed her apron. "I'm not angry. But Elise and I never like strangers to know our business." Even as she uttered these words, she realized they must sound odd.

"I'm not a stranger," said Lowri.

"Of course you're not." Annora knew she was floundering; she tried another tack. "But you see, there are people from our past, people we wouldn't want in our future."

Now Lowri and Efa *both* regarded her with keen interest.

Annora twisted her newly smoothed apron between her hands. "You can appreciate not wanting the wrong sorts of people in your life. As a woman of experience, you can sympathize."

A look of comprehension spread across Mistress Lowri's face. "By the Blessed Trinity. Annora, you used to be a prostitute. Why didn't you tell me before?"

"What?"

"You weren't? Then Elise was."

"Don't be an idiot."

Lowri wasn't offended. "But when you say you don't want the wrong sorts of people in your lives, you must mean men. Women aren't as worrisome as men usually, are they? So you must mean bad men, like Sir Nicolas. Or jilted lovers."

Annora sighed. "Not exactly, but something like that."

Lowri nodded knowingly. "Men," she said. "A few can be beasts, as I well know. But most are lambs. There's always the Devil's own luck or lack in games of the heart."

"So you won't mention Conwy is our destination, if anyone should ask?"

"I've already forgotten we spoke of it."

After Lowri strolled back to her house, Efa said, "My silly neighbor poses an interesting question, friend."

Annora felt her headache from the previous night crowd back into her skull. "What do you mean?"

"I mean, who are you? Who is Elise? What are you running from?"

Annora squared her shoulders. "I can only give you my word we are honest women. That ought to be enough for anyone who claims to be my friend."

Efa rushed forward and hugged her. They were much of a height and much of a plumpness. "Of course it's enough. It's more than enough for me."

That evening Elise and Annora ventured to Mistress Lowri's house to recompense her for her hospitality during their stay. But she would accept no coin.

"We're friends," she said, wiping away a tear as she stood in her doorway. "I hope we'll always be friends." After a low, cajoling voice caused her to glance over her shoulder into her house, she turned back to the women and spoke more hurriedly. "But one of my favorite clients showed up out of the blue just a while ago, and it's been a loveless month for the boy. So Godspeed and come visit anytime—during the day." The door closed.

Annora and Elise went on to the church to offer prayers for their journey and for the future. Father Sefyl handed each a rosary made of cored, whittled dice. "During the Pestilence," he told them, "one of my flock collected all the dice 'round about here. He had been to London, you see, and heard tales that claimed gaming displeased God so much He sent the Great Death."

"Was it true, Father?" said Annora. "Could it have been a thing as frivolous as gambling that provoked the Maker to dispatch so fierce a chastisement?"

"Surely many things forced His hand, daughter. But this whittling of dice was a desperate rage in London. So my parishioner chose to imitate it, hoping he might help in some way. I've a casket full of rosaries to attest to his optimism."

Annora raised the new rosary to her forehead; her skull pounded more painfully than ever. "I'm afraid his efforts were futile," she said. "So many souls still perished."

Father Sefyl smiled but with a hint of reproof about his mouth. "We shouldn't presume to opine at the Lord's doings. He reckons every effort into the brilliance of His judgment."

As they said farewell and left the church, Annora was astonished to feel her headache abruptly desert her. Did Jehovah perform this tiny miracle by means of her new rosary, to confound her doubt? Yes or no, she chose to interpret it as a favorable omen.

Going back down the ridge toward the widow's cottage, she had a private question to pose to Elise; such things were easier to remember now that her head didn't ache. Her query echoed a notion put forth earlier by Efa. "How will you cope if we cross paths with Gwydion in Conwy?" she asked. "That manor Sir Nicolas purloined sits outside Conwy's walls. Gwydion is sure to be in the neighborhood, for it's his manor now or ought to be. He'll want it back."

Elise was slow to reply. She minded her steps as they approached the bottom of the ridge. Overhead, twilight's earliest stars appeared.

"Well, child? What do you say? Gwydion is much like you. He can prattle readily in English and come and go as he pleases in Conwy without worry. He must have spent at least a portion of his early years in these parts and probably knows scores of people. One of the women here in Llanrhychwyn even told me his father was an important man in Conwy, though he was fully Welsh. Did you know?" She pursed her lips. "I suppose you did."

"His father was the justiciar of North Wales."

"Then he *was* important."

"He answered to no one but the King of England. In North Wales every lesser man, the sheriff and the constables and their underlings, had to go to him for vital judgments."

"If he was so powerful, why has that Sir Nicolas been allowed to murder him and steal his manor?"

"You said it yourself, Annora: Gwydion's father was Welsh. English rivals at Conwy don't seem bothered by his murder. They may have been secretly glad."

"You learned that from Gwydion? Or was it Thomas?"

"Gwydion."

"I'd say he was very confiding, then."

"He wasn't. Not really."

The older woman heard censure in Elise's voice and drew her to a halt so they could continue to speak without being overheard. Efa's candlelit window shone just ahead.

"You say he didn't confide in you, child. But it sounds to me as if he did."

"He only told me of his father's murder. And his sister's."

"His sister?" The great shock on Annora's face was evident in the modest light.

"And her husband, on their way from Cornwall to Conwy. They were the ones found near Dolwyddelan."

"Sweet Mary."

"Gwydion believes de Breauté thought they might become inconvenient, so killed them too. Or had them killed."

"And you're just now bothering to mention it?"

"He told me on the night you and Efa drank the giant woman's ale. The next morning you were so sick it slipped my mind. Since then days have flown."

Annora cringed, recalling the day after Nela's ale. "Never mind that. But it still sounds like he was remarkably frank, considering his usual way. Yet you say he didn't confide."

Elise's voice was void of emotion. "He was forthcoming about some things. Of course he didn't tell me about his betrothed."

"Ah. Why would you want to be told about such a personal thing?" Annora asked. But she knew why.

Elise ignored her question. "He didn't tell me that when she died, he went straight out to find a whore. He told Thomas whores are less bother than decent women."

"It's interesting you should choose that particular bit of information to dwell on." Then Annora searched her mind, for she too had been told this tale of the dead betrothed. But what she knew didn't quite jibe with what she'd just heard. "Thomas offered you such an unsavory story? I wonder why."

Elise wished she hadn't spoken. "He was trying to sound worldly, I suppose."

"You think so? I'll wager he forgot to mention that Gwydion never laid eyes on the woman he was pledged to marry."

Elise strained to see Annora's face but said nothing.

"Such arrangements are commonplace as you well know. You never beheld Maelgwyn before you married him, did you? Anyway, I had *my* information from Gwydion, in case you wondered. We were chatting one day, our one and only confidential chat. But it sheds new light on Tom's tale, doesn't it?"

Elise let the dice rosary run through her fingers and coil into her other palm. "I suppose it could."

"Excess grief would have been surprising, in truth, although I'll admit some consolation other than a whore's bed might have been more seemly. But Thomas had a game of his own to put forward by telling you only part of the tale."

"Surely not. Thomas isn't so selfish," said Elise. Her words lacked conviction.

"Was he painting his cousin in unflattering colors to further his own suit?"

"No."

"You were never a good liar." Annora's eyes suddenly widened. "Did that young rooster offer you a position as his handy-woman? Don't be ashamed to tell me."

Elise's silence gave the answer.

This disconcerted Annora into a silence of her own. Eventually she said, "Mistress to the son of an English earl. The summit of some women's ambitions. He must be fairly keen then, poor Thomas. No wonder he felt need to make his cousin out to be less than the hero you imagine."

"Tom is only a boy, Annora."

"He isn't. He's a grown man, though clearly a man in need of tempering. You refused him, I take it."

"Oh, no, for Thomas offered to let you chaperone me if I agreed. I thought it would be the perfect solution to our problems."

Annora made a noise like a riled hen as they finally proceeded toward Efa's. "Very funny, child. But he still didn't need to blacken Gwydion's character, smitten or no."

"I'm surprised you wax so indignant on Gwydion's behalf."

Annora knew it was a guilty conscience that made her indignant, but she couldn't admit that to Elise. She said, "It's unjust, that's all."

"Thomas didn't mean to lie, I'm sure. It's only that he didn't tell all of the truth."

Nearing the widow's cheery window, Annora was better able to see Elise's face. "I declare, you seem pleased," she said. "Is it because you thought Gwydion was a heartless scoundrel before, but now you think it may not be so?"

"If I seem pleased, it's only because it doesn't matter to me if he's heartless or not."

"No?"

"Of course not. Why should it?" The tone of Elise's voice altered. "But let's go inside now and celebrate our last night in Llanrhychwyn. Maybe Efa still has some oak beer."

Annora shrugged and did her best to match Elise's mood. "A fine notion. Oak beer would be a treat."

"And you know, I think I'd like to get a cat and a dog and some rabbits when we finally settle into a real home."

The girl had refused an offer to be Thomas's mistress, she claimed to have no feelings for Gwydion, and now she wanted a menagerie. What next? "Fine. Get ten of each and fifty pet nightingales, child. I'm only pleased you're so optimistic."

"I always complicate things or imagine things, don't I? Meanwhile you're so patient and sensible. But I understand better now. Maelgwyn was my only real problem, and now he's gone forever."

They entered the cottage.

Efa came toward them, with a pitcher. "Dear friends," she said, "stop that whispering and join me. Sip some oak beer to thank the Maker for the kindnesses He's shown us all."

"Oak beer? You never told us you could read minds, Efa," said Elise, bending to kiss the wrinkled cheek of the bride-to-be. "I'll take a cup, with the greatest pleasure imaginable."

39

TREATS ON A STRING

The next morning Annora and Elise said their good-byes to Efa. She charged them to visit Bleddyn in Trefriw, to meet the good and handsome man she would soon marry. "And be warned," she told them, "you'll find I'm on your doorstep in Conwy before you even have a chance to miss me."

"Before you marry?" said Annora.

Efa blushed, as Annora had hoped. "Well, soon after. On a market day."

With their staffs and sacks, Elise and Annora departed Llanrhychwyn. Along with clothes, sundry items, and a bladder of oak beer, each sack held a loaf of bread, a baked onion hollowed out and filled with mustard, bundled in waxed cloth, and chestnuts from Gloucester. The nuts were a parting gift from Efa, who had naturally obtained them from Bleddyn.

Deep in her sack Elise tucked an item she wouldn't have wished to discuss—the letter Gwydion left at Efa's.

Annora still refused to allow Elise to carry their coins, although there were more now since Gwydion had left such a stack. She said, "I told you it's not likely anyone will look between my legs, so that's where these bags will dangle. Don't pester me anymore about it."

The downhill path from Llanrhychwyn to Trefriw was forested and rough. By this route the adulterous Princess Joan had come and gone to worship on days her royal schedule had brought her to these environs over a hundred years earlier. But Joan had apparently wearied of toiling up from Trefriw—from Gardd-y-Neuadd, one of several retreats her husband claimed in North Wales—to Llanrhychwyn's church on the ridge. So in 1230 the doting but at least once deceived Llewelyn ordered a more convenient chapel built in Trefriw. Dedicated to the Virgin, the chapel still yet enjoyed use by the townsfolk.

"Will we stop to visit Bleddyn, as Efa said we ought?" asked Elise as they navigated a steep part of the path. "I'd love to meet the man who causes her to color at the mention of his name."

Anchoring herself first to one tree trunk, then another, Annora zigzagged down the hill. "Hush," she said. "I can't spare breath from this damnable path."

They were both glad the weather was dry, elsewise the ground would have been even more treacherous. So many people had trekked between Llanrhychwyn and Trefriw over so many years that the path was no longer at ground level in most places. Worn and furrowed, it had become a hollow-way, a scooped-out passage below the surface of the land it traversed. Walking there was like walking on the slanted bottom of an earthen bowl.

Eventually they reached a more level spot where Annora could catch her breath and brush cobwebs and twigs from her tawny cloak. "No wonder the princess wanted a church nearer Trefriw," she said. "Imagine having to go back and forth on this path. It must be a treat in rain or snow."

"Efa comes this way to visit Bleddyn."

"The dumb muscles of love."

"Cynic," said Elise. "Don't you want to meet him?"

"If he's at home. And I'm not a cynic. I'm probably just jealous because *my* love muscles are so withered."

Little by little the path became less steep. Cottages came in sight, then the church built for a princess. There was a mill by a gurgling stream. In the distance the Conwy River flowed, marked by the trees that grew on its banks. Just as Efa had described, there stood Bleddyn's stone house, banked with red flowers. At a reasonable distance from its front door was a pond, with a circle of pigs lounging in it.

The women approached.

"Hello," Annora called through the open door. "We come to pay respects to Bleddyn the merchant."

No one replied.

Elise sniffed the air wafting outward through the door. "What *is* that?"

"Spiced fruit? Whatever it is, it's lovely."

A white-haired man came hurrying toward them from the interior of the house. He possessed remarkably large ears, and golden powder dusted his blue shirt and his chin. "Ladies," he said, looking guile-

lessly from one visitor to the other, "you're those dear friends of my
Efa, the ones who saved the life of the man felled by outlaws. Efa
promised you'd call. I'm Bleddyn, you know."

At his cordial bidding they entered his home. It was large and untidy, with sacks in every corner and stacks of goods between. Against a
wall three fat brown puppies slept atop a bed of folded marbrinus—
silk woven to resemble marble. Brass goblets spilled out of a rough
bag next to the silk. On the floor beside the goblets sat a crate, its lid
pried open to reveal silver cloak fasteners fashioned like figure eights,
the sign of eternal love. There were two sets of oars leaning against a
wall, a brass bell as big as a crouching dwarf, baskets of pears, three as-
trolabes, a battlefield banner depicting a floating thumb beside a
phoenix on an azure field, a lute, and peacock feathers.

All these items they beheld, but there were many others—too
many to take in at once.

"Heavens," said Annora.

The merchant chuckled. "Efa threatens to put me to rights."

By then the smell the women had encountered at the threshold
had been replaced by an odor less savory.

Elise turned toward the rear of the house and her eyes widened.
"Are you cooking, sir? Smoke drifts this way, I fear."

"Shark dung," he cried, and sped away.

"Shark dung?" said Elise. "People roast such things?"

"Let's go find out," said Annora, following their host.

Bleddyn's home consisted of the goods-stuffed room in front and
another large area in back, to which the women now hastened. Above
these rooms was the space where Bleddyn had his sleeping chamber.

In the rear downstairs area was a hearth built into a wall. Here
wreaths of smoke were beginning to dissipate. As they entered the
room, his guests beheld Bleddyn standing hearthside examining
something as long as he was tall, and the mere width of two fingers.
The thing draped between his hands. Whatever it was, it was thoroughly charred.

"Not your midday meal, I hope," said Elise, coming to his side.
"Surely not shark dung either."

"Shark dung?" He looked puzzled, then smiled sheepishly. "Oh,
that's just an expression I use, my dear. I was roasting dainties to take
to Efa's tomorrow." At her name he blushed as brightly as his future

wife did when she uttered his. Even his ears went red. "I should tend my tasks better."

"Let us help," said Annora. She rid herself of staff, sack, and cloak. "What exactly were you roasting?"

"Dates, almonds, and figs."

"Ah. Treats on a string. At least we're not in Lent."

Dates, almonds, and figs were imported from warmer lands. So in demand would they be—to sweeten menus in place from Ash Wednesday until Easter, to alleviate the monotony of no meat, chicken, eggs, or butter, but only fish and more fish—their prices would quadruple in Lent.

Bleddyn tossed the burnt string into a bucket. His ears had returned to a normal hue. "Don't worry. I've sufficient ingredients," he said, pointing to a table. On its surface sat three heaps—almonds, dates, and figs. "A friend brought in a shipload of luxury stuffs to Caernarfon a fortnight ago, and the price was too good to pass by. Actually I sold the lion's portion of almonds to the Brothers at Maenan Abbey. They're so fond of almond milk, they use it in nearly everything."

"Lucky fellows," said Annora. Never before had she seen so many foreign fruits and nuts in one place, excepting the market in Beaumaris.

The women set about helping Bleddyn with his chore of love. He was a cheery host who told droll tales of his travels. He also plied them as they worked with slices of square, snow-white bread usually enjoyed by the very wealthy. He told them he often bought a loaf from a baker near the village of Tal-y-bont, downriver. Such bread was made of the same smoothly ground wheat as Eucharist wafers.

Between bites, Elise used a needle to string Bleddyn's delicacies on a woolen thread. Then she wound the thread around a spit and readied it to set over the hearth. Meanwhile Annora studied the spices her host had at hand. She marveled at his chaotic shelves, crowded with things most cooks only dreamed of. He even boasted wooden boxes jammed with pomegranate seeds, galingale, dried lemon peel, and grains of Paradise.

Finally, with a horn-bowled spoon whose handle was topped by a golden mouse, she set about beating eggs, milk, cloves, saffron, and bits of ginger.

Elise laughed when she glanced over at her friend. Annora's cheeks bore traces of the yellow powder that decorated Bleddyn. It was dust of saffron, made from dried crocus stamens.

"For sweetening," said Bleddyn, handing Annora a grainy cone the size of a baby's shoe.

Her eyes went wide. "Sugar? I haven't seen any since before the Mortality, and not often then."

He seemed pleased by her reaction. "I'm acquainted with a Venetian who ships it here from Cyprus."

Annora turned the cone in her hands, pondering how best to use it.

He offered her a blunt knife. "Hold it over the bowl and run the blade down the side. Grains will fall."

She did just as he told her until a coating of sugar grains sat atop the batter. Then the little gold mouse went 'round and 'round as she stirred. Soon Annora drizzled the sweetened concoction spoonful by spoonful over the string of dainties, as Bleddyn turned the spit. Heat from the fire thickened and cooked the confection until it grew golden and crispy. The house once more enjoyed a delicious scent.

Cooking chore completed, the women tried to say farewell. But he begged them to stay, offering tempting fare. "You see, I never know when business guests might arrive," he said, producing from a larder several things already prepared. "So a local couple keeps me in provisions." He brought forth pots of braised carrots with Portuguese bay leaves, white beans and bacon, custard colored with violets, and hippocras—red wine steeped in spices, just waiting to be heated. "All this might otherwise go wasted, dear ladies. Grant me the pleasure of your company. Efa would wish it, you know."

Elise and Annora resisted, feebly. They told him they carried mustard-stuffed onions in their sacks. Bleddyn only nodded and warmed hippocras as they talked. Then he readied plates.

It was the purple custard, Annora said, that finally persuaded her. So the table was cleared, and all three sat down to an early supper.

By the time they finished, the sun hung low in the western sky. It was too late to journey on as they'd planned. As it would have been improper for Bleddyn to invite women guests to stay the night at his house, he escorted them to his cousin's cottage, nearby.

An old lady with familiar oversized ears greeted them with a sour glare. "Who might these fancy pieces be?" she asked.

Bleddyn's ears naturally went crimson. "Cousin," he said, "where are your manners?"

"A stick for manners. Why do you all stink of wine, eh? And where are their menfolk?"

"Fate constrains us to undertake a journey," said Annora, too annoyed to keep politely still. "Or should we stay in one place until we rot, just because we are women?"

The crone pursed her thin lips. "Decent females would."

Elise watched Bleddyn slip something into his cousin's wizened paw.

Instantly the woman's demeanor reversed. "What was I thinking?" she said. "My kinsman's friends are welcome as springtime in my home. Come in, come to the fire." She held the door wide. "Evenings aren't half so warm now as at the summer solstice, are they? Michaelmas will be here before we know it."

"For your information, madam, we've had only a modest drop of hippocras," said Annora, still vexed.

When her ruffled feathers were finally smoothed, she and Elise entered the crone's cottage and settled in for the evening. Bleddyn hurried back to his house.

After her bribe the cousin was a sufficiently affable hostess. She showed off her collection of rings set with gemstones and colored glass. Rings were her passion, she told them, and she hoped God would not judge her too harshly when she arrived in Heaven. "I can't help it," she said, wiggling gnarled fingers, "if I was born with pretty hands."

The guests slept by the fire on a bed of straw, using their cloaks as cover. Both fell asleep quickly, and the hippocras bestowed dreamless rest. But Annora awoke to a chilly sunrise with a kink in her back and stiffness in her limbs.

"I'm too old to sleep on the ground like a nesting grouse," she said, as she pulled on her shoes. She groaned when she stood. "In Conwy we'll get feather beds."

Their hostess was too engrossed brewing ale to offer more for breakfast than old baked eggs, but Elise and Annora ate all they were given.

Then Bleddyn came to escort them to the edge of the village. "Efa and I will be sure to visit you in Conwy, my dears," he said.

"After you're husband and wife, you mean," said Annora, waiting for his ears to go red.

She didn't wait long. "Yes, after that," he replied.

He handed each woman a gift. Annora's was the spoon topped with the golden mouse, for he'd noticed it amused her. Elise accepted a small book filled with pictures of such grotesque creatures as griffins and Harpies. "From Cologne," he told her. "Drawn by a noble Beguine."

Then he waved them on their way.

40

THE EVIL EYE

Maelgwyn rested in the bed he once shared with Elise. A day and night he lay, after he killed the shepherd. The murder did not trouble him. Considered rationally, it was Elise's fault. If she hadn't stolen the cache, the shepherd wouldn't have gone berserk and needed to be killed. Besides, the shepherd was vile. He believed in three-breasted angels, fairies, and more—blasphemous things. Now Maelgwyn nursed his hurts and considered his choices. He was still master of a fine house, but he had no riches. Without riches how could he survive?

Perhaps he could sell an item or two. But the notion didn't please him. His last horse had been stolen by a servant long ago. Could he bear to wander afield acting as his own pack animal, dragging coverlets, tapestries, or brass candlesticks?

Well, there was no other choice. He'd be forced to go on foot to the closest village, Ysbyty Ifan, and hope for the best. But when formerly he'd ventured to that benighted hamlet, the villagers were loath to speak. Their mouths clamped shut as soon as he appeared. Even hospice priests were unfriendly. He knew why. They considered him evil and believed his foulness could infect them most easily by way of an incautiously open mouth. The fools. It was this sort of idiocy that had often compelled him to send a servant, when he still had one, to transact business in the village.

Maelgwyn's mother had also been locally disliked. The foolish peasants resented their family's higher standing in the world, she told him. Take no heed, she advised.

As a child he had occasionally suffered doubts about the worth of their high standing. What good was superiority if no one else acknowledged it? He remembered when his father died, when Maelgwyn was five years old; although they were rich, Mother and her fatherless son had few admirers. The only people who ever visited Gray Hill, after

Father's death, were Mother's male friends, and the tutor, and one rouged, sloe-eyed woman who claimed ties to local gentry. Could these wine-swilling characters possibly conform to anyone's idea of superiority? As a solitary, precocious child, Maelgwyn wondered.

Before slinking secretly away nearly two years ago, his last remaining servant had maliciously informed him that the villagers at Ysbyty Ifan believed he possessed the evil eye. They had believed it of his mother before him too. That's why they spit three times whenever Maelgwyn's gaze fell their way—one time each for Father, Son, and Holy Ghost. That's why they hid their babies and cows, and why men shielded their genitals. Those with the evil eye were well known to be ruinously envious by nature, envious of beauty or goodness. Their malevolent glance could simply *drain*—drain milk, health, or manly vigor. Vulnerable things had to be hidden from sight.

Maelgwyn understood that this nonsense was actually a pathetic reversal of the villagers' envy. Victim became villain in the self-serving court of doltish public opinion. But how outrageous that the villagers despised *him*, not Elise. That sneering servant had said they pitied her, though they'd rarely beheld the bitch. The idiots pitied *her*.

But wasn't it often the righteous who suffered, while the corrupt throve?

His reflections, however, accomplished nothing.

And there were things that had to be done. He had to secure his home against trespass during his impending absence and choose a belonging or two to take to the village to sell. After that he needed to buy food. It was a shame he'd been too overwrought to think of butchering one of the shepherd's fat ewes. Then he would have had meat *and* made a sacrifice to God, as Abraham had done. But it was too late to bemoan this lack of foresight. He must endure his ordeals, like Job before him.

Things were certainly less than perfect.

It would have been pleasant to denounce Elise publicly in Ysbyty Ifan for her thievery and his attempted murder. But that was hardly feasible. She'd only lie to the constables when they caught her. After all she was an accomplished liar, just like his mother had been. And how would he explain his survival without mention of the shepherd? That might lead to other questions. If the fool's dead body came ashore somewhere—as his own live body had—things might get thorny. Who would understand?

So he would track down the murderous whore himself and pronounce sentence on her, wherever she might be. But first he would slit her servant's throat, in leisurely fashion, while Elise cried for him to stop. Elise was fond of the hag, he knew, so he would not stop.

After that it would be his dear wife's turn.

Another vital detail: he'd have to find out what happened to his cache. Elise could not be allowed to die until she told.

Resolved on this plan, Maelgwyn got up from his bed. Smiling, he folded the fox coverlet and set the chair neatly against a wall. As he did, he caught sight of his face roughly reflected on a remaining glass pane. His nose looked swollen. He touched it and winced. Thank God, he'd always been one who healed quickly. Already the reopened wound on his groin had begun to mend.

With sudden apprehension, he pulled back the neck of his tunic and studied the scar on his throat. The shepherd had said it looked like a pink caterpillar. But it did not. It was pink, and red at one side where he'd torn it afresh, but it wasn't comical or dreadful. The glass was not a perfect mirror, but it worked well enough to tell him that much. The shepherd had only been tormenting him, as had been his way.

Maelgwyn felt relief. He admitted to himself how unhappy it would have made him to be regarded by strangers as defective in any way.

"Lord," he said, hands palm to palm at his chest, "once more You show me compassion."

There were mundane household matters to be seen to in preparation for his eventual homecoming and return to normalcy. Firewood had to be collected and stored. The beetroot cross on his door wanted thorough scrubbing. To deter potential robbers, the old padlocks and keys for the doors would have to be located.

There were also things to be disposed of under a pile of rocks far behind the house. He found an empty grain sack and stuffed it with the torn shift, false Pestilence cloths, rushes and rags sodden with blood, and bits of broken glass from his window. He had used the rags to wipe off the roasting skewer and to sop up the mess the shepherd had made on his floor. What a lot of gore the old heathen had spilled.

His money box he replaced under the floor plank. One day soon he would fill it again.

Maelgwyn's day continued in this manner. Before supper he lit the central hearth and one candle. As sunlight waned, he went to the buttery and found a loaf of moldy bread and a wrinkled apple. These he ate willingly enough, as they were no more unappealing than the food the shepherd had dispensed. However, the ale in his best brass ewer had gone far too sour to drink, and there was no more to be found. Boiled water from the river had to suffice. He hoped it would not pain his gut, as it sometimes did. Since two goat bladders and a leather beaker were missing, he assumed Elise had pilfered the greater part of his ale when she fled. Other things had vanished—cutlery, two yew staffs. Thus the list of grievances against his wife lengthened.

Night fell. Near the fire he dropped to his knees to pray. He asked for courage while hunting his bride. "For I will be like Moses on the mountain for forty days, or Elijah traveling forty days before reaching the cave where he beheld his visions. O Father, dare I compare myself even to the Son, who wandered forty days in the desert among wild beasts with only angels to minister to him? If Satan tempts me, as he did Christ, snatch me from his wiles, I pray."

Later, as he again lay content in his bed, the fickle river sang him a soothing lullaby. An owl hooted. Out on the Migneint Moor, wolves howled.

41

Wallowing in Carnality

Llys Garanhir had been a handsome, orderly house. Under the regime of Sir Nicolas, however, its grandeur sadly and rapidly diminished. Twenty-two mercenaries camped in its great hall with their ragtag assortment of easy women, fornicating openly whenever their needs overcame them. Mice raced across the banquet table, cats stalked the mice, and a quartet of bloodhounds padded the halls searching for their master, Gruffydd ap Anarawd. But the search was always in vain, for Gruffydd was dead. There would be no corpse to discover either; Sir Nicolas had burned it on a shoddy bier far out in the woods.

In spite of their restless pacing and occasional baying, Nicolas grew fond of the bloodhounds. He even chose to overlook that there were four—four, that number he usually considered disastrously unlucky. The fact was he found the creatures' soulful eyes nigh irresistible. But the dogs' wariness frustrated his attempts to win their affection.

"Why will my hounds not come when I call?" he asked Dexter one dank afternoon.

Dexter finished a roast chicken leg and threw the bone toward the manor's door. He wiped his mouth with the bottom hem of his tunic, thereby exposing a portion of pale, concave torso. "Willful animals, bloodhounds," he said. "Could be they know it was us stuck a sword in their poxy master's windpipe, even if they didn't see it happen."

"How long will they bear a grudge?"

Dexter scratched his armpit. "Kill 'em, and get new ones."

Nicolas lunged forward and grabbed Dexter by the ear. "I like these particular dogs, you hapless afterbirth. I don't want another set."

Dexter squirmed away.

A squat, swarthy mercenary leaned against a wall a few feet off, watching and snickering.

"Are you well entertained, Walter?" Dexter called angrily to him. "Think you'll carry on laughing when I stick my foot halfway up your backside?"

"No, probably not then," said Walter, ambling away.

"I mislike that Walter," Dexter snarled.

"He's no favorite of mine either," said Sir Nicolas, fondling his crucifix. His annoyance with his longtime servant had vanished as quickly as it came. "He's neither use nor ornament."

"Let me kill him, sir."

"You're so intent on murder today. Well, I've no objection. One less mouth to feed. But do it out of doors, for the manor grows too squalid."

Dexter skulked away.

The bloodhounds just then loped past Sir Nicolas. They ran in tandem. Their tongues lolled out as they went, and their eyes searched everywhere. Nicolas watched, shaking his head.

That evening one less man came to the crowded table, but he was not much missed.

When he finished his meal, Sir Nicolas stood. "Friends," he said, "did you enjoy the furmenty? The venison? What of the pears, ladies? I know how ladies esteem baked pears."

There was a murmur of approval.

"Be sure to thank Cook," said Nicolas. "Now, we need to talk about practical things, and the first is money. Gentlemen, this evening you will each receive your promised usual portion."

Cup banging greeted this news.

Sir Nicolas acknowledged the approval with an inclination of his head. "Yes, you're welcome. But the second practical thing is duty. Some of you, I fear, spend too much time wallowing in carnality. Mind you, carnality is not to be sniffed at. But men ought to do other things than just moving their rumps up and down, oughtn't they?"

As this was apparently perceived as a rhetorical question, it garnered no reply.

Nicolas continued. "Now I'll tell you a thing you'll find unpleasant. You men, all of you, if you don't make more effort to guard this house and Conwy's gates more diligently, day and night, I'll see to it you don't live to celebrate the Yuletide this year."

The room went suddenly quiet.

The nobleman asked, "Is my threat idle, Dexter?"

Looking up from his plate with his mouth still full, Dexter shook his head.

"I appreciate your capture of the gentleman with the warrant," Nicolas went on. "However, your abdication of duty more recently may have allowed other undesirables into Conwy. That grieves me."

A man stood. "We caught a pair of fellows last week, your lordship," he said.

His employer nodded. "I beheld their remains. Unfortunately neither was anyone whose life or death meant anything to me. Neither carried a warrant. Both were unremarkable fellows."

The man sat down.

Nicolas stepped away from his chair. He walked to the hearth and held his hands toward the flames. "I'm not just being tedious. You see, I've heard rumors a troublesome enemy of mine could be lurking nearby." He pointed to a grinning man with a red mustache. "You."

The big man's grin disappeared as he scrambled up. "Sir?"

"You were in that whorehouse village with us. Do you know the man I mean?"

"Aye. Dexter stuck him with his dagger when we left, sir."

Nicolas swung his astonished gaze to Dexter. "You stabbed him after—after I warned you he was the rooks' prey?"

Dexter squirmed. "I barely touched him. Just a jab."

His master regarded him searchingly. Then his face relaxed. "Maybe I should have let you kill him, now I've had time to reconsider. But I was concerned about the rooks."

The man with the red mustache sat back down as inconspicuously as he could.

Sir Nicolas paid him no mind. "But now I've heard my enemy has apparently escaped being eaten by rooks, gentlemen. He's a tall, ill-mannered Welshman—hence my instructions about such characters—whose father once lived in this house. Have I mentioned that?"

Half the men nodded, the other half looked confused. The women stared down at the table.

Sir Nicolas told them more. "It's possible this person, Gwydion son of Griffith son of a pig-faced slut—no slur intended, ladies—may be in Conwy gathering men to his side to seize my new home."

"Bastards," said Dexter, pushing his plate away.

"Bastards indeed, Dex. But you know, I intend to keep my house and the chestfuls of money I found inside it. It was promised to me and I've earned it." He scrutinized the company. "Is that unreasonable?"

"No, my lord, it surely isn't," said Dexter. Then he pounded his fist on the table.

Others did the same, with less fervor.

"Good," said Nicolas. "You'll all be on guard for the Welshman, and for other wretches who might carry a warrant for my arrest. By the way, the Welshman is left-handed, a sure sign of devilish collusion." He suddenly leaned to one side to grab at a woman's half-exposed bosom. She let out a yelp. "Shush, sweetheart," he said. "I've been admiring your nipples. So earthy. Would you like to sleep in my bed tonight?"

"If you please, your worship," she said, looking appalled.

"I promise you'll be pleased."

She did not appear reassured.

Nicolas then picked up a carving knife from the table and used its tip to clean his fingernails. The silence in the room suggested a collectively held breath.

When he finished, he made as if to toss the knife back down. Instead he whipped it across the table. It pierced an inattentive fellow's sleeve, pinning his hairy wrist to the back of his neighbor's chair.

An oath escaped the target. But when he saw who threw the knife, he gave a chuckle and nodded too heartily, as if he'd been expecting a flying blade to miss his flesh by a hair.

"Next time heed me better, fool," said Sir Nicolas. "Now, there's one other thing. In the morning a pair of the most well-spoken of you will accompany me for the short ride into Conwy to learn if there's further word of the foe I just mentioned."

"I'll go," said Dexter.

"You will not, for your beguiling face would not engender affection in Conwy's townsfolk. Stay here to supervise a cleanup. My friend who has visions may be arriving any day, you know. And just look about: the place is a sty."

"You *truly* think she'll show up here?" said Dexter, not hiding his bile.

"Of course. She swore she'd come, and a woman like that doesn't break promises. Besides, we have a deep understanding, my lovely friend and I."

"She only said she'd come to humor you, my lord, so we'd go away. She's no soothsayer either. I swear, she's a fraud."

Sir Nicolas's face took on a threatening cast. "Fasten your jealous mouth. Do you really presume to suppose your judgment is superior to mine?"

Dexter was the first to look away. "No, sir."

"I was certain you did not."

Nicolas stayed among his servitors a while longer, doling out pay from a great chest that had belonged to Gwydion's father. Coins chinked. Spirits rose. When the last man had his portion, the nobleman crooked his finger at his chosen bed companion. She came hesitantly forward.

"It's late and yet early, darling," he said, leaning toward her. But when he kissed her hand, he grimaced, then jerked her close to sniff at her neck. "Have you bathed since Easter, my dear? Or since the Feast of the Purification?"

"I had a proper bath at Christmas, sir," she whispered. "Soaped my hair twice too."

He hesitated, then shrugged. "Well, never mind. I always keep a barrel of water in my chambers."

The woman gazed at him as if he were a snake charmer and she a helpless asp, as with unctuous ceremony he led her toward the staircase.

42

BATCHES OF GOSSIP

Thomas and Gwydion arrived in Conwy without mishap and with little cordial conversation. But after a few days passed, Thomas's mood improved. Gradually he stopped treating his kinsman with the icy formality that tested Gwydion's unreliable patience twice as much as it diverted him. Neither man spoke of Elise.

They rented a house with a stable, between the church and the market square, and created false, bland names for themselves. Anonymity, they agreed, would be sensible while they tried to discover if de Breauté's tentacles had reached into Conwy.

A single message had come to them from the constable in Caernarfon, the man Dexter slammed into a tree trunk. Delivered by an elderly Welsh fishmonger on market day, the missive warned that de Breauté might be watching Conwy's gates for anyone he considered a threat. The constable wrote further that the dangerous English nobleman resided at Llys Garanhir unhindered by Conwy's authorities. A score or so louts dwelt with him, but few ventured into town. The constable had garnered his news from rural rumor that always found a way to his Welsh ear. But the fact de Breauté remained a free man was no accident. A warrant had been sent from Caernarfon a fortnight earlier naming him as Gruffydd ap Anarawd's killer, but it had never reached Conwy's bailiff. As was customary, the messenger who carried the warrant had worn the arms of the king emblazoned on his tabard. Like the warrant, the messenger had vanished. Ominously, two other men had recently disappeared as they went about their unrelated business near Conwy. The constable speculated that Nicolas was simply waylaying anyone who looked at all as if he might be carrying news that he preferred not be delivered.

Nicolas de Breauté, the constable concluded, was shaping up to be an increasingly worrying character. The constable was not disposed to send another warrant yet, to put another messenger at risk. He might try again to use the elderly fishmonger—who was actually his wife's uncle—but first he'd have to let him rest a while back in Caernarfon. Old Uncle traveled slowly, by donkey, but there was no other suitable man to send instead.

Gwydion doubted that his own sworn word as the murder victim's son would be sufficient to induce the English bailiff to arrest an English noble. He was essentially a stranger in Conwy, having been away for years. The current mayor had been a friend of his father's, it was true. Unfortunately Gwydion had not seen him since his boyhood. He knew he bore some resemblance to his father, as sons do; Gruffydd had also been tall and dark. But it was unlikely the resemblance was enough to be called utterly convincing. Even if it had been, a warrant would still be necessary to arrest a nobleman for a crime like murder. Nicolas was not a peasant who had stolen a neighbor's hen. He was a member of a prominent family, albeit an infamous member.

Gwydion had first learned that his father was dead from the letter his sister sent him in Paris, a letter he had received a few days after being freed from La Cerda's keep. As he read it, a cold, logical portion of his brain took control. Simple enough to bring the malefactors to justice, he at first believed.

But when he actually arrived in London with a notion of confronting the effete noble Elizabeth reported had hired de Breauté as paid assassin, logic fell away.

Surprised in his velvet-hung apartments, the noble was clearly vexed by the arrival of an uninvited caller; he'd been occupied with a delectable but difficult female. He reached for his sword when Gwydion told him his name; the Englishman made no attempt to pretend the name was unfamiliar. "This is odd," the man said, as his hand hovered above his sword's hilt. "I'd heard you were, let us say, permanently abroad. But how fortunate you are to be back in England."

Then he must have reconsidered any idea of appearing overtly belligerent, for he let his hand drop to his side. Recovering his insouciance, he gave a perfunctory apology and even feigned sympathy for the death of Gwydion's father. He crossed the room as he spoke and sauntered behind a stout table. With that length of protection from his caller, he proceeded to place the blame squarely on "that madman de Breauté" for the whole affair. It had never been his intention, he averred, for Gruffydd to be killed. Merely he'd hoped to persuade him to take a well-deserved rest from patriotic duty.

The self-exoneration continued. Finally, perhaps convinced by Gwydion's composed demeanor that he intended no violence, the Englishman grew bolder. He suggested to his impassive guest that his deceased sire would not have wanted more blood to be spilled. "After all, harming me would accomplish nothing, if that was why you came," the man said. "My appointment as justiciar of North Wales is virtually assured now, you must realize, and it's too late to undo that. Things are going forward, as things do." Then he misread Gwydion's intentions so badly as to offer him an embossed leather pouch filled with coins to assuage his "unfortunate loss."

Gwydion ignored the pouch. "You ordered my father harmed so you could take his place as justiciar. Tell me, am I right in thinking that was your sole reason?"

As a hint of rage had now become evident in Gwydion's voice, the Englishman decided to be much more forthcoming. "Not—not quite. Someone threatened *my* family, you see. So I'm really not at fault."

"Someone?"

"A man I met in Paris when I acted as a negotiator for King Edward."

"Charles of La Cerda."

"You know him. Of course you do. So you know only a fool would say him nay. When he sent me a letter making his demands, what else could I do?"

"He told you to order the killing of an innocent man."

"Perhaps. But it wasn't my fault. It's true I coveted your father's position, but I wouldn't have harmed him to attain it. Then that fiend Charles said he had a score to settle with you. He said you didn't treat him with proper respect. Well, these damnable Castilians. But he told me you were safely out of the way in Paris, forever. He told me if I didn't do his bidding, he'd have my sons taken—"

"You followed his orders like a dog."

"Could I do anything else? He made such threats, you can't imagine."

"You could have informed the king."

"Which king? Who would have cared about my little problems?

And if I *had* told, I would have paid the price later in some even more horrible way."

"By God. At least it would have been honorable."

That made the nobleman laugh, a bit hysterically, until Gwydion told him to unsheathe his sword.

"You're serious? You can't be serious. What of my wife and sons?"

"What of my father?"

The fight was brief, punctuated only with frenzied curses from the Englishman. At the end he pleaded for mercy and received none. But he was able to keep his pouch of coins, temporarily, for Gwydion spilled them across his dead face.

One other person chanced to witness this confrontation—a disheveled girl not yet in her teens. She stepped from the shadows, gazed at the blood soaking into the carpet, then spit on the corpse. Gwydion merely raised a brow and wiped his sword on his foe's velvet curtains. As he turned to go, a last look showed him the girl harvesting coins from the dead man's face.

Now, in Conwy, Gwydion sent letters to Caernarfon asking for another warrant for de Breauté's arrest. But he also sent word to certain of his acquaintances, fighting men he hoped to enlist to help defeat Nicolas in case no warrant arrived. His messenger was a laconic soldier, a friend from the French wars. This fellow, Jack, rode a swift horse and had a singular way, Gwydion knew, of avoiding detection by ill-wishers.

Gwydion still hoped Nicolas would soon dangle in Conwy's sea breeze. Death had come too easily to the man in London, he believed, and he wanted the end to be more excruciating for Sir Nicolas. But if a hanging proved unworkable, any method of execution would suffice.

On those occasions when he could bring himself to think of his sister, and her death on the Trackway, his resolve hardened. Grief and bitterness choked him. No one had witnessed the murders, with the likely exception of Nicolas's stooge, but Elizabeth and her husband would be avenged.

A decent couple was hired to cook for Thomas and Gwydion in Conwy and see to their mundane needs. There was no reason for this couple to suppose their new masters were not the respectable English gentlemen they seemed. If either wondered why Gwydion dispatched letters some mornings by a taciturn messenger, why he paced in the yard between the house and the stable, or why he stared bleakly into the fire, their conjectures remained unspoken. They were far from stupid and weren't paid to pry.

Keeping to themselves, Thomas and Gwydion nevertheless made a conscientious effort to return any greetings they received from the friendly, inquisitive people on their crowded Conwy street. This stab at cordiality came quite effortlessly to Thomas.

For their part the neighbors supposed the new arrivals were prosperous knights freshly returned from the French wars and in need of recuperation. The dark, quiet man stayed indoors and had an interesting pallor, as if recovering from an injury. Both apparently had unnamed but noble relatives in Conwy, but it would have been rude to ask for details. This was what Thomas gently implied to the neighbors, and his manner was so cordial and credible, no one thought to doubt him or be offended.

Thomas was a stranger to Conwy. Gwydion had naturally been there many times before, although a decade had gone by since his last visit. And he was much changed. Except for his height, few townsfolk would think to connect him with the impetuous, laughing son of the Welshman Gruffydd ap Anarawd, the justiciar of North Wales, now deceased.

Others within Conwy's walls might sometimes speak with communal pride and nostalgia of that young man's mother, the elegant and independent Philipa of Born, an Englishwoman gone peacefully to her reward a year or two earlier. But talk of the young man's father was newer and more shocking. The recent death of Gruffydd ap Anarawd hadn't been from natural causes, it was rumored. In fact it had been murder of a most alarming sort.

Violence was an everyday consideration for those who traveled or lived outside the protection of Conwy's limewashed walls. Not even Gruffydd's high place had exempted him from that violence. Welsh thieves had killed him and his retainers, burned the bodies, then stolen everything worth having from Llys Garanhir, his house. They *must* have been Welsh wrongdoers, for Englishmen could not behave so viciously; on this point Conwy's townsfolk were in righteous agreement. Besides, no one could deny that the Welsh lands outside Conwy's walls were wild and ungovernable.

Of course the culprits had escaped. Likely they had connivance from one of Gruffydd's servants or from the barbarous natives who lived in the valley beyond Conwy.

During his lifetime, Gruffydd's situation had been unique. He was Welsh, related on the distaff side to the house of Ednyfed Fychan, a general who long ago served Llewelyn Fawr, husband of the unfaithful Princess Joan. Ednyfed's coat of arms bore three bloody, anonymous English heads, in remembrance of his removal of them in battle. Despite his aggressive ancestor, Gruffydd's reputation for acuity and fairness earned him his appointment as justiciar of North Wales over all other candidates, English candidates at that. For twenty years he served as the king's administrator, wielding considerable power.

Welshmen were prohibited by law from living in the town of Conwy. But Gruffydd's noble wife had been English, and his own position exalted. An exception would have been made for him with alacrity if he had asked to make his home inside Conwy. But he had not asked. He preferred to reside in his ancestral manor, a short distance from town. His family had lived in the manor since before Edward I conquered Wales. So he chose to make the daily trip into Conwy, when his work did not compel him to ride to Caernarfon or elsewhere in the region. In Conwy he heard grievances and flattery, gave counsel, and oversaw everything that might affect the king's peace. In a handsome timber and stone building at the western side of the castle he toiled behind a desk laden with books, writs, letters enumerating debts, and so forth.

Days and nights must have provided decided contrast to each other, for Gruffydd. Days were filled with Conwy's noise and commotion, while nights were spent in pastoral tranquility at his manor—until his violent end.

Conwy folk privy to rumors of his death considered it strange his Welsh murderers had made no allowance for Gruffydd's Welshness. But then, murderers aren't known for nicety of feeling. Or perhaps the killers reasoned he deserved his fate for having dealt too closely with the English. It was well known that Gruffydd had once even been invited to meet the king himself and his oldest son, in London. That son, Edward of Woodstock, fought against the French in 1346 at Caen and Crécy, though only sixteen. He became Prince of Wales a year later. Although the prince was too busy living a warrior's life in France to set foot in the wayward realm his great-grandfather had conquered, he earnestly made it his business to keep abreast of events in faraway Wales.

While there had been Englishmen jealous of Gruffydd's authority as justiciar, he had been on friendly terms for years with Thomas Upton, Conwy's mayor, the only man in the region who could rival him in power. Gruffydd had also been respected by most other English folk over whom he'd had jurisdiction. As for the Welsh who lived outside the English-colonized towns of Conwy, Caernarfon, Criccieth, Beaumaris, Harlech, and Bala, they admired their prominent countryman and took pride in his lofty reputation.

But now he was gone. Gossip said his manor had been sold off— with indecent speed—by an unsentimental daughter who lived far away in Cornwall. The new owner was an English nobleman from somewhere near London. This man was described as eccentric but genial, with a wish to live in the tranquility of the countryside. Few had yet encountered him in person, this Sir Nicolas de Breauté. But ambitious Conwy citizens with maiden daughters were eager to entertain him, as he was reportedly unmarried and handsome.

But how could Llys Garanhir have been sold to a stranger by Gruffydd and Philipa's rapacious daughter? By rights didn't the manor belong to their long-absent son?

No, for corpses can't inherit. Gwydion, the only son, had been killed in France. Alas. Father and son, both dead. A shame, really. The young man of memory was gone—so ran the rest of the tale told on Conwy's streets. Gwydion must have been a fine fellow, people said, since he died defending the English crown. Half-Welsh he may have been, but he knew his duty to his mother's homeland, a country that had made his father even wealthier than when he was born.

No one in Conwy could say where all this interesting information originated, but it had been repeated often enough to attain the ring of accepted truth by the time Thomas and Gwydion arrived.

If anyone *had* bothered to ask where the rumors about Gruffydd and his family came from, no clear answer would have emerged. The rumors had the same obscurity of origin as those concerning Llys Garanhir's new owner, Sir Nicolas de Breauté.

The truth was sordid and predictable: both batches of gossip had been brewed by Sir Nicolas. He enjoyed finding an outlet for his latent creativity, he'd told Dexter. Someday he might even be tempted to pen a few lines of poetry, if ever he found a spare moment.

Through his tailored gossip Nicolas hoped to paint himself as an innocent victim in any future contest with the man whose father he'd murdered. But he hoped, before that, to convince Conwy's citizens that Gwydion was dead and that any fellow who showed up calling himself by that name was a vile opportunist.

Sir Nicolas considered his methods remarkably clever. On two consecutive Fridays he dispatched to Conwy a pair of the more intelligent prostitutes enjoying Llys Garanhir's hospitality. His instructions were simple and not unpleasant. He told the women to go to taverns, inns, also the marketplace, as Friday was the designated day of the town's bustling market. Be friendly and confiding to everyone, he directed. Be forthcoming to town officials or soldiers. Whisper stories in their ears.

The females were happy to obey. They enjoyed the pleasant walk to Conwy, away from the ceaseless lecherous demands of their current paramours. Friday's market was lively too, with tempting goods on display. There were beads, silks from across the sea, scented oils, and crystallized bits of ginger. Strong ale flowed in the taverns. Best of all, the ladies had an unprecedented supply of coins to squander, for Nicolas made their mission well worthwhile.

What did it matter to the women what fairy tales Sir Nicolas chose to have them spread, as long as he paid generously? They learned his tales by rote, knew nothing of the people involved, and cared even less. Their gossip was surely just as Sir Nicolas assured them—an amusing bit of theater. It was the sort of pointless mummery their peculiar host found entertaining. What harm could playacting do?

In taverns and shops Thomas soon heard the results of the women's diligence. A week after their arrival in Conwy, he brought the news to his kinsman. Gwydion had rarely left the house until that time, choosing to pace in their garden or drink ale at a table near a window.

"Cousin, you'll be surprised to hear that you're dead," Thomas informed him. The servants had gone to bed, and Vort dozed by the hearth.

Looking up from his ale, Gwydion frowned. "I'm what?"

"Everyone in Conwy thinks you're dead."

"Do they?" Gwydion kept his eyes on his cousin's face. "Then tell me all of it."

"They say—"

"Who does?"

"Half of Conwy. I visited two taverns tonight, then a dice game by the quay. To be sure, I ingratiated myself with some ancients sitting on barrels by the mill. All tell the same tale."

"That Gwydion ap Gruffydd is dead."

"You died fighting in France. And Gwyd, you'll hate the rest of it."

"Go on."

"All right." Thomas sat down beside him. "Welsh villains killed your father and escaped. Then your uncaring sister, who supposedly lives like a queen somewhere in England, sold Llys Garanhir for a pretty profit to the innocent, eligible Sir Nicolas."

Gwydion bent to stroke Vort. The dog rolled to his back.

Thomas grew impatient. "Cousin, some reaction might be considered natural. You're dead, your sister is heartless, *Welshmen* murdered your father, and all the well-born girls in Conwy want to be Lady de Breauté. Make some comment."

Gwydion settled back in his chair. "More than ever, Tom, I don't believe the constable's missing messenger is still among the living." He finished his ale and poured more.

"Yes, that's a reasonable assumption. And?"

"*Cwrw Conwy gorau pei bellaf.*"

Thomas glared at him. "English, if you please."

"A local adage. 'The ale of Conwy, the farther the better.' Wretched stuff it is too." He took another swallow. "This town is famous for wretched ale."

"Then why bother to drink it?"

"Good question." Gwydion stood. He went to the door and pulled it open. "Why indeed." Onto the nighttime street, with its irregular paving stones and tamped dirt, he poured all the ale remaining in the pitcher.

Thomas folded his arms across his chest. "You're in a strange mood tonight."

Gwydion came back and sat down. "Not so strange."

"So now make another interesting comment. Something pertinent would be nice."

"Well, Tom, I also believe Nicolas de Breauté is partly mad. But not a fool."

"No, not a fool. He's unleashed a whole pack of plausible lies on Conwy somehow."

"Grease a lackey's palm and send him into town to spread tales. Simple enough. Gossip, the Devil's delight."

"What do you mean to do about it?"

Gwydion rose once more. He walked across the room, then walked back, ducking to avoid low beams. "I mean to see him dead. Nothing has really changed." His voice was unemotional. "But we may not get any help from Conwy's bailiff, because another messenger with a warrant could easily be intercepted. That's been demonstrated. So we'll have to go to Llys Garanhir and mete out the punishment ourselves."

"The pair of us?"

"I told you I've sent for some friends as a precaution. Mercenaries and soldiers on leave. I'm hoping they'll arrive in a week or so. If they all come, we'll be fourteen."

"The constable's letter said de Breauté has at least twenty. Hardly good odds."

By the firelight Gwydion read apprehension on his cousin's young face. "Don't worry, Tom. My friends enjoy a fight."

Thomas stood. "I'm not worried. Given the choice, I'd naturally prefer to live a while longer, but I'm happy enough for a battle. But are *you* well enough to fight?"

"I'm well enough."

"I know you've sent off messages with that surly crony of yours, the fellow with the wild-eyed courser."

Gwydion smiled. "The horse is definitely wild-eyed, but Jack isn't surly. He's merely frugal with words."

"If you say so. But if the constable's man didn't make it past de Breauté's lookouts, and it's fairly obvious he did not, why should your friend go on being so lucky?"

"What they lack in finesse, Jack and his horse make up for in shrewdness and speed. Nicolas will never even see him."

43

LINGERING NEED

After this discussion the men retired.

Alone in his room Thomas thought of his life back in England. Home seemed far away. He wondered how his parents and his stolid older brothers and their wives had been occupying themselves since he rode off with Gwydion. Did his three doting sisters miss him? Had late summer been golden and sweet? It would soon be harvest time on the estate. There would be singing, cider drinking, and dimpled milk-maids to show gratifying appreciation for the compliments they received.

He yawned and pulled the blanket to his chin. Nights on the Welsh coast could be damnably chilly, he was learning.

He remembered how eagerly he'd volunteered to help Gwydion find his father's murderer. He had barely given his half-Welsh cousin a choice in the matter when Gwydion had arrived in Ipswich, looking haggard, with news of Gruffydd's death. The idea of a quest for justice had been compelling to Tom. It would be a great adventure, he thought.

He had heard of Gwydion's exploits and daring from the time he was a boy. There were rumors his fluency in French made him a valuable spy for England and that his Welsh made him useful in dealing with the English army's obstreperous longbowmen. Marvelous enough, such talk. But Thomas also saw how the ladies simpered and sighed on those rare occasions when his dashing cousin visited Ipswich. How Tom had yearned to be thought valiant and mysterious, to have women cast inviting looks his way.

But the reality of a quest for justice was proving less exhilarating and more worrisome than he'd anticipated. It wasn't that he feared the fighting. As an earl's son he had been trained from boyhood to fight. But Gwydion had nearly died at Llanrhychwyn. His blood spilled as readily as any man's; Thomas had seen it with his own eyes. Yes, anyone could fall, anyone could die. There'd been no magic or glory in Llanrhychwyn's mud, as far as he could tell.

How would things transpire at Llys Garanhir? With the odds against them, any unthinkable thing might happen. At twenty-one Thomas naturally considered himself much too young to die—or be crippled. He had a dread of being crippled.

Another matter weighed on his mind: he'd made a fool of himself over Elise. Worse, he'd behaved like a knave. He knew that now. She offered him no encouragement, yet he made indecent advances. He gushed to her about love. In his darkened room in the house at Conwy, Thomas felt his face grow hot with the memory. His only excuse, a feeble one, was that he wanted her to find him strong and compelling, as women seemed to find his cousin.

When she rejected him, he reacted by insulting her. Then he tried to blame Gwydion for her rebuff. He saw the two were drawn to each other but had no reason to assume they were lovers. Yet he implied as much to both. It didn't comfort him to imagine how foolish that accusation must have sounded, as indeed it must have. Surely lovers would not have parted from each other as coolly as Gwydion and Elise did in Llanrhychwyn.

Someday he hoped to apologize to Elise. Maybe even to his cousin.

Things might not be turning out as he had anticipated, but he couldn't abandon Gwydion now. That was out of the question. But secretly Tom almost wished he hadn't come to Wales. When he returned to Ipswich, he wouldn't leave again anytime soon. Adventure had its place, but he'd had enough to last for years. He agreed his cousin was honor-bound to avenge his father's and Elizabeth's deaths. But what then? Would Gwydion return to France to face more peril, perhaps die alone on foreign ground? Or would he land in some hellish French prison?

If he were Gwydion, Thomas was sure, he'd want nothing but peace. And a warm bed with a loving wife snug in it. But he was not Gwydion. In the past weeks he had learned his cousin was as admirable as he had always supposed him, and right-hearted. But he could also be distant, unapproachable. Maybe his years in France, his wounds, and his grief all caused him to be guarded. If so, who could blame him?

But Thomas knew now that he wouldn't have traded places with him for all the emeralds in the East. He didn't envy him his complex and apparently solitary soul. He didn't envy him at all.

On that thought he fell asleep.

Meanwhile Gwydion, across the hall, found his own hindrances to rest. His mind and body were restless, each alternating between cool and hot.

Outside, the wind changed direction and buffeted the eaves. He thought of his mother. Then he thought of his father and sister. It made him wild with anger to even imagine de Breauté uttering their names, telling his lies about them.

He remembered a long-ago evening when he and Elizabeth played chess while their parents talked softly by the fire. That night the hall at Llys Garanhir smelled somewhat of wet dogs—Father's well-loved assortment, which had spent that afternoon frolicking in a light rain—and it smelled of quinces and apples the cook had simmered all day for preserves.

But his memories turned darker when they stretched too far past childhood. He thought of meetings he had witnessed between jaded courtiers, princes, warriors. He recalled battles he'd fought in, and the stench of dead men and dead horses.

Gwydion thought of his recent captivity in Paris and his host there. He knew they would one day have a reckoning. For the first time in weeks he examined memories from his Parisian imprisonment and let himself grieve for the singer of French ballads. Never once had he caught a glimpse of her, but her voice cheered him. Why had she been thrown into the Castilian's dungeons? Oh, yes—for giving comfort to the enemy. Still she sang. She sang until despair drove her to take her own life.

Gwydion's fever had raged throughout the day the guard told him she was dead. He had suffered hallucinations. Fireflies danced on his eyelashes, and before his startled eyes his hands became fish, then wicked moths. The walls heaved with tapestries only he could see, tapestries portraying pig-faced men who mounted weeping angels. As his horror grew, the moths flew away from his hands. But when he saw they carried his dismembered fingers, he screamed. Roused from a nap, Yves, the crueler guard, had come to the cell and thrown filthy water in his face.

But all that was in the past.

Now, beyond Conwy's wall, a nightjar gave its churring cry.

Weariness bore down on Gwydion, but he couldn't rest. He put his hand to his side. His wounds still ached. His thoughts went to Elise—her slender, gentle fingers, the way she stood straight and forlorn at Efa's window when she thought no one observed her. He remembered their long conversations and her gray eyes, so fathomless and true. How he had wanted to hold her, to lift the burdens he sensed in her.

There was more he wanted. He remembered her unbound hair, and that instant of trust and surrender in her eyes.

His lingering need disturbed him, but he struggled to put her from his mind. She had been damaged by life, by a cruel man, and would never come willingly to his embrace. Besides, how likely was it that they'd meet again?

No matter. The world was full of women.

Still . . . what would it be like to live in honest contentment with a warm and devoted partner, as his parents had done? Would he ever know?

His thoughts stayed fixed on Elise and refused to be diverted—the way she trembled against him, and the sweet scent of her hair. He remembered the shape of her mouth.

Impatient with himself, he tried to imagine some other woman, the obliging, sophisticated sort he usually pursued. But the thought of any woman but Elise held not the least allure.

Again the nightjar cried. The night seemed cold and endless.

44

PEARLS

Some mornings Vort wandered to the Conwy River, to Porth Isaf, the Lower Gate. He made friends with the royal guards who manned the gate, one of three built into the town's all-encompassing stone wall. The men gave him bread crusts and allowed him to come and go through the gate, to the quay, as often as he pleased.

At quayside sat a wattle and gorse hut where mussels were brought in from the mouth of the river. Here Vort was welcomed by the Welsh folk who labored with the shellfish.

An iron pot of water hung over a fire in the hut, and heaps of mussels were dropped in to boil. When the shells opened, the slimy bits were picked out and put into a tub of cool water. Fishermen's barefoot children jumped up and down in the tub until everything grew mushy and murky. Animal matter floated up and was used as food for ducks. Sediment sank to the bottom. The sediment was collected, dried on cloths, then placed on a tray. Finally, pearls—if fortune smiled—were separated from the sand and pebbles on the tray by a pretty young woman with a goose feather. The pearls were smaller than a pea but beautiful. Blue or gray, sometimes purple, they were placed gently in bags and taken to Chester or Liverpool to be sold.

Vort sniffed the hut's fishy air as mussels danced in the boiling water. He capered when the children splashed in the tub. Then he watched silently when the woman plied her feather. His good manners earned him bits of herring, and hugs from the children.

One day, the day after Gwydion threw his ale into the street, the woman with the feather tied a green cloth around Vort's neck, kissed his nose, and called him handsome.

When he returned home, Thomas removed the cloth to examine it. "What have you been up to, Vort? I wonder."

The next morning Tom followed the dog through the Lower Gate, then to the hut by the water. Tom was restless, with an excess of time on his hands as he awaited the arrival of Gwydion's military friends. Sometimes, in spite of himself, he dwelt on Elise's rejection of his amorous overtures. A voice in the back of his mind reproached him for his foolishness and pride, but he ignored it. After all, she had rejected the son of an earl.

It also galled him to suppose sometimes that Gwydion had merely snapped his practiced fingers to inveigle her. *Had* she been his lover? Had their coolness at parting only been a ruse? An opportunity for intimacy had existed for them several times in Llanrhychwyn, surely. Perhaps she was a wanton. Even so, why hadn't she seen how callous his cousin was where women were concerned? He remembered how indifferent Gwydion had seemed when speaking of his fiancée's death. And what about the many other ladies he was said to have bedded?

But other times Tom's conscience smote him. He was at fault, not Elise. He'd behaved badly. He had indulged in unkind thoughts against her, and against Gwydion, out of simple pique.

Nevertheless he promised himself the next time he gave his heart away, it would be to someone mindful of his worth—if ever again he could bring himself to give his heart away.

But at the quayside hut the remnants of his rancor fled. He, like Vort, found the pearl fishery intriguing. He found the young woman with the feather even more so. That she spoke no English and he little Welsh perturbed him not at all. Any language uttered by her pink lips would have been acceptable to Tom.

"*You're* like a pearl," he told her when no one else stood near. "That's what I'll call you."

She smiled, understanding not a word. She was willing to be told anything by the handsome young man. Her parents always said to be wary of blandishments from Englishmen, but she chose to disobey them in this instance. After all, this Englishman had such a sweet smile, such gallant manners.

The two communicated sufficiently to arrange a tryst that evening on a treed hillside beyond Conwy's walls. At that tryst all went enormously well. Each learned a bit of the other's tongue, and more than that, and resolved to meet again whenever they could.

Their rapport helped Thomas forget Elise as if she'd never been. If the organ he offered Pearl was not precisely his heart, it still afforded them both satisfaction. Each dusk he met Pearl beneath the trees, then returned home with a dreamy grin on his face and leaves clinging to his clothes.

Gwydion couldn't help but notice and was glad. He envied Tom his changeability.

45

INTERCOURSE WITH THE DEVIL

At Ysbyty Ifan Maelgwyn was pointedly shunned, as he had supposed he would be. Panicky hags scurried into their thatched cottages. A striped cat hissed at him, then leaped over a mossy stone wall. Children were scooped into their parents' arms and carried from sight. Hunching their shoulders, men and women turned away up and down the lane. The miller slammed his door. One young fellow held a pot in front of his private parts as he strode off.

In front of the famous hospice run by the Knights of Saint John, two old monks in black frocks and cowls watched as Maelgwyn approached. One monk was gaunt, the other more so. When Maelgwyn returned their stare, both made the sign of the cross.

"Where in Ysbyty Ifan do you decant the milk of human kindness, brothers?" Maelgwyn called from the edge of the pebbled lane, disguising vexation under a veil of humility. "All I've been offered so far is vinegar and vitriol. Am I not a neighbor?"

The less thin monk replied in a reedy voice, " 'Even as Sodom and Gomorrah and the cities about them in like manner, giving themselves over to fornication, and going after strange flesh, are set forth for an example, suffering the vengeance of eternal fire.' "

Maelgwyn sucked in his breath. What did they know of his life? He hadn't been near this sorry excuse for a village for most of a year. It was more than a righteous man should have to bear. But he reminded himself again that God tests hardest those He loves best. So he managed a forgiving smile. "The Epistle of Jude? Ah, glee for my ears."

The second monk spit.

Maelgwyn decided to beat them at their own sanctimonious game. "You are partial to Jude? You know this verse? 'But these speak evil of those things which they know not: but what they know naturally, as brute beasts, in those things they corrupt themselves.' "

The second priest raised a stick-thin arm. " 'Raging waves of the sea, foaming out their own shame; wandering stars, to whom is re-served the blackness of darkness forever.'"

Maelgwyn sighed. But he knew it would be remiss of him not to remind these allegedly upright men of the danger of their malice. He said, " 'Thou hypocrite, first cast out the beam out of thine own eye; and then shalt thou see clearly to cast out the mote out of thy brother's eye.' Words uttered by our Lord, and I pray they ring in your ears."

" 'Even so every good tree bringeth forth good fruit; but a corrupt tree bringeth forth evil fruit,'" the thinner monk shot back.

The first monk spoke again, but not in verse. "Enough! You are unwelcome here, Maelgwyn ap Peredur. Your father was a good man, too soon gone by unholy means. *You* are the well-loved son of a whore. The milk of human kindness would curdle on your tongue, if your eyes did not pollute it first."

The scar on Maelgwyn's throat throbbed. He could kill the monks with two blows from his fist, one each on the temple. He could.

Of course he did not smite them. He knew he'd be apprehended if he did. So he repeated the Commandments, silently, in his seething mind.

He carried a staff and a sack of things he expected to find useful during his hunt for Elise. He also carried an antique footed basin made of silver. Its shallow bowl bore the intaglio likeness of a wild sunflower, called an elecampane, surrounded by a rim of polished hematite. Concealed in the basin's foot was a hollow space secured by a little hooked door. Inside, a scroll of brittle vellum rested.

Some long-dead hand had penned on the vellum these cramped instructions, in archaic Welsh: "Visit the woods on Thursday dusk. Stick a knife in the flower known as elecampane. Say a litany. Leave the knife and go. Next when night and day divide, offer good inten-tions to God with prayer. Return to the flower. Say a litany. Dig up the plant while the knife is still in it. Lay plant and knife under a church altar. When the sun is full up, remove the knife, wash the flower, shed its petals into a bowl of wine mixed with lichen. Boil the wine thrice, once each with sheep milk, cow milk, goat milk. Pour holy water in it now, three thimbles. Sing GLORIA IN EXCELSIS DEO. Make four crosses on the quarters of the wine bowl with a sword's tip. Say a litany. Drink. All will be well."

Beneath these words their author gave names to the evils the guidelines were meant to dispel: "Against elfkind and nightgoers and those who have intercourse with the Devil."

The bowl escaped being stolen by Elise, Maelgwyn was sure, because she had not known of its existence. He kept it hidden in a secret place atop a rafter in the barn. But he did not keep the bowl from affection, although it had been a gift from his father to his mother, and then from his mother to him.

When he was twelve, Mother told him why Father first gave her the bowl. "It was to protect me from myself, darling," she said. "What a fool your father was."

Then, and now, the basin, and most especially the vellum, made Maelgwyn uneasy. He abhorred their apparent fusing of the pious with the profane.

Finally, these two dozen years later, he would find some use for the repugnant antique. He would sell it so he could afford food and lodging until his riches were reclaimed. He hoped it would fetch a good price in Ysbyty Ifan. There was no use in being sentimental, since Mother had left the bowl to him only because she knew he disliked it. It had been in her nature to indulge in such provocative tricks.

As a boy, even as a man, he sometimes tried to imagine the moment Father gave the bowl to Mother. Father said it was to protect her from herself. Had he suspected she dealt in bewitchments and needed to be shriven of their coils? What had Father known? Did he believe she had intercourse with the Devil?

Like many of Maelgwyn's thoughts, these did not bear close scrutiny. As ever, he recalled only what he chose. His parents were dead, after all. It was foolish to dwell in the past.

His mother told him the intaglio flower, an elecampane, represented Helen of Troy, a martyr of beauty like herself. But Maelgwyn had read something of Helen since then and knew she had been a whore, running away from her good husband, Menelaus, with Paris, her lover. What strife she had wrought. How kind the cuckolded Menelaus had been. No, Helen had not been a victim. Rather she had made victims of the men in her life.

Tertullian of Carthage, blessed Church father, had stated it well more than a thousand years ago. He understood the real face of women, the face behind their beguilements, Maelgwyn thought. Tertullian wrote of Eve and her swarm of daughters: "You are the Devil's gateway. You are the unsealer of that forbidden tree. You are she who persuaded him whom the Devil was not valiant enough to attack."

As he watched the two monks disappear into their hospice, Maelgwyn felt a jolt of righteous anger. Yes, it was a Devil's gateway, a vile persuader and stinking rose, who had now forced him to endure the monks' abuse. Elise had done this. She'd likewise forced him to kill the shepherd. Here in Ysbyty Ifan she had turned everyone against him. Even cats ran away. Now she drove him to barter his belongings. Elise was the bitch who had done it all.

A puffy-faced young man came around the corner of the hospice, nearly colliding with Maelgwyn. The plump stranger wore black hosen and a tight-sleeved cote-hardie, half white, half black, with tippets nearly to the ground and gilt buttons from his neck to his garment's hem. A wide belt encircled his hips under the shadow of his belly. Completing the ensemble were red gloves and black shoes with exaggeratedly long toes.

What a tailor's victim have we here, thought Maelgwyn. And he smiled ingratiatingly.

"I'm fresh arrived in this place, friend," said the stranger. "But you look like a man who'd know his ass from his ankle. Can you direct me to a decent inn?"

Maelgwyn's smile widened. "The inn is just there, with the ale stake and the bumpkins jabbering before it. They must be commenting on your costume, sir. Ysbyty Ifan does not often see such splendor."

The fellow's chest swelled. "Not surprised. From Cardiff, you know. On my way to Denbigh, visiting kin here and there betwixt. My only brother died recently—"

"May he sleep with Jesus."

"His chances of that are as good as anyone's, I suppose. Poor soul succumbed to apoplexy, and I am his heir, as he departed childless and without a wife. I go to Denbigh to receive his worldly goods."

Maelgwyn eyed the dandy's fat purse. "A long journey. Do you worry for your safety in these rough parts?"

"I suppose I do, now and again."

"Friend, then Heaven favors you." With a flourish Maelgwyn pulled the silver bowl from his sack. "For this basin and its sanctified scroll were blessed by Thomas à Becket himself, expressly to protect good travelers."

After a long discussion that found Maelgwyn extolling the remarkable properties of the basin and its wonderful scroll, the dandy, no scholar, was persuaded to become its new owner. A goodly sum of money went into Maelgwyn's hands, and the bowl into the dandy's.

"I'll admit I've been uneasy, sometimes, on these wild byways," said the dandy, admiring his acquisition. "But how can you bear to part with it?"

"My highest duty as a Christian is to be of aid to others. God will see to my welfare, I'm certain."

The gullible stranger was not totally convinced of that. But he hurried away with his prize before the seller could change his mind.

A little later Maelgwyn left Ysbyty Ifan. He had bribed a bleary-eyed rascal to go into the shops and procure him provisions for his journey. Now his sack was weighted with bread and salted beef. Strapped to his shoulder was a wooden jug of beer.

Considering which route he should take, he decided to travel northwest. He would follow the Trackway of the Cross. Elise had often shown interest in tales of the Trackway. Maelgwyn now suspected her curiosity had everything to do with her diabolical plans and nothing to do with interest in the history of the Trackway. It made a twisted kind of sense. He believed she would use or had used the Trackway, at least at first, to take her toward her old home, the heathenish island of Anglesey. Didn't mongrel bitches always try to find their way home? He wasn't certain, by any means, of her intentions. But for now the Trackway seemed a more reasonable course than any other.

He passed Bryn Llech, Hill of Flat Stones. Heaven gave sureness to his gait, he knew. Penmachno would be next. Across the river, then on to Bwlch-y-Groes, Pass of the Cross. Then Dolwyddelan. He might reach Dolwyddelan by nightfall. He could make discreet inquiries of the locals there. Had anyone seen a gray-eyed slattern, he'd ask, and her crone of a servant? He had coins to buy information and lodging now. He could ask some foolish woman, for women love to chatter about the doings of others. "Women rattle on and on because they are made of bone, not good earth," Maelgwyn said to himself.

Of course some few days had gone by since Elise stabbed him. She might already be back near Beaumaris, on Anglesey. But perhaps she tarried somewhere along the way. She might even have decided

Beaumaris would be too obvious a choice for her, in case she fell under suspicion for his supposed murder.

She believed him dead, he was certain. But what a resurrection he'd show her, when they met. Again he pictured how shocked she would be to behold him. It was his most constant and happy daydream. Ah, what a fête of love they'd enjoy.

He laughed aloud, startling a thrush on a nearby branch. The thrush flew off without singing.

Simple logic told him to ask at every place he visited until he heard firm word of his wife. He would soon possess good facts to take him surely toward her.

Should he go to Trefriw? She might be headed toward Conwy, as she spoke English so adroitly. That was another idea. He spoke English himself, well enough. As a child he'd been to the Friday market at Conwy several times. If that was her plan, to hide there, it would be insufficient to thwart him. He could never pass for an Englishman in either Conwy or Beaumaris, but he could walk freely enough through their city gates on any market day.

Suddenly he bethought himself to offer prayers in honor of the pilgrims and holy men who had followed the Trackway before him. Kneeling in the dust, he felt their encouraging presence hovering above him. Then he thanked God for sending the plump dandy to Ysbyty Ifan.

46

A Harbor of Stilled Desire

Before going on toward Conwy, Annora entreated Elise to stop at Ffynnon-bedr, Saint Peter's Well. The well was not too far from Trefriw, and the day was young. Saint Peter's water, Annora had often told Elise, cured her father of ruinous worms in the belly when he was only four years old. It had been a famous tale in her family.

"My grandparents made the trip from Anglesey to take Father to the well, as it was acclaimed a last hope for afflicted children," she told Elise as they went cautiously over a stream by way of a great fallen tree. "Father was so weak they despaired. His mother even hung coral around his neck, in the old way, to keep the evil spirits from closing in entirely."

"But the holy water saved him?"

"If it had not, I never would have been born. Father was essential to Mother in the endeavor of my begetting."

Elise smiled. "I'm happy they felt the inclination."

They traversed the flat path down the valley. Saint Peter's Well lay outside the village called Llanbedr-y-cennin, named in Welsh for Saint Peter, like the well.

"Were you ever sick as a child?" asked Elise, to make time pass as they walked. "I've rarely known you to be ill."

"I suffered terrible pustules in my mouth when I was about six. I don't recall it, but Mother cured them. My brothers always teased me that the pustules came from talking too much."

The friends froze, startled by rustling in the undergrowth. When a pheasant hen burst from the grass, dashed across the path, then plunged into a tangle of wildflowers, they went on with relief.

Elise shared her own recipe to eradicate pustules. Hearing it, the older woman threw up her hands. A debate on the efficacy of other potions and plasters ensued, with each healer claiming superiority for her cures. Opinions diverged, by and by, on how to rid a body of warts.

"The inner bark of willow, creamed with vinegar," said Elise.

"Folly. Wash warts in water from a font in which the seventh son of a seventh son is baptized. Should you have seven sons, and the seventh has seven, you might one day test it."

This assertion turned their banter less jaunty.

"I'll bear no sons," said Elise, her face changing in an instant. "Nor daughters either."

Her brothers had been right, Annora thought, to say she talked too much. But she attempted to relieve the gloom. "God may have sweeter plans for you than you suspect," she said.

Elise didn't reply. They walked on toward Llanbedr-y-cennin.

The well was easy to find, just beyond a gentle brook with stepping-stones to cross it. On the edge of the quiet village, Saint Peter's Well burbled, protected by a tiny windowless building. The shrine was marked with brown and yellow mosaic crosses on either side of an east-facing door. Emerging cool and appealing from the earth, the spring had long ago been decorated with polished stones to create a kind of child-sized, bubbling bath. The water gushed upward from so mysterious a place, human eyes had no way to judge its depth.

Next to the well sat a chapel. After immersion in Saint Peter's spring, children were rushed to the chapel for supplemental prayers. Crutches, eye patches, and other abandoned paraphernalia of affliction lined the walls, testifying to the mercy some had received. A caretaker's cottage stood nearby, traditionally housing an elderly monk from Maenan Abbey whose job it was to collect pennies from supplicants.

The current caretaker hobbled to the well from his snug cottage when he saw the two visitors arrive.

Annora dropped coins into his outstretched hand. "Good day to you, Brother."

The man made the sign of the cross. "I see no little ones," he said. Then he turned his rheumy gaze on Elise's middle. "Or do you come to say prayers for a babe still in the womb?"

Roses bloomed on Elise's cheeks as she denied impending motherhood.

Annora laughed too heartily. "No, Brother. We came to honor my father, for he was brought here as a child and found a miraculous cure."

"Our spring boasts many such tales. They say at the Abbey even Vikings brought their offspring here for Peter's blessing. Vikings and other pagans."

Elise regained her poise, for the man seemed guileless and entertaining. "What is the most wondrous sight you have seen here, Brother?" she asked him.

He peered into her face as if to weigh her earnestness, then said, "Your eyes suggest you are sincere, so I will tell you something quite amazing." Now he stared into the distance. "I have twice seen Peter, Saint Peter himself, floating on the evening mist. He journeys to the lake where no waves lap and he beckons me to follow. But my feet are too heavy as yet to lift me from the earth. Still, the sight fills my heart with joy."

Unexpectedly moved, Elise leaned toward him and touched his angular old shoulder.

He jerked back. "I am God's man," he cried, the rapture on his face changing to distaste. "A harbor of stilled desire. Jesus keeps me from lust, so I've no use for females whatsoever."

Elise's face also changed, but subtly. It showed a hint of the imperious disdain she had once before exhibited, when the innkeeper at Dolwyddelan mistook them for women of bad repute. She put more distance between herself and the monk and shook out her skirts, while Annora clicked her tongue.

The monk bid them an affronted adieu and shuffled back to his cottage.

As they left the well, Annora gave vent to indignation. "Deluded dodderer. Ass." She imitated his voice. " 'I've no use for females whatsoever.' Lucky thing for the old toad his mother didn't feel the same about males, at least once. I'm of a mind to complain to his betters at Maenan Abbey."

Elise shook her head. "Let Heaven deal with him."

Still Annora fulminated. "But he's ruined my family tale for me and left a bad taste in my mouth. Why do some of these wretched men, supposedly godly men, so often imagine women are panting for their favors?"

Elise thought of Maelgwyn but did not utter his name, for she recalled how Brother Gerald translated the Latin words of the lunatic in Dolwyddelan: "Of the dead say nothing except good." Annora's excoriation of the imperfect monk eventually dwindled to desultory aspersions. Then the subject was allowed to drop.

The women went on to the north in the direction of Caer Rhun, an old Roman fort. There, nothing was left to recall the ambitions of dead Romans but the broken foundations of their fortification. Elise and Annora sat on an old stone wall, nibbling chestnuts and bread. The mustardy onions had to be eaten too. And they were, but they did not inspire pleasure. Still, the sun was pleasantly warm and no other person, living or dead, disturbed the humble repast.

"I'm less stiff and sore than when I rose this morning," said Annora when they finished.

"Ready to go on?"

"Of course. You told me I have the stamina of a horse. Don't you remember?"

"That was a hundred years ago, I think."

"A thousand. But where next, child?"

"Through Tyn-y-Groes and Gyffin. Not far. Then to Conwy. The land ahead should be pretty and rolling, easy to traverse."

"Conwy? Today?"

"Tomorrow. Before sunset."

"And no more wells or onions. I've had my fill of both."

Annora thought of the featherbeds they would soon purchase, and the new shoes. They could afford what they liked, including a place to live. Reaching discreetly down to touch the money pouches hanging against her thighs, she imagined what tasty thing she and Elise would have for their supper the next night, in Conwy. An image presented itself—roast beef, steaming on a platter beside a hillock of peas. Next to the peas sat a prune tart dolloped with cow's cream.

Elise didn't think of lodging or food. She thought of Gwydion. She prayed he was well, that he was behaving sensibly. He probably wasn't, she supposed. Were his wounds healing as they ought? She truly hoped she wouldn't see him in Conwy, even from a distance. It had been sufficient to bid him farewell once.

She said another prayer for his safekeeping and begged God to remove all thoughts of him from her heart.

How wonderful it would be if one could leave memories and ruined hopes at a special spring, the way cured children cast aside crutches and bandages at Saint Peter's Well. If such a place existed, perhaps one could leave longing there too.

For now, longing remained Elise's companion and showed no inclination to leave her.

47

THE FLYING PHALLUS

Sir Nicolas and two of his men took the short ride to Conwy to see how matters stood. The nobleman did not fear he would find grim-faced, sword-brandishing soldiers waiting for him at the gate. If he were known to be a wanted man, Conwy's constable would have surely gone out to Llys Garanhir and tried to arrest him there. Besides, the harlots he'd sent into town to spread rumors denied hearing any untoward talk attached to his name.

As he had supposed, he entered Conwy without hindrance. In fact he had an amiable chat with the four guards at the gate. When he gave his name, these fellows evinced interest in a most flattering way.

One said respectfully, "I fear you'll have to hide yourself from all Conwy's good ladies, my lord."

"Now why is that?" said Nicolas, at his most unassuming.

"They say in the taverns every fine lady in town wants to meet you."

Maintaining his seat on his eager sorrel without effort, Nicolas clutched his crucifix and looked nonplussed. "Why would fine ladies want to meet an insignificant fellow like myself?"

Another guard spoke. "You're all the ladies talk about, my lord. If you've need of a wife, you can choose from twenty of the best-born girls in town—meaning no impertinence."

The two scapegraces accompanying de Breauté snickered.

But Nicolas gave a serious answer. "One lady will be sufficient. I only hope I don't prove too great a disappointment to Conwy's maidens when they behold me in the flesh. But I've tried to make myself presentable, for it is true I'm desirous to wed." He lowered his voice so his next words sounded confidential. The guards would remark later on his cordiality and condescension. He said, "Friends, the time has come to set up my nursery. I need an heir, a bright-eyed lad to carry on my name when I go to my reward."

The guards murmured appreciation at being recipients of such manly candor. They all looked forward to telling the tale in the barracks and taverns as soon as their duty at the gate ended.

Sir Nicolas was grand in his attire, as befitting a nobleman on the lookout for a bride. Since the morning in Dolwyddelan when Gwydion cut a jagged line through his kerseymere cloak, he'd had another fetched from London. He wore this new cloak now. It resembled the other but with golden trim. On one shoulder he'd affixed a pilgrim's badge.

This badge he now pointed out to the guards with solemn pride. "To bring me luck in my bride hunt. It came to me from a man who claimed he stole it from the Bishop of Paris. Naturally, when the fellow bragged how he purloined it, I dealt with him in the only way I could." As the guards nodded uncertainly, Nicolas tilted the brooch so it caught the sun. "But I take as good care of it as any bishop, for it represents the happy season of Lent," he went on. "So I've been told. You'll think me strange, but I sleep with it beside me on my lonely bed."

The guards stared up at the jewelry. It was the size of a man's thumb and depicted a winged phallus with legs. On the head of the phallus rested a tiny crown.

Sir Nicolas smiled. "You men are struck by its holy beauty, I see. I hope ladies will know by my wearing of it that I am a godly man. And so, perhaps, a worthy bridegroom."

The senior guard nodded slowly, his face blank. The ways of the nobility, he told himself, were not for him to understand. If Sir Nicolas wanted to wear a golden penis on his cloak, he could wear it and Godspeed. "A handsome badge, my lord," he said.

Nicolas inclined his head and in regal fashion rode through the gate and into the town.

His two men soon came abreast. "You're the most complete jokester, my lord," said one. "You had that badge from Cicely the whore last week."

"Yes, big-bottomed Cicely," said de Breauté. "She says it reminds her of me. Such an acrobat that girl is too."

The other man said, "Are you hunting for a wife, sir?"

"I am. A rich, fertile wife. Someone untouched, to polish my sword and fill my declining years with domesticity."

All three men laughed.

Then Sir Nicolas grew serious. "I do find the idea of an heir appealing. Any boy of mine is bound to be handsome and intelligent."

Of course his men agreed.

They made the rounds of Conwy's taverns. Sir Nicolas told his tale of wife-hunting everywhere they went. On the streets finely dressed ladies were much in evidence, as if they had all been awaiting his arrival. They simpered at his greetings. Men welcomed him to their town. He even received three invitations to come to dinner as soon as he could spare the time.

Although some people stared with bemusement at his pilgrim's badge, no one remarked on it aloud. Like the diffident guard, they supposed a nobleman was entitled to wear whatever odd thing he liked.

As they rode back toward Llys Garanhir in the late afternoon, Sir Nicolas said, "What have we learned today, friends?"

"That Conwy's filled with ladies warm to make your acquaintance, sir," answered one.

"And it's filled with a few more who might want to make mine," said the other. "None so rich or pretty as yours, sir, but I wouldn't object to letting one or two polish *my* sword."

Nicolas frowned. "Your sword may be of interest to you. Unfortunately it is of no interest at all to me."

The man's sly grin drooped.

"What I was asking," de Breauté continued, "was what have we learned today about my situation?"

The first man who had spoken now said, "There's no talk of your enemy in Conwy, sir, the one Dexter jabbed. Not a soul knows about the warrant either. Everyone thinks the owner of Llys Garanhir was murdered by Welsh criminals, and they think the manor was sold to you by kin." He essayed a deferential smile. "And the townsfolk all want to have you as guest at their tables."

Nicolas inclined his head. "That's what I learned too. I'm glad our observations tally."

"What happens now, sir?"

"We'll continue to watch for unsavory characters and warrant servers, and we'll be ever mindful of the need to consider God's good opinion in all of our affairs."

If his two companions wondered precisely how God would view homicide, robbery, and orgiastic reveling, neither asked.

"Furthermore," said Sir Nicolas, "I must have all my hosen laundered and my teeth polished with sage leaves and salt."

"Why, sir?"

"Because my saintly friend will soon come to call, for one thing. It will be my first attempt at entertaining a worthwhile person."

The lackeys said nothing.

Nicolas went on. "But for the most part, I'm simply making myself presentable for my future bride, whomever she may be. Oh, what a fine wedding I shall have. My in-laws will be thrilled, and my bride will learn the art of love from the foremost practitioner in Britain." He peered down at the winged phallus and smiled.

His men concurred enthusiastically.

48

COLD-BLOODED CREATURES

Annora and Elise met a young woman and her toddling daughter on the path north of Caer Rhun. They exchanged amiable greetings. When Elise complimented the woman on her youngster's beauty, the mother stayed longer to chat. On hearing that the strangers did not know where they would rest their heads that night, she invited them to her home.

"My husband wouldn't mind," she said, "if he knew. But they took him off to try his longbow against the French, so he's been gone since before Lent."

"We'll repay your kindness, never doubt it," said Annora, glad of the offer of a bed. "You must be in some need, with your man away."

The woman's downcast eyes betrayed the truth of this. "It's not been easy. To say true, Cadi and I were out hunting for cowberries just now. But we found nothing."

"Cowberries?" said Elise. "They're so bitter."

"But they do make a tolerable jam, mixed with sea holly. And my aunt and uncle live nearby and bring vegetables when they can. This morning they surprised us with a pot of onion stew, so we won't go hungry for the rest of the week. We'd be pleased to share."

"How lovely," said Elise, covertly watching Annora.

"A treat, indeed," that diplomatic lady said. "A body should never be ungrateful for a pot of onion stew. Healthful, I always think."

So they went with the woman and her little daughter to a Spartan hut in the woods. When the sun sank behind the trees, they ate onion and fennel stew and sopped their bowls with the bread that remained in the travelers' sacks.

Since the cottage had no proper bed, all four slept atop piles of green bracken on the floor by the fire, but not close enough to be singed by occasional sparks. In the morning, contrary to her expectations, Annora was not so achy as she'd been the day before. She supposed the warmth of the young mother's hospitality had made her rest serene, even in the poor, smoky cottage. She'd also been comforted by the sound of the toddler's even breathing in the dark.

"It's too much," said their hostess, seeing the coins Annora put in her hand when the visitors were ready to leave. "You were with us one night, not half the year."

Elise scooped Cadi into her arms. The child giggled and hid her face against her captor's neck. "You could buy this poppet a doll," Elise said. "And perhaps you could get a cow and some chickens to keep you in milk and eggs. That is, if you'd like."

"But, ladies—"

"Hush now," said Annora. "Without your kindness we would have slept out in the cold and damp last night."

"We're obliged to you, so let us pay our debt," said Elise. "It will make us happy."

The woman wanted them to be happy, so took the coins. They parted company with the best of good feelings.

"How far to the next place?" asked Annora, when they'd walked for a time in the cool morning. The ground undulated gently, and bird-song sounded. Behind them loomed gray, mist-draped slopes and the daunting peaks the Welsh called Eryri, Abode of Eagles. The English used a different name, Snowdonia, mountains of snow. No white mantles covered them now, but from October until late spring they would earn their Saesneg title. "I forget the name of the place," Annora continued. "Will there be an inn?"

Elise didn't answer. She'd stopped to stare blindly ahead.

"Child, are you ailing?"

But Annora soon understood that Elise didn't ail in any way she could endeavor to treat. All she could do was guide her to an ash tree and lower her gently against its broad trunk.

When the noise of the wings came, Elise's heart commenced to pound. It was a vision: she knew it, even as her conscious mind re-treated. She had been praying for weeks to be delivered from these unwanted trances, but her prayers had not been answered. So she felt once again the sensation of nearness to Heaven, or some equally un-knowable place, and experienced growing clarity of inner sight. All notion of any different reality vanished. Anxiety faded as well and was replaced by great calm as the world behind her eyelids changed to azure blue. Everything was now in its place. Why resist or worry? Everything was as it was meant to be.

Then a woman's nude form took slow shape before her. The woman was beautiful, red-lipped and smiling, with golden hair tumbling to her waist. She raised white hands to her cheeks, pretending to be shy. But her wide gray eyes told a thousand wicked stories only partly echoed in the words she now spoke to the air.

"I dreamed of water and knew what my outcome would be."

Elise's glance fell to the necklace of tiny starfish the woman wore.

The lady looked down at her jewelry, as if sensing Elise's regard. "Cunning, isn't it?" she said. She touched her breast and continued in an altered voice. "Spiritual milk is the easiest to digest, though cold-blooded creatures will take none. Yet if you rip a starfish in two pieces and throw it in the sea, it will not die. It's not so passionless as that, for it sprouts new limbs and makes another of itself. Strange, is it not?"

"Who are you?" said Elise.

The woman did not hear, or feigned not to hear. She spoke again. "I've practiced divination by thunder and by lightning. I know the language of foxes and seven secret uses for mandrake root. With an unguent of boiled semen and virgins' blood stirred with bones plucked from hawk's dung I've preserved my face and form. And I've gathered spell books from the four cities of old knowledge—Thebes, Toledo, Naples, Athens. Yes, the *Book of the Flowers of Celestial Teaching* was my boon companion in the summery hours that are only memory. Even the angel Hocroël came at my midnight urging."

"Don't speak these evil words," said Elise, as she tried to fight through the azure clouds swirling about her. She had to reach the woman, to silence her. But she could not.

"Let me tell you a secret, listener." The fair woman lowered her voice to a shivery whisper. "If you place a holy wafer beneath your tongue, then kiss an unknowing man as the wafer melts, that man will triple in his lust." She licked her lip. "He'll be hot to take you whenever you will have him."

The azure changed to indigo, pricked by particles of white like stars in an icy sky.

The woman tilted her head. She glowed pink, ivory, and gold

against the darkness. "Your mind is sealed when it oughtn't be," she said, no longer whispering. "But heed me now. The figure of Venus has a grid of seven. Seven rows of seven. Each row summed equals one hundred seventy-five. Up, down, across, slantways. The corner numbers are eight, one, sixty-four, fifty-seven. Work magic with it on a Friday, for it is the figure most proper to the delights of females—and of sex. Write it on parchment with a dove's blood and put it 'neath your bed. You'd be a fool not to."

Elise tried to cry out, but words fell useless from her mouth. "Spare me hellish sums," she finally struggled to say. "Rather than live as Satan's pawn, I'll die lonely and cold and blameless."

The woman's lips curved in a joyless smile. "Lonely, cold—but not blameless, I think. I do wish you joy of your winter."

A handsome man appeared at the woman's side. He seemed confused, misplaced in the darkness surrounding her. But he immediately seized her and kissed her hungrily on the mouth. She broke away, laughing. "Poor husband," she said. "So tediously good." Her starfish necklace changed to a rosary. She began an obscene prayer, fingering the beads one by one. Clutching his chest, the man fell. He writhed and cried out, then went still. His body turned to dust and blew away.

A second man appeared. When he pushed the woman to the ground and mounted her, her laughter stopped. She reached up to claw his shoulders. First in whispers, then screams, she begged for mercy. But he rode her wildly like a hellish satyr. Finally he finished and stood. Blood poured from between her legs as she sprawled in the dirt. As the red pool spread around her, the woman's agonized gray eyes narrowed.

"You think my death will free you," she said. "But you will never be free, for you've learned too well at my side. We'll dance this dance four thousand times more, you and I."

"No, we'll not be partnered again," he answered, "for Heaven now guides my steps. The Lord told the Pharisee, 'Your inward part is full of ravening and wickedness.' I say the same to you."

The woman conjured into her fingers a pessary shaped like a man with cupped hands. She pushed it between her legs to staunch the flow of blood, but it had no effect. Her eyes grew crazed as she searched the dark sky. "Come to my succor, Marastac, Baal, Mayrion, Troion. Come to the aid of your servant."

The man shook his head as a roiling river appeared at his feet. "Your demons will not come. They've made a fool of you, Procreatrix. They've used you and are done. Go take joy now from the pomps of Hell." He produced a knife and hacked her apart even as she screamed. Soon all became silent, and he tossed the pieces of her body into the river.

Her bloody face appeared for an instant in the river, in the starlight. Tiny fish jumped nearby—her necklace come to life—and waves lapped at her mouth. Her hair spread around her on the surface of the water, entangling the fish. She disappeared with them beneath the flow, leaving no ripple or wake.

The man turned to Elise.

"I would not want it tallied against me," he said, "that I suffered the woman Jezebel, which calleth herself a prophetess, to seduce God's servants to commit fornication."

His face blurred. As the sound of beating wings returned, the sky spun 'round and 'round.

Elise felt the tree against her back and opened her eyes.

Annora stood before her, wringing her heads. "Sweetheart, another vision. I know, I know. You cried and trembled until I despaired."

Elise stood, but light-headedness forced her to lean against the tree once more. "Maelgwyn."

"Maelgwyn? No, he's dead. No vision can change that."

Gorge assailed Elise, rising in her throat until it filled her mouth. The taste of bile and onions surged against her teeth and slid under her tongue. Doubling over, she vomited into a patch of flowering horehound. Her friend fussed around her as she was racked by wave after wave of nausea. Finally she straightened and wiped her mouth.

Annora took her hands. "What was it? Oh, what sickens you so?"

"I'm all right now. But we're a pair for wasting our food, aren't we?" Elise said, pulling gently away. She tucked strands of hair back under her kerchief and checked her skirts.

"Cariad, tell me."

Elise went still. "Are you sure you want to know?"

"If you can bear it, I can."

"Then if you're sure, I'll tell you. What I saw was a scene from Hell. Maelgwyn's mother killed her husband. She boasted skill with evil craft and murdered him with magic."

Annora made the sign of the cross and touched her dice rosary. "Heaven help us, but . . . I suppose, I suppose it might be true. It might well be true. It would explain why Maelgwyn was so full of hatred."

"There's more, and worse."

"Worse than murder?"

"She and Maelgwyn were not as a normal mother and son should be."

"Not normal? What do you mean?"

Elise looked away.

Annora tried to smile but failed. "Impossible. It has to be. I recall similar rumors of some neighbors when I wasn't yet twenty. Everyone gossiped of a twisted brother and sister, but—"

"He killed her. He cut her into pieces."

"No." Annora placed her hand flat against the tree. "She killed her husband with craft, took her own son as lover—and then Maelgwyn killed *her*?"

"Before he killed her, she said he knew dark ways too."

Annora only shook her head.

"I know it sounds mad."

"Couldn't your vision be wrong? Really, it's not even a vision, since it didn't tell of the future. It only told the past, Elise. Why would you need knowledge of the past?"

"I don't know. But I saw the woman one other time in a vision. Only it wasn't like this. It frightened me, but not like this."

"You never mentioned it, child."

"There seemed no point. I didn't know then she was his mother."

"Maybe it's the Lord's way of comforting you. It proves we were right to rid the world of Maelgwyn. The diseased branch of a diseased tree ought to be chopped off, and both burnt."

Elise didn't reply.

Annora put her arms around her. "Can you try to put it out of your mind?"

"I can try. But I don't know. God help me, I don't know."

"It doesn't change anything, after all."

"But it's so horrible." Elise leaned against her friend. "No wonder Bryn-llwyd felt so foul. Imagine the things that must have happened there."

Annora pushed her gently away to look into her face. "Yes, but Maelgwyn had a choice in his life, cariad, and chose to be cruel and evil like his mother."

A shiver ran up Elise's spine. "You're right. I know you are."

"Of course I'm right. Now rinse your mouth, say a quick prayer, and let's be on our way. Let Heaven deal with him and his mother. Or Hell rather. Either way they've both gone past earthly consideration."

49

THROUGH CONWY'S GATE

Annora and Elise walked on toward Tyn-y-Groes, Farmstead of the Crossroads. By midafternoon they reached that small but congested place, ate a modest and blessedly uneventful meal at the busy hostelry, then carried on to the north. As the sun began to sink, they came to a mill on the Gyffin River. They passed beyond it, still going north.

Soon Conwy's thick walls loomed before them, enclosing the colonial town in a rough triangle more than a mile in length. Viewed from nearby hills, the shape of the walls was akin to a Welsh harp. Bitter Welshman said Longshanks, Edward I, ordered his masons to form it thus to heap further scorn on the people he had conquered and on the many bards and minstrels he'd allegedly silenced forever. Calmer heads denied that, concluding the shape was an accident of topography.

Twenty-one towers guarded the wall, each with a battlemented parapet and arrow slits. Except on the side facing the Conwy River, the town was also surrounded by a steep moat.

Far to the women's right, Longshanks's great castle sat on its bed of gray rock. The castle's limewashed mass, barred windows, long stepped ramp and drawbridge, and the eight identical towers anchoring it to its rock—all were intimidating and dramatic in the waning light, as they were meant to be.

The double-towered gate through which Annora and Elise would attempt to enter Conwy was called Porth y Felin, Gate of the Mill. It guarded the southern part of the wall and was one of three places of ingress and egress. The others were Porth Isaf, the Lower Gate on the Conwy River, and far opposite it, Porth Uchaf, the Upper Gate.

The women stopped some distance from the Gate of the Mill and consulted.

"We've actually arrived," said Annora. "I can hardly believe it. But do test your English before we go in, child. Just to get back in practice. I've been dreaming of roast beef for supper, so why don't you say roast beef and peas and prune pie? Go on."

Elise obliged her by reciting this menu easily, perfectly, in the language she had so often spoken with her mother.

Annora sighed. "I still think it sounds better in Welsh."

Light faded. Conwy's gates would close at sunset, so the friends hurried forward.

"Tonight we'll raise cups to our new lives," said Annora, her voice confident.

"I think I'll have wine. Conwy's ale doesn't enjoy a happy reputation, or so Mother said. She brought me here once as a child, though I don't recall much of the visit."

"I stayed at home."

"That's right, I remember. You stayed to mind Rhodri and Cadog. But for now, darling, you'll have to hobble your tongue unless we're alone. I'll say you're unable to speak."

"Why am I unable?"

"When you were young, you were kicked by a donkey, I fear. So stay silent no matter the provocation."

"Perfect. A donkey."

The wall's shadow swallowed them. The gate was high and wide enough for two riders to pass if they met.

A pair of guards stepped from the gatehouse to hail them as they came near. "What lovely ladies are these, soothing my eyes at the gloaming hour?" said one, in friendly fashion.

"An honest Englishwoman and her servant, from near London," replied Elise. "We come to Conwy to grace it with refined herbal skills, if there is occasion for such endeavors."

"Occasion enough, I think," the man answered. "We had a fellow who knew remedies, but he perished. Now all that's left is his drunkard son, and a blowsy midwife. So you're bound to find a welcome."

The other guard addressed Annora, who stood with head bowed. "What of you, old woman? Nothing to say?"

Elise put a protective arm around her and gave the second guard a look of reproof. "She is mute and can't answer."

"Aye? Scant good a mute crone will do Conwy."

"One needn't have a voice to pick herbs or make fine salves." Elise squeezed Annora's shoulder, glad her friend could not understand the man's rudeness and perhaps take noisy and unthinking offense. "She is a gem among servants."

"Why'd you come all the way out here from London?" the guard said, still aggressive. He was peckish and dry from a long afternoon, and intent on belligerence. "Something happen in London you didn't like?"

Elise raised her chin in the way Annora was beginning to recognize. She wondered what the guard had said to annoy her.

"Is this how you treat decent women?" Elise asked, her voice now imperious. "Perhaps I should speak to your superior to learn how I have been misinformed, for I was told respectable Englishwomen would be graciously welcomed in Conwy. Perhaps your orders differ."

The impolite guard looked less sure of himself.

"Yes, fetch your superior," Elise told the more genial guard. "I would confer. Tear him from his evening meal if you must, for this ought to be discussed." She recalled the name of a wealthy English acquaintance of her mother's, a woman who lived in Beaumaris. "Tell him the daughter of a friend of Lady Joanna fitz Norroy has arrived, but this other all-wise fellow implies she is unfit to enter."

Annora watched the guards' faces. She had no idea what Elise was saying but hoped the girl wasn't getting carried away. Her tone had gone so haughty, her posture so unyielding—exactly like her father at his most irked.

The pleasant guard tried to smooth things over. "Jarvis don't mean nothing, miss. He talks to everyone that way, so there's no need to take offense."

"He calls my servant a useless crone, then suggests I am some ne'er-do-well run out of London, yet I oughtn't take offense? Is this the usual greeting honest folk find in Conwy?"

The bullying guard cleared his throat. He'd reconsidered his attitude as soon as Elise's manner grew icy. "Sorry, miss. It's just we have orders to put sharp questions to anyone who passes. There's a parcel of Welsh thieves and murderers and whatnot running around in the forest and on the roads."

Elise allowed her voice to thaw the veriest bit. "Murderers? We beheld none."

"Some's not been so fortunate, miss."

"I see. Am I then to assume you mistook me for a Welsh thief or a murderess? Or possibly a whatnot."

"Surely I didn't."

The moderate man said, "Please, come in and be welcome."

Elise looked from one guard to the other. She tapped her foot. "All right," she finally said. "We will enter."

Annora noticed the Adam's apple of the less prepossessing fellow bobble as they passed. She wondered why. But it didn't matter: they were inside the walls of Conwy.

"One last thing," said Elise, pausing.

The men hurried to her side. The rude guard trod on Annora's toe in his haste. "Miss?" he said, while Annora scowled at his back.

"Can you recommend an inn of genteel reputation?"

The guards spoke over each other in their eagerness to please. Their advice was to go straight ahead, toward the Church of Saint Mary. Bear right. On the left would be The Otter and Roe. "That's your place, miss. No low company. Just clean beds and famous victuals."

Elise inclined her head and walked forward.

"What did you tell those fellows?" whispered Annora, at her heels. "That you were the queen of England?"

"Hush. And don't turn around. Just follow me and I'll lead you to the best meal Conwy has to offer."

Annora quickened her step. Elise smiled to herself, for the guards hadn't even asked for her name.

Behind them the men shut the gate until morning.

"Your stupid mouth nearly got us in the stew again, Jarvis," said one. "Can't you be civil?"

"How was I to know she had high connections? You ever hear of a well-born female turning healer? Surprised me, is all."

"What do you know of decent women anyway? You know leg spreaders, that's what you know. *That* was a lady. No common female could talk so uppity as her."

"Maybe so. But something else I never heard of is a well-born woman walking all the way from London."

"She never said she did."

"She never said she didn't."

"Jarvis, you're an ass. Maybe she had a ride in a fine cart to Mae-nan Abbey, crossed the river, and walked from there."

It took both men to haul up the drawbridge spanning the moat and to drop two long, heavy bars across the closed gate. Jarvis ran chains through loops on either side of the bars and secured them in the middle with a massive lock. Soon six fresh guards would arrive to climb the stone steps to the top of the double watchtowers—three men in each tower—to look out on the countryside for signs of Welsh deviltry.

"I'm for ale," said Jarvis, rubbing his palms. "You?"

"Aye," replied his colleague. "The Otter and Roe, is it?"

Jarvis gave a guffaw. "In a rat's mitten. You'll not catch me drinking ale with any cold-assed fancy women."

"As if you'd even be let in, or me. Anyway, I bet she ain't so cold. I bet she'd warm up fine, under a clever hand."

Jarvis laughed again. His mood always improved swiftly when his workday ended. "Dream on, hardy."

They hurried off toward a common alehouse and forgot all about the two women.

50

The Wages of Sin

Penmachno and Bwlch-y-Groes soon lay behind Maelgwyn. He marveled at the speed with which he was able to go forward on the Trackway of the Cross. Nothing had the effrontery to impede him, not weather or man or beast. As Dolwyddelan came into view at sunset, he intoned another effusive prayer. If further proof had been needed to illustrate God's favor, the ease of this journey provided it.

The lipless maid saw him coming across the meadow toward the inn and decided she didn't care for his quick swagger. Few knew better than she that it was prudent to avoid certain sorts of men. Although this man's sort was not immediately discernible, she suspected it would prove unpleasant. Pleasant men did not bear themselves so self-importantly, walking or riding. So she recalled a chore she had to tackle in the buttery and hurried there to do it, out of harm's way.

From the doorway of her inn, Ieuan ap Morgan Goch's wife hailed Maelgwyn as he approached, for she was not so astute as her maid. "Good traveler," she called, "look nowhere else for accommodation. You behold the finest establishment in Dolwyddelan."

He condescended to inspect the inn's rooms, negotiated the price downward in a hardheaded way, then agreed to stay.

After a repast of chicken stew, buns, puréed apples, and ale, he leaned back in his chair and swallowed a belch. It was the most extravagant meal he'd had in years. No other guest was about, and the innkeeper and his wife stood outside the closed front door indulging in a domestic discussion. As Maelgwyn lounged in the public room, the red-haired lad came to tend the fire.

"Here, you," said Maelgwyn.

The boy came obediently to the table.

Maelgwyn studied the child. "Tell me your name."

"Alun, sir."

"Well, Alun, do you profess to be a good Christian person? Mind you don't offer me a bold untruth if you are not."

The child wished he had taken Marged the maid's advice and stayed out of this scowling man's sight, but he answered as bravely as he could. "I go to church as much as my work permits me, sir. And—and my favorite uncle is a monk. Mother made a belt for him once, of hemp."

"You know what happens to liars, then."

Confused by the malice playing over the stranger's face, the boy dropped his gaze to the floor. "I suppose I know."

"You only suppose? Well, I'll tell you without flummery so you won't just need to suppose. Alun, liars are pulled down to Hell by demons. Demons' fingers are cold as icicles but hot as fire and coated with slime and hair. Down in Hell, lying boys and girls are stripped naked and roasted over flames made from puppies and kittens."

Round-eyed, the boy jumped backward, but Maelgwyn grabbed him by his shirt and dragged him to his side. "Stay, and know the truth. Where was I? Oh, yes. When they're cooked, yet somehow still alive and sobbing for mercy, the wicked children are placed like charred meat on black platters. Then they're sliced up and served to Lucifer's angels. Their fingers are devoured, their toes, their belly meat and backsides, then their dirty little private parts. Lastly, their eyes—so they can watch it all happen, you understand."

Alun whimpered.

Maelgwyn went on. "The most dreadful thing about it is that the next night it happens again. Every night children are roasted and devoured, roasted and devoured. How the demons do roar with delight as they sink their fangs into that tender oozing flesh and wipe grease from their chins. And though He's far up in Heaven, boy, God sees the whole proceeding, every night, and is sorely grieved."

Tears streamed down the boy's face.

Maelgwyn sighed. "I think that's the worst part, Alun, that God should be so grieved. Don't you agree?"

Lip aquiver, the child nodded wildly. Thinking his ordeal had ended, he spun around to flee. Again Maelgwyn seized him. "Wait, I have a question."

"Please, sir"—the plea was breathless and barely audible—"I've many tasks to finish."

"Don't be in such a rush. I merely want to ask if you've recently seen two particular women in Dolwyddelan. One is old and round, the other young. The younger one is pretty, in a falsely modest way, with brazen gray eyes. Women with gray eyes are often evil, Alun. You'd be wise to remember that. Anyway, this pair probably had no respectable escort."

The child knew immediately. He knew this awful man meant the two women whose forgotten walking staffs he had carried across the meadow. What business could someone so mean as this have with such kind-faced ladies?

Maelgwyn caught the boy's elbow. "I see by your hesitation you know exactly the females I mean. I also see you're thinking up a lie to hurt God."

"No!" Alun tried to pull away, but Maelgwyn was too strong.

"You are. You want to join the roasted children in Hell, don't you? You want demons to gobble you with gravy." He grabbed the boy's fingers and bent them backward.

"I'll tell, I'll tell," the boy gasped, as he tried to wriggle away.

Maelgwyn released his hand but kept hold of his shirt. "I knew you were a good boy, really. Your uncle would be proud."

After he'd heard everything Alun could think to tell, Maelgwyn hunched over the table, muttering. The boy tiptoed away. He had almost reached the rear door when again he was commanded to halt. "Stay, you. I have one question more," Maelgwyn said, raising his head. "Are you certain there were no men with these slatterns?"

"There were no men, sir."

"You seem unsure. Think again."

Alun, too frightened to do anything but what he'd been told, strained to think back to the brief time the ladies had been in Dolwyddelan. He remembered the Englishman's blue plume, the white dog, and the tall man with the silver sword. There had been crazy fellows at the inn too, with a monk. He took a shaky breath and told Maelgwyn about these visitors.

"Very good, Alun. This tall man—why is it you remember his sword so particularly? Was it so unusually fine you thought perhaps he had stolen it?"

Alun squeezed his eyes shut to jog his memory. He reopened them. "No, I think it was truly his."

"But why?" This person with the sword interested Maelgwyn greatly. Of all the men Alun described, he seemed the most reasonable choice to be the lover of a whorish wife. "What sort of man was he?"

"Rich, I think. Well-spoke and goodly dressed, but held his spoon with his left hand." Alun's words spilled out, for he hoped if he answered quickly, he might be the sooner released. "Mayhap he was a knight, for he had a great destrier. And I recall more: he tossed me a coin for seeing to their horses, and the other man gave Ieuan more than was needful for tariff." Alun made no mention of the murders near Dolwyddelan Castle only because he didn't think to do so.

"What were their names?"

"The tall one was called Gwydion, I think. Mistress figured they were rogues."

"Mistress must be more intelligent than she looks. Did the tall man, this Gwydion, know the slatterns? Did they converse?"

Alun tried to remember. It seemed so long ago. But Maelgwyn's face was so close, he could smell chicken stew on his breath, and he knew some answer was required. "Y-yes."

"Stammer me no lies. Yes or no?"

"Yes. They did speak."

"Did they seem intimate?"

The child didn't understand.

"Stupid boy, you know precisely what I mean. Did their eyes meet, the tall man and the younger woman? Do you imagine they might have lain together secretly that night?"

By this time the boy could have imagined nearly anything. All he knew for certain was that he wanted to get away from his inquisitor. "I . . . I think I did see them talking together." The lad swallowed and became more creative than precise. "Indeed I think I spied them nuzzling near the stairs."

Maelgwyn's head hummed and throbbed. As his mind's eye formed a sudden picture of Elise servicing a tall, handsome man with her mouth, his manhood stirred. It stiffened painfully, shaming and confounding him with a mixture of lust and rage. He was glad the table hid the evidence of his bewitchment.

He put a hand over his crotch, beneath the table. "Where did the women say they were traveling? Tell me and you may go."

"I heard Mistress tell Ieuan they were going to Rhuddlan, only she didn't believe them."

"Why didn't she believe them?"

"Mistress mostly doesn't believe anyone. And she doesn't ever like ladies much 'cause she thinks they're all out to lure Ieuan away. Marged says that's why she puts so much work in his suppers."

"What direction did they head, the two slatterns?"

"Toward Dolwyddelan Castle, on the path that goes by the trolls' waterfall and over the stepping-stones toward Trefriw. I saw them go that way."

"Fine. Good." Drawing his ale toward him, Maelgwyn crossed his legs at the ankle. His manhood was reverting to its unprovoked state. "You may leave me now, Alun."

The next morning Maelgwyn set off north. Before he left, he had a farewell conversation with Ieuan ap Morgan Goch.

"You've paid for your bed and your meal now, so we'll call it quits. But after this day don't bother casting your shadow on my wall again," the innkeeper told Maelgwyn as soon as the tariff was settled. "Not ever again."

Maelgwyn had reached the door but now flung around. "What's that? What Parthian shot have you unloosed?"

"Yesterday you filled Alun's head with a lot of bilge about demons who roast children and eat them for supper, and you hurt his hand. Don't deny it. That boy was up half the night weeping. What were you thinking, to be so cruel to a child?"

Maelgwyn's eyes narrowed. "My, what a fearsome pretender. I merely told him a tale from the Scriptures. Guilt must plague him if he chooses to pervert divine stories. Best carry him to church immediately. Compel him to make a confession if you want to save his soul."

"Save your own damned soul, if you're able," said Ieuan. "But I wager you'll not be able, for a truer son of Satan I never before did see. My wife shouldn't have let you in here."

How he found the wherewithal to contain his temper, Maelgwyn was later unable to explain to himself. The Holy Ghost must have flown unseen to his aid. Likewise the Lord must have stayed his right hand to keep him from ripping the tongue from Ieuan's head.

Celestial assistance aside, it took tremendous effort to leave the inn without resorting to violence. But Maelgwyn gripped his staff fiercely, as Moses must have done. "I'll depart, never fear," he said. "But I will pray for you and for the child, and I will turn the other cheek."

Ieuan brandished his broom like a quarterstaff. "Turn both cheeks, and trundle 'em off my property. Imagine—scaring kiddies for your own twisted pleasure."

Maelgwyn stalked out of the inn and crossed the meadow as fast as any man without a horse had ever crossed it. He took the well-traveled path past the deserted castle but paid the ghostly edifice no mind at all; he was too wroth. Again he had been reviled because of his slut of a wife. Again the truth was distorted against him. But Elise's judgment day approached. The sooner he found her, the sooner she would pay her reckoning.

He reached the point where the Trackway of the Cross and the Roman Road became one and the same for a distance. His head cleared. He soothed himself by recalling stories of joyous pilgrims and of the Christian emperor, Constantine.

These thoughts improved his outlook. "Praise God I have recovered full use of my legs, after so nearly dying," he told himself. "Indeed I'm stronger than ever. Like good men before me, I'll follow Heaven's course without any petty complaint."

He came to a forest full of flowers and pleasing smells. After he had walked there for a while, he heard the roar of the Foaming Falls. Nothing else could have caused such a din, he was sure. As he moved toward the sound, the world filled with noise. Soon the falls themselves burst upon his sight. Dropping to his knees, he listened to the song of the water and felt its kiss on his face. "This is a work of wonder," he cried. "If the almighty God who shaped this liquid mountain is my champion, who can stand against me?"

Renewed in spirit, he hurried on. He came to Castell-y-Gwynt but spared little thought for the Roman ghosts said to inhabit the area. After all, God wouldn't imbue heathens with the knack to reappear to mortal eyes a thousand years after death. Why bring idol worshippers back for a second chance?

Speeding on, he paused once to cast acorns at goldfinches in a cherry tree. Every shot went wide. The birds flew off twittering, but Maelgwyn only shrugged his shoulders and watched them go. His mood had certainly lightened since leaving Dolwyddelan. Crossing the Llugwy River at the stepping-stones, he hummed.

Shadows lengthened. Countless hills and hollows finally brought him to Llanrhychwyn. Striding across the ridge to the church he saw from the path, he pulled open the door and called out for a priest. None appeared, for Father Sefyl happened to be waiting beside a deathbed at a parishioner's hovel in the village. So Maelgwyn knelt to pray alone, and his surroundings comforted him.

Soon he strolled down into the village to hunt for fresh information about Elise and to find a bed.

Spying an unknown man from her window, and glad for it, Mistress Lowri sped out of her house. She'd had no custom all day and was bored. This fellow looked respectable but not intimidatingly rich like Sir Nicolas of horrible memory. Lowri had learned her lesson about wealthy men and was now content to find patrons solely from among less volatile regular folk. Some had sufficient money and were grateful to trade it for love, which suited her very well.

She straightened her scanty bodice as she went.

"Good evening, sir," she greeted Maelgwyn. "You're fresh to our village. Are you hungry? I have food. Do you need a bed? Mine is clean, I promise, and very warm." Two early cups of ale had made her even less subtle than usual.

He frowned at the vision before him. Half-exposed breasts, painted lips, vulgar dress and headscarf. How did these people suffer such a creature to remain among them?

He scorned her advances with a few harsh words and without a trace of diplomacy.

She put her hands on her hips. "No need for insults, Master High-and-Mighty," she called after him as he stalked off.

He walked here and there, asking for lodging at each likely cottage in Llanrhychwyn. Everywhere he was denied. "We've no room," the villagers told him. Efa refused him likewise, shutting the door in his face. Like her fellow villagers, she decided on the spot that she didn't care for his cold blue eyes.

As night fell, he was forced to go back to the church for refuge. The priest was still absent. Of course holy surroundings gave Maelgwyn consolation, but they didn't assuage his irritation. What a rude lot of bumpkins these people were, as bad as the fools at Ysbyty Ifan.

He ate a cold supper of bread and salted beef from his sack, then slept on the hard floor near the altar.

At sunrise Father Sefyl returned, having successfully ushered the old tanner past the threshold of the next life. "Good morning, my son," he said, to rouse his unexpected and unknown guest. His voice was as chilly as the interior of his small church, for he was not a man who appreciated surprises.

"Ah, Father, well met," said Maelgwyn, rubbing his eyes and getting to his feet.

"No one in the village could accommodate you?" Disapproval colored the priest's question.

"I regret to say your parishioners proved an uncouth and unobliging lot. Even with funds, I found no bed and no polite conversation. In fact the only welcoming words I received came from a painted whore. A sorry state of affairs indeed. One would hope for better."

Father Sefyl had been well educated at Basingwerk Abbey, farther north near the English border. He too often found the superstitious ignorance of his flock quite irksome. But who was this smug stranger to criticize them? And upon closer examination, the priest saw why his awkward lambs shunned the fellow; he had such chilly, off-putting eyes and an odd wound on his throat.

"Well, I'll be extraordinarily busy today," Father Sefyl said, hoping his uninvited guest would take the hint and leave as soon as could be. "I'm afraid I've no time to dawdle."

From experience Maelgwyn sensed the churchman's burgeoning antipathy and knew he was being dismissed. Such a shame, he thought, for a spiritual advisor to be as unreasoning and ill-mannered as those he ought to instruct. Nonetheless he set aside his pique. But he showed no inclination to perform a timely exit; he still had a vague hope his host might drop some useful kernel of information.

"My dear, sweet sister," he said musingly, as he considered his belongings without making any move toward them. "She also journeyed this way not too long ago, I believe."

The priest took the bait. "Your sister?"

"With her old servant, yes. Elise is my sibling's name. A lovely young woman. Has she perchance stopped here?"

Father Sefyl frowned. "Why did *you* not travel with her?"

Maelgwyn kept his tone carefully regulated despite the sudden bubble of hope in his belly. "You see, hardship forced the poor girl to leave her home, south of here." This seemed reasonably plausible and imprecise. "I dispatched a letter to her there, but the messenger arrived too late. So she had no idea I would be coming to her aid, as I always have since she was a child."

The churchman did not reply, nor did his face give any clue as to his acceptance or rejection of Maelgwyn's hastily concocted story.

Maelgwyn continued, talking faster—for this fellow knew something, he was sure. "I only wish I had definite knowledge of her destination. The poor girl will surely have need of a brother's protection more than ever now." He shook his head and gazed toward the altar. "So alone and defenseless."

Could this vexatious character actually be kin to the clear-eyed woman who had recently been amongst them? Father Sefyl pondered the question. Watching Maelgwyn's hopeful face, he absently put a hand to his lower back, for it ached from bending over the moaning septuagenarian through the long night.

Then he straightened and sighed. Why couldn't the two be siblings? Siblings frequently did not resemble each other. The man sought out God's church to sleep in, didn't he? He'd surely been offered a bed at Lowri's. Besides, what reason would a fellow have in pretending someone was a sister who was not?

The priest said, "Is she a widow, your sister?"

Maelgwyn's eyes gleamed but he answered calmly. "Yes, poor thing."

"Then, aye. She's been here."

Maelgwyn crossed himself. "Oh, what welcome news! Is she well?"

"I think so."

"Now I tremble with hope. But, kind sir, did she speak of her destination?"

"Not to me, but I've heard the villagers talk of it." The priest saw no need to inform his visitor that the "painted whore," Lowri, had careened drunkenly around the village one recent evening, spewing details of Elise and Annora's plans to everyone she met. So the plans were hardly a secret, as the whole of Llanrhychwyn had been made privy. He went on, while Maelgwyn's eyes blazed brighter. "Your sister has gone to Conwy."

Maelgwyn clasped his hands together. "Praise God, we will soon be reunited." Then he frowned. He'd considered the notion before, but why precisely would she go to Conwy?

Father Sefyl provided an answer. "She means to set up an apothecary, and I expect she'll do well. She and her old friend, her servant, as you say, nursed a wounded man back to health, here in Llanrhychwyn. But you would naturally possess knowledge of your own sister's healing talents."

"Oh, yes. She is very adroit." And very busy and devious and scheming, Maelgwyn thought. "But who was this wounded man?"

Nonplussed by the intense look on his visitor's face, the priest suddenly wondered if he'd been misled into saying too much. Was he heedless and loose-lipped, spilling information about decent men who left sizable donations for the church? So he answered, "Dear me, I don't know his name." God would surely not object to a judicious falsehood. "He left when he recovered. But he was a generous and dutiful Christian." That was true, at least.

"Did he have a silver sword and wear it at his right side?"

"Eh? Oh, no, he had no sword."

But the flicker in Father Sefyl's eyes told his questioner he lied.

The triumphant look on Maelgwyn's face made the priest even more uncomfortable. Yes, he had definitely said too much. For wasn't this cold-eyed man displaying a peculiar surfeit of curiosity about a stranger's weapon?

Without fully understanding his own motivation, Father Sefyl attempted to throw him off the scent, whatever it was. "You sister's patient was aged and half-blind, poor fellow. He would hardly have use for a sword. Anyway, his wound was not the result of swordplay, but only a fall from a horse. He broke his . . . wrist."

"You relieve my mind." Maelgwyn smiled as he picked up his sack. "It would be dreadful to think of my sister involved with violent swordsmen. But now I really must go, sir. I'm keen to find Elise and put an end to all her hardships. In the meantime I thank you for your hospitality."

He went straight out the door.

Uneasiness swirled around Father Sefyl for the first part of the morning. Had he inadvertently given information that would cause that pleasant young woman or her magnanimous patient difficulty? If he had, he surely hadn't meant to.

But his guilty conscience was eventually soothed by the arrival of a local couple bearing fresh butter, a warm loaf of bread, and an itching need for marital counseling.

Only later did his mind stray back to the stranger. Was the man truly that quiet girl's brother? Did he have some quarrel with the generous Gwydion?

He knelt before the altar and put the matter in God's hands, asking to be forgiven for the double sins of spreading gossip and lying. When he rose, he felt relieved. After all, he told himself, one could only do one's best. The worst part of sin was always in its intention, and he had certainly intended no harm.

Maelgwyn reached Trefriw and went on without even slowing. He was pleased. Thanks to his subtle probing, the priest had provided a mother lode of fascinating information.

He now knew Elise had stayed in Llanrhychwyn. She was passing herself off as a widow, as indeed she must believe herself to be. She had nursed a man. This man had a fine sword, judging by the priest's inexpert attempt at dissembling. Most significant of all, Maelgwyn learned his quarry had gone to Conwy. The bitch had run to Conwy. That was something of a surprise, for he had supposed she would head for Anglesey. But the firsthand information was heartening and welcome.

The man Elise nursed was of course the same man she'd lain with in Dolwyddelan, the man sniveling young Alun told him of. The puzzle pieces were all coming together in a lascivious whole. She must have known him, this fellow with the fine sword, for some time. Perhaps the two met somewhere, some midnight, and planned his murder months ago—while he, her righteous husband, slumbered on in innocence in his bed at Gray Hill. Such a debauched character as Elise's swordsman must have more than one enemy. Hence his wounding at Llanrhychwyn. Another enraged husband, perhaps.

But Elise and her lover wouldn't triumph in the end. God was steadfastly at Maelgwyn's right hand, and God would never fail him.

These sanguine thoughts gave him pleasure and helped hurry him toward his destination with even more determination. Places that might have tempted him to idle investigation on a more mundane day now held no lure to draw him from the path. Ffynnon-bedr, Caer Rhun, Tyn-y-Groes—all were soon behind him.

Long before sunset he reached the walls of Conwy. It was Wednesday, but he knew Conwy held its well-attended markets on Friday. As a boy he'd been there several times as escort to his mother. All manner of things had gone home in their cart. Mother bought wine, spices, cloth. She also patronized a house in a dark lane near the castle but never allowed him to accompany her inside. She emerged with bundles she said were filled with ribbons and ladies' nonsense. But he had wondered. Why would she never let him carry those bundles? Could ribbons be so fragile?

One of her acquaintances, a handsome, strutting Irishman he had much disliked, once teased Mother at dinner about love potions and the mysterious ingredients she probably stirred into them to tempt men. "Do you use rat whiskers or roosters' testicles, darling?" the man said, as his emerald ring sparkled in the firelight. "Do you wait until the moon is full?" The other guests stayed silent as the Irishman laughed at his own drunken wit. Spying at the door of the hall, Maelgwyn heard it all. Mother had not looked amused. Her answers were cold.

The next morning the man failed to appear at breakfast. Maelgwyn asked where he had gone, as the weather was stormy and had been since the night before. But Mother waved her elegant hand dismissively. "He's . . . gone. The Irish, you know, have a way of always leaving."

Maelgwyn wondered if the contents of Mother's secret bundles had anything to do with the Irishman's sudden departure.

But that was history.

Now, on this Wednesday in the late summer of his thirty-fifth year, he could not pass through Conwy's gate. He was a Welshman. He'd have to wait until Friday, the only day of the week when his kind was allowed. Lurking behind a tree, he watched a few dreary travelers come and go. He listened to the guards' conversations and was pleased to be easily able to understand everything he heard. His grasp of English had not deserted him. Still, he knew his accent was too obviously Welsh to fool the gatekeepers into granting him admittance on any day but Friday, market day.

When the guards became distracted by the arrival of a garrulous comrade, Maelgwyn abandoned his tree and dashed farther away to hide in a coppice. He needed time to think and rest his feet. Sinking down, he put his chin in his hand. Should he retreat to the closest inn outside Conwy's high walls, probably the inn at Gyffin, and wait there until Friday? There was money enough for that scheme, although he preferred not to spend unwisely.

Afternoon sun beat down. Bees buzzed. His eyes closed as he considered his next move.

Moments later a bag dropped over his head and a rope was looped tight around his neck.

"Don't say a word now, slack-ass," said a rough English voice in his ear. "Or we'll cut you in pieces and leave you here for seagulls to gag on."

The pink scar on Maelgwyn's throat pulsed. To show he'd cooperate, he bobbed his head. He was thrown over a horse's rump, secured, and ridden away from Conwy's gate.

"What are we going to do with this great ox?" said another voice, in a while. "He can't be carrying a warrant, being without a horse. Or you suppose he skipped all the way from Caernarfon?"

"Quiet. If Sir Nicolas wants results, we'll damn well provide him results."

"Results? He's more likely to take one look at this pudding-faced oaf and give him to Dexter for dagger practice."

"At least somebody'll be happy. That Dexter's a proper vicious bastard and dotes on his dagger practice."

Maelgwyn tried to take a full breath. He tried not to wet himself. And he prayed to the Maker to deliver him from evil.

51

FIRST NIGHT AT CONWY

The Otter and Roe proved to be the perfect place for a meal and a bed. The landlord greeted Annora and Elise with immediate courtesy, for he recognized in the younger woman the sort of good breeding he liked to see in his clients but too often did not. In spite of her lack of male companions or rich dress, her way of speaking was formal and considered, her posture patrician, and her face fair.

When she asked about Conwy's need for an apothecary, he was taken aback. By her demeanor she didn't seem the type of female one would expect to seek out work for money. But he reminded himself that life for everyone had changed drastically since the Mortality had swept the land more than two years before. Many fortunes had also changed.

A sudden and romantic assumption of his—that Elise was a noble English lady fallen upon straitened circumstances—created sympathy in his benevolent, snobbish breast. He resolved to help the young woman find a comfortable place in the beleaguered harbor of English life that was Conwy. It was the least a fellow countryman could do.

The mute maid also made an impression on the landlord. Of course only a true noblewoman would have the grace to endure such an afflicted servant so uncomplainingly. It was obvious the woman in the brown dress had been with her mistress forever; he could tell by the maid's watchful concern for her charge. Once, the old woman even made a squawking sound, like a half word, when she accidentally splashed ale on her employer's dress, as if she'd forgotten she was a mute. By the look on her worn face, her squawk shocked even herself. Her antics, however, didn't stop her from devouring roast beef sufficient for a man twice her size.

How magnanimous it had been, the landlord thought, for her young mistress to offer to pay extra for her companion's intemperate appetite. "My maid has a peculiar approach to food," she explained.

"She often eats ravenously like this for several days, then quits altogether for no apparent reason. I wish she could speak so she might explain why."

The innkeeper naturally refused additional money for the maid's odd affliction. His business was robust and could bear occasional benevolence.

Alone that first night in their chamber, the women communicated by whispers and hand signals. Light shone beneath the door and through chinks in the shutter at a small window. Sprawled across the bed, Annora gave a sigh. "That was a meal fit for a queen."

"Or a she-bear."

"Don't be mean. I was famished."

"I don't deny it was tasty. But now the landlord thinks you have a tapeworm."

"Let him think it. What other things did you learn from our host, cariad? I think you impressed him. He hovered so."

"He says there's a shop available at the end of this street. It may work out well. Conwy's old apothecary died and his son is too fond of drink to be trusty. He keeps a place by the church, but no one goes near it unless they're almost dead. Then it's convenient to the graveyard."

"Is there a midwife?"

"Yes. Lucy. Our host claims she nearly killed a few ladies with her strange regimens. But he's probably exaggerating. He says Conwy's better class doesn't care for her manners, so that's likely the real problem."

Annora raised her eyebrows. "That must mean he thinks *you're* one of the better class."

Elise laughed softly. "I think he does."

"Good. He could be a help." Annora jingled the pouches under her skirt. "If we can entice the town's rich folk, we'll make more money sooner."

"Then you won't have to work anymore."

"Nor you. We'll buy a cottage on Anglesey and collect all the cats and dogs and rabbits you want. I'll be glad to go. This place isn't bad, but it's too Englishy here to be content forever. All these foreigners make me nervous."

"I'm part foreign."

"I'm used to you."

Sounds drifted through the window. Men wished each other loud, ale-soaked good nights. Somewhere near the inn a girl began a sad, sweet song.

"What is she saying?" asked Annora. "It sounds forlorn."

Elise listened to the English lyrics. "The usual lament," she said, as she began preparations for bed. "Lost love. Her man went away and will never return."

Annora detected a hint of longing in that answer and felt an echo in her own heart. "Cariad?" she whispered.

Elise didn't seem to hear as she combed out her hair in resolute fashion.

"Cariad."

The younger woman looked over her shoulder. The room was too dark to see clearly. "Did you say something?"

"Are you all right? Are you . . . happy, happy enough?"

"Of course I am. Fortune is finally smiling. It will be good to pick herbs again and make medicines. We'll both enjoy that. We might even be able to cure a few ailments."

"That's a sensible way to look at it." Annora rose slowly to make her own preparations for sleep. She knew she'd been gently rebuffed. It made her a little sad, as the girl had always been so candid in the past. She accepted that for now, at least, Elise wouldn't be wheedled into revealing anything personal. But maybe that was just as well. Maybe fortune really was smiling at last. They had funds and a reasonable plan. The future was much less bleak than it had been for a long while.

Elise pulled back the blanket and climbed into bed. "Everything will work out perfectly if you can actually manage to stay silent in public. But I know that will be tricky."

"Don't worry. I'll be the best servant anyone ever saw but didn't hear. The perfect servant, in fact."

Both drifted to sleep with nightjar cries for their lullaby.

52

MEN OF THE WORLD

Gwydion's friends arrived in Conwy. Three came one day, two the next, then two more the following week. These first seven were English, so rode through the town gates with their weapons and without interference. All were nevertheless careful not to say or do anything to draw attention to themselves.

"We caught sight of a pair of sneaking thugs just before we reached the wall," the fellow named Cob told Gwydion as they all drank ale in the rented house's low-ceilinged main room. "But there were three of us and we're so damned good-looking." He winked. "Off those rascals galloped, totally flummoxed."

The mood was mellow. There was plenty to drink and they'd all partaken of a hearty supper before the two servants withdrew.

"I'll wager those thugs were de Breauté's men," said Thomas importantly. He was the youngest, least seasoned of the company and felt a need to show himself worthwhile. Also his dalliance with Pearl caused him to be more swaggering and outspoken than before.

"Aye, lad," said Cob, "that's who we supposed they were."

Thomas didn't much care to be called "lad." He didn't care to be patronized. After taking an irritated gulp of ale, he lurched forward, choking and sputtering in his chair.

Cob grinned and slapped him on the back. "Careful with that brew, lad. Conwy's ale has a nasty reputation."

"You'll have to forgive Tom," said Gwydion. "His ladylove keeps him so fatigued, it surprises me he's still awake."

Thomas wiped his mouth and grinned sheepishly. He'd blurted the news to Gwydion of his romance with Pearl soon after he had begun it, and now was glad he had. Thanks to Gwydion's remark, these men would think more highly of him. They wouldn't dismiss him as a *lad*. He was a man of the world like they were, a man who conducted *affaires*.

Vort was a favorite with the visitors.

"Gwyd, is this handsome whelp really Vortigern, that pile of bones you plucked off the street in Paris?" asked a fellow with black hair and gleaming eyes. He looked down at Vort, who looked back with a canine grin. "I swore he'd be dead in a week. But look at him now."

"Like his master," said another man. "We thought he'd be dead in a week too."

"A pair of survivors," said Vort's admirer.

"Here's to Gwyd," said a third man, raising his cup. "Lucky devil. And to fine dogs everywhere. Oh, and to dead Frenchmen, live Frenchwomen—any kind of women, in fact."

A man who had been silent rose and went to peer out the window. Then he turned around. "When do the others arrive? How many more?" he asked abruptly. He spoke English with a Northern burr and had a scar down the center of his forehead.

"Soon, William," said Gwydion, not treating the questions lightly. "Several men more. Some are Welsh and can't pass through the gate until Friday. They can't bring weapons either, so we'll have to find blades for them here."

"Welshmen?" said Cob, pulling a face. "We're to fight arm to arm with damnable pagan Welshmen? Lord, they'll likely talk us to death or argue us to death. Then they might just steal our horses—or our favorite whores."

Again they all laughed, including Gwydion. It was clear from Cob's tone he meant no offense. These men had all fought together in France and forged bonds that could not be easily broken. For money or glory or both, some would soon cross the Channel to fight once more. Whether their brothers in arms were English or Welsh made no difference. They shared a common enemy and understood the worth of a stalwart comrade.

"Twelve or thirteen of us, then," said William, not one to be long diverted from an important discussion.

"And Jack," said Gwydion, "if he chooses."

"Jack would be a good one," added Thomas, eager to prove he was not wholly ignorant. He'd forgotten he had recently described the messenger as surly and his horse as wild-eyed.

"Against twenty?" said William.

"Maybe a few more," admitted Gwydion.

"But the villains don't know you're in Conwy."

"I don't think so."

Cob rubbed his hands together. "Sounds easy. We'll serve 'em their brains for their breakfast. So cheer up, William. You know you always like a nice massacre."

For the next hour they discussed strategies for retaking Llys Garanhir. With the odds ostensibly in Sir Nicolas's favor, a measure of surprise would be critical. So it was understood Gwydion's friends would have to stay out of sight as much as they could until the confrontation. They'd take what exercise they might in the weedy garden behind the house and perhaps go out only occasionally, after dark, for ale or minor errands. Otherwise the enemy might somehow glean too much about their numbers and possible plans.

Gwydion had already apprised them of the reasons they'd been asked to come. He spoke briefly and with a certain detachment about his father's murder and his sister's. After that, those crimes were not mentioned again. The men understood Sir Nicolas and his horde were dangerous and violent.

"So this bad nobleman's put it about you're dead, Gwyd," said an older man in a worn cloak. "He likewise killed the man bringing a warrant against him. Yet he's still managed to paint himself as an innocent, peace-loving fellow?"

"I think he has, Malcolm."

"Crafty. He's keeping the law well off his doorstep."

Thomas poured more ale. "He won't keep *us* off."

A couple of the men exchanged amused looks at this, but Thomas didn't notice.

"I'm grateful you're all here," said Gwydion. "I know some of you just returned from France and others will go back soon. But you'll be well paid, whether we win or lose."

"What if you're dead?" said William. "Who'll pay us then?"

"Shut up, Will. You'd help him for free and you know it," said Cob.

"Aye, I would. But I'd rather have the money—no offense intended, Gwydion."

"None taken, Will."

They drank and talked until late. Gwydion had advised the servant couple they wouldn't be needed for the next week or more and had given them extra wages to ensure their discreet allegiance. The pair was content enough to go off for a respite, and to keep their mouths shut. Why not? The tall, quiet-spoken man paid them generously and treated them well. They also suspected he'd be the wrong man to cross.

Gathered around the fire, the soldiers swapped stories and spoke of fallen friends. Then, to lighten the mood, they compared swords, daggers, and other deadly toys. They threw dice. As the hour advanced and candles burned low, some bragged about female conquests.

"I lately tested a pretty piece of goods in York," said William, finally content to set business aside and put his feet up on the table. "What a horsewoman."

"How so, Will?" asked the black-haired man.

"Rode me like a good saddle, is how. Rode me till I thought I'd die of the joy of it."

Cob laughed. "There's the William we know and love. Why didn't you marry her, man? Most women don't take half so keenly as that to the pommel."

"Oh, I couldn't marry her. If I married her, she likely wouldn't let her doe-eyed, big-bosomed friend sleep in our bed with us like she was used to. Cozy, that was."

After the hoots died down, Malcolm said, "I hope we're not too long indoors here, snug as it is. It's not healthy for a man to be without female company too long. Throws the humors off."

"Sleep with your mare," said William.

"I'm in earnest. How are *you* coping, Gwyd? Been slipping out to the brothel, I'll wager. You're a man likes lifting the skirts on a regular basis, I know."

Gwydion shrugged. "The brothels here don't really have any woman who suits me."

"What?" said Cob, scratching his head. "By God, the lad there"— he jerked his thumb at Thomas, who was now too far gone in drink to be offended—"found himself a skirt, and *you* ain't had one because none suits you? What shite is this?"

"The choices here are limited. That's all, Cob." Gwydion stood and Vort came to his side. "But I'm for bed. Sleep where you can, gentlemen. Someone put that screen on the fire so the house doesn't burn down." He picked up a flickering candle stuck on a small pewter plate and walked to the foot of the stairs.

Thomas suddenly sat forward in his chair and said, rather more loudly than was needed, "Thing is, my famous cousin's smitten. It's true. He doesn't want any common whore now because he's smitten. We both wanted the lady in question at first, but I lost interest once I found another. Isn't that so, Gwyd? Aren't you smitten?"

William turned to watch Gwydion's face across the dim room. He detected no emotion but wasn't surprised. Gwydion had never been a man to betray much emotion.

Thomas stood up and would have promptly fallen over if Cob hadn't steadied him. "Tell 'em, cousin," Tom called, swaying a bit. "I don't mind, now I've got my own cozy armful. Tell 'em about your ladylove. Go on, we're all men of the world."

His kinsman did not respond but remained unmoving near the stairs. Some of the men quickly busied themselves with other things, chatting self-consciously, pulling off their boots, trying to ignore the young man's gauche outburst.

Thomas persisted. "Go on. You can pretend it's not so, but we know better, don't we?"

Gwydion went up the stairs without another word.

Cob looked at the man with the black hair, who looked at Thomas, who was looking at nothing in particular and grinning in an unfocused way.

"Damnation, what's the world coming to?" said Cob.

"To shite," said William, grabbing Thomas by his arm.

"Where are we going?" asked Thomas.

"To dump water over your empty head," replied William, leading him to a side table where a big pitcher sat.

Thomas tripped and bumped into the wall.

"Don't drown him," said Cob. "They're kin."

"He's still a stupid shite," said William.

Cob frowned. He lowered his voice. "You've got to admit, Will, it's a rare piece of news if it's true. Gwyd? Smitten?"

"Maybe so. But rare or not, Gwyd's a good man, a good friend. He deserves his privacy if he wants it—which this shite should have the sense to know, drunk or sober." With that, William raised the pitcher and poured water over Tom's head.

53

THE SPIRITUAL ADVISOR

When his hood was yanked off, Maelgwyn blinked, then gulped lungfuls of air. He'd been deposited on a chair in a large, high-ceiling hall. Four brown dogs sat in a silent row at the other end of the room, a fire blazed in a great hearth, and a group of unknown men ringed him. Some grinned. Grating feminine chatter smote his ears from nearby, but he couldn't see the women responsible for it.

"Your face is a little battered," said a cultured English voice. "And I think you've wet your clothes."

Maelgwyn looked around to see who spoke.

"Over here, to your right," the voice said. "I'm your host, Sir Nicolas de Breauté, a God-fearing nobleman. These idlers are my assistants."

Locating the handsome, well-dressed man who spoke, Maelgwyn tried to sit up straighter. He held out his bound hands. "Why am I a captive? What God-fearing man abducts and terrifies innocent strangers?"

"A fair question. I'll answer if you promise not to urinate inside my house."

Maelgwyn looked down at his hosen. What with his great apprehension and the bone-rattling ride he'd endured, he hadn't realized until now they were damp. His face grew hot. A pox on his treacherous bladder.

Sir Nicolas tapped his foot. "You have to promise."

Maelgwyn wondered if he had been dragged into an asylum. Everything was so strange, especially this Englishman who called himself Sir Nicolas.

"I don't have all day," said de Breauté. "A naked woman is waiting in my chamber with a cup of warm honey. After that, I have to consult with Cook about dinner."

A scrawny man with beady, close-set eyes approached Maelgwyn's chair. He squatted in front of him and peered into his face. "He's waiting for a promise, Piss-Pants."

"Dexter, don't call our guest names. Can't you hear by his accent he's Welsh? Some Welshmen have awkward customs, but we ought not to mock them."

"He's still waiting," said Dexter.

Maelgwyn swallowed. "Yes, I promise."

"You promise what, Piss-Pants? Speak up."

"I promise not to . . . to urinate."

Sir Nicolas toyed with his necklace. "Oh, you may certainly urinate. But not indoors." Maelgwyn watched with sudden sharp interest as the nobleman lifted the crucifix from his chest and kissed it three times. "Now I'm off," de Breauté said, sauntering away.

"What should I do with this lump?" called Dexter to his master's back. "He's got a foul air about him, seems to me."

Nicolas turned. "Of course he does: his hosen are wet. They probably chafe. But he wasn't carrying a warrant, was he?"

"No."

"Then get him some dry clothes and we'll fix on his fate tomorrow. It's too late now for tiresome decisions."

"Wait! You say you're God-fearing," cried Maelgwyn, anxiously watching de Breauté's face. If his ploy worked, he might potentially avoid a grim fate. "Wouldn't a God-fearing nobleman treat a guest with kindness? For thereby some have entertained angels unawares."

"You don't strike me as angelic, however," said de Breauté. "And how do you know what every good man would do? Some may behave less traditionally than others, after all."

This was not the response Maelgwyn expected, but he kept on. "God sets clear limits for men, traditional or not. I know, for I am a man of God, a . . . a priest of God."

Nicolas looked slightly more interested. He walked back to the circle of his men. "Then why aren't you in proper holy robes?"

Maelgwyn thought fast and hard and came up with an answer. "My sect goes unheralded among the people. We believe we can do more good dressed as simply as our flock."

"Oh, really. Recite the Ten Commandments."

Maelgwyn rattled them off.

Nicolas raised his crucifix and kissed it again. "And which is your favorite member of the Holy Trinity?"

This presented Maelgwyn with a dilemma. How could he utter the sort of blasphemy this oddity seemed to want to hear? He sent a silent inquiry skyward and received an instant reply. "I've no favorite," he said. "The One God in Threeness can never be sundered by a wretch like me."

"A good answer," said de Breauté. "Smarmy but adroit." He came to Maelgwyn's side, produced a knife from his boot, and cut through the rope that bound his wrists. "I've a sudden happy notion. Would you like to be my spiritual advisor? I have a cook, grooms, harlots, and an array of other employees. But no spiritual advisor. What say you?"

Maelgwyn rubbed his wrists, then placed his trembling hands in prayer position. This was better than he had hoped. "It would be my honor."

"Wonderful. I won't pay you much, because it would have been cheaper to let Dexter kill you, after all. But you'll have free meals and a woman every night."

"Oh, no. I practice celibacy."

"Well then, practice all you like. I shan't, however. I enjoy ladies. You don't reckon that a sin, do you? By the way, what name shall we call you?"

"I am Maelgwyn. And I don't consider your consorting with women a sin, since *you* have not made vows of chastity."

"Another superior answer, Maelgwyn. You could have been a statesman, and we all know what they're like. Also I assume you don't object to discreet execution either, if the victim is deserving?"

Maelgwyn cast about in his head for a fitting verse and soon found it. "To everything there is a season—a time to kill and a time to heal, Sir Nicolas."

"I only asked because I have an enemy who impugns me for crimes I did not commit. At least not all of them. He even wants to take away my house"—he gestured to the surrounding walls—"and have it for himself."

"Heinous," said Maelgwyn.

"Indeed." Sir Nicolas looked into his new advisor's face, then stared at his throat. "Now that I look closely, and I see your funny pink scar, I believe there may be a special name for a man like you. But I'm not quite sure what it is." He glanced at Dexter, who still squatted nearby. "Dex, do you know of a name for men of Maelgwyn's stamp? He has an odd aspect."

"Aye," Dexter said without hesitation. "Oily-tongued weasel."

Sir Nicolas put a playful foot to his chief henchman's shoulder and pushed him over. "You're incorrigible, fair Dexter. You never like anyone." The nobleman then went toward the staircase again. "But I'm definitely neglecting that poor darling who waits patiently upstairs. You men get my new advisor clean clothes and tell him about Gwydion ap Harlot ap Pig Droppings, our left-handed foe. I'll see you all at supper."

After the nobleman left, Dexter led Maelgwyn to a pile of straw in a corner. "Here's your nest, holy man. I'll fetch you hosen later."

"Wait," said Maelgwyn, as Dexter moved away.

The impatient lackey turned back with a string of invective that strained Maelgwyn's English capability to its limit.

"Dear friend," said Maelgwyn, shrinking a bit from the man's ferocity, "I was just wondering about the name of Sir Nicolas's sworn enemy. What did he say it was?"

"I'm not your friend, Weasel, but he said it was Gwydion ap Pig Droppings. So what?"

Maelgwyn smiled. "Nothing, friend. I just wanted to be sure I knew what name to use when I pray to the Maker to rain down vengeance."

Dexter spit into Maelgwyn's new bed of straw. "As if the Maker would be at the beck and call of a lumpen thing like you," he said, and stalked off.

With hurried strokes and a hidden smile, Maelgwyn brushed away the pool of spittle with a clump of straw. He was elated; he'd been miraculously delivered to the very hall of the foe of his foe. Then he looked up to behold a man and woman coupling atop one end of the long dining table. The man's face was bright red. Beneath him the woman moaned theatrically.

Hunkering to one side, Maelgwyn watched the writhing pair. His breath grew rapid.

Like an angry apparition Dexter reappeared at his side. "You like to watch, Weasel? That your little game?"

"What?" Maelgwyn dragged his attention from the lovers. "Oh, no. I'm just a bit taken aback. I assure you I make no judgment, friend."

"See you don't. And if you ask me, you look more randy than taken aback. Too randy for a God-botherer."

"Your aspersions are unfounded."

"See they stay that way or you'll answer to me. You'll answer hard."

"But Sir Nicolas—"

"Is too good and grand to keep a watch out for lying swine like you. But *I'm* not, never fear."

54

CURIOSITY AND CATMINT

Elise rented the shop near The Otter and Roe two days after she and Annora arrived in Conwy. Her new landlady was a half-blind harridan who didn't care who her tenants were and what they sold as long as they paid on time and let her be. The place had one large unglazed window with shutters and a sturdy door. Formerly it had housed a fishmonger, and it required a fair amount of cleaning to be rendered habitable. But the women didn't mind.

As they dusted and scrubbed, a succession of folk peeked through the door to see what was afoot. "What's it to be, your shop?" a young woman asked from the threshold.

"We're makers of salves and decoctions and medicines," said Elise. "My servant can't speak, but she's a wonder at diminishing pains of the head, at chasing wrinkles and women's monthly complaints, and easing a hundred other ills."

"What of you, miss?"

"I make rinses for the hair, wart creams, syrup for a child's barking cough, powders for itch-mites. I can help rid the face of freckles, firm the lips, and blend perfumes out of flowers."

The visitor's face brightened. "If you can do all that, the ladies of Conwy will flock here. The men too, I should think."

"Tell your neighbors. Tell them we will welcome their first visits two days hence or three. First we need to harvest certain herbs and fetch vital items from the spice merchant."

After that, interest grew even more rapidly. Women ventured into the shop-to-be with their friends or servants. Everyone wanted to see the apothecary and her silent assistant.

Elise's self-appointed champion, the host at The Otter and Roe, informed all his clientele that the young newcomer was a mysterious, well-born lady as intelligent as she was gracious. Of course it was the Mortality that had forced her to earn her own way. Her deceased father had been a duke. At least so the innkeeper suspected. She might even be the natural child of someone higher-fixed than a duke. But *that*, the innkeeper warned, was only hearsay and ought not be randomly repeated. In any event, one could see that the lady possessed admirable bearing and manners. Her speech had the careful, well-enunciated tone of the English aristocracy. How fortunate were Conwy's citizens that she had chosen to settle amongst them.

His intriguing words fanned the sparks of curiosity.

Ignorant of the grand past she'd suddenly acquired, Elise simply supposed Conwy's citizens were rather friendly and rather odd. Folks poked their heads in the shop's door so often, she finally had to bar it to get any work done.

"I think some of our would-be customers are plaiting their hair too tightly," said Annora when she and Elise were alone. "I never saw so many nosy, silly creatures."

"That big blond woman who came this morning told me the last apothecary didn't like to deal with females," said Elise. "He'd get flustered if their complaints were of a womanly nature. But now he's gone and his son just stays drunk all day, so they're pleased we've arrived. There's a barber-surgeon, Master Plumstoke, but he only does tooth pulling, boil lancing, and cupping. His main job is ferryman. He takes a boat to Deganwy."

"Busy fellow. But that explains why everyone's so interested, I suppose. Have you heard any talk of the midwife?"

Elise finished dusting a cabinet in the back of the shop, behind the thick curtain that separated the public area from the room where she and Annora would sleep and eat. "The ladies I've talked to hail mostly from Conwy's richer classes. They speak of the midwife with disdain."

"Then are we prepared to deliver babies too?"

"I tell everyone it's absolutely not our usual business."

Later that day they had a chance to meet the midwife in person, when an aggressive knock sounded. Elise rushed to let whoever it was in, thinking it must be an emergency.

"Do you mean to rob me of my livelihood?" said the new visitor without introduction.

Annora came forward in case there might be trouble; this female seemed agitated.

"Have we met?" said Elise. "My apologies if I've forgotten. So many ladies stop by."

"I'm Lucy Atwall, as if you didn't know. I'm midwife here, a good and honest midwife, so you can stop pretending you never heard of me." She folded her arms over her chest. "The women say you're a prince's by-blow. I for one don't believe it."

Elise inspected Lucy. She was fair and not ill-favored, in her middle years, and somewhat rumpled. A closer look at her face revealed more bluster than hostility. "People say a lot of strange things, Lucy, but we have absolutely no intention of taking away your livelihood. We aren't midwives."

"What are you?"

"We deal in herbs, healing creams, flower medicines."

Lucy glanced at Annora, who had gone back to brushing cobwebs from the ceiling with a cloth fixed to the end of a long stick. "Why doesn't the old one say anything?"

"My maid is mute."

Lucy still looked suspicious. "Then you swear it? You're not here to steal the bread from my mouth?"

"I swear it. Now come and sit. Share a cup of ale and a bite of *our* bread as a token of accord. Then we'll be able to chat with more ease."

Lucy perched on the rough chair Elise offered. "Well, everyone talks about your fine manners," she said grudgingly.

As the midwife grew comfortable, she commenced to give Elise hints about difficult clients she might encounter and about which women or men would be likely to want certain medicines and which might want other things.

Leaning back in her chair, Lucy peered at her new acquaintance. "I hear you're a widow."

"Yes."

"Already had enough of men?"

"I suppose I have."

"Me too. My husband went down in a ship, just off the coast here. It was hard at first, but now I'm glad to make my own way. Less trouble."

Elise smiled and stood, trying to bring the conversation to an end. There was much work left to do.

Lucy ignored the hint. She held out her cup for more ale, which Elise of course politely provided before taking her seat again. "Still, we've got a new crop of men about just lately," the midwife said, sipping ale as if she might stay forever. "There's a rich man lives just outside of town. I've heard he's virtuous and easy to look at. Then my neighbor told me of another. This one has a boy's face and a winsome smile. I haven't seen him yet either, but boy or not, he's dallying with some Welsh tart from the quayside. They meet in the woods and do things even married people oughtn't. Likely they think no one knows. But it's hard to keep those sorts of secrets in Conwy, I promise."

"I'm sure it is," said Elise, rising once more. She had grown impatient with her garrulous new friend. "But I should really get back to my cleaning now. Besides, I've taken up enough of your valuable time."

The midwife finally rose. "I suppose you're right. I've a patient who wants a baby but can't get one, so I told her to sit naked over a pot of catmint tea. She's still at my place, steeping. But it's been nice to meet you and listen to your tales."

"Thank you. And don't fret about losing customers. You needn't worry for a moment."

"I'm relieved." Lucy looked out into the street to be sure her next words were not overheard. Then she looked back at Elise. "Tell me honestly, are you a royal bastard?"

Elise frowned. "I am not."

"Oh, well. I thought it sounded like a fool's tale."

After she'd gone and the door was barred again, Annora set her cobweb stick aside. "That one liked the clatter of her own tongue," she said, sinking into the chair Lucy had warmed. "Who was she?"

"The midwife. She was fretting we might steal her business."

"You assured her we wouldn't?"

"I did. But she's an odd sort of person. Still, she's friendly enough."

"Good. No harm in having more friends."

They returned to their work. The fishy odor had been nearly vanquished, as had most of the grime from the walls. Tomorrow they would buy bowls and jars, spices, and other necessary ingredients. When all of that was accomplished, they'd go beyond Conwy's walls, to the woods, to gather herbs and flowers.

55

Dragon Eggs

With Annora trailing behind like the perfect mute servant she pretended to be, Elise walked down to the shops the next morning. A ship had arrived in Conwy the previous week with a cargo of rare spices and other unusual items, so there was much choice.

The women found camphor, mandrake root, cloves, quicksilver, milk of aloe, galingale, musk oil, and verjuice made from unripe grapes. "It's a treasure trove," Elise whispered when a spice merchant disappeared to the back of his shop to find a larger basket for their purchases. Annora nodded, then sneezed when she held a pot of dried red ants too close to her nose. Insect bits flew everywhere. She hastily set the pot down to brush at her dress.

"Good lady, you must have some of these ground emeralds," said the merchant, returning. He held a basket in one hand and a vial filled with green powder in the other. "Effective against the most deadly ailments, even the Pestilence. Why, if a poison toad turned his glance upon this vial, his very eyes would shatter."

Elise shook her head. "Thank you. But in my experience emeralds cannot save a soul from the Pestilence. If it wants you, it will have you."

He produced other expensive possibilities. "Greek tortoise eyes, borax, dragon eggs?"

She refused his exotica. "Tempting as they are, I doubt I have the necessary knowledge to use them to best advantage."

The merchant later told his spouse that he appreciated the new apothecary's humility but wished he could have sold her dragon eggs at least. "We'll never be rid of the things, I fear."

At another shop Elise purchased bowls, bottles, cups, and linen and string to wrap wares for their customers. Then at the cobbler Annora had a frustrating time describing the footgear she wanted without opening her mouth. Her hands fluttered and flew in pantomime. But when the two friends left the shop, she wore sturdy shoes of soft leather with a brown ribbon sewn down the front. This pair had been ordered months ago by a lady who had since died unexpectedly of some stomach ailment. Happily they fit Annora well. If the cobbler was surprised the smiling young lady was willing to spend so much for her servant, he didn't say so. He wished he had a hundred more like her with fine taste and ready money.

Annora threw her old shoes into a midden beside a scruffy ale-house.

Elise hired a boy to carry their packages, for there was still more to buy and their arms were already full. Then they bought two wool blankets, measuring spoons, a small scale, and fresh aprons. At a stall near the church they found honey in clay pots and bunches of dried heather. The boy walked ahead, weighed down with his burden but happy for the coin he'd been given.

Annora glanced around to be sure they wouldn't be overheard. She said in a low voice, "We ought not spend any more, child. You've already been too reckless."

"But it's such a good feeling."

"Yes, but now we need to get to work, or we'll be living here until you're as old as I am."

"We won't. We'll be in that cottage before next summer."

"Not if you fritter away every penny. You know, we didn't really need new aprons. We didn't need heather either."

"Oh, Annora, the heather wasn't that dear. I want our shop to be sweet-smelling and homey, that's all. Is that wrong?"

"It's not wrong. But remember, this place is temporary."

Elise gazed around her at the cottages and shops, the church, and the looming castle. "Everything is temporary now. Sometimes I just want things to seem familiar. And lasting."

"Patience, cariad."

They still needed to pick wild herbs and flowers. On their list of wants were agrimony, betony, nettle, iris, lily, borage, chamomile, mustard seeds, pimpernel, flax, wild roses, ivy, the inner rind of an elder tree, and pennyroyal.

They dropped their purchases at their shop and dismissed the parcel boy. After that they walked over to the inn to enjoy a good meal — their last indulgence for a while, Elise promised. Shopping had made them hungry, and there was nothing in their new place except honey, stale bread, and half a pitcher of indifferent ale. The innkeeper was glad to see them, as usual, and told Elise her shop was bound to be a success, judging by the interest it had created. His words buoyed her.

Their visit to Conwy's merchants had not gone unnoticed. Recovering from too much ale and feeling sorry for himself, Thomas had gone down to the quay to see Pearl. She always made him feel so good, so manly. But she wasn't there. No one was in the mussel shed. That happened occasionally when the catch was poor. He decided to wander around the streets for a bit, as anything was better than returning to the house, where the men would probably treat him like an irksome child.

Tom's day had begun badly. He received a private earful from Gwydion's friend William as soon as he woke up. The man with the scar down the middle of his forehead was standing in the doorway of his room when Tom first opened his eyes. "Remember what you said last night, lad?" William asked. He looked grim.

Lad again. Truly, Tom was beginning to loathe the word. "Not much of it," he said, sitting up. He had a sudden sinking fear he may have been a bit free with his talk. He hoped, he prayed it wasn't anything too horrible. "What did I say?" Then he felt a chill and looked down. "Damn, why's my shirt wet?"

William leaned on the doorjamb. "You told us about Gwyd's ladylove. Then you had a little bath courtesy of me and Cob."

Queasiness assaulted Thomas. He groaned.

William nodded. "Coming back? You're lucky the man didn't split your skull. I would have."

Tom struggled up from his bed and somehow found the nerve to look William in the eye. "What else?"

"Oh, that was the worst of it. Gwyd wasn't any too pleased, but he went to bed without saying anything much because that's his way."

Thomas shuddered, imagining the scene. "Should I apologize?" He hated asking advice from this rough fellow.

"Up to you. But don't ever do it again or you'll answer to me. He's my friend, a damn fine friend, and doesn't need his business blathered around by drunken puppies."

Thomas wanted to vomit. He felt like running back to Ipswich and crawling into a deep, dark hole.

Watching him, William relented a little. "Don't take it too hard, lad. Learn from your mistakes, since you're likely to make more. We all do. But if your brain can't keep up with your mouth when you're drinking, you know you've likely had enough."

William had left him alone then to wonder what dreadful things he'd actually said. But Thomas still hadn't found sufficient courage to seek Gwydion out and tell him he was sorry.

It was at the spot where two lanes meet in front of the old church that he caught sight of Elise and Annora. He thought at first his guilty conscience had conjured them, but that notion only lasted a moment. It really was Elise, smiling, perhaps a bit pale, with her arms full of heather.

He trailed them to a shop and watched Annora take a key from a chain around her neck to open the door. So this was their place. Guessing by their packages, they were in the process of furnishing it as a shop or a home or both. A boy held even more things and carried them in.

Thomas considered this new knowledge. He sat on the garden wall of a house in the next lane until a woman came outside and gave him a meaningful glare. Then he decided to backtrack to The Otter and Roe, where the host had a reputation for gossip. Sure enough, at the inn he learned all about Conwy's new arrivals.

Here was a way to make up to Gwydion for whatever embarrassment he had caused him the night before. He could tell him that Elise, his ladylove, was nearby.

He hurried back to the house. A few men sat in the main room, but not Gwydion. No one greeted Tom. He went out to the back and found his cousin alone, grooming his horse.

Deciding to approach the thing without roundaboutation, he said, "I made a fool of myself last night. If I embarrassed you, I'm sorry. I won't do it again."

Gwydion barely looked over his shoulder. "Fine."

Thomas bit his lip. *Fine?* Nothing more? No, he still felt awful. He cleared his throat and tried again. "I've begun to realize you might have real feelings for Elise, and I had no business talking about her in front of your friends. It was stupid of me and I hope—"

"Be still, Tom."

"I can't just be still. You have to truly accept my apology, Gwyd. Otherwise I'll keep talking. I'll talk all day because I can't even start to tell you how sorry and ashamed I feel."

Gwydion turned and looked into his cousin's worried face. Then he shook his head and finally, reluctantly, he smiled. "All right. I formally accept your apology because I know full well you're capable of talking all day."

The queasiness Tom had felt since waking began to subside. He returned his cousin's smile. "Thank God. But Gwyd, there's something else I have to tell you."

"Good Lord. What now?"

"Elise is in Conwy."

Gwydion's brows drew together.

"With Annora. They've rented a shop two lanes over from here, with a yellow door and yellow shutters. It's to be an apothecary and they'll open in a day or two."

Gwydion gazed over his cousin's head. "Well then, may they prosper."

"May they prosper? I might be a *lad*, and I might behave like a fool sometimes, but I know one thing, cousin: I know you and Elise like each other. Don't you even want—"

"Don't talk to me about what I want, Tom. I don't want anything." He moved toward the house. "Your imagination is frenzied."

Thomas stared after him. "I was just jealous, you know," he called, suddenly desperate to disclose everything. "I asked her to be my mistress to get her to take me seriously, that's how stupid and jealous I was. But she never even looked at me. All she saw was you."

"Mistress?" Gwydion turned around. But when he saw his cousin's young face, earnest and a bit alarmed, he fought down the awful rage that had suddenly enveloped him. He took a moment to calm himself, finally saying, "You misjudged Elise very badly, didn't you?" He ignored the mocking voice in his head that accused him of precisely the same crime.

"I know that now. But I thought you and she were . . . I thought she might be—"

"We weren't, Tom. And she isn't."

"But didn't you want—"

"Enough. I accepted your apology; now let it be."

Later that afternoon, after an intense solitary struggle in his chamber, Gwydion set out alone for the place Tom had described, Elise and Annora's shop. He was completely unable to stop himself. But he made sure no one saw him leave.

Luckily the streets were quiet and he found the place easily. But the yellow shutters and the door were firmly closed. It appeared no one was home. He just stood there, staring, until a passerby gave him a curious look. Calling himself the greatest fool who had ever been born, he went back the way he had come.

What would he have done, he asked himself, if Elise had been there? Strolled casually in and requested more honey for his wounds?

He opened the door of his own rented house and went in. It was safer and simpler to drink ale and talk about the impending confrontation at Llys Garanhir than to think about Elise. From now on he'd stay well away from her new home.

However, that resolve proved to be not in the least steadfast. For when everyone else retired or was occupied with other business in the house, he came back down the stairs. By now, so late, she would have surely returned from wherever she had been. Maybe if he just caught a glimpse of her—maybe it would be enough to see her one more time and know she was safe. Or perhaps he might even apologize to her for his cousin's insulting proposition. Or would that only embarrass her?

Without any fixed idea of what exactly he would say when he found Elise, he set out.

56

ROSES AND JAWBONES

As helpful and talkative as her husband, the innkeeper's wife told Elise where to look for the best flowers and herbs. But a visit to this place required a trip across the Conwy River.

The day was warm, so Annora and Elise left their cloaks behind and took the ferry to the place called Deganwy. Master Plumstoke, the barber-surgeon, was their pilot. His loutish and sweat-stinking son was the first and only mate and the women the only passengers, although there was room in the boat for four or five more.

Master Plumstoke was gnarled and leathery from the sun, and full of talk. "Mostly folks cross here to be on to somewhere else. There's not much in Deganwy to tempt a body to loll. But you two're off to pick herbs, eh? 'Ware the stinging nettles on the slopes," he told Elise. "Meaner than most. The Welsh grow 'em special to bedevil us English, you know."

"We'll be mindful," she said.

"Mind any Welsh you see too. Dark and crafty. A godless pagan lot, worship trees and eat babies. Sacrifice virgins too." He gave her a lecherous grin. "Best be extra careful, miss."

The smelly son sniggered.

"Since I'm a widow," Elise said, shielding her eyes from sunlight and spray, "I'm sure I'll be safe."

"Mayhap the savages aren't as fussy nowadays, with so few fresh virgins left. Keep your wits about you if you don't want to prance naked in a Druid's orgy or bubble in a stew."

Again the son laughed. "Druids. Oh, you're a rogue, Pa, you are," he said, using the flat part of his oar to splash water on his parent and sprinkling Elise in the process.

She gave him an irate look, but he feigned not to notice.

Master Plumstoke told his passengers to come back before sunset and not be late or he'd leave them stranded until the next day. "You won't like sleeping on the beach, if you're late. It's haunted by weepy ghosts, they say, and crabs'll pinch your feet."

After disembarking, the women crossed a meadow to a hill the innkeeper's wife had described. Along the way they picked ivy, penny-royal, and chamomile. On a shady slope where a brook danced over mossy pebbles, they found pimpernel.

As she stepped easily across the little brook, Elise said, "This isn't much like the river in Penmachno, is it?"

Annora was relieved to be able to speak Welsh, or any language, without fear of being overheard. "But it's such a melancholy place. Pretty, but sad."

"It is. You can almost hear echoes. But of what?"

"I don't know, child. It's probably best not to think too hard on such things."

Not a soul was about. There was reason for that, though Annora and Elise were ignorant of it: every man, woman, and child in De-ganwy had died in the Mortality. Without its minders, the vineyard that once flourished there, close to the river, was now a tangle of greenery and bare stalks. Boats rotted on the shoal and empty cottages kept hopeless vigils. Jawbones and femurs of all sizes lay shielded under veils of sea holly. Wheeling high above, ever watchful, were seabirds, guardians of a hundred tragic stories they could never tell.

"Anyway, the ground is good, fertile. Our sacks will be overflowing in plenty of time to get back for the ferry," said Elise. "We'll be waiting on the spit before Master Plumstoke has a chance to utter another word about ghosts and Druid orgies."

"Was that what he was saying?"

"Oh, yes. He's quite a storyteller."

They climbed the hill. At the summit they sat on a log to share the quince tart the innkeeper's wife had kindly given them. Borage grew all about, along with wild mustard and flax.

"I'll search for iris now," said Elise, when they finished. "But I sus-pect it's too late in the season." They wanted the oblong fruits of that flower to make drinks for stomach complaints.

"There's safety in numbers, so I'll stay with you. We can protect each other from ghosts and nasty Druids."

"Father always spoke of the Druids with respect."

"Did he ever meet one? No, and they've all vanished now. But it's better to be safe than sorry, though I'm more worried about common criminals than I'd ever be about Druids."

They merged into the deeper woods that guarded the hill's far slope.

Wild roses were plentiful, if past their prime. Each woman plucked a score, just the limp flowers, and placed them in her sack. But though they searched in every likely place they came across, they didn't see a single iris.

Stopping by a holly tree, Elise breathed in deeply. How quiet it was. The scent of the greenwood soothed her. In this secluded glade no one could know her heart or judge her.

Again she thought of Gwydion. How did he fare? Had he yet confronted de Breauté, or was he residing temporarily in Conwy itself, perhaps even on the next lane over from theirs, or the next? She supposed she could quiz the innkeeper to see if he knew anything of the matter.

But why bother?

She took another deep breath.

Gwydion. Would they meet on a market day, exchange cool greetings, and move on? Probably not. In all likelihood they would never meet again.

The late afternoon found the women waiting for the ferry with their sacks full of herbs and flowers. Neither spirits nor men had molested them, and the bright sun had shone all day. An uneventful ferry trip across the estuary brought them safe back to Conwy just before nightfall.

But their arrival at the town gate was secretly witnessed by one pair of close-set eyes and one pair of icy blue.

Dexter lurked outside Conwy's wall, dutifully watching from the nearby woods for a bailiff or any other of his lord's enemies who might come or go. That day there hadn't been much to see. But he came to excited attention as the two familiar women disappeared into Conwy.

He smirked. Sir Nicolas would be so hurt to know his "sister" was in the neighborhood but hadn't seen fit to visit him. Oh, yes, and he'd taken such a fancy to her. Didn't he go on and on about their marvelous spiritual bond? More important, hadn't the little bitch sworn up and down she'd come visit as soon as she could? She certainly didn't appear to be on any vital mission that might forestall her, as she went through the gate smiling, carrying flowers.

Beside Dexter, Maelgwyn crouched in the shadows. His fists clenched as Elise and her servant passed through Conwy's gate. His heart pounded. Yes, it really was Elise. Elise, his wife and would-be slayer.

Maelgwyn followed her progress with his eyes. The bitch was snickering, carrying yellow flowers and snickering. How lighthearted she looked—a jaunty little murderess.

Earlier that afternoon when Dexter had forced him to come along to keep vigil outside Conwy, Maelgwyn had been furious. But he was powerless to do anything except whatever the lackey decreed. "You come with me, Piss-Pants," Dexter said, "because I don't like to think of you festering indoors, on your own. It'll be easier to keep an eye on you if you're right here by me. Truth is, I don't trust you any more than I'd trust a mad dog."

Sir Nicolas, of course, gave Dexter his blessing. "By all means, Dex, take poor Maelgwyn for an airing. I'd be grateful. I fear I was hasty in giving him employment. He casts a pall over the house, I think, with his gloomy face and verses. Best to put him to better use."

But now fate had turned Maelgwyn's fury to joy. Elise was found! He, Maelgwyn, could erase her smile forever. The fool de Breauté could help him do it.

Neither Dexter nor Maelgwyn commented aloud as they watched the women enter Conwy. But each man was well pleased with his outing and his discovery.

57

THE PAST AND THE FUTURE

Light showed beneath the yellow door. Gwydion approached. The hour was advanced, but someone was still awake.

He knew he wouldn't sleep for the rest of the night if he didn't try to see Elise. And he knew he was a fool. When before had he ever pursued a woman who didn't come to him when he beckoned? He'd always walked away without another thought.

Everything was different now.

"All she saw was you," Thomas had said. Perhaps this late-night visit wouldn't be altogether distasteful to her. He hoped.

He raised his hand, hesitated, then knocked.

The noise startled both women, who were busily sorting and preparing the simples they had collected. Who could be at their door so late? Perhaps the well-meaning innkeeper or his wife brought some surplus treat from the inn's kitchen or stopped to see how the trip to Deganwy had gone.

Annora raised the bar and opened the door a crack.

Then she opened it wider.

"This is a surprise," she said, torn between consternation and inexplicable relief.

"Annora. I hope I find you well." He looked past her.

"And I you. You came here specially to ask if I'm well, did you? How did you even know where to find us?"

"Tom and I took a house nearby. He mentioned he saw you walking near the church, so I thought I'd come by to pay my respects."

The strain in his voice and his slight lack of certainty would have probably gone unnoticed in another man, but Annora heard, and saw, and was astonished. She took pity.

"Elise," she called, "look who's here."

Elise already knew, as she'd been hovering near the curtain that separated front room from back. She came slowly forward.

"It's good to see you, Gwydion," she said, smiling uncertainly. "Have you been well these past few days?"

Both unknowingly thought the same thing: Had it only been a few days?

He said, "Very well, thanks to you. I mean, to you both."

Unspoken words hung so palpably in the air between them that Annora was confronted once more, and forcibly, with the notion that she'd been wrong to tamper with their lives. So strong was that notion, she resolved to let them muddle through on their own from then on, without her dubious help.

She yawned. "You won't mind if I lie down? I'm exhausted. But Elise, I promise I'll help you finish with the herbs tomorrow morning before we pop in at the market."

Gwydion and Elise were both surprised by this announcement. But neither tried to stop her from retiring. She wished them good night and disappeared behind the back curtain.

"The sun must have tired her," said Elise, watching the curtain swish into place. She turned back. "We spent the afternoon across the river gathering herbs and flowers."

"Then it's understandable. Did you find everything you needed?"

"Oh yes. Well, almost. There were no irises."

Silence fell. She fiddled with a string she'd tied around her wrist to remind herself to ask the innkeeper's wife if marshmallow grew anywhere nearby. The roots could be used in babies' teething ointments and in a cream for sore muscles. Gwydion watched her. He desperately wanted to speak, to say something, anything. But he was dumbstruck, and maddened by his strange new lack of sangfroid.

Finally he struggled to say, "Does it chafe, that string on your wrist? Shall I loosen it?"

It didn't chafe in the least. In fact, it hung slack. But she said, "Yes, please."

He took her arm carefully, as if fearful it might break, and worked at the knot. Their heads met over the endeavor. Tugging and twisting lightly, he tried not to let his fingers touch her skin.

"It's stubborn," he said, frowning.

"Don't worry then. It's fine." She drew away.

"Elise, I—"

"Truly, it's fine. I'll snip it off tomorrow."

"But I want—"

"It isn't bothering me, actually—"

He pulled her into his arms. She made a small sound, then went still and stared up at him. As he looked into her eyes, the things Annora told him came flooding back.

"I'm sorry, I had no right," he said, immediately releasing her. "I seem to have formed a habit of forcing myself on you. But I'll go now and leave you in peace."

"I wasn't struggling."

"I know about your marriage. I know I'll only upset you."

She read the tangle of emotions on his face. Whatever he wanted from her, at least no one watching his expression could think him indifferent.

Then maybe the truth wouldn't disgust him or drive him away. Was that possible? Maybe she could confess her sins, try to make him see how she came to commit them, then hope he could still want her afterward—for anything at all.

She would accept whatever he offered of himself. Elise knew that now, knew it with shameless certainty. What she spurned from Thomas, she'd welcome eagerly, with joy, from this man—this man only. "Will you sit?" she said.

He did reluctantly, and she took a chair across from his.

Her voice was low, so it wouldn't carry to the back. "I'm not upset. I promise."

"Annora told me—"

"I know. She meant well, but she was wrong. It's true I'm the widow of a cruel man. But it was only my husband I feared, only Maelgwyn. And now he's dead."

"Then why did Annora warn me?"

"She was just trying to protect you, and me."

"From what?"

She gathered her courage. Even if it meant risking her one small, very small, chance at happiness, the moment had come to tell the truth.

"I began having visions when I was eleven," she said. "I don't know why I have them or where they come from. Sometimes they don't seem to mean anything at all. But sometimes they foretell the future. Sometimes they reveal secrets."

He watched her eyes. "Go on."

"At home my visions didn't really matter. People on Anglesey are more tolerant of such things, I think."

"But then you left Anglesey."

"When my family died, yes. My father, a dear, good man, saw a chance to provide security for me just before his death. So he arranged my marriage to a widower who lived near Ysbyty Ifan."

"Maelgwyn."

She nodded. "I journeyed to his house and we were wed."

The lines of Gwydion's mouth tightened a little. "How did he react when he found his new wife was subject to visions?"

She gave a small, ironic shrug. "Not well."

"He punished you."

"It was his way. But gradually his temper grew more violent."

He leaned toward her. "Why didn't you leave?"

"And go where? Women don't have such ease in the world as men. We don't strike out into the unknown without direst need."

"If he hurt you, your need was surely dire."

"You're right. In the back of my mind, I did dream of the cloister."

"Would that life have suited you, Elise?"

She blushed. "Perhaps not. But in the end fate intervened."

He kept his eyes locked on hers. "Fate? Maelgwyn died, you mean."

"He died." She took a deep breath. "But not a natural death." Her voice grew even softer. "I killed him, Gwydion." She waited for shock and revulsion to register on his face.

But he only folded his arms across his chest and leaned back in his chair. He gave her a crooked smile. "You? A killer?"

She looked down. "It's true."

"All right, it's true. Tell me how it happened."

He hadn't been overwhelmed by her confession—yet. She went on. "I wasn't an adequate wife, Maelgwyn told me. I had to die. So he choked me, but I found a jagged piece of glass." She gazed beyond Gwydion. "I stabbed him. Twice. Then, to be rid of his body, I pushed him into the Conwy."

Silence fell.

She stole a glance at his face. "Now do you see why Annora tried to warn you? I'm a murderess."

"You're sure he was dead?"

"What? Of course."

"You really think you should be blamed for saving yourself from a monster?"

"I—"

"At least now I understand why you'd have reason to be leery of men."

She gripped the arms of her chair. "You still don't know everything."

"Tell me. I'm not so fainthearted as you seem to suppose." He smiled at her with great kindness.

How fine he is, she thought. How brave and good.

He interrupted her silent cataloging of his virtues. "Tell me, Elise."

"Yes." Everything. "After Maelgwyn died I saw, in a trance, that he and his mother practiced dark crafts. But I think he wiped the memory of all that from his mind, for he constantly boasted of his own piety. Perhaps he was trying to convince himself of it."

"Your tale is surprising and not comfortable," he said. "But truly, why did you suppose it would give me a disgust of you?"

"Hear it all, to the last detail. About Maelgwyn and his mother. You see, I believe he killed his mother sometime before our marriage was arranged. He cut her in pieces and threw her in the river."

"But why? Why would he kill his own mother?"

"Their relationship went beyond what is . . . acceptable for a mother and son. That's what a vision showed me." She felt herself flush. "Maybe he couldn't bear the weight of guilt."

At last he looked shocked, but only for a moment. "And now they're both dead. But how can you possibly blame yourself for their sins? Wasn't it enough that you suffered at his hands?"

She stood, and so did he. "I was wed to a foul, evil man and I killed him. I have visions. How could any decent man want to know a woman like me?"

"None of it matters."

"But you shouldn't risk my friendship. Someday my crime may come to light."

"Your risk is greater than mine. For all you know, *I* might be a rogue."

She gazed up at him. What she saw brought a tremulous smile to her lips and she slowly, hesitantly, held out her hand. "You, a rogue?"

He drew her to him then and she felt the hard, steady beating of his heart. He pulled her still closer. When his lips brushed her brow, she pressed herself against him.

"If I'm not a rogue yet, you'll soon be making one of me," he said in a harsh whisper.

Reluctantly she freed herself.

He watched as she moved to the makeshift table where she and Annora had been sorting herbs. Combing trembling fingers through wilted leaves, she waited for her breath to return to normal, or near normal. When she could speak sensibly, she changed the course of the conversation by asking about de Breauté.

Sharing her wish to take their talk down less perilous paths, he obliged. For now he'd have to cultivate patience, that virtue for which he had so little liking.

"No warrant reached Conwy, I fear," he told her. "But friends have offered to help me deliver de Breauté to the gallows. After they all arrive, we'll ride to Llys Garanhir."

Her cheeks lost some of their rosiness. "How soon?"

"Three days, perhaps sooner."

"You'll take good care."

"I will. But now I think you need to rest, Elise. I'll come back after de Breauté's safely in jail waiting for the hangman."

Hesitating before raising the wooden bar across the door, he silently wondered what it was he really wanted from this lovely creature.

Yes, that. But so much more.

Then he knew. Or rather he finally admitted to himself what he'd already known for days.

He brushed his hand against her cheek. "I'm so truly sorry about what Maelgwyn did to you. More than you know. But I won't ever let anyone hurt you, Elise. Not ever again."

After he left, she undressed in a dream and slid under her blanket in the back room.

Annora sat up. "You were too quiet for me to eavesdrop. What did he say?"

"Hm?"

She poked Elise's arm. "Cariad, what happened?"

"Oh. I told him. Everything."

"About Maelgwyn, and the visions?" Annora poked her again. "Don't you dare just sigh and go to sleep. What does he intend to do? What does he want from you?"

"I'm not sure. But whatever he wants, he can have. Anything. For as long as he likes."

As Elise fell quickly and contentedly asleep, Annora lay in a pother.

58

SAINTS AND SINNERS

Sir Nicolas lounged at the head of Llys Garanhir's table. "I'd relish a tidbit of news," he announced to no one in particular. "Nothing ever happens in this dull place. Someone tell me something interesting."

A woman in a provocative dress stood and threw him a dazzling smile. The effect of this was somewhat lessened by her deficit of teeth. "Rebecca and me showed a few of these fine gentlemen a new trick today, your worship. I put a string of beads . . . somewhere nice and private. Then she retrieved it with her mouth while I—"

"That's not interesting." Nicolas lolled back in his stately chair and propped a foot on the table. "Nor is it news. I've seen that trick at least seven times."

She dropped back down, red in the face.

Across the table Dexter mined his ear with a rabbit's rib bone. He said nonchalantly, "Master Piss-Pants and me loitered around the woods and dales today, over by Conwy."

Sir Nicolas looked petulant. "*Who* loitered?"

Dexter flipped the bone to his empty plate. "Piss-Pants. Weasel face. You remember, you told me I could take him along."

"Oh, you mean my spiritual advisor. And what amazing things did you two ill-assorted comedians observe, fair Dexter?"

"I saw a pair of females. One had a bunch of yellow flowers."

His master stifled a yawn. "Thrilling, Dex. Did you also see boats and butterflies and clouds shaped like sheep?"

Halfway down the table, Maelgwyn sat grinding his teeth. A lack of options had forced him to take a chair between a prostitute who kept squeezing his thigh and shrieking with amusement and Percy, a bald man with no eyebrows who constantly knocked into him with his elbow as he gnawed and slurped his meal. Maelgwyn was upset. Why did Dexter mention the woman with yellow flowers, Elise? She was *his* tale to tell.

So he erupted. "I saw the woman too."

Sir Nicolas took a deep swallow of wine. "That's not interesting either."

Dexter glared down the table at Maelgwyn. "Piss yourself, Weasel. And shut your mouth."

"Ho hum," said Sir Nicolas.

"I, however," continued Maelgwyn, "was not merely loitering, ogling trollops. As it happens, I bear news. Sir, I learned something today which will gladden you immensely."

Nicolas drummed his fingers on the table. "I doubt it."

Maelgwyn pushed his chair back and stood. Thumbs hooked behind him, he took a ponderous stroll the length of the table and back.

"For God's sake," said de Breauté, suddenly lobbing his half-full goblet in Maelgwyn's direction. "Cease your perambulations and tell me your great news, man, or I'll rip off your holy feet and drop them in the privy."

Everyone laughed but Maelgwyn. "Sir," he said, brushing wine from his sleeve, "my news is momentous. This afternoon I beheld a woman—indeed, the woman with the yellow flowers—who knows the whereabouts of your greatest enemy."

Sir Nicolas raised his brows. On the table before him sat a golden, lion-shaped saltcellar he had inherited from Llys Garanhir's dead owner. He stroked the lion's mane. "Go on."

"This woman is actually your enemy's lover, his whore."

The nobleman considered his spiritual advisor out of suddenly narrowed eyes. "Really. And what is the identity of this mysterious female? Where is she?"

"What are you yammering about, Weasel?" said Dexter. "My lord, the woman *I* saw was your precious friend, the one who swore up and down she'd come visit you. Your saintly supposed kin."

Maelgwyn frowned. "Dexter is deluded. The woman, Elise, is a cunning female who has intercourse with Satan. She claims to have visions and know the future. Besides her regular hellish occupations, the bitch has intimately consorted with your left-handed enemy so they might destroy you."

Dexter wagged his head in woeful disgust. "How do you figure all that, Piss-Pants?"

Thugs and harlots murmured. But de Breauté watched Maelgwyn's face intently. "Is she pretty and gently spoken?" he said. "Does she have an old servant who vomits?"

Maelgwyn looked momentarily confused but recovered. "She's pretty enough, my lord, with mouth and gray eyes full of faithless sincerity. And I believe she does employ an old servant woman. These females almost certainly have their lair in Conwy, for I watched them enter the gate this evening."

"You watched?" said Dexter, rising, going toward Maelgwyn. "Just you?"

Sir Nicolas went to stand by the fire. "Sit down, Dexter. It's obvious you're both referring to the same woman."

Dexter glowered, while Maelgwyn's eyes followed his strange employer.

Nicolas stared into the flames. "But I don't believe for a moment she consorts with Satan. No one with eyes as guileless as hers could be what you say, Maelgwyn. By my sweet soul, she and I have a bond."

"Isn't that how Satan conducts his cruel custom, my lord? Would her wiles be so effective if she appeared hideous, if she were not so convincing?"

Sir Nicolas tilted his head. "Precisely how do you, dear Maelgwyn, happen to know of my friend?"

"I regret to say she earned a vile name in our former mutual village. She has a reputation as an evildoer."

"Does she?"

"To her shame, sir."

"Duck fodder," said Dexter, quick to imagine rivalry for his master's approval. He was happy to see Elise discredited, but the praise for her downfall should be his own, not Maelgwyn's. "This is just some fishy trick of Piss-Pants's."

Maelgwyn sent the lackey a cutting, dismissive look, then turned back to his employer. "Sir, would you not rather take the word of a minister of God?"

"Perhaps, perhaps not. But I have a plan." Sir Nicolas approached Maelgwyn. "Tomorrow is Conwy's market day. You and Dexter will go there in the morning and search discreetly for my friend. Harold Munceny will accompany you, since he'll be less off-putting to the populace. And as he may actually possess part of a functioning brain, he'll smooth the way at the gates." Nicolas wasn't wholly confident about Harold's ability to be cunning. After all, the man had had a chance to eliminate Gwydion ap Gruffydd at Dolwyddelan and had been unable to seize it. But he believed Harold, though imperfect, would seem more reassuringly normal to guards and townspeople than either Maelgwyn or Dexter. "When you locate my friend, you'll bring her here, unharmed. Then I'll determine the truth."

Maelgwyn dropped his chin to his chest and closed his eyes. "Your wise decision has made Christ joyous, sir."

The nobleman grabbed Maelgwyn by the hair and jerked his head up. "Don't dare presume to say what makes Christ joyous. My friend may be a saint, after all. And you may be a sinner."

"The both of them are sinners," said Dexter. "That's what I think."

"I've told you repeatedly, fair Dexter, I don't keep you about to think." Sir Nicolas released Maelgwyn and sauntered back to his chair. "Still, there *is* something piscine about his tale. Your relentless misanthropy may yet prove to be instructive, Dex."

Dexter grinned. "Ain't I grand."

"Don't toot so hard on your own scrawny horn. You are certainly not grand. Foul-smelling, ill-favored, violent—loathsome in general—yes. However, you're also consistent and ludicrously loyal. Those qualities are a comfort to one of my mercurial nature."

After everyone else wandered off to pursue their own business—including Maelgwyn, who stood alone at the end of a dim, isolated hallway to avoid heckling from the other men—Sir Nicolas and Dexter spoke privately.

"How do you figure Piss-Pants knows of your sorry saint?" said Dexter. "I mean, truly?"

"Don't dare call her sorry until you know for certain she is."

"Aye, my lord. But there's no denying she's acquainted with Lord Pig-Droppings, is there? We saw 'em have words. Mayhap Piss-Pants got that part right. Mayhap your saint likes to ride the pink bone."

Sir Nicolas struck his lackey fast and hard across the face. Dexter snarled and fell back a step. "You can be unbearably coarse, toad," said de Breauté. "Usually I appreciate that, but not now. Speak of my friend with respect until you have reason to do otherwise."

The lackey tested his jaw. "As you say, sir."

"Now—now I'm wondering if my dear sister is actually dallying in Conwy to assist me. She and I have such a rare and wonderful kinship, you know, and she'd surely wish to assist me. Oh, I realize she swore she'd come to Llys Garanhir, but perhaps she intends to lead Lord Blade astray before she does."

"And perhaps pigs'll fly."

Nicolas raised his hand. "Must I pummel you senseless?"

Dexter cowered. " 'Twas a jest."

"I'm happy to hear you say so. Now, what I find most puzzling is that our tedious Maelgwyn should be acquainted in *any* way with her. It's peculiar. And if you dare to say she likes riding his pink bone as well, I shall throttle you without a qualm."

"No, sir. No woman still breathing would want to ride that slug. But you want to know what I'm really wondering?"

"Go on. I pride myself on my forbearance."

"What if Piss-Pants has been hunting for your friend to settle some old score with her?"

"Possible. He did say they come from the same village."

"He's the kind to hold a grudge."

"Undoubtedly."

"That doesn't mean she's still not thick as thieves with Sir Blade too. We saw her talk to him, and Piss-Pants says she's his doxy."

"There does seem to be a connection. But it might well be innocent. Maelgwyn knows Sir Blade is my enemy and may just be pointing the finger at my friend for his own foul ends."

Dexter shrugged. "Could be. Piss-Pants is a shite."

"He's not endearing. If he's accusing my friend falsely, there will be no word to describe his regret."

"What if he's not lying?"

"Then they'll both be sorry."

"Both?"

"My dear friend for taking advantage of my good nature, and Maelgwyn because I've decided I don't like him at all. I am increasingly repulsed by him. Aren't you? Most of all I dislike his eyes. So I've decided whatever happens, as a spiritual advisor he'll make a fine cadaver."

They both laughed, but Dexter winced and put his hand to his jaw. Sir Nicolas poured more wine to take to bed.

He turned back as he prepared to mount the stairs. "I'll be overjoyed when Sir Blade is dead, you know. Then I can finally settle in without a worry. I think I'll give a fête to celebrate Michaelmas and I'll invite all the gentry. We have a month to prepare."

"Can we have roast peacock and birds that fly out of pies?"

"Too vulgar."

The lackey looked crestfallen. "Jellies shaped like ships?"

"No."

"Then what?"

"Thirty courses and good wine. Everything costly but understated. I mean to be the new arbiter of taste in these parts, and my taste is always exquisite—as my rich bride will be, when I choose her."

Dexter leered. "Think she'll mind all these whores we got flouncing around?"

"We can encourage a few to make other arrangements."

"Not Buxom Barbara."

"Oh, no, Barbara is so cheerful. On that happy note, I leave you." He resumed his ascension.

Dexter went to hunt for Buxom Barbara. He all at once felt rather amorous.

In another part of the manor Maelgwyn rubbed his hands together in the dark. When the bloodhounds padded by at the end of the hall, the last dog in the procession paused. It sniffed the air, then growled. The other dogs returned. All looked toward Maelgwyn.

"What do you want, you beasts? Go away."

The dogs stayed.

"There's nothing for you here. Go, or you'll regret it."

Losing interest, the dogs loped off.

Maelgwyn resumed his ruminations. "Tomorrow my wife will arrive, I hope, to be revealed as the evil slattern she is," he told himself. "The fool de Breauté will surely let me have her so I may administer the punishment she deserves. Afterwards I'll reclaim my riches. Perhaps eventually I'll even remarry. As the Apostle Paul warned us, it is better to marry than to burn."

Maelgwyn was glad events had transpired as they had. It had angered him to be forced, like an errant child, to go with Dexter to lurk in the brush near Conwy's gate. But just look what had come of it. Now he knew for certain where his wife was hiding. Now she would die, her left-handed lover would die, and he would get his cache back.

And never again would any righteous man be seduced by Elise's deceitful gray eyes.

59

SAINT AGATHA'S RELIC

Friday morning Harold Munceny, Maelgwyn, and Dexter saddled three steeds from the stables at Llys Garanhir and rode to Conwy. Their entrance to the town was trouble-free. Welsh folk streaming in from the countryside, merchants on brawny packhorses coming from far and wide, and local farmers with goods to sell or barter—the line of this motley collection of marketgoers was too long to allow gate-keepers the luxury of prolonged individual interrogation.

Designated by Sir Nicolas as unquestioned leader of their trio, Harold announced his first decision: they'd head to an inn for a quick cup of ale. A drink would relax them. Then on to the marketplace at the opposite end of town from the castle, where they'd weave casually through the crowd and dig up information about Elise. Harold would chat with English people who seemed inclined to gossip, and Mael-gwyn with Welsh. Dexter was not to say a word.

This discriminatory stricture did not sit well. Standing in a quiet spot beside their horses, at the edge of the market, de Breauté's main lackey objected.

"What about Piss-Pants? Look at that face, those eyes. Damn it, Munceny, nobody likes him. I don't, you don't. Nobody'll want to speak to him. So why does he get to gibble-gabble, but I don't?"

Maelgwyn stood to one side, waiting for the argument to end in his favor.

"He parleys Welsh, Dexter," said Harold. "We don't. I agree with you about his face, but it can't be helped."

"So he speaks Welsh. What of it? If the slut's living here in Conwy, it'll be the English who know it. Welshies are only here for market day. They won't know about her one way or the other."

Harold looked thoughtful. He shook his head. Then he nodded. His vacillation lasted for a few moments, until he finally said, "You're right, Dex. When you're right, you're right. The archbishop can keep his prosy mouth shut too."

To his indignation Maelgwyn was ordered to stay silent.

"But I speak English, not just Welsh," he said.

"It's not the tongue, Archbishop, it's the face," replied Harold. "Do you agree, or should I tell Sir Nicolas you wouldn't follow orders? We can go back now and tell him."

Maelgwyn didn't want to return without Elise, and he certainly didn't want Sir Nicolas to think he had been difficult. Irately he agreed to stay silent.

Leaving their horses in the care of an eager urchin, the three men went to a nearby inn and downed ale. They then returned to the market gate and paid the usual admittance fee.

It looked as if every inhabitant of Conwy had turned out to buy and to gawk alongside the Welsh. Young and old meandered through a hotchpotch of stalls and permanent shops. Geese waddled to and fro, honking, while children munched plums or apples. To beguile customers, an old Welsh beekeeper drizzled a thread of nectar from a spoon to a pottery plate. Sun rays struck the golden cord, making it glisten and glow. "Honey," she cried, in English. Then, "*Mêl*," in Welsh.

Girls sold wildflowers and fresh berries. Cobblers and minstrels; beggars on crutches; monks; vintners; scribes for hire; butchers and roasters; coopers; fletchers; pardoners; weavers; sellers of furs and glass and Eastern gemstones; dairymaids with armfuls of cheese; glove makers; spice and nut men; brewers; a boy with a cage of frantic songbirds; a dealer in the bones, tears, and blood of saints; several cutpurses; a cross-eyed alchemist who performed inconclusive and malodorous demonstrations; two rival astrologers; a sword maker; a goldsmith; a poulterer; and an eel peddler—these and more vied for the attention and coin of fickle marketgoers.

Mundane vegetables and grains sat in baskets in the shade, watched over by gruff rustics. A sloe-eyed dancer titillated the crowd from her little platform. In a nearby corner a booth housed a long-bearded physician who did brisk business pronouncing verdicts on men's health by judging their urine's color. If piqued by the popular sobriquet given to those in his profession—piss-prophets—his rancor didn't show. Certainly he suffered no shortage of patrons.

Another popular profession was in evidence; painted women whispered their fees and specialties, paused, then moved on.

The air bore a stew of odors. There was roasting meat, fish of fresh and not-so-fresh varieties, woodsmoke, musk, cloves, sweat, wine leaking from casks and from overindulgent guts, roses, onions and wild garlic, rotting fruit, and sewage.

Harold bought a meat pie from a chesty, snub-nosed girl. "You're a sweet thing," he told her as he paid.

"You're not," she replied.

"Ah, and bold. I wonder if a pullet like yourself can say if a new lady's come to town."

The girl curled her precocious lip. "Look about you, scholar. There's lots of new ladies in town. And some old ones. And some are here as are not ladies, if that's what you're after. But don't look in *my* direction; you're not hardly my sort."

His cocky grin slipped. He wondered if his smooth way with females was on the wane. "You mistake me, darling. The lady in question is my niece. Pretty, with big gray eyes. She has an old servant woman, and they would not have been long in town."

"Go ask up at the castle," said the girl. "Maybe they know. Tell 'em your granddad's the king's jackass and your nephew's a potentate." She then turned away, shouting, "Pies, meaty pies!"

Maelgwyn, listening from a few feet away, came to Harold's side. "I'm so glad it's you who has charge of this sortie," he sneered. "It's clear you have a winsome, wily way with strangers. Far superior to mine."

"Shut your mouth, Archbishop. That one was a hard-tongued viper, that's all."

Maelgwyn gave a derisive snort. "Ah, yes. The tongue can break bone, though it itself has none."

"Just shamble about and try to look normal and sharp. That'll keep you busy. I'll find out the damned woman's whereabouts before you can catch your next bellyache."

Dexter rejoined them. He said nothing, just spat a glob of phlegm toward Maelgwyn's foot.

"One of these days, *Master* Dexter," said Maelgwyn, "you just may choke on your own putrid habits."

"Not before you're food for worms," said Dexter.

Harold left them to their brangling. He ventured away, shouldering through the crowd. He smiled, he winked, he nodded at the women. He bought a cup of mead.

Dexter soon followed, staying near enough to watch his colleague's antics. He liked the bustle of the market, the color and noise. A prostitute sidled up to him, acted as if she might say something, then sniffed and passed by. He leaned forward and gave her backside a malicious pinch. "You don't know what you're missing, dumpling," he jibed. She fled.

For his part Maelgwyn strained his eyes to catch some glimpse of his wife. But he was distracted, disturbed by the sea of chattering humanity. Whores and dancers, vacant-eyed priests. Children careened into his legs, then ran off. There was even a flaxen-haired woman peddling animals hearts, sweetbread, tongue.

It was too much. All at once he couldn't breathe. Staggering to the nearest wall, he sagged against it, chest heaving.

The seller of saints' bones studied him, then approached. "Some miracles can indeed be bought, my friend," the man said.

Maelgwyn waved him away.

The man did not go. "Friend, your need for a miracle is as plain as the torment on your face. But I think I can help."

"Leave me, false dealer, or God will strike you dead."

The peddler frowned. "If you're in so good an odor with God, ask Him if you ought to buy this." He held out a small open box containing a shriveled pink circle the size of a coin. "He'll tell you yes, I promise."

Maelgwyn stared down at the object, curious despite himself. "What is it?"

The merchant made the sign of the cross. "The blessed right nipple of Saint Agatha."

"Charlatan!"

"Lower your voice, for I am no charlatan. This is a verified holy relic. I've a sworn letter from Pope Clement right here in my pouch. Aye, I've refused a dozen offers from wealthy men for this divine object, because I found them all undeserving. But you're different."

"I warn you, take your trickery elsewhere."

"I choose to persevere, friend. I sense you're the proper owner for this holy thing, because you comprehend the rapture of agony.

Blessed Agatha is the opposite mirror of your heart. She died in agony, did she not? Dragged to a brothel, then racked, roasted, rolled in hot coals. But faith stayed with her even unto the end." He dropped his voice to a whisper. "Even when they hacked off her breasts."

Heady and strange sensations washed over Maelgwyn—wrath, ecstasy, and grief. He could not speak.

Dexter appeared at his side and squinted at the box the merchant held. "What's this, Weasel? Lady-bits from the graveyard? By God, if you need relief as bad as that, there must be some half-blind female hereabouts. Still breathing, even. But maybe you like your females better when they can't complain, eh?"

Maelgwyn drew back to strike his tormentor. His arm knocked the box from the merchant's hand. The three men stared downward as a quick-witted witness, a brown terrier, sneaked between Dexter's legs and snatched the relic in its teeth. The dog scampered off while the merchant chased after, shouting obscenities.

"Well, that's that," said Dexter. He grinned at the furious relic seller when he returned empty-handed. "But all's not lost. Mayhap you've got one of Saint Dymphna's kneecaps. No? Her nostril then?"

At that instant Maelgwyn swore to himself he'd kill Dexter as soon as it proved convenient. This resolve brought a degree of tranquility absent only an instant before.

"Don't you want to hit me, Piss-Boy?" said Dexter, smirking.

"You're not worth the bother. But perhaps I'll say a prayer on your behalf—later."

Dexter scowled. "Lucky me."

The relic merchant stalked away as Harold reappeared. He looked smug. "A milkmaid took a liking to my face and gave me all the local gossip, and a kiss. I know where your girl has her lair—in a house with a yellow door and shutters, three lanes from here. But my milkmaid said she saw her and her old servant arrive here at the market just a while ago. So they're probably still about."

"Then let's go fix up a homecoming surprise," said Dexter.

They left the market, remounted, and easily found the house with the yellow door. The streets were nearly empty, as the townsfolk had almost all flocked to the market.

"Looks like nobody's home yet," said Dexter when they arrived. "All right and tight."

Maelgwyn massaged his throat. He stared at the door as they decided what to do next.

"We'll just slip in quick as can be," Dexter went on, "wait inside till she shows up, then give her a harmless tap on the head and carry her out in a blanket."

"Assuming they have blankets," said Maelgwyn, his hand still on his throat.

"Of course they have blankets, fool. Women always have blankets," said Dexter. "I never met a woman yet didn't have at least one blanket. And a pot."

Harold pushed his sleeves up. "When we get to the gate, I'll tell the guards she's dead. They won't look too close. But what about the maid?"

"I say we conk the hag and truss her," said Dexter. "If we finish her off, it'll raise too big an alarm. But truss her, and it'll seem more like plain old robbery. By the time she's found, we'll be long gone."

"And no one would think to connect Sir Nicolas de Breauté with anything dastardly," said Harold. "But wait. Maelgwyn, does the maid know you by sight, from before?"

Maelgwyn pretended uncertainty. "Oh, I fear she may."

"She'll likely know me too," said Dexter.

"Then both of you keep your faces hid till she's smacked. Now then, the door's surely locked. What's the quickest way in? We don't want to have the sergeants down on us."

They dismounted, tied their horses to a post and walked toward the yellow door. The lane was deserted. "Leave it to me," said Dexter, pulling a short metal pick from his boot.

"What a versatile villain it is," said Maelgwyn under his breath.

A bit of jabbing and coaxing, and the lock succumbed. Dexter grinned. "Easy-peasy," he said.

Then they were in, with the door neatly shut behind them.

Maelgwyn examined the place that was his wife's new abode. It was unimpressive—a room in front obviously being set up as a shop, and a smaller room in back with a bracken bed and a cabinet.

"Don't gawk about like a halfwit, Archbishop," said Harold, watching him.

"Aye, find a nook and squeeze your ugly self into it," said Dexter. "When the females come in, let Harold conk the hag, then you and me'll burst out and grab the other."

Harold hid behind the door. But first he searched around and found a piece of cloth to use as a gag. Maelgwyn and Dexter skulked to the back.

It wasn't long before female voices sounded, just outside.

The women stood for a moment at their threshold after they opened the door. They were examining the lock. "But I'm certain I locked it," said Annora as they entered.

As soon as they were inside and the door was shut again, Harold rushed forward and slammed Annora into the wall. She staggered but didn't fall, so he hit her in the face. A second blow sent her down.

Maelgwyn and Dexter swarmed to the front, where Harold now struggled with Elise. He was attempting to stuff the cloth into her mouth while she kicked wildly.

Then she saw Maelgwyn and went absolutely still.

"Dear Elise," said her husband, coming to her side.

Dexter looked from one to the other.

"No," whispered Elise.

"A miracle, isn't it?" said Maelgwyn.

"You're dead. I saw you in the water." She spoke Welsh, as he did.

"Aren't dead men cold? But just see how warm I am."

When he tried to grab her hand, she jerked away in terror.

"What game is this?" said Harold, frowning.

As he replied in English, Maelgwyn's eyes never left Elise's face. "No game. As I told Sir Nicolas, she is well known in my village as a cunning whore. See, she remembers me too."

Elise took a shuddering breath and met Maelgwyn's gaze. "You're alive. It's not possible, but somehow it's true." Then she broke into rapid, panicky English, so all could comprehend. "But I know about your mother now, what you did to her. I know you were her lover until—"

Maelgwyn went for her throat, but Dexter dragged him back. "Careful now, Piss-Pants," he said. Then he wrinkled his nose. "So. Hail from a close family, do you?"

"You'd believe a whore?" cried Maelgwyn. "You're mad."

"Not me. But we'll sort it later, be sure. Just shut her up for now, Harold, and let's show this place our heels."

Maelgwyn abruptly launched himself on top of Elise, tearing at her dress, making strange growling noises. Her sleeve ripped at the shoulder.

Dexter rushed to Maelgwyn's side and pressed a dagger against his ribs until he released her. "Unharmed, Sir Nicolas told us. Don't you remember, sonny boy?"

"But she'll try to spew out an evil spell. I know her, I know her," said Maelgwyn, panting. "Filthy, lying whore."

Elise crouched wild-eyed beside Harold.

"Christ, it's hard to know which of you is more sickening," said Dexter. Without warning, he bent forward and smashed his dagger's hilt against the side of Elise's head. She collapsed into Harold's arms. "Easy-peasy. But for now, Piss-Pants, truss up the hag. Can you manage that one little job? Make sure she can't give a warning when she wakes up."

Maelgwyn nodded stiffly, his color hectic.

Harold found a blanket. "See? I told you they'd have blankets," said Dexter. Then he and Harold bundled Elise into it, carried her outside, and draped her over Harold's horse. Two children came around the corner. Their eyes grew wide. "Come over here, boys," said Dexter. "Want to see what a dead person looks like up close? Mind you, there's a lot of pus and maggots. But step up, don't be babies." The boys fled.

Unsupervised inside the shop, Maelgwyn bent over the now trussed Annora. "Where's my money, hag?" He lifted one of her eyelids, then the other. "Tell me or I'll mutilate your precious angel soon as ever I can. Is that really what you want?"

She didn't respond. Her head rolled sideways.

He considered the situation. "What would be the last place you would look?" he said to himself. He straightened, then knocked crockery, bundled herbs, a ball of string, and six candles off a shelf. He searched further but found nothing. In the back room he discovered the carry-marry sacks and scattered their contents on the floor. Picking up the little book made by a Beguine, he furiously ripped out all its pages. But when he caught sight of Gwydion's letter, and scanned it, he sneered and tucked it in his boot. Then he tipped over the cabinet and kicked apart the bracken bed. Nothing. No cache. He returned to the front of the shop and scowled down at the moaning old woman— at her frayed wimple, her new shoes, her apron, her dress.

And he knew.

He pushed her skirts up and saw the two sacks hanging from their cords. "Praise be to God," he said. "Not one sack but two." He cut the cords and stuffed the sacks under his tunic. Belatedly he gagged Annora. Then he aimed a hard kick at her side.

"That didn't look like something a spiritual advisor ought to do," said Harold, quietly reentering the shop. "Or was it part of some little game you used to play with your mama?"

Maelgwyn flushed and jerked Annora's skirts down. "She tried to force herself on me."

Harold's lip curled. "I bet she did, Archbishop. Best get your sorry self out of here now, or she might revive and have at you again."

Maelgwyn quit the shop. Harold stayed a bit longer, checking all was well. Then he came out and pulled the door shut. From the street everything looked as it had when they arrived.

Arranged over the horse, Elise didn't move.

"That went smooth enough," said Dexter.

"Except for that granny in there trying to have her way with the archbishop," said Harold. "He must be irresistible to mature ladies."

Dexter's beady eyes opened as wide as they could. "You mean—"

"I do," said Harold.

"Well, you miserable excuse for mucus." Dexter glared at Maelgwyn, forgetting he once considered molesting Annora himself. "You make me heave, you do. I bet this whore's tales about your mother are all true." His gaze shifted to the lumps at Maelgwyn's midsection. "Wait, wait, what's this? You suddenly in the family way? Oho, I think I begin to see. I think I do." He smiled. "But don't fret, Weasel. Your friend Dexter will deliver that babby for you just as soon as we get past the gates."

60

HIDDEN DEPTHS

Harold was right. The guards did not show particular interest in examining the corpse—who just happened to be Harold's dear sister—especially once they were informed the poor girl had died in agony, fevered, hysterical, covered in hideous welts. But at least the Pestilence hadn't been what felled her. No, this ill-fated female had eaten spoiled shellfish.

One guard did ask where the men supposed they were taking her. "You want a hallowed churchyard, surely," he said. "Where will you find such a thing outside these walls?" No sane person would bury a loved one in unconsecrated earth.

Harold now demonstrated why de Breauté had chosen him to be leader. "An old monk long ago showed us a place, beyond the far hill up ahead." He gestured vaguely in that direction. "He said a chapel was erected there a hundred years ago to try to bring proper religion to the Welsh. It had a cemetery and a marble cross. But what do you think those murdering foreigners did?"

The guard looked blank.

Harold crossed himself. "They burned down the chapel. They struck down God's monument and smashed it, and they hanged the English priest. We can only thank the Lord they left the graves intact."

Maelgwyn did not look pleased with this bogus and defamatory history. But he was in no position to refute it.

A second guard entered the conversation. This fellow looked less easily convinced. "I never heard of such a tale."

Harold shrugged. "Few have. It isn't pleasant, is it?"

"But why would your sister want to be buried in a place like that instead of in Conwy?"

"Anne intended to become a nun, you see. Heaven had other plans." Harold paused to brush away an imaginary tear. "But just before the end she made me promise to bury her out there, in that sad little graveyard. Brave, pious soul, she said she hoped her spirit might chase away the scent of tragedy that has lingered there so long."

Dexter sniffed and wiped his nose on his sleeve.

The guard was still dubious. "What about a coffin?"

"I've brought my friends to help me. We'll make a coffin out of weeping willow, Anne's favorite tree."

"Bad idea," said the guard. "Willow rots in a trice."

"It does, of course." Harold looked pained. "But how could I deny the sweet girl her final wish? She asked so little of life. And after all, her soul will be with God."

Still the guard was skeptical. "How's she going to chase off scents in the churchyard if she's gone up to be with God?"

Dexter suddenly rose in his stirrups. His beady eyes blazed. "You've got no heart, man," he cried, anguish in his voice. "I loved my sweet Anne since she was a child, but I could never tell her because her only wish was to be Christ's bride, not mine. Now you're telling me she died for nothing? Is that what you're saying?"

"That's not what I meant. I only—"

"Go on through," the other guard said abruptly. He stood away from the gate. "Sorry we detained you. Go on and Godspeed."

The men and poor Anne passed through the gate.

The guards watched them until they vanished over a rise. "It's always the good ones that go too young," said the fellow who bade them Godspeed. "Someday maybe I'll go find that graveyard. I could bring flowers. You should come along, Simon. It might be good for you, Doubting Thomas that you are."

Simon swore as he closed the gate.

Down the path Harold and Maelgwyn both gave Dexter curious looks.

"What?" he said, catching them at it. "What are you gawking at, you ugly buzzards?"

"You," said Harold. "You have hidden depths."

"Don't be an idiot. If I hadn't spoke up, you'd still be blabbing. Willow coffins and holy smells. Well, Christ and the Virgin defend me. I could just about imagine your dear sister coming miraculously back to life and settin' up a screech."

Harold grinned. "Fair enough."

"Anyway that's that, so close your yapper. Now we'll go on for just a bit, then we'll see what sort of babby Weasel's brewing under his clothes."

Maelgwyn rode on in anxious silence.

Just before they reached Llys Garanhir, Dexter dismounted. He walked to Maelgwyn's side and yanked him from his horse. "Come on, Weasel, let's take a peek at your babby. Why so shy? There now, consider me your own kindly nurse."

"Let me be." Maelgwyn stumbled backward and fell. He gaped up at Harold. "Tell this maniac to let me be."

Harold only looked annoyed.

Dexter stuck his hand under Maelgwyn's tunic. Maelgwyn resisted until he received a sudden angry fist to his gut.

"You filched these off that old pudding, didn't you?" said Dexter, dangling the sacks by their snipped cords. "You stuck your nasty hand up her dress and stole all her money. What else did you do, I wonder?"

"Nothing, I did nothing. And it's my money."

"Yours? Then why was it under the pudding's skirt?"

"That's enough," said Harold, already urging his mount down the path. "Just hold on to those sacks, Dexter, and let's go. Poor Anne could resurrect any time now, and I don't want to have to smack her again."

Dexter remounted and followed. With no other choice, Maelgwyn trailed. Heavenly intervention, he reminded himself over and over as he rode, followed its own mysterious schedule. At least he still had the letter he'd found in the back of Elise's shop. At least Dexter hadn't taken that. What a piece of persuasive evidence it would be when he showed it to de Breauté. Especially now that Elise was telling lying tales about his mother—now she had to be silenced as soon as could be. The letter might help silence her forever.

61

URGENT QUESTIONS

Lucy Atwall, the midwife, stopped by Elise and Annora's shop to bring them four duck eggs she'd purchased at the market. She had decided furthering her friendship with the newcomers would be more sensible than not.

But no one answered her knock. Or her call. She knocked again. This time the door swung slowly inward.

"Mercy!" she cried, beholding the mute servant sprawled on the floor with her feet and hands bound and a rag jammed in her mouth.

She hurried inside and untied her. She removed the rag. The poor old woman's mouth was swollen and bleeding, as was the side of her face.

Lucy ran to the rear of the shop. Everything was strewn about as if a great wind had blown through. She rushed back and knelt at Annora's side. "What's happened to your mistress?" Then she remembered the poor thing couldn't speak. "Oh, this is terrible," she said. She helped Annora up and led her to a chair. "Don't worry, I'll get help. I'll go to the inn and get help. Oh botheration, why am I telling *you*?"

Hearing a footfall, the midwife looked up. A man towered in the doorway.

"Who's that?" she cried, frightened by the look on his face. "Who are you?"

He went to Annora's side without answering. "Elise?" he said, taking the old woman's limp hand in his.

"She can't tell you," said Lucy, seeing he wasn't violent. "She's mute. But Elise is gone. I came to bring them eggs and found the place like this. But who are you, sir?" she asked again. Something in his demeanor suggested she treat him with civility. He certainly didn't look like a criminal.

Annora roused and gripped his hand. Clutching her side, she

struggled up. On her cheek was the imprint of her dice rosary; she'd been lying on it since Maelgwyn kicked her. "Thank God you're here. Oh, thank God."

He clasped her wrinkled hands. "I came on a whim, to see Elise."

"Thank Heaven you did. Someone was here, I didn't see who." She was barely able to get the words out of her damaged mouth. "Oh God, where is my poor Elise?"

"She speaks," cried Lucy. "Gibberish, but she speaks. It must have been the shock."

"You're hurt. Are you well enough to cope if I ask this person to stay with you?" Gwydion asked.

Lucy stared. No, not gibberish. Welsh. She'd heard that tongue at Friday markets all her life and couldn't be mistaken.

"I'll cope," said Annora, beginning to cry. "But is she truly gone? Is my girl gone?"

"She is."

"Who took her?" She moaned and hung her head. "Oh, it had to be de Breauté. I didn't see who hit me, but who else could it be but him?"

"I'll bring her back." His words were spoken softly.

Annora lifted her head. "Oh, Gwydion, what will he do to her?"

Still his words were soft, but now they were tinged with menace. "He'll not harm her." He pulled his hands free. "I'll see that he's not able."

Her breath came in shallow gasps. "But you know how wicked and strange he is. Take care. Please take care. For yourself as well as Elise."

"I will, I swear it."

He turned to the stunned midwife and spoke in English. "Will you stay to look after this woman? You'll be well rewarded."

Her head bobbed in consent. "With pleasure, sir, like she was my mother. Are you going to search for Elise? Do you know who took her? When will you be back?"

He pressed coins into Lucy's hand and went to the door. "You promise you'll take good care of my friend?"

"Solemnly, I do."

He turned to go.

"But, sir," Lucy called. She wanted an answer to one urgent question at least. She had to be able to tell anyone who asked her—and everyone would ask her. Even the innkeeper and his conceited wife would have to come to her for this thrilling information, for only she would know it. So for the third time she asked, "Who are you?"

He gave her a grim sort of smile, as she would later tell anyone who listened.

"I am Gwydion ap Gruffydd of Llys Garanhir," he said, and went out the door.

Lucy stared after him. "The justiciar's heir?" She turned and looked at Annora. "He can't be him. He's dead. Everybody knows he's dead."

Annora lowered herself to a chair and stared unseeing at the floor. Professional obligations recalled, Lucy set about comforting her as best she could and seeing to her hurts.

62

EVISCERATION, THEN SUPPER

Harold carried the still-unconscious Elise through Llys Garanhir's wide door. Sir Nicolas sat at the head of the long table trying to entice the bloodhounds to his side with bits of raw sheep liver.

"Finally," Nicolas said. "Put the poor thing in a chair. Gently. By God, I hope you haven't damaged her."

When the blanket was pulled back, de Breauté bent forward to examine the captive. "Yes, that's my dear friend, my sister. She looks a bit worn, but she's breathing."

"No thanks to the archbishop, my lord," said Harold.

"My advisor?" Nicolas looked around the hall. "Isn't he with you? What rock has he crawled under?"

Muffled shouts sounded. The main door slammed. Dexter appeared, urging Maelgwyn before him at the point of a dagger.

"Here's trouble," said de Breauté.

"You don't know the half, my lord." Dexter tossed the two sacks of coins on the table. "Our fine, pious boy put his hand up the hag's dress and stole her money. But I stole it back. That's it there. Seems he has a fondness for old ladies."

Sir Nicolas frowned and emptied both sacks. He raked his fingers through the coins, then examined the four jewels and the spoon with the golden mouse. "Rather a grand cache for a hag, isn't it? I assume when you say hag you mean my friend's hag."

"The one that cast up her bubblings."

"We're making progress. So, Maelgwyn stole money and jewels from a defenseless old woman."

Harold added a bit. "He may have done worse, for he had her skirts hiked up. Besides that, he kicked her. This female here said he killed his own mother too, amongst other things."

"Other things?"

"Well, sir, his mother and him, they were, they, uh—"

"Good God. Honestly? And I thought *my* family was revolting."

Maelgwyn stood quietly with his palms together at his chest. He was conserving his energy, concocting a brilliant defense.

Sir Nicolas arranged the jewels in a neat row on the table. Then he noticed his spiritual advisor's pose. "Are you waiting for the lions to be released?"

Elise moaned.

Nicolas went to her and took her hand. "Bring wine," he told a servant boy. "And water and food and a cushion."

The boy went running.

She moaned again, but her eyes remained closed. The nobleman stayed by her side for a moment, massaging her fingers to no useful purpose. Then he put her hand gently in her lap and went to quiz his advisor.

"First things first, Maelgwyn," he said in a cordial voice. "Why did you take that money and lift the hag's skirts? I thought you practiced chastity. And what's this about your mother?"

"It's my money," said Maelgwyn, eager now to make his case. "And I didn't touch the crone in an improper way. Likewise the accusations about my mother are heinous, worse than heinous. But this one"—he gestured with sudden fury to Elise—"*did* steal those two sacks, in our village. They're mine. She gave them to the crone for safekeeping, but I saw through their conspiracy."

"This slip of a female took your money, Piss-Pants?" said Dexter. "How? She attack you with a stinkhorn? Have at you with sticks?"

Maelgwyn hunched his shoulder against the lackey and addressed only de Breauté. "She asked me to pray with her. How could I refuse? We were both on our knees at my fine house. I begged God to wrench her from the maw of Satan, her master. But while my eyes were closed, she struck me with a meat skewer and took my money."

Some of the harlots wandered in from other rooms to see what was afoot. One approached Elise and examined her face. "One of us, sir?" she asked de Breauté. "Dead?"

"No on both counts. But go away now and play with your toes like a good girl." He turned back to Maelgwyn. "You know, I'm afraid you have a rather naive idea of the sorts of stories other people find plausible. For instance, your tale of being struck by my friend. I don't find that particularly believable. Harold, Dexter, do you find it believable?"

Both men chuckled.

Sir Nicolas shook his head. "In fact, everything you say strikes me as suspect."

Maelgwyn held out his hands. "But it's all true."

The boy returned with a cushion under his arm, a beaker of water in one hand, wine in the other. He presented these to de Breauté. "Cook's bringing food, sir," he said, bowing.

When Sir Nicolas flicked drops of water onto Elise's face, her brows drew together and her eyes fluttered open.

"You're awake. Wonderful. But pray don't be alarmed," he said when she shrank at the sight of him. "You're with friends. You know me, Nicolas de Breauté. You saved me from the rooks. Yes, I see you do remember. My men have brought you here for a little visit, and to help us solve some riddles."

When she sat up, he slipped the cushion behind her and offered her a cup of wine, which she rejected.

"No wine? Water perhaps?"

She accepted the water with a trembling hand.

"Calm yourself." Nicolas waited while she drank. "Better? Ready for riddles? Good. First I'd like you to explain why you haven't come to see me when you've obviously been so close by. You swore you'd come. We're nearly family, after all." His mouth curved suddenly downward and sparks of anger glittered in his eyes. "You swore you'd come, Elise. I thought we shared a bond."

She took another sip of water and tried to gather her chaotic thoughts. Glancing up, she saw Dexter lick his lips like a dog waiting for a banquet.

De Breauté's face was uncharacteristically grim. "What answer can you make? Don't lie to me, please, for I'm a bad man to deceive." Then his eyes grew wide and he slapped his hand flat on his chest. "You've had a vision of me, haven't you, haven't you? And after you swore you wouldn't. That's why you didn't come." He pulled a dagger from his belt.

She cowered in the chair. "I have never had a vision of you. And I *did* come here," she said, sure only a lie would save her. "But a man turned me away. He wouldn't listen."

"What man? When?"

"Yesterday, at your door, in the morning. A man with greasy hair and a squint."

Voices around the room suggested possible culprits.

Dexter hopped up and down. "More lies! All of us have greasy hair."

"True, Dex," said Nicolas, looking thoughtful. "But not everyone squints. Do details like that simply fly from the sky right into people's heads?"

"Aye, they surely do," said Dexter. "Liars' heads are stuffed full of false things."

"Actually it's possible you're being unfair, Dex, because of jealousy. And I'll make allowances for that." Nicolas folded his arms across his chest. "But now, Elise, do you perchance see that man here, the one who denied you entry?"

She gave the room a quick, pretended inspection. "He . . . he's not here."

All at once the anger left de Breauté's eyes completely. "Then the fool must be out hunting my enemies." He put his dagger back in its place and reached for her hand. "I knew it. I knew you wouldn't let me down, and I'm so sorry I doubted you. I'm also sorry you weren't allowed in but overjoyed you tried. But never mind that. When the rude man returns, I'll have his skull split open."

"Oh, no, he surely meant no harm, sir. It would distress me to think of a man suffering for so little cause."

He thought for a moment, then gave her a boy's shamefaced grin. "Your compassion rebukes my temper. Hence I will not kill him."

"I'm glad."

"But, sir," said Dexter, red-faced.

"Quiet, Dex. Now Elise, there's another matter, I fear. You see that fellow over there?" He directed her attention to Maelgwyn, who stood ten or so feet away, behind her.

She turned. Her eyes widened and she gripped the arms of her chair until her knuckles went white.

Sir Nicolas nodded. "Just so. I don't like him either. But he claims you stole his money." He gestured to the coins on the table, and the jewels. She gasped when he held up the spoon and made it move as if the golden mouse were dancing. "Oh, dear," he said, watching her. "That's a dismaying reaction. Could my advisor be telling the truth?"

Pushing aside the blanket, she rose from the chair and lurched against the table. She fixed her gaze on Maelgwyn. "My servant carried that money. My friend." Her voice shook. "What did you do to her? If you hurt her, I'll—"

"Calm down, dear," said Nicolas. He took her arm to steady her. "Leave the mayhem to the men."

Elise again sat down.

The nobleman watched her. "Now, he also claims you have a lover, Gwydion by name, who happens to be my enemy. You remember Gwydion? He's the man I fought in the little village with the whorehouse."

"Of course I remember him. But he's not my lover."

"You don't mumble spells and sacrifice frogs to help him defeat me?"

She looked bewildered. "Spells?"

"I thought not."

The nobleman went to Maelgwyn's side. "I can't say any of this surprises me. You steal, you assault females, you lie. I don't believe you practice celibacy either, and I don't think you'd know a Commandment from a catamite."

Maelgwyn gazed about the room. Encountering not a single friendly face, he swallowed rising panic. It was no use telling de Breauté this lying whore was really his wife. No one would believe him, he knew. He made a frantic sign of the cross. "But she's turned everything around," he said. "She's Satan's most apt pupil, I swear. Look into her eyes. They're gray. Women with gray eyes are always evil, it's well known."

"Be quiet," said de Breauté. "You're an ass."

"I have proof! A letter written to her from—"

"Spare me any more of your lies."

"Only read the letter, sir. You'll see. You'll believe me."

Maelgwyn tried to reach for the letter. But Dexter prevented him. He gave him a prod with his dagger, just enough to pierce the fabric of his hosen.

"Admit you only came here for free food and a cozy bed, why don't you, Piss-Pants?" said the lackey.

Maelgwyn looked over his shoulder. "I *came* here? I was dragged here, you ape. I sleep in a corner on filthy straw."

"Enough whining, Maelgwyn. You know what I'd really like you to do?" said de Breauté. "I'd like you to go to the little room near the buttery, the room where the wine is kept, and think about your sins. You'll have all this day to be penitent."

Maelgwyn took an unthinking step backward, until he once again felt the tip of Dexter's dagger.

Sir Nicolas continued. "After you've asked forgiveness for being such a hypocrite, such an incompetent criminal, and God knows what else, someone will fetch you to the courtyard. At which time I'll say a eulogy. Then Dexter will disembowel you."

Maelgwyn gave a shocked cry. Dexter kicked him in the rump.

Nicolas addressed the assorted men and women who had trickled into the hall. "Anyone who wants to watch Dexter at work certainly may do so. He's something of an artist. A sculptor, if you will. And there will be a bonfire. After that we'll have a lovely supper."

The men gave a bloodthirsty shout of approval.

"When those fellows out hunting for my enemies return later on, share the news with them. And you, my dear?" Nicolas smiled at Elise. "Does my plan meet with your approval?"

"I'd like to return home, sir," she said, more certain than ever that de Breauté was a lunatic. "I'm worried about my servant. I'd like to take her money back to her and make sure she isn't hurt."

"She'll be fine. Someone is bound to come by and assist her."

She opened her mouth to try again, but he raised a hand to prevent her. "Actually, Elise, I've decided you must stay until Michaelmas." He gave his most winsome smile. "I intend to host a fête then. If you're worried I'll molest you in the meantime, have no fear. You don't appeal to me in that way, if I may say so without causing hurt."

She gaped at him. "Until Michaelmas?"

"Did I tell you I'm considering marriage? Ah, but to whom?" He remembered another detail and turned to Harold. "Was the crone properly gagged? Did she see anyone but you?"

"No, sir, just me. Maybe not even me. No one else in Conwy took our scent either."

"Good. Elise's servant will have to tell her rescuers she has no idea who took her mistress, won't she? They'd never suspect me." He chuckled. "This is working out well."

Maelgwyn was dragged off to the storeroom by Dexter and locked in. But because he immediately set up such a ruckus, he was dragged out again, bound at the wrists, and gagged with a dirty cloth.

"Shut your face, Weasel, and make your peace with God," said Dexter, as he locked the door a second time. "Not that it will keep you out of Hades."

Back in the now-quiet hall, Sir Nicolas offered Elise a plate of sardines, two kinds of cheese, and an apple. She stared down at the food.

Leaning back in his chair, the nobleman gave a contented sigh. "Two dear friends, sardines, a fine afternoon. You know, I haven't a care in the world."

Her head ached. She could not reply.

He didn't notice. "Actually I do have one care. But after I kill Sir Blade, I'll have none."

The smell of the sardines was sharp and unpleasant. Elise pushed the plate away.

Nicolas continued. "This was his father's manor, you know, but now it's mine. I earned it." He caught sight of the bloodhounds across the hall. "Those are my dogs."

She looked at his strange, handsome face. "How exactly did you earn this house, my lord?" She took care to sound only curious.

"Hard work, my dear. There's no substitute for hard work, as my indolent father was wont to say."

She probed further. "If this was his family's house, mightn't this Gwydion logically suppose he has some claim to it?"

He picked up a sardine, put his head back, and dropped the fish in his mouth. "He might. But he was in France, so I've heard, when he should have been here protecting his property. That's only common sense."

"Did he cross the water to fight for England?"

"What if he did?" Nicolas looked a trifle sulky. "I find that entire soldiering nonsense a bit flamboyant for my taste. And yet so plebeian. Anyway, his loss is my gain. But please, let's not talk about such dull things or I'll think you really do have a fondness for the man. Let's discuss my fête. Did I tell you I'm planning a fête for Michaelmas?"

"Yes."

"Only a few weeks away. Let's consider a menu, shall we? I'd enjoy that above all things. Our aim, at my fête, is to impress the local beauties with my style and taste. Will you help me inspect them as they arrive, for bridal potential? That's only proper, as you stand in the stead of my sister."

They both looked up when muffled banging erupted from the back of the house.

"Ah yes, Saint Maelgwyn," said de Breauté, "thumping on the storeroom door. Really, he's quite a disturbed man. By the way, I realize you two have some unpleasant mutual history which hasn't been fully divulged. I'm not obtuse. And that's fine. People are entitled to lead their own odd lives, after all. As for me, I've known him only briefly but already detest him. I'll be relieved when he's gutted." He offered her a piece of runny cheese.

She declined.

"You must eat, my dear. At least have some wine." He stood and busied himself putting the coins back into their two pouches. "Speaking of fêtes, I've a small favor to ask."

She picked up the apple and scrutinized its smooth red skin but said nothing.

"I know I ordered you not to have any visions about me, but now I've reconsidered. I have an intriguing idea." He cleared his throat. "Dear Elise, could you try to envision my bride? I've lately grown enamored of the idea of marriage, but I have such discriminating taste in women. If you were to concentrate, and consider my preferences, you might conjure the perfect wife. Then I'd know what to look for." He suddenly knelt before her, took the apple and set it on the table, and seized her hands. "Try?"

She pulled away. "How? I can't control my visions."

He grabbed her hands again and squeezed her fingers. "Would it be so onerous to try? Picture an elegant young woman, fair-haired, with a generous bosom, lusty inclinations, and—"

"You're hurting me."

"Forgive me." He released her. "I'm so agitated. Sister, may I share a confidence? I think about an heir, often. I'll call him Young Nicolas and buy him jolly cloaks and chapeaux. So please, will you try, just try, to envision my bride? For the sake of that Young Nicolas to be."

Was any other answer possible? "Yes," she said. "I'll try."

63

TOOLS OF THE TRADE

Maelgwyn slid to the ground and leaned against the door. The rope at his wrists was not tight and came away after a few moments of frenzied struggle. Then he pulled out the gag. He wept. How had he arrived at such a pass? Was this truly how his life would end, beneath Dexter's filthy paw, slit down the middle like a helpless fish so his innards could come bursting forth shiny and pulsing, flopping to the ground in a hot heap? What about his heart?

Elise would be there, smirking. She'd peer into the steaming red cavity that had held the workings of a good man, and she would laugh. His eyes might close forever upon that view of her triumph. Afterward she and her friend de Breauté would drink wine, bandy lewd jokes, and retire to his chamber. Of course. The smell of blood would whet her appetite for coitus—it didn't matter with whom. Wasn't that her way? Hadn't that always been her way?

He shook his head, suddenly befuddled.

Elise grew excited at the sight of blood. Didn't she? Yes, yes, of course she did. He tried his best to recall specific instances, but his thoughts now seemed tangled. He propped his head in his hand to let remembrance better do its work.

He again tried to remember the many instances when the sight of blood excited Elise. But he began to realize that his recollections were faulty and treacherous, for obscene images formed behind his eyes and a strange distress in his gut expanded to include his lungs and throat. His scar throbbed.

In his head images took shape—dead doves, hares, goats, funeral wax shaped like a child's doll, pages of vellum scrawled with foreign symbols, piles of bones and hair, a staff of hazelwood, four nails pounded into an aspen tree, and a disk of bronze glinting at the bottom of a shallow stream.

These mental pictures assaulted and grieved him. But they would not stop. All of these images were culled from a witch's bag of tricks, or an evil conjurer's. Why should he, Maelgwyn, be bombarded with such talismans of foulness?

"No more," he cried, thudding the back of his head against the door. But more sights assailed him.

He beheld himself, fully grown, lying naked with a woman. They thrashed. Drenched with sweat in the moonlight, they merged and drew apart a dozen times. When the woman rose and gave a mocking laugh, he snarled and grabbed her by the throat.

The scene blurred, then became clear once more. He now lay alone, facing the wall with his knees drawn to his chest. Beside him rested the stump of a slender white arm, blood dripping from its fingertips. Nearby was its mate. Other gory body parts decorated the room.

Scrambling to his feet to escape this nightmarish inner landscape, Maelgwyn lurched across Llys Garanhir's storeroom. The only light came from beneath the door. Losing his balance, he careened into a row of wine barrels stacked three high. As he crashed to the stone floor, casks toppled. A seam on one cask split and wine gushed forth, forming a spreading pool by his side. Like an animal he bent forward and lapped greedily. He prayed the wine would be potent enough to slake his thirst and chase away the grotesque, monstrous lies his imagination had forced him to witness.

He drank and drank. And in a while the wine brought great relief.

Horrid images and scenes still clawed the inside of his skull. Lurid tableaux encroached. But their power waned—for he now understood they were false shadows, afflictions sent from Satan to confuse and dishearten a foe.

Who but Satan could conjure the false and hellish mirage of Maelgwyn's own mother as his lover, and as his bloody victim? Who but Satan and his handmaiden, Elise? After all, Mother hadn't died at his hand. That was a vile, ludicrous notion. She had drowned in the river, accidentally.

It was true he had hated her, yes, but only because she'd been unkind, sometimes cruel, and because he suspected her of behaving immorally with the various men who came and went at their home. But he certainly hadn't hated her because of some perverse secret union between them. Mother hadn't been capable of such foul iniquity. Nor was he.

It was Elise who was foul. It was Elise who was iniquitous.

Yes, but Elise would not triumph. Hadn't God already provided a pool of sweet wine to comfort him? Maelgwyn's belly was now full, his gut's roiling temporarily masked and becalmed, and the false images had faded.

When he stood, the storeroom spun. But then it righted. His hands tingled, and the corners of his mouth turned up.

Elise had finally gone too far. In abetting her master, Satan, in helping somehow to send her innocent husband the hideous mock memories he had just borne, she had unintentionally cleansed him of his lust for her. The beleaguered, bewitched part of him was now nearly mended. He was delivered from his wife's spell—or would be before the day ended. He was confident of it.

The rout of the false memories was a clear sign that victory in *all* matters was imminent and certain. Still, he had to play his part. He couldn't simply dally in a storeroom. But what *could* he do?

When raucous female laughter pealed from some other part of the manor, his head jerked up. Then came the clatter of pots, closer by. He heard, as well, the slow trickling of the wine.

The wine. The damaged cask—a wooden slat that could be pried away and fashioned into a stake. Yes, a wooden stake. Simple. Perfect. Fitting.

The Messiah had been a carpenter. He, Maelgwyn, would be a carpenter too.

64

RED SKY AT NIGHT

The sun grew large and red as it slipped nearer to the earth. Wood for a bonfire was brought to Llys Garanhir's courtyard. At the great table in the hall, Dexter sat sharpening knives of various lengths. He hummed tunelessly as he worked, occasionally trying a blade edge on a large raw turnip. A long-handled axe leaned against the wall by the hearth.

Near the foot of the stairs, two women argued over a glittery necklace. One pinched the other's upper arm, snatched the jewelry, then fled screeching and laughing down a hallway.

Sir Nicolas escorted Elise to a room off the hall. He told her it was his pondering chamber. "There was a glut of books and letters here when I claimed the house," he said. "But I had it all taken away except this desk and this Bible. Other people's belongings are so dull."

She sat in a deep chair near the window. Llys Garanhir had glass in many of its windows, including this one. Strips of lead divided the panes into small diamonds of blue, yellow, or violet. The diamonds were handsome but made it hard to judge the color of the sky beyond. She could only see that daylight had begun to fade.

She wondered if Gwydion had spent much time in this room as a child, as a young man. Had he watched the glass change colors in the twilight? Perhaps on winter evenings his father read stories to him and to his sister. Perhaps his mother sat in this very chair gazing at her husband and children.

Now they were all gone, except Gwydion.

"What are you thinking?" Nicolas asked. "You look melancholy."

She turned from the window. "I'm concerned for my servant."

"Oh, pooh." He frowned. "If one of my servants is inconvenienced, I don't give it the slightest thought. Why should you?"

"She's more than a servant. She's taken care of me since I was a baby."

"I daresay. When I was a baby, my father bundled me off to live with his sister. I wailed quite a lot and never slept, I've heard, but Auntie couldn't refuse. She was dependent on Father. Still, she gave me a hand mirror and a set of rooms and Dexter."

Elise listened with half an ear. The day had been dreadful, she thought, and the night would be worse. Nicolas would make a speech in front of a bonfire, then signal his henchman to murder Maelgwyn. She would finally, truly be a widow. But how could she rejoice? It was impossible to wish Maelgwyn anything but ill fortune, but his death would be so horrible and barbaric.

She said, with a defiant look, "I'll stay indoors when Dexter ends that man's life."

"I was afraid you'd say that, but I wish you'd join the festivities. Pretend it's a pagan ritual. What fun." He smiled. "My dear, when did you last throw caution to the wind?"

The blow she'd taken from Dexter's dagger hilt had produced a painful knot above her ear. She massaged it lightly. "I'd find no pleasure in the show."

He threw down the stylus he'd been using to write menu ideas on a board coated with green wax. "I've said over and over again how excited I am to entertain you. But if you insist on moping, stay here and mope. It's your loss."

"Thank you."

"Nevertheless, I insist you come to supper afterwards. I've asked Cook to roast a boar's head, for a joke. Cook has a delicious sense of humor when she's sober. As she brings the boar's head into the hall, she's going to hide behind it and pretend it's reciting Commandments." He assumed a falsetto. "Thou shalt not be a sham holy person. Thou shalt not molest old dearies. Thou—"

"I understand."

He scowled, for he didn't like being interrupted. "There are eight more."

Dexter came to the room's open door, shuffled his feet, and coughed for attention.

"What is it, pest?" said his master.

"Sun's headed down, my lord. Red sky at night, shepherd's delight."

"Are you a shepherd, fair Dexter? Is shepherding another of your well-hidden talents?"

"No, sir. It just appears like it'll be a fine red sunset. You're partial to good signs so I thought you'd want to know."

"That's considerate. But I believe everything is going smoothly and will continue to do so because my friend has come to visit, not because of the color of the sky. How backward you are."

The lackey shot Elise a dark look. "Could be, my lord," he said. "Even so, the men are peckish. Females too. Fact is, everyone's out in the courtyard waiting for the show. Only ones not there yet are Cook and the lookout fixed by the main road, I think."

"Well then, tell Harold Munceny to go fetch the—what does he call my advisor?"

Dexter sneered. "Archbishop."

"Ask him to fetch the archbishop. While he does, slip out to light the bonfire and arrange your tools."

Touching fingertips to forelock, Dexter hurried away.

"Now, dear, I must run off to ready myself for the evening. You know, I may even recite some poetry later." The nobleman rose and took Elise's hand. "Ah, this delightful extremity is a bit warmer than when I kissed it in that muddy village. Do you remember?" He released her and went to the door. "Just be sure you're ready for supper. In an hour, let's say."

He left but came back almost immediately. "Don't attempt any melodramatic escape, Elise, to run to your servant's side. A lookout is posted, as you heard. Just resign yourself to gaiety for the remainder of your stay. After all, family ought to enjoy the company of family whenever and wherever possible."

He blew a kiss across his palm and sauntered out.

She went to the window and stared at the colorful triangles. It was not yet dusk, but flames from two candles on the desk reflected on the panes. She leaned her forehead on the cool glass as moments dragged by.

Maelgwyn lived. In her heart, had she ever really believed he was dead? Hadn't her visions tried to warn her?

Would he scream as Dexter began his work? Would she be able to escape from the sound of his cries? Then, after the slaughter, a grand supper. Gaiety, recitations, a talking boar's head. Already the smell of roasting meat wafted through the house.

She was determined to induce de Breauté to set her free the next morning. How could she bear to stay longer in his madhouse? Somehow she had to persuade him, perhaps with an invented vision. Fearful as he was about her visions, that could surely convince him.

Perhaps someone had already gone to Annora's aid. She prayed so. Where was Gwydion? He said it would be a few days before he attacked Llys Garanhir with his friends. As soon as Annora was able, if she were able, wouldn't she try to find him to tell him what happened? Annora would understand it wasn't common thugs who spirited her young friend away.

It would be better, Elise was certain, to get away from Llys Garanhir herself rather than wait to be rescued. Then she could go to Gwydion and tell him what she had learned in his father's house before he came to confront de Breauté.

The likelihood of an impending battle alarmed her. She hated to imagine Gwydion in danger and tried to put all thought of such things from her mind. But the new miracle of his seeming regard was an entirely different matter. She took a long time, a long, sweet time, to recall the night before. As she allowed herself to relive the particulars, her face grew dreamy and warm.

But after a while she forced herself to abandon her daydreams; this wasn't the proper time to entertain them. She crossed to the desk, for diversion. The wax board was covered with dozens of ideas for de Breauté's upcoming fête and his wedding. Could such a man actually induce some young woman to marry him and bear his children? Anything was possible. Hadn't she married Maelgwyn?

A fine Bible lay on the desk. Gwydion's father's? She ran her hand over its cover, trying to recall the last time she cast the sacred lots. More than two years. How many times had she cast lots on Anglesey at the urging of some neighbor or friend? Perhaps now would be the perfect time to attempt it again, but on her own behalf.

She made the sign of the cross, then set the Bible gently on its spine and let its pages fall open. Holding her right hand over the two pages of Latin words thus revealed, she closed her eyes. Her hand drifted downward. Of its own accord her forefinger found a place. She opened her eyes to translate the verse her hand had discovered.

" 'He shall fly away as a dream, and shall not be found: yea, he shall be chased away as a vision of the night.' " She thought she understood what the words meant, and she could not grieve: Maelgwyn would die and all memory of him fade.

She went back to the window and stared out without seeing. It was fortunate this chamber faced away from the courtyard. Otherwise, the bonfire could be blazing merrily within her view by now. The colored panes would fracture the flames into dozens of flickering tongues.

From behind her came a sound. Before she could turn, a hand clamped over her mouth.

"Elise," a low voice hissed as her scarf was yanked off. "Lamb, it's your husband come to fetch you." His breath stank of wine. "Don't dawdle now, love. I'm eager to get you alone."

Maelgwyn choked off her scream with his own dirty gag, bound her hands with her scarf, and dragged her to the door.

65

DISRUPTED REVELRY

Maelgwyn dragged Elise through the hall without meeting a soul, for the revelers were out in the courtyard. The pair had reached the bottom of the staircase leading to the upper level when a voluptuous woman came toward them from another hallway. She paid scant attention to her surroundings as she walked. Smiling, she peered down at the gaudy necklace adorning her cleavage.

The woman almost collided with Maelgwyn before she saw him.

His lip curled as he appraised her. "Another whore of Babylon," he said and drew a sharp stick from his belt.

When she stumbled backward and turned, he drove the stick into her back. Without a sound she fell onto her side and did not move. Maelgwyn gave a satisfied grunt, then kicked her over so she lay on her back. Her necklace gleamed in the light of the dozens of candles Sir Nicolas had ordered lit early in the hall.

Maelgwyn tucked his bloody wooden weapon back under his belt. Then he snatched a torch from a nearby sconce and pulled Elise up the stairs by her hair.

A few moments later Dexter looked up from fanning the bonfire. He noticed Cook standing in Llys Garanhir's wide main doorway. She took a wobbling step.

"Look there, sir. Cook's cleaned her gums with the wine again," he told de Breauté, beside him. "Supper'll be a rare botch-up if she trips down those steps and cracks her fat head."

Sir Nicolas frowned. "That woman drinks like a gravedigger." He crossed the courtyard and ran up the dozen steps to her side. "Cook, it's understandable you want to join our festivities, but duty calls you back to the kitchen for the time being. Go, or I shall be cross."

She reached out her arm and clutched his velvet sleeve, then his embroidered glove. "Kitchen," she said.

He flicked her hand away. "You're touching me."

"Kitchen."

"Yes. Get back to the kitchen where you belong."

She dropped to her knees, then sprawled facedown at his feet. He saw the red stain down her back. The crowd saw too. A woman screamed, then everyone went silent. Dexter hurried up to his master.

"See if she's dead," said de Breauté, smoothing his sleeve.

Dexter knelt and located the source of the blood; it was a deep wound between her shoulder blades. He turned her over, listened in vain for a heartbeat, then nodded.

Nicolas scanned the assembly. "Which of us is missing?"

Men and women gazed around with apprehension.

"Clay's not here," said a fellow. "But he's out guarding the road."

"Harold's missing," said another. "Harold Munceny."

Dexter had been laboriously counting heads. "I sent Munceny to get Maelgwyn like you wanted," he told his master.

"Wait," cried a woman. "Barbara's not here either."

"Damnation," said de Breauté, clutching his crucifix. "I suspect Munceny may have shared Cook's fate since I don't think *he* would have murdered the old girl." He raised his voice so all could hear. "Friends, my spiritual advisor has escaped, I'm afraid."

Men grumbled and swore. A woman swooned and nearly fell into the bonfire.

Sir Nicolas ignored them all, saying, "There's a generous reward for the one who finds my advisor first and brings him to me—alive."

"Best leave a few men to keep watch here outside, my lord," said Dexter. "The females can huddle in the hall with a couple of fellows to guard 'em."

Sir Nicolas considered this. "Fine. But I fear for my friend Elise. We'll have to be sure she's safe before we hunt down Maelgwyn. Otherwise he might harm her."

Dexter went back to the fire to get his longest knife and the axe. As he returned, he said, "Could be he already has, my lord."

Frowning, Sir Nicolas pulled his sword from its sheath and went through the door. The women followed, also all the men except the three chosen to keep watch in the courtyard.

The pondering chamber was empty. "Bad luck," said Dexter, crowding the chamber's doorway with half a dozen others.

Nicolas pulled off one of his gloves and slapped it against the desk.

"You've always spoken disparagingly of my friend, so spare me your two-faced solace. But I see no sign of blood in here. Do you?"

Dexter inspected the room. "None."

"He's clearly taken Elise off somewhere else in the house, unless she's hiding. Either way, Dexter, you'll help me find her before she's harmed or you'll greet tomorrow as Cook's hellish scullery boy." He pulled his glove back on.

They found the body of the woman with the necklace. "Now this is beyond the pale. Poor Buxom Barbara," said Sir Nicolas, shaking his head.

"Aye, she was always a good one," said Dexter. As he stepped over the corpse, he discreetly yanked off the necklace and stuck it in his hosen.

They found Harold Munceny in the wine storeroom, dead, as de Breauté had expected. He bore an ugly puncture wound like Cook's in his breast, and a neater cut below it. Nicolas inspected the broken cask. "It seems Maelgwyn is using wood from this barrel as a weapon. But see that second wound? Now he has a sword or a knife too, stolen from Munceny. He must have been hiding behind the door when Harold came to escort him to the ceremony."

Blood decorated the kitchen floor. At the ingle the boar's head was already noticeably burnt on the snout side; it hadn't been turned on its spit since just before Cook staggered to the front door. Sir Nicolas shouted for the servant boy to come tend it, so that at least the supper's main course might yet be salvaged.

The door leading from kitchen to rear yard was still barred from inside. "The bastard didn't go out here," said a fellow, "unless he asked Jehovah to put the bar back down after."

They broke into three groups of five. "My four men and I will go upstairs," said Nicolas. "Dexter, take the cellar. You others, search the rooms here on the main floor. If you find him, whether he has my friend or not, keep him talking until I arrive. He likes to talk."

Three men watched the courtyard, three men guarded the females in the hall, and the rest, fourteen others, did as Sir Nicolas instructed.

Outside, the lookout had been leaning against a pine tree, near the place where Llys Garanhir's long pathway met the road into Conwy. He was imperfect in his duty, however, and didn't hear misfortune approach him from behind. Now he lay beneath a thicket on a bed of overripe blackberries and irritated snails. His eyes were wide open, but he saw nothing.

The three men in the courtyard should also have looked behind them. If they had, they might have seen trouble coming. Instead they looked toward the windows and doors of Llys Garanhir, hoping Maelgwyn might appear and give them a second chance at the reward.

In the cellar Dexter swung his axe through spiderwebs and kicked over stacks of books de Breauté had relegated to the nether regions. He and his companions used torches to illuminate every corner and passage but found no holy man, no frightened female.

The main floor also yielded no red-handed escapee. Frustrated searchers ran from room to room. They thrust rushlights into alcoves, storage rooms, and cupboards.

Both these groups of men were soon back in the hall, thwarted and unsettled. Where had Maelgwyn hidden himself? Where was de Breauté's friend?

By this time the sun was a great orange sphere suspended just above the horizon. For reasons known only to them, the four bloodhounds had taken it into their collective head to arrange themselves around the now raging bonfire and produce loud, soulful howls. Once they began howling, they did not stop.

Dexter stood near the hearth in the hall. "Someone go slit those mongrels' throats," he said, hands over his ears.

"Clever idea," said the mustached man who'd fought with him in Llanrhychwyn. "Won't the master be tickled if someone kills his precious pups? Why don't *you* do it, Dex?"

"Ah, piss and shite," said the lackey, kicking a table leg. "I hate those dogs."

Upstairs at the front of the house, Sir Nicolas finally found a possible murderer's lair. Every door save one, at the far end of the hall, was unlocked. He now stood outside this last door. "We may have cornered our rat," he whispered to his companions. They crept back down the hall to confer near the top of the stairs. "But how best to catch him so he doesn't harm Elise? Assuming she's with him and still alive."

Percy said, "We could get a log and ram the door, my lord. He wouldn't have time to do aught."

Nicolas considered the girth of Percy's chest. The others too were not saplings. "Yes, Percy. Good. We'll slip downstairs and find a log. Then we'll smash the door and snatch the rat."

"Quick as pie, sir."

"Finally we'll be able to go on with our evening. But let's hurry before my advisor commits some other mortal sin. He seems sadly bent in that direction."

66

BLOODSHED

Gwydion took the steps of Llys Garanhir two at a time and walked calmly into the hall. A man returning from a side passage spied him and crept forward with knife raised. Gwydion turned in time to deflect the blade and put his sword through the fellow's gullet.

The bloodhounds stopped baying. Dexter looked up, wondering why.

"Shite," he said.

A dozen other men surged into the hall. Women screamed. At Gwydion's side, William frowned. He was shocked to see so many scantily clad females. "All you pretty partridges out," he shouted, waving his arms. "Fly to Conwy." He doubted they'd make it there before the gates closed at nightfall. No matter, they could head to Gyffin. Wouldn't the innkeeper there be surprised?

The women didn't need to be told twice. Most knew how quickly male business could turn into a bloodbath. And none was so loyal to her current intimate partners that she was prepared to share their uncertain fates. So the prostitutes streamed out the door, shrieking and crying as they ran.

"You, swine of a Welshman, how dare you barge into my house?" said Sir Nicolas, arriving in time to see the last of the women depart. He halted halfway down the stairs, his four men behind him.

Gwydion barely looked his way. "Where is she?"

"She?" A momentary trace of wrath flared in de Breauté's eyes but was immediately replaced by stony contempt. "To which *she* do you refer? We've had so many women here."

Dexter inched along the side of the room toward his master. "I'll wager he means your precious friend, my lord," he said. "It's just like I warned you: she's his whore."

"Shut your mouth, fair Dexter. Your suppositions wouldn't interest a gnat."

Thomas now stood at Gwydion's other side. "Where is Elise?" the younger man said.

Descending the last few stairs, de Breauté frowned. "The English puppy again. You do keep poor company, boy."

Thomas opened his mouth to make an angry retort, but Gwydion spoke first. "Just tell me where she is."

"Ah, yes. Elise. Let me think." Sir Nicolas touched an index finger to his chin. "No, I can truthfully say that I'm not absolutely certain where Elise is just now. She might be upstairs. *Might* be. My spiritual advisor carried her off somewhere."

Gwydion came forward.

"Where are you going?" said de Breauté, taking an exaggerated step back at his approach.

"He means to fetch your precious friend, my lord," said Dexter with a malicious leer. "He misses her, I think."

"You will *not* fetch my friend—if she is actually my friend. For now I'll give her the benefit of the doubt. Good God, man, she and I are siblings of the spirit." He flourished his sword, slicing the air with a graceful loop. "I'll die before I let you tear her away from me."

"Great Jehovah," said Cob, his voice loud and clear and his words in plain English, "the man's a lunatic."

Dexter's narrow face went muddy pink. "Don't you say that, vermin," he cried. "Don't you slur my master."

"Enough!" Gwydion roared. He swung his sword, slicing through two candles on a table. The flickering tops fell to the rushes, igniting a small fire, which Thomas stomped out.

No one spoke until de Breauté said, "Temper, temper."

Gwydion stared at the smoldering rushes, then raised his eyes slowly to de Breauté's. "After I find Elise, you and I will talk about my father. We'll talk about Elizabeth."

Dexter broke in. "*I* killed your damned father. Not my master."

"Laudable, Dex," said de Breauté. "But your heroics probably won't impress Sir Blade. I don't think he's interested in details."

Dexter went on. "Sir Nicolas don't much care for bloodshed. Only sometimes. So it was me killed your father. Your squealing sister too."

Sir Nicolas sighed. "Strictly speaking, that's true. Of course I've killed dozens of other men. Just now and again, as he says. But it doesn't thrill me like it does Dexter. He finds it stimulating."

"You're a maniac," said Tom. "He's your servant. You're the one giving orders."

Sir Nicolas bit his lip. "Are you suggesting if he commits a crime, I'm responsible?" He fondled his crucifix. "Odd. But if it's true, I'll need to find a very good pardoner."

As Gwydion's men fanned out along the walls by unspoken consent, de Breauté watched them with grim interest.

Gwydion took two sudden steps forward, grabbed Dexter by his throat, and hurled him across the table. The lackey slid on his stomach, tumbled over the side to the floor, then scrambled up and darted to the end of the hall. Meanwhile three of de Breauté's minions fled out the door and kept on running.

"Rot in Hell," the nobleman shouted after them. "Poltroons."

The odds were now nearly even.

For the first moments of the mêlée, Tom's heart beat wildly. But he forced his mind to go blank, engaging the closest foe he could find—a sweating fat man. They circled. Grinning and oinking wetly, the fat man waved a long-handled boar catcher. "Here, piglet," he sang. Goaded, Tom ran straight for him. The man's blade tore a hole in his mail and grazed his side but did no drastic damage. Shouting senseless words, Tom struck back with a savage blow from his sword hilt that hit exactly between the fat man's eyes. The man dropped to his back like a great white rock and stared up at the ceiling, dead. Startled by his own prowess, Tom gaped down at his sword. Then he gave a whoop and went in search of more targets.

In another part of the hall William fought a fellow who jigged about like a minnow in a boiling pond. "Stand still, fool," he said. "I didn't ask you to dance." William soon grew weary and shoved him against the wall. Pulling a dagger from his belt, he bent down and efficiently sliced through both of the fellow's hamstrings. "Try hopping now," he said. The man dropped, screaming.

Jack was there too. He had returned to Conwy the previous night, brusque as always but well pleased to fight. Near the stairs he and Cob dispatched two opponents with the ease of veteran campaigners. Jack rolled his dead prey under the long table to get him out from underfoot, and Cob kicked his down the stone steps by the main entry.

Fighting raged around the hall. Gwydion's two Welsh friends had arrived in Conwy only that morning, earlier than anticipated. One carried a bronze-headed mace, which he put to good use—until Percy fatally split his skull. Malcolm saw it happen and charged Percy like a bull. A moment later he too lay dead, his windpipe crushed between Percy's enormous hands.

Iago, the other Welshman, approached without hesitation. He had a knife in his hand but held it discreetly. Smiling, he stared up at his friends' executioner. "Quite the lad, aren't you?" he said in Welsh. Percy frowned, unprepared for strange syllables. Still smiling, looking Percy in the eye, Iago brought his knee up hard to the place where Percy's legs met. Percy toppled, clutching himself. Iago kicked him in the gut, but Percy reared up and locked his arms around Iago's waist. "Aye, quite the lad," Iago rasped. Grappling in the embrace, he maneuvered his knife toward his foe. Sucking in his breath to create a space between them, he punched down on the hilt as hard as he could. The blade sliced deep into Percy's belly. The big man grunted and collapsed, taking his adversary with him.

When Percy went still, Iago untangled himself and struggled up. He told the bald-headed corpse, "That was for Prys and Malcolm, you rotten, stinking bastard."

Gwydion had no patience for a long fight. He knocked his head against the head of a man as tall as he. Dazed, de Breauté's creature lashed out with his dagger, but Gwydion grabbed his hand and bent it backward until he heard a snap. Then he dragged the howling man to the door and hurled him down the high stone steps to join Cob's victim. The man remained there, moaning, one leg twisted at a strange angle.

Dexter reappeared and sought out Thomas. "Little lads shouldn't play at being men," he said, waving his dagger.

Thomas had learned enough to keep his mouth shut and his eyes open.

"What's wrong, boy? Cat got your tongue? Mayhap that pig-shite Welshman does all your talking for you. Or mayhap you've got a bad ear."

Thomas raised his sword and waited.

Not for long. Another of de Breauté's men grabbed him from behind. "Enjoy yourself, friend Dexter," this fellow said, as Thomas kicked and struggled.

Dexter grabbed him by the hair, saying, "Easy-peasy," as he sliced off his ear.

Thomas cried out and broke from the grip of the man behind him. Pain forced him to his hands and knees.

Dexter bent over him. "Here's another present," he snarled, aiming the blade at his back. When Tom shifted away at the last instant, the dagger sank into his shoulder.

Closing his eyes, Tom felt himself float over his own body. His sisters and mother took sweet shape below him, in Ipswich, laughing at the table. He saw his father, staring out over his lands, gazing to the west. The images faded. He opened his eyes again. He smelled roasting meat, and heard—from far away—the sounds of fighting. His mangled ear rested a few feet in front of him but didn't seem important. Nothing seemed important. Again he closed his eyes.

Dexter laughed and bounded off.

Moments later Gwydion found Thomas and carried him to a corner. He ripped sleeves from a dead man's tunic and wound them around Tom's head to staunch the flow of blood. Then he went to find Dexter; he thought he recognized his handiwork.

Nicolas had been busy. He had killed two of Gwydion's friends and wounded another. Now he stood near the bottom of the staircase, looking for more prey. William approached. "I heard your mother got you by a swineherd, de Breauté," he said, with a look of innocent curiosity.

"You're thinking of someone else. My mother hated rustics even more than she hated Father."

William shook his head. "You really are a lunatic."

"Some people find me disarming."

William raised his sword. "Not me."

"I'll have to endure that. In any event, it's unhealthy for mice to investigate the workings of the grindstones."

"A mouse, am I? Better a mouse than a fancy madman."

Nicolas frowned. "That's not an insult I need to tolerate," he said, brandishing his sword. "Especially from a mouse."

Across the hall Gwydion located Dexter. "I'm going to kill you now," he said calmly. "For my father, for my sister."

"No, you're not," said Dexter.

Gwydion's greater height gave him an advantage, but Dexter dodged and wove, managing at first to avoid his sword. Nevertheless

Gwydion soon lunged forward and took a notch off the lackey's ear-lobe. Then he took a notch off the other. "And *that* was for my cousin."

Blood dripped onto Dexter's shoulders.

But his friend reappeared to aid him. The same man who had grabbed Thomas now threw a rope around Gwydion's chest. Gwydion wheeled. He brought his sword up in a wild arc, severed the rope, then sent the man sprawling with a well-placed fist to the windpipe.

Thinking he heard Thomas moan, Gwydion glanced up. Dexter saw his chance. He dove forward and stabbed him below the ribs, through mail and jupon, just where he'd stabbed him in Llanrhych-wyn. Gwydion staggered but stayed on his feet as the lackey slashed him again, on his left arm below the shoulder.

"So mighty now, are you?" said Dexter, dancing back on the balls of his feet. "I'll kill you like I did your fancy sister—almost. Oh, that was sweet, that was. Afterwards I'll go find your saintly whore and fin-ish her too. But first I'll have some sport."

Gwydion's sword slipped from his wet glove just as he noticed an axe on the floor beside him. Swooping, he grabbed its handle in his right hand. He reared back, taking aim.

Dexter's eyes widened as his own weapon hurtled toward him. He ducked, but not quickly enough. When the axe blade ripped into his chest, he gave a final, high-pitched wail.

Across the room Sir Nicolas still fought William. Hearing his lackey's awful cry, he frowned. "Dexter?"

Gwydion called out to him, "Safe in Hell, de Breauté. Look around. You've lost. Surrender and save your own sorry life."

Nicolas counted survivors. Three of his men and himself—four, that ominous number. Four against seven. He cursed. "Save my life temporarily, you mean."

"Or die here, now."

"Dexter's really dead?"

Gwydion came toward him. "Yes."

"So he has betrayed me too." Nicolas flung away his sword in dis-gust, then pressed his crucifix to his forehead.

William slumped onto a chair, gazing at de Breauté with bewilder-ment.

But Gwydion said, "Elise. Where is she?"

"Apparently locked in a room upstairs with my spiritual advisor—or rather, my former advisor."

"A priest?"

"I think not."

"Why is she with him?"

"You'll have to ask them yourself. But don't expect the truth."

Gwydion put Thomas in William's charge, then sent Jack to the cellar for rope. Sir Nicolas's men, those still breathing, were taken out to the courtyard and tied to trees.

Back inside, Gwydion searched de Breauté for hidden weapons before binding his arms behind him. "That's too tight," said the nobleman, struggling. "First you killed Dexter. And you killed my other men. You needn't now maul my wrists."

Gwydion gave the rope a brutal yank. "Better?"

Nicolas went silent.

"You're going with us," Gwydion said as he dropped a loop of rope around his prisoner's neck like a leash, "so I can be certain of your safety."

"Thank you, Sir Blade," said Nicolas. "You're so thoughtful. But before we go upstairs, be candid with me: did my dear friend Elise really lead you here? Did she actually play Judas?"

"I don't have the slightest idea what you're talking about," replied Gwydion. He yanked the rope again and dragged Nicolas toward the stairs. Jack and Cob and Iago followed.

"Wait, there's something else," croaked de Breauté as he was pulled along. "You give lip service to precepts of fairness, but is this truly fair? Trussed up as I am, I'm quite defenseless. And Maelgwyn has no sense of decency. He kills women and—"

"Maelgwyn?"

"Yes, fool. My spiritual advisor."

67

REVELATIONS

Nicolas was right about the locked room; Maelgwyn was inside with Elise. She stood with her arms above her head, attached by bound wrists to a ring set into the wall. The room was large and bare except for a beautiful tapestry of birds and fishes on one wall. A west-facing, unglazed window let the sun's last golden-pink rays through its open shutters to spill across the floor.

Maelgwyn had wedged the torch into a crevice in the stone wall near a dim corner. He stood beside it. The torch flared and flickered, casting shifting shadows over his face.

"Calm yourself, my dear. I won't kill you yet," he said. "You're still useful. If your favors have pleased de Breauté, as I'm sure they have, he won't want to see your mangled corpse plummet from this high window. Therefore he'll return my cache and give me a horse. You and I will gallop away to hunt down your other lover, Gwydion. Then you'll watch me end his life. Afterwards you'll join him in Hell. But for now let us enjoy each other's company. We haven't had sufficient time to be alone of late."

A sneer twisted his mouth. "Wait, I'd almost forgotten. I've a treat for you. I tried to show it to de Breauté, but he was too big a fool to heed me." He drew Gwydion's creased letter from his tunic. "This is really quite poignant. Listen. 'Madwoman, I wanted so badly to chase the shadows from your eyes.' It's from your left-handed lover, as you well know." He dropped the letter. "Did you mean to use it in another of your evil rites, Elise?"

The gag didn't allow her to speak. She could only stare at him, transfixed.

"You think you'll disconcert me with your evil gray eyes. But the infatuation I bore for you is waning. I don't even mind that you've made de Breauté into another slave. What's one more? His lust may keep him from barging in here and jeopardizing your wretched life."

He came across the room and stood before her. "You see, your whore's habits have turned out to be a boon." Lifting her skirt, he let his large, bloody hand roam up her thigh. "There, that's lovely, isn't it? You must stay in practice." His hand moved higher and his breathing grew more rapid. "You adore that, don't you, my stinking rose?"

She stomped on his foot.

He stifled a roar, then cuffed her across the face. Her legs buckled but her bonds kept her from falling.

"Oh, your pretty cheek is bleeding," he said through clenched teeth. "I'm so sorry. But I know: if I seal the wound with fire, it will heal more cleanly. Fire purifies, doesn't it? Let me get the torch."

Silently she begged Saint Michael to protect her and banish her fear. But the prayer had no effect. Sobs swelled in her throat, and she knew she was a coward. Had God or the angels answered her prayers when she and her family suffered on Anglesey? At Gray Hill? No. Heaven had no use for cowards.

Maelgwyn flung away to seize the torch. "Harsh medicine. Harsh medicine is best, Mother always said."

He froze and jerked toward the window. "Those hounds have stopped baying," he said. "Why?"

Shouts swelled from the rooms below and a woman screamed.

He hurried to the window to peer out. The hand holding the torch shook. "I see nothing," he said. "Nothing but the bonfire. Wait, no. Whores are running away down the path."

He jammed the torch back into the crevice.

Returning to Elise, he freed her from the iron ring. Wrists still bound by her scarf, she collapsed to the floor with a muffled cry. "Something is going on," he said, as if to himself. "A fight?" He pulled her up and dragged her to the wall near the door. "Come along and keep still. No tricks. Stand here by me and we'll just wait and see what comes to pass." He leaned forward and turned the key. "There, it's un-locked. If it *is* a fight, perhaps the victor will come upstairs and peek in here. But if they do, they'll see no one, because we'll be safely hid-den behind this great door."

She leaned against the wall near the door's hinge to keep herself from falling, as new sounds came. Crashes, curses, a bellow. The clamor below grew more widespread. Maelgwyn stood behind her, clutching Munceny's sword. His moist breath fanned her cheek. She shrank from him but he jerked her back, pulling her hair aside to press his hot lips to her neck. "Aren't you excited?" he whispered. "You know how we love the sight of blood."

As moments passed, the noise increased. Whole armies must be clashing, she thought. Had the constable finally arrived from Caernarfon to arrest Sir Nicolas? Was Gwydion downstairs?

Gradually there came a lull.

Then footsteps sounded on the stairs. Men consulted in low voices at the other end of the hall, before all went quiet. Maelgwyn's sweaty hand stroked Elise's throat. He squeezed lightly.

Again footfalls sounded, moving closer.

The door swung inward, toward them. But no one entered. Elise felt her husband's breath quicken against her cheek. His hand on her throat trembled, as a hum like a thousand angry bees started in her ears.

A man came cautiously into the room with his sword raised. Elise was just able to see the side of his face. She saw he was a stranger. He went to the window—and considered the torch.

Maelgwyn tightened his grip. A red shroud floated up before her eyes as the dirty gag pressed on her tongue and the back of her throat. Suddenly she gasped for air.

The man wheeled toward the sound. "They're here," he cried out in Welsh. The words barely left his mouth before Maelgwyn dashed forward and lanced his side with Munceny's sword. The stranger crashed to the floor.

Dashing back to Elise, Maelgwyn hissed, "Now you'll be my shield." He pushed her before him to the open door but immediately staggered back.

Gwydion stood outside with his men, and with de Breauté, restrained by his rope collar. Nicolas gaped at Maelgwyn, for once at a loss for words.

"Elise," Gwydion said, searching her face, "can you move away from him? Can you come to me?" His voice was composed.

Maelgwyn's grip on her arm tightened. He shoved her forward half a step. "You'll let us leave this house unhindered or she dies," he said. "I swear it's true, I'll kill her." Elise stumbled but he kept her upright as they edged into the hall.

Gwydion didn't move. He said, "Everything is finished, Maelgwyn. It's over. Let her go."

His calmness unnerved Maelgwyn. He pressed Elise against his side and stared at his new adversary. Only the width of the hall separated them.

"Let her go," Gwydion said again.

Cob said, in English, "I'm not sure, Gwyd, but I'd say this fellow's none too quick. Let me knock some sense into his head."

"No," said Gwydion. "Take de Breauté." He shoved the nobleman toward Cob.

De Breauté staggered against the wall but recovered with swift grace. As he did, Cob jerked on his rope and sent him sprawling.

From the floor Nicolas cast Cob a venomous glare. Though he couldn't see Elise for the maze of legs, he cried out, "So you led these murdering louts straight to my door, dear sister. And it's true, he's your paramour. How could you betray me?"

Elise didn't reply. All she heard was the buzzing in her ears.

Jack bent and stuffed a glove into de Breauté's mouth. "You talk too much," he said.

Maelgwyn felt an urge to laugh. Wasn't the haughty Sir Nicolas droll as a humiliated captive? But his amusement quickly left him, for he had another pressing dilemma. He dug his fingers into Elise's arm and turned his attention back to the man before him. "How do you know my name? And by what right do you meddle in a man's dealings with his wife?" Perceiving the fine silver sword, his mouth hardened. "Ah, yes. Her left-handed lover."

Soon his expression altered subtly, growing less hostile. He squinted as if to see Gwydion more clearly. "Are you unholy too? Perhaps not." Words now spilled out rapidly. "She holds you in thrall, I think, as she once did me. She had a letter of yours meant for future dark craft, but I seized it. Perhaps you really don't know she's Satan's whore, but it's true. Hear me, if you have any hope of Heaven."

"Enough." Gwydion's voice was low and wintry. "Before God, enough."

Elise tried to take a full breath but could not. The noise in her ears grew into a cacophony, like the Foaming Falls, like a cascade of broken glass. Her face burned and her legs felt numb. Wouldn't it be easier to just go to sleep forever? Surely it would be easier.

She closed her eyes and let herself fall.

Maelgwyn clutched at her hair, her arms. But she slipped away, to the floor. He looked up and saw Gwydion's eyes on her unconscious form. His eyes were black, unreadable.

Backing into the room he'd just abandoned, Maelgwyn's breath came still faster. He looked over his shoulder as a gust of wind whistled through the open window, extinguishing the torch. Just then a great flock of dark birds rose cawing out of nearby woods and swept off to the glowing west. Their cries made a harsh, fierce din.

In the hall Nicolas spat the glove from his mouth and tried frantically to rise. Jack knocked him senseless with his fist.

Maelgwyn swung back around, fearful his enemy might be creeping up behind him. But Gwydion knelt beside Elise. She had revived, and he'd removed her gag.

Words from the ancient vellum concealed in his mother's bowl came drifting back to Maelgwyn. "Against elfkind and nightgoers and those who have intercourse with the Devil." Had he been wrong to sell the bowl? Did he have need of it now?

No, no, it was pagan blasphemy. He brandished his sword.

Gwydion untied the scarf at Elise's wrists. She clung to him. Touching her cheek with the back of his hand, he raised his eyes to Maelgwyn's. "What sort of man are you?"

Maelgwyn stared down at his wicked wife resting so tenderly in another man's arms. She had ensnared this fool with her gray eyes and her ungodly ways, it was clear. And now no righteous man could hope for help or understanding.

Taking a step backward, Maelgwyn tripped over the man he had wounded, Iago. Gwydion let him get to his feet again unhindered. "Hear the truth," Maelgwyn said, edging to the window. He jabbed a finger toward Elise, who now watched him solemnly. "This woman is sin incarnate. Oh, I grant you she appears sweet and blameless, as women often do. But she forced me to join her in debauched revels with other men and made me help her with unholy spells. No twisted practice is beyond her. I swear by the Holy Father, she should be . . . she should be cut apart and thrown into the river."

Gwydion helped Elise rise. When she stood, with the wall as her support, he moved away from her and came slowly into the room. He came toward Maelgwyn.

Seeing him glance at the window, Gwydion halted. "Would you take the coward's way?"

Maelgwyn drew a shaky breath, raised his chin, and stood straighter. His blue eyes flashed. "Why should I? God Almighty stands by my right hand."

With a half smile Gwydion said, "Did He stand by your mother too? When you hacked her to pieces and threw the pieces in the river, who was at her side? Who was at yours?"

Maelgwyn screamed and slashed the air with his sword, missing his foe by an arm's length.

Still Gwydion wore a goading smile. "Your mother taught you her unholy ways, Maelgwyn. Don't you remember? Perhaps you even enjoyed them. But then you killed her. Did you enjoy that too?"

Maelgwyn lunged at him but slipped in Iago's blood and fell. His sword clattered to the floor. Scuttling after it, he spun to face his accuser. "My wife's foulness has won you," he said. "I see how cold and merciless your eyes are. 'If thine eyes be evil, thy whole body shall be full of darkness.'" He raised Munceny's sword in his right hand and advanced.

Gwydion took his own blade in a surer grip. "Your mother awaits you," he said and walked forward to meet him.

When Maelgwyn swung his weapon, Gwydion raised his own to deflect it. Metal struck metal, filling the room with sound. Then Gwydion attacked, battering Maelgwyn's sword even while his right arm still quivered from the first blow.

Maelgwyn careened backward, crashing into the tapestry-covered wall. He clutched the thick fabric to save himself from falling. "The one I serve won't suffer me to perish," he gasped, slowly straightening.

"He will. As he did your mother."

Final rays of the sun danced across the tapestry's woven birds and fishes, lighting them as if they were jeweled. Maelgwyn's blue eyes glittered. His mouth opened but no sound came. Then he launched himself toward his enemy, whipping his sword before him like a scythe.

Gwydion's sword crossed Maelgwyn's. The force of the blow shook Maelgwyn's hand open, and his weapon fell at his feet. Then Gwydion swung his blade.

When the cold metal bit into Maelgwyn's neck, he screamed. Blood spattered across the wall as bone, vein, and muscle surrendered completely. His scar was halved.

His body slumped to the floor, and his head dropped beside it.

The scream died away. There was no sound but the crackling of the bonfire below.

Gwydion moved to the open window. The last of the sunlight glowed on the hills and a thrush called from the woods. He threw back his head and gave a low, triumphant cry.

Elise closed her eyes and put her head in her hands.

After a moment Jack came into the room to hoist Iago over his shoulder. But he collapsed to his knees with the effort. Eventually he managed to pull him up in an awkward, lurching bear hug. Stopping every few feet, he half carried, half dragged his comrade down the stairs.

Cob did the same with Sir Nicolas, who mumbled woozily. Naturally Cob was not so careful with his burden as Jack.

Gwydion gathered Elise in his arms and held her tightly.

68

PATIENCE IS REWARDED

In the room where his body lay divided, Maelgwyn's mouth remained open. No living muscle or wish survived to instruct it to shut.

A large black spider sat in the corner. It sat motionless for a long while, as patient and watchful as the rest of its kind.

Quiet soon reigned. Darkness fell.

The spider assessed Maelgwyn's bloody head. It considered it from all angles. Finally it approached. It climbed the severed red throat, crossed the chin, and gained the bottom lip. Pausing, it raised two legs. Then it lowered the legs and crawled into the mouth.

69

HEALING

Sir Nicolas and his remaining men were delivered to Conwy that night, and their crimes made known. Afterward Annora was fetched to Llys Garanhir.

She burst into tears when Efa arrived at Llys Garanhir two mornings later. Against Annora's advice Gwydion himself rode to Llanrhychwyn to fetch her. Efa had her chores cut out for her; Annora's side was bruised, her face swollen, and one front tooth was missing. In spite of her injuries, she'd been bullying and nursemaiding Elise, Thomas, Gwydion, and everyone else in the house. It was Efa's job to look after Annora and try to keep her from exhausting herself. For her part Elise was little use. She sat by the fire like a ghost, all but silent, with Vort at her feet like a self-appointed paladin.

Lucy Atwall was also requested to come to Llys Garanhir and went gladly. Unlike Efa, she didn't mind the sight of blood in the least. And she did her best to help, racing importantly from one patient to another.

After five days Lucy returned to Conwy with the other three women. Annora had the two money pouches back and her little spoon. Once Thomas Upton, the town's shocked mayor, learned the whole tale from Gwydion the Welshwomen were granted special permission to abide inside town walls for as long as they wished. It didn't sit well with the mayor to think Gruffydd's son might suppose him heartless or guided by anti-Welsh bias. But then, this Gwydion was so reserved and distant, so unlike the carefree youth he remembered, that Upton didn't at first feel comfortable initiating a conversation about such sensitive things as Anglo-Welsh relations.

Of course, Gwydion's father and sister had been brutally murdered. With such cause, who could blame him for erecting barriers?

It was quite true that Upton had known nothing of de Breauté's crimes, and he was honestly dismayed to suppose it could be thought otherwise. After staying silent for almost a week, he finally told

Gwydion, "Your father was a fine man. We were friends for many years, and neither his Welshness nor my Englishness ever concerned either of us. So his killer will pay the ultimate price, you may be assured of it."

Back in Conwy, Lucy had dozens of fascinating snippets with which to beguile her fellow citizens. Her tales even helped improve her midwifery business; everyone wanted to hear about the events at Llys Garanhir, so they flocked to her door. Women with pretended or implausible complaints came. Some brought their husbands. Anyway, since the shop with the yellow shutters seemed unlikely to open soon, or ever, those who had been anticipating new medical guidance had to resign themselves to Lucy's tender mercies after all. Other than the drunken son of the deceased apothecary, she was all they had. Fortunately, watching Annora concoct unguents and soothing drinks for five enlightening days at Llys Garanhir, and observing her reassuring manner, had proven instructive to the midwife. She certainly went about her work with more confidence and proficiency than she had evinced before her short stay at the manor.

It was Lucy who helped spread the word about the crimes of the detestable Sir Nicolas. She also told tales for her rapt clients—and for the innkeeper of The Otter and Roe and his snippy wife—of the very-much-alive Gwydion ap Gruffydd, Llys Garanhir's rightful owner. In inventive detail she told how he rescued Elise from de Breauté's henchman, a fiend who masqueraded as a man of God. She told how he parted that man's body from his head, how the head rolled across the floor like bloody, misshapen fruit. Of course Lucy had not actually witnessed the decapitation, but she thought the fruit comparison made a nice dramatic tidbit for her repertoire.

When the innkeeper's wife asked why Elise was carried off to Llys Garanhir in the first place, Lucy looked lofty and implied it had to do with Elise's regal relatives. "I am not at liberty to divulge the whole story," she said, striking a mysterious pose. "Dear Elise relies on my discretion." The innkeeper's wife itched to slap her, but everyone else was enthralled.

Iago's wound healed quickly. He thanked Gwydion for a memorable time and went back to South Wales carrying many coins. Half of the money was earmarked for the widow of his friend Prys and her three children.

Jack left too, on his wild-eyed horse. "I'm for France in late spring," he told his friends as he departed. "By Sandwich way. Come if you want."

Gwydion's left arm mended. His side still ached, but Annora made him a supply of strong salve and some potions. "If you intend to have more epic battles," she told him on the day she went back to Conwy, "get your other side damaged. This side has had enough. As it is, those scars will never fade completely."

The constable's uncle finally arrived from Caernarfon by donkey. For his trouble he was given a nice fee, a meal, oats for the donkey, and a place to sleep. The warrant he delivered, however, was thrown into a heap of parchments to be scraped and reused, for the man named on it, Sir Nicolas de Breauté, was already locked in jail. He awaited trial.

De Breauté's high-placed relatives proved to be no help to him, contrary to what might be expected in the case of a nobleman accused of such serious crimes. His brothers, uncles, and cousins had all washed their hands of him many years before. Besides, he stood accused of not one but several murders. So heinous were the crimes, even those crimes committed on his orders by his dead lackey, that a special judge was coming from London to oversee the case.

Since the loss of his new manor, Dexter's death, his imprisonment, and what he perceived as Elise's betrayal, Nicolas had fallen into gloom. "I am already a dead man," he told his interested jailers as he rose from prayers in his cell. "When I am gone, take my boots, my mantle, my brooches. Have my horses. None will be of any use to me. Just leave me my crucifix." The guards promised to oblige.

Some of Conwy's most foolish maidens expressed disgruntlement with the whole Llys Garanhir debacle. After all, Sir Nicolas was so handsome. He dressed so well and had even been seeking a wife. He'd have made quite an admirable husband too—if only he hadn't turned out to be a homicidal fraud.

The man now residing at Llys Garanhir, though tall and handsome and unmarried, did not seem to be angling for a bride, more the pity. On the occasions he'd been seen in Conwy since the now famous bloodbath, he had paid no heed to the many available girls who smiled coquettishly in his direction. It must be his half-Welshness, the ladies sniffed, that gave him such ungallant manners. And if, as rumor suggested, his heart had already been won by the woman Elise, then he had remarkably deficient taste, the Conwy maidens whispered. After all, how could Elise's pitiful wardrobe, her apparent lack of jewels or coin, and her tiny abode compare with any of their own assets? Even if she *did* turn out to be a royal by-blow, which they highly doubted.

Thomas was still at Llys Garanhir, recovering in body if not in spirit. "Just look at me, Gwydion," he said. "What will my parents say? What woman will want me now?"

"No one will even notice, once your hair grows over it. You're a man with a past now, Tom. You fought bravely for a just cause. You didn't lose an arm or a leg, after all, and you're alive." He clasped Tom's shoulder and looked into his troubled eyes. "You have my thanks and respect as well, if they mean anything to you."

Thomas blushed but spoke gruffly. "A man with a past? Is that what I am? All well and good, but I'm not going back to England until I don't look like a freak."

"Then stay here as long as you like."

Gwydion went daily to the shop with yellow shutters that was not a shop at all. He brought seashells, lace, dried lavender—things he hoped a lady might take some small pleasure in. But Elise sat by the window, with shadows beneath her eyes. She still said little.

With apologies and thanks, Annora or Efa always rushed forward to unburden him of his packages. The women urged Elise to go for a walk with him in the lovely valley or up to the windswept hills that overlooked the sea. She needed to get some color in her cheeks, they told her, and he was so kind to visit. But Elise refused politely and steadfastly.

Annora worried, for Elise now had dreadful nightmares. Nightly they came, even though her troubles, and Maelgwyn, were finally, truly no more. She and Efa often consoled her when she woke in terror. They asked her what her dreams were, but she would never say.

Efa tried a stringent approach. "We know you're dreaming about that Maelgwyn. But Elise, he's dead, carted off to the mountain crossroads with de Breauté's lackey to be dined on by beasts and birds. Wouldn't it help to talk about it instead of only brooding?"

Elise couldn't tell them her dreams. The words would have been too ghastly. For though he was unquestionably dead, her memories of

Maelgwyn were still alive and monstrous. They crouched at the edge of her mind to assail her as soon as she closed her eyes. Nights were torture. He returned to her—his blunt fingers, muscled trunk and ox's neck, his scars, his hot breath on her neck. And his cold blue eyes. But now there was a twist. Now he carried his own bloody head in his arms and filled her dreams with hideous garbled sermons. Sometimes his dead mother walked at his side, simpering, mocking, lewd.

Elise couldn't tell her friends these terrible things. They might go mad, as she believed she might. Her only consolation, a secret one, was reliving her rescue at Gwydion's hand. Every night as she tried to sleep, she clutched to herself the memory—only without its bloody finale. She believed somehow that remembering the rescue might comfort or protect her. So far it had not.

Conwy's Honey Fair took place in early September. The town filled with merrymakers. Honey bread, honey cake, mead, even honey ale—everything sweet and golden was offered. Gwydion brought the ladies a copper bowl full of the nectar said to be sweetest of all, gathered from old hives on Conwy Mountain. But much to Annora's chagrin, Elise barely even acknowledged the gift. She just stood near the window and watched children running in the lane before the shop, while Gwydion stood beside her with the smile dying on his lips.

This time he didn't take her lack of response with as much apparent insouciance as he had taken all her previous rebuffs. Now an undeniable touch of his old aloofness showed in his eyes as he bid the ladies a cool adieu.

Annora was not happy. The night Gwydion came so late to their door, the night before the battle at Llys Garanhir, she had worried he meant only to make Elise his mistress—and with the girl's ardent cooperation. But since then his tenderness toward Elise had been so extraordinary and incontestable, Annora had been encouraged to hope for more.

Now she wasn't so sanguine. Her great hope that the pair might one day be honorably joined was fading.

As for Gwydion, he understood Elise needed time for all her old inner wounds to heal. But how long? It felt like years since she had spoken warmly to him—she who had apparently saved the insignificant note he'd left for her at Llanrhychwyn. Didn't such a telling action show she must have cared, a little? Had he only imagined that his desire and yearning were reciprocated? But she seemed so different now from the woman he'd held in his arms.

Perhaps the things that had happened to her since that night in her shop—her abduction and the consequent discovery that the perverted, dangerous man she had married was not dead—had indeed damaged her past healing.

How dearly Gwydion wished Elise hadn't been witness to Maelgwyn's violent death. Perhaps she now associated the man who truly, passionately loved her—and it had become pointless for him to deny to himself that he loved her—only with overwhelming memories of bloodshed and horror. If that were the case, it was no wonder his visits to her seemed all but unwelcome.

On the day of the Honey Fair, when she could barely bring herself to look at him, he abruptly resolved not to approach her with further impositions. His scant store of patience was depleted and his pride badly hurt. He was a heartsick fool but could just as well be a fool in private. If she wanted him, she could come to him. He'd tried long enough.

He decided to go to France and take his revenge against Charles of Spain. Had it not been for Charles, his father and Elizabeth would still be alive. Dexter and Nicolas, the nobleman in London—they'd been the Spaniard's deadly puppets. But he'd have to go soon, for the Channel crossing was only prudent between May and October. He'd hire the efficient couple who cared for the rented house in Conwy and leave Vort and the bloodhounds in their care until his return.

So if Elise did want him, time was running out for her to let him know. If she allowed him to leave without one kind word, he'd find some other, more amenable woman in France. Or anywhere. He'd find fifty women, if it took fifty to forget her. But he wouldn't wait forever, and he wouldn't pine alone in a cold bed. He would make himself forget.

Gwydion rode back to Llys Garanhir to drink and brood and wait for the judge to arrive from London. And the sun went down on the Honey Fair.

After Gwydion left, when she thought no one saw, Elise took a drop of honey on her fingertip. She closed her eyes and tasted. She smiled.

But Annora saw. She dragged Efa aside and hugged her; it was Elise's first smile in days.

*   *   *

Michaelmas arrived. Thursday, the twenty-ninth day of September.

At sunrise Elise shook Annora awake.

"What is it, cariad? Are you ill?"

"Last night there were no nightmares. No blood, no horror."

Groggy, Annora struggled up in the bracken bed. "What?"

"No nightmares. Oh, but I had such a beautiful dream. I dreamed honeybees made a great hive in a rock wall, and then honey poured down the rocks like a waterfall. Violets grew all around. Children tucked violets in their hair and bathed in the honey."

Annora rubbed her eyes and smiled. "Didn't they get sticky?"

"No, they just laughed, because everything was golden and sweet. I was there too, Annora. I bathed in honey with the children, and I wore flowers."

Efa was roused and told of the dream. "You'll have to go to church now and pray to Saint Michael," she said. "This is his day, so your dream must have been his gift."

70

RECKONING

Tom's hair grew long enough for him to once more be seen abroad. When he wandered to the quayside and was enthusiastically received by Pearl, he right away became more cheerful and even started to consider going home to Ipswich. Efa had already returned to her impatient Bleddyn but had promised to come back to Conwy soon for a visit.

Elise and Gwydion didn't meet again until a Monday in early October. On that day both were summoned to the great hall of Conwy Castle to appear at the trial of Nicolas de Breauté. A distinguished judge with bushy white eyebrows had arrived from London to preside.

By then Sir Nicolas had acquired a small group of female supporters who bribed guards to be allowed to watch, through arrow slits in a wall, as he took his brief airings. Around nones, in midafternoon, he emerged from the Crown jail to circle the enclosed terrace section at the eastern end of the castle. He was the only man then confined there, as lesser detainees languished in another nearby building paradoxically known as the Free Prison.

Bound hands clasped before him, de Breauté daily walked three times around the terrace, praying aloud. This trio of laps was his request, a change from all previous prisoners' set number of four. Three laps had the further benefit of echoing the blessed arithmetic of the Trinity—or so he told his skeptical guards.

So handsome was he, so affecting his prayers, that his admirers felt their hearts go aflutter in their bosoms as they watched him. The prisoner never spoke directly to his enthusiasts, other than once crying out in their general direction that such lovely women should not waste pity on a hopeless wretch such as he. His supporters were the opposite of deterred. They afterward tossed flowers over the wall and cried even more loudly in sympathy.

One young woman, a flamboyant blonde, gave a guard three coins to bring Nicolas a lock of her admirable hair. The next day he was seen to sport the lock, fixed 'round his upper arm with a cord. The blonde saw it as a mark of singular favor and galled her friends with preenings. "I've won his affection above you all," she said. " 'Twas my golden hair."

The morning of his trial de Breauté sat calmly with the judge on one side and Thomas Upton on the other. A dozen guards watched from the room's perimeter. Mayor Upton was no gullible maiden to be charmed by a glib tongue and meek demeanor. He had taken the accused's measure early on and understood the man needed to be assiduously guarded, always.

Annora didn't go to the trial because she couldn't speak English and no uninvolved, fully trustworthy person could be produced to translate her testimony. She didn't mind. She knew Nicolas was guilty and was confident judge and jury would soon know it too. Besides, she said, a roomful of English busybodies would only make her nervous.

An avid throng of townsfolk, a hundred or so, including the smug blonde, squeezed into the courtroom until no more could be squeezed. The less well connected or less pushy waited outside beyond the moat, where disobliging guards herded them.

A jury of sixteen wealthy townsmen had been assembled, a few with orders from their daughters to be as lenient and unprejudiced as possible. "I implore you, Father," one young woman instructed, "to oppose the execution of Sir Nicolas. On his lonely walks he prays so sweetly and casts such a manly shadow. He cannot be as guilty as 'tis said."

More objective folk also believed Nicolas should not be treated overharshly; by the beginning of the trial it was rumored his dead henchmen had actually done the foul deeds for which he stood indicted.

So the proceedings began.

Elise and Gwydion, who had not yet conversed privately that day, each gave testimony. Elise spoke of the bodies at the Castell-y-Gwynt and said all she knew of Nicolas de Breauté. Later Gwydion told what he'd learned of the man who hired de Breauté to kill his father and said without apology that he had fatally confronted him. In a flat voice he recounted Dexter's boasts concerning his sister's murder. Shocked murmurs rippled across the courtroom at this, but de Breauté sat in impassive silence. Thomas then came forward and corroborated his kinsman's statements.

When Sir Nicolas was finally questioned, his rapidly diminishing pool of supporters waited breathlessly to hear his defense, a defense that would surely prove he'd been the victim of unfounded assumptions and false accusations. Soon the handsome nobleman would be declared innocent. Soon he'd be free to grace their banquet tables.

But it became immediately and spectacularly apparent that *innocent* was not the right word to describe him.

The judge asked him simply, "Who murdered Gruffydd ap Anarawd?"

He replied, "My lackey, Dexter, whom this man"—he pointed to Gwydion—"slew savagely with an axe. Poor, loyal Dexter was practically defenseless."

"Did your lackey act on his own?"

"No, on my order. One might say, however, he was overconscientious. I never asked him to kill anyone, only to render them nonthreatening."

"Why did you give such an order?"

"Judge, I promised an ambitious man in London I would see the Griffith person removed as an obstacle to his schemes. It wasn't my idea, but I like to be helpful. But that man in London is now as dead as Dexter, again by the hand of your witness. Yet you would punish *me*? Which of us, I ask you, has the most ungovernable temper?"

And so on.

Playing with the lock of yellow hair fixed to his arm—as in the audience the flamboyant blonde's eyelashes shadowed her apple cheeks—Sir Nicolas assigned all of the actual murders to Dexter and Percy, both conveniently departed. On further probing, however, he shrugged and admitted some responsibility for the death of Lady Elizabeth's servant, Eadric.

"He meant to do me harm. And he was only a servant, after all," de Breauté said, after he had coolly described the circumstances of Eadric's death. It was a tale that caused Gwydion to abandon his chair and walk stony-faced toward the front of the room—before Thomas and several guards deterred him. When peace was restored, Nicolas remarked with grim satisfaction, "You see what I mean about that man's temper? Anyway, I don't think the dispatch of a difficult servant should be held against a nobleman. Do you?"

When the judge evinced disgust and amazement at such an audacious attitude, Nicolas looked shocked. "You're disgusted?" he said. "Come, many of us in this room are noble or wealthy or both. Do you expect me to believe that any of you care about the death of a servant with violent tendencies? What nonsense."

On that score he won no favor among the jurors. No one liked to suppose that he himself shared any of the accused's callous notions.

Each known murder was considered: Gruffydd, Elizabeth and Nevill, Eadric, Herv, the two unknown men waylaid near Llys Garanhir, and the constable's warrant bearer. The judge even brought up an unrelated case involving the unsolved slaying of a courtesan in London. But although Nicolas did not flinch from admitting at least partial culpability for all the other charges, he reacted indignantly to that last accusation.

"I don't murder women," he said, "especially women with skills." Then he amended his declaration. "Perhaps I did, once. But she was ill-favored and a servant as well. Her harsh soap ruined a favorite shirt of mine."

The jury soon filed outside to confer but returned before anyone grew restless. Their unanimous verdict went against de Breauté.

The prisoner's well-formed mouth fell open when he heard. When the mayor asked if he felt any speck of remorse, Nicolas snapped, "If any of you is without sin, let him cast a stone."

The judge did his best to give the condemned man a stronger sense of how his actions might have affected the victims and their loved ones.

"Yes, but hanging me won't change anything, will it? It won't bring anyone back from the dead. I think I should merely be released with a stern warning" was de Breauté's response to this homily. "Truly I'm dumbfounded by your cold reception of all my candor. My soul is cleaner than many of yours, I'm certain. Furthermore my defense has not been adequately heard. For instance, that creature"—he indicated Elise—"swore she'd have no visions of me, yet she might have. She swore she was my sister in spirit, yet she probably isn't. And she swore she was not in intimate collusion with your left-handed hothead, yet she was and likely still is. See how she shrinks in her chair. Then who is the greatest sinner—my false friend or myself? Which of us takes care to almost always speak the truth?"

The judge glanced at Mayor Upton. He then said to Nicolas, "*Almost* always?"

"Dear sir, no truth is absolute. This speaks directly to my point, if I may. You all seem to believe everything my would-be sister tells you. Why? After all, my deceased spiritual advisor claimed she was his lawful wife. Peculiar, is it not?"

"Your advisor's wife?" said Upton. "What are you carrying on about? How does it relate to the crimes you're now convicted of?"

"It relates just . . . as a glove relates to its wearer." Lifting his arms, struggling as if his metal restraints caused him great discomfort, Nicolas displayed spread-fingered hands for the rapt courtroom.

"Spare us your foolery and get to the point," said the judge. "If you have one."

"I do. I'd like you all to speculate upon the credibility of my false sibling. Upon her motivation. She married my advisor, Maelgwyn, whom your witness slew. But what caused her to desert Maelgwyn? True, he was no paragon. But if every wife deserted every unsatisfactory husband and took an obligingly murderous new lover, or vice versa, where would we be?"

The judge's splendid eyebrows bristled. He looked a warning to the spectators, who began to whisper and crane their necks in Elise's direction.

Encouraged by the crowd's interest, Sir Nicolas slid to the edge of his chair.

The mayor humphed. "Even if that were so, de Breauté, how would it undo your guilt? This nonsense stinks of death-door revenge, nothing else." He flung one hand up in a contemptuous, dismissive manner, then turned to the judge. "Lord Judge, the jury has spoken and I recommend our business here be finished. You're too busy a man to be endlessly subjected to a scoundrel's rant."

As many in the crowd nodded agreement, Nicolas stomped his feet.

The weary judge always found Upton an interfering sort of character. Why must the man undermine his authority at every blessed Conwy trial? The judge knew his job and had been preparing to adjourn when know-all Upton snatched away the reins. Traveling from one town to another, one trial to another, had been easier in the judge's younger days. Mayors had known their places in those more decorous times.

Then the judge remembered the meal awaiting him at The Otter and Roe, his favorite hostelry in Wales.

He stood. "Quite right, Upton. You've had your say, de Breauté."

"I haven't finished!" cried Nicolas. "Hear me out. It's your duty."

"Let him speak," said the blonde, springing up, shaking off her mother's pleading grip on her elbow. "You permitted a Welsh harlot to testify"—by now, everyone knew Elise was half Welsh—"so why shouldn't an English nobleman be allowed to defend himself completely, he who has all at stake?"

"Remove that female," said Upton, "and fling her in the moat if she gives you bother. Maybe that will teach her better civic manners."

Two guards waded into the crowd to escort the uncooperative young woman outside. Her chagrined mother trailed behind, glancing over her shoulder apologetically as she vanished through the doorway.

"Thank you, brave maiden," de Breauté called after his advocate.

"Her, a maiden?" came a rude voice from the back of the room. There was a scattering of laughter. The blonde's habits of swain baiting and self-admiration robbed her of any willing champions. Then the court grew quiet.

"Yet she spoke fairly," said Nicolas, rising, filling the silence. "I fervently beg you would hear me. And I do not lightly beg. Before his death, my advisor claimed Elise was his wife. For his pains his head was chopped off by your witness, Gwydion. Severed altogether. So consider a real possibility. Consider that this pair's crimes are worse than anything I may have done. In fact, I only defended myself from a rogue lackey. But I'm certain these two illicit lovers cold-bloodedly conspired to do away with her poor unpleasant husband."

The guards tensed as Gwydion again came to his feet.

"Ah, Sir Blade. Would you chop off my head too?" One corner of de Breauté's mouth turned up. "And thereby cheat the hangman?"

Near the front, Elise, eyes downcast, sat beside the innkeeper's wife. That matron looked dismayed and a bit confused. But she reached over impulsively and took the younger woman's hand.

"Men of Conwy, I beseech you," said Nicolas, his voice growing hoarse, "observe the lovers. Observe them closely." His gaze swept from Gwydion, on one side of the courtroom, to Elise on the other. "Deny you love Sir Blade, *sister*," he called. "And swear you're as innocent of Maelgwyn's murder as you pretend. Let us hear your oaths. Swear on those two things by the Scriptures."

Elise unhesitatingly raised her eyes to his. Her voice was remarkably sure. Nor was there shame or doubt in her mien. "I gladly swear it. I swear by the Scriptures I have never conspired to harm any man."

From across the room Gwydion watched her. His gaze was steady and intense.

Nicolas shook his head frantically. "No, no, you've used trickery in your words. You didn't swear properly. You must—"

"I've heard enough," said the judge, to beat Upton to it. "I've rarely been subjected to such nonsense as this, Nicolas de Breauté. Convicted privy shovelers deport themselves with more dignity and sense." He nodded to a brawny fellow who strode to his side. "Sergeant, prepare to remove the prisoner the instant I render sentence."

The sergeant turned to Nicolas. But Nicolas dodged him, then coiled to one side and smashed his manacles against the man's head. The sergeant fell. Four men took his place before he hit the ground, each restraining de Breauté with grim-faced zeal. One applied his fist to the nobleman's handsome nose, thereby rendering it bloody and much less handsome.

As two men helped the moaning sergeant from the room, de Breauté was slammed back into his chair.

By then the judge was utterly convinced that de Breauté was two things: guilty beyond redemption and mad as a rabid boar. Regarding the prisoner from beneath beetling white brows, he said, "Nicolas de Breauté, you are found guilty of murder. For your sins I sentence you to public hanging four days hence, on Friday. Your body will remain at the place of execution for one month to provide example for the populace and sustenance for gulls. May God have mercy on your soul."

Blood from his restructured nose streamed over his lips as Nicolas clutched his crucifix. "Four days? Four?" he cried. "Can it not be five?" But he was quickly taken away, spitting extravagant threats.

71

NECTAR

Excited townspeople streamed from the castle and over the moat to spill news of the nobleman's conviction. No one gave credence to de Breauté's claims concerning those who testified against him. The mayor was right, folk said, to declare the accusations wicked revenge. All believed justice had been served—with the possible exception of the flamboyant blonde. But since she had finally been persuaded by her long-suffering mother to retire to their home and cease making a public fool of herself, her opinion hardly mattered.

The courtroom slowly emptied. Delighted to spy the proprietor of The Otter and Roe in the crowd, the judge took him firmly by the arm and marched him out the door. With a peck on the cheek for Elise, the innkeeper's wife dutifully followed.

As she stood alone, Gwydion approached Elise. Some who remained in the room dragged their feet on the way to the door to try to observe the interesting pair. But Gwydion's forbidding expression, turned upon them, soon ended their loitering. Tom too had the good sense to go out and find himself a tumbler of ale.

At last no one was left in the courtroom except Mayor Upton and two elder townsmen, friends with whom the mayor began to exchange opinions on the day.

"We should speak," Gwydion said to Elise. No one overheard, for the other three occupants of the room had moved to the back and were deep in conversation. "But not here."

She stared at him, then looked hastily away. "Come to our house. Annora would be happy to see you."

"Annora. Of course."

Again she met his eyes. "Besides, I wanted to return your bowl."

His next words were exasperated and harsh. "God save my sanity. What bowl?"

"You brought us honey in a copper bowl." She tripped over her words. "From the fair. I never thanked you. I think, that is, I'm sure it's too good a bowl to deprive your cupboard—"

"The devil fly away with my cupboard."

They stared at each other, both breathing harder, as Upton and his cronies chatted away behind them.

Gwydion spoke again. "Monday next I leave for France, while the crossing can still be managed. Before winter."

She forced her lips into a stiff smile. "Journey well, then. We'll pray for your safety."

"As you would for any tolerable man of your acquaintance."

She flinched and pulled her mantle closer.

His tone immediately softened. "You're cold. Are you yet unwell?"

She looked toward a window and essayed a lighter tone. "Oh, no. Merely I felt a draft. Perhaps these joists are not in good repair."

Without warning, an unholy smile twisted Gwydion's mouth. "Mayor," he called out. "When I was a boy I sometimes played in the King's Hall. Is it as I remember?"

Upton turned from his friends. "The King's Hall, Gwydion? You're welcome to inspect the old place, if you like. If a sentry stops you, say you go at my behest."

"Thank you, sir. The lady expresses interest in architecture, you see."

"Does she?" The mayor chuckled, for he was a wise, well-tested man. "Admirable."

Gwydion took Elise's hand and led her out.

"Then de Breauté had his story partly right," said one of the cronies, after the couple left.

"I doubt it," said Upton. "There's bad blood in de Breauté but not in Gruffydd's heir. That girl's no harlot either. Not with those fine eyes."

Gwydion and Elise passed a group of guards, who watched their progress with interest but made no move to stop them. A small interior drawbridge led the pair to the private section of the castle, the Inner Ward, marked at its corners by the Stockhouse Tower, Chapel

Tower, Bakehouse Tower, and King's Tower. Between the latter two lay the King's Hall. A sentry guarded its door, but when Gwydion advised him they came at Upton's bidding, the fellow moved aside.

Then Elise and Gwydion stood alone in the great chamber.

He watched the play of emotions on her face.

"I was champion at *kayles* here," he told her. "And sometimes on rainy afternoons English friends and I shared a box of battered toy soldiers."

She nearly smiled.

He surveyed the room. "*These* joists are superior, don't you think?" he said kindly. "Though it's true that poor hearth hasn't often seen a fire."

She moistened her dry lips. "Has it not?"

"It was never warm here, I recall," he said. Then he sighed. "But perhaps that's enough talk of joists and children's games. Shall we speak of other things?"

She moved toward a tracery-adorned window.

Following her with his eyes, he suddenly grew stern. "Face me, Elise, so we may better discuss these other things."

She obeyed, turning to him slowly. "I'm not unaware of my debts to you, my omissions. I realize full well how kindly you treated us when we returned from Llys Garanhir. You brought gifts and asked after my health."

His dark eyes never left her face.

"You must wonder at my manners," she continued, "after everything you've done. And the most valiant thing of all, your rescue of me from Nicolas, and from—"

"Don't. I don't want gratitude."

"From Maelgwyn. I couldn't thank you, before, because I could hardly move from one day to the next. Nightmares plagued me." She swallowed and rushed on. "That's my sad excuse. I couldn't sleep without seeing Maelgwyn's face. Every night he came. Every night, until I dreaded sunset. Mornings brought no peace, because I knew night would soon return."

A muscle flicked in his jaw. "Now? How fare you?"

"The nightmares have stopped. Now I can finally thank you, for everything—before you go away. I only hope you'll forgive me and accept my gratitude."

"Why didn't you tell me about your dreams?"

"They weren't your burden. They were solely mine."

"I see. Well, then I'll take your thanks and apologies and we'll speak of it no more. But since I am inclined to be so gracious, you must tell me a final thing before I leave you."

"If I can."

"Tell me why you swore only one oath of the two de Breauté demanded today."

She colored. "What? I answered sufficiently."

"You swore you never conspired to harm any man, yes. But he asked for a second oath. In that, you didn't oblige."

"It was nonsensical. It didn't matter."

"You're wrong. So I'd have you remedy your oversight now, since we are alone. After all, the law must be served. I will be your witness." He crossed the room to her side and looked down at her intently. "Swear you don't love me, Elise. Swear it with all your heart."

She didn't meet his gaze, nor did she reply.

"Come, won't you bring our business to a proper, tidy end? It should be easy enough."

"Why do you press this, sir? I never expected you to be cruel."

"I only want the truth."

She took a ragged breath and bowed her head. In surrender.

"You couldn't lie." Cupping her chin, he forced her to look up. "You love me."

"Yes! Yes, from the start. There, now you have your truth. Now you can go away."

"You're not afraid of me?"

She frowned and shook her head. "Never of you. Only of needing you."

"But I want you to need me, madwoman, as much as I need you." He dragged her into his arms and took her mouth with his. She was still, for a moment, then gasped and arched against the length of him, returning his kiss with urgency.

When he finally drew back, she saw that his eyes were fierce and black, and she looked demurely away. A tiny smile curved her lips.

He watched her with bemusement. "You'll lead me a merry dance, won't you?" His voice was low and not quite steady. "But you almost sent me away, you little fool. We almost lost each other."

Her smile fled. "I thought it was my punishment, to live without you."

"It would have been my punishment too. But not now. There can be no other woman at my side, in my bed, in my heart. I mean to guard your happiness forever. Elise, don't you understand how much I love you?"

She gazed at him then with such sweet and honest joy, such trust, that he groaned and took her back into his arms. "How can I leave you here to brave the winter alone?" he said, his decision already made. "France will have to wait."

Glossary

AP, AB — son of (Welsh)

ASSES' FEAST — a celebration on either Christmas or January 14, commemorating the prophecy of Balaam's ass (Numbers 22) or the flight into Egypt (Matthew 2:13–15)

BECKET, THOMAS (1118–70) — archbishop of Canterbury, assassinated during the reign of Henry II, canonized in 1173

BOETHIUS (480–524) — author, philosopher, influenced by Christianity, also by Aristotle and Plato, tortured and executed

BY-BLOW — illegitimate child

CADWALADR (615–64, approx.) — King of the Britons, born in Wales

CANDLEMAS — Feast of the Purification of the Virgin Mary, February 2 or 14

CARIAD — dear, darling (Welsh)

CARRY-MARRY — coarse serge cloth

COOPER — barrel or cask maker

COTE-HARDIE, COTTE — long, close-fitting overgarment for men or women, held by a belt

COURSER — a swift horse

DAGGES — decorative edging on garments

DESTRIER — warhorse or charger

EDWARD OF WOODSTOCK (1330–76) — Prince of Wales, oldest son of Edward III, later called the Black Prince, probably because of his black armor at the Battle of Crécy

FLANELLA — woolen fabric, the origin of *flannel*

FLETCHER — a person who makes or deals in bows and arrows

FULLER — a cloth craftsperson. Fulling is the process of thickening newly woven fabric by beating and washing.

FURMENTY (or FRUMENTY)—a dish of hulled wheat cooked in milk, colored with saffron, sweetened, and thickened with egg yolks

GALINGALE—aromatic rootstock of various Chinese and East Indian plants of the ginger family, used in medicine and cooking

GARDEROBE—a privy, or a closet or wardrobe

GONG RAKER—someone who cleans privies or gutters

GOOD KING HENRY—spinachlike plant, *Chenopodium bonus-henricus*, named for a German woodland creature

GRAINS OF PARADISE—cardamom seeds

HANDY-DANDY—children's game in which guesses are made as to which hand holds a small object such as a pebble

HAROLD GODWINSON (1022–66)—Earl of Wessex and last Anglo-Saxon king of England. He reigned for less than a year and was killed at the Battle of Hastings.

HOSEN—fabric or leather stockings (or breeches) of varying lengths

JORDAN—chamber pot with lid, or a flask for collecting urine for medical examination

JUPON—sleeveless surcoat worn over armor, or a close-fitting tunic worn under armor

JUSTICIAR—a very high judicial and political official

KAYLES—like skittles, a game in which players knock down pins by rolling balls or disks

KNUCKLEBONES—a game like jacks, played with small animal bones

LIRIPIPES—extravagantly long fabric tail of a hood, wrapped around the head or swung over the shoulder, often decorated with bells, semiprecious stones, or fringe

LLEWELYN FAWR (THE GREAT) AP IORWERTH (1173–1240)—ruler of Wales. He fought for Welsh independence and supported bards and poets to stimulate a Welsh literary renaissance.

MATINS—between 2:30 and 3:00 in the morning but sometimes later; the first of the seven canonical hours

MICHAELMAS—Saint Michael's feast day, September 29

MYRDDIN (or MERDDYN)—Merlin, King Arthur's advisor and magician

NONES—midafternoon prayers, the fifth of seven canonical hours

PARDONER—a church official (or self-appointed fraudulent official) who grants indulgences in return for offerings

PATERNOSTER—the Lord's Prayer (Latin, "Our Father")

PESSARY—vaginal suppository

POULARD—fattened hen, especially desexed

PROCREATRIX—contemptuous or legal designation signifying only literal motherhood

SAINT AGATHA—virgin and early Christian martyr, Italian

SAINT BRIDGE (BRIGID, BRIDE)—sixth-century abbess of Kildare, baptized by Saint Patrick

SAINT DYMPHNA (DYMPNA)—seventh-century martyr, supposedly the daughter of a Celtic king who desired her incestuously; patroness of the mentally ill

SAINT SEBASTIAN—Roman martyr ca.300. Often represented with arrows in his flesh, he was invoked against the plague.

SAINT SEIRIOL—sixth-century abbot, one of Anglesey's principal saints, founder of Penmon Priory

SIMPLE—a plant or herb used in medicine

SIMPLER—herbalist, a person who gathers simples or is skilled in their uses

SOLAR—a private room, a bedchamber

STINKHORN—fungus *(Phallus impudicus)* which secretes green slime to attract flies and looks remarkably like a penis

SURCOAT—overgarment, knee-to-floor length (shorter for riding), sleeveless or half-sleeved

TALIESIN—Welsh bard and visionary of the sixth century

TERTULLIAN—priest and ecclesiastical writer born about 160 at Carthage. He began life as a pagan.

THOMAS AQUINAS (1225–74)—Dominican theologian, canonized 1323

TIPPET—a hood's long liripipes or sleeve's pendant streamer

VERDULET—bright green with bluish tones

VERJUICE—semifermented sour liquor made from unripe fruit, used as a condiment or as a base for medicine

VESPERS—sunset prayers; the sixth of the seven canonical hours

VORTIGERN (VORT)—British king of the fifth century

WOAD—broad-leaved herb used to make blue dye

Nectar from a Stone

1. In Chapter 1, Elise wonders if her servant's, Annora's, stories about spiders are true: that "to their webs spiders entice fallen souls who only appear to poor human eyes as trapped moths or mites, before herding them to Purgatory." But, she recalls, Annora also said the "creeping things were a blessing in the house, because they could miraculously absorb the poisonous Pestilence vapor, bind it to the spots on their backs." What stories have you heard about spiders? What is the significance of the spiders in this book?

2. What kind of tone does the opening chapter set? How did the author maintain that feeling throughout the novel?

3. Why does Jane Guill choose Elise and Gwydion as her main characters? In what ways do these two people reflect their time period, social standing, and cultural norms? In what ways do they defy them? When they first meet, it seems Elise and Gwydion are repelled by each other. Yet they grow to love each other deeply. What do you think Elise and Gwydion have in common? What about them is very different?

4. The medieval church approved doctrine that established woman as the bearer of Original Sin. How do you think this affected the household dynamic between husbands and their wives? Do you think we are still feeling the effects today? How did the Church's stance touch the lives of the men and women

in *Nectar from a Stone*? Compare some of the marriages and couples in the novel.

5. Elise puts up with Maelgwyn's abuse for two years. What are some of the reasons a woman might stay with such a man? Compare the situations of medieval women in abusive marriages with abused women today. Do you think Elise had any other choice but to kill Maelgwyn? Imagine yourself in her time and place: what would you do? Why do you think it took her so long to kill him? How does her marriage to Maelgwyn affect Elise's feeling about men and love?

6. In chapter 11, Elise and Annora meet a monk and his flock of lunatics at an inn in the village of Dolwyddelan. In the fourteenth century, those branded as "insane" may actually have been suffering from a wide variety of illnesses, both mental and physical. Some may not have been ill at all. Do you think these men are really mentally ill? Why or why not? What about Maelgwyn and Sir Nicolas? How do they compare to the monk's patients and to each other?

7. The author seems to imply that Maelgwyn suffered some abuse at the hands of his mother. How much do you think this affected his adult behavior? What other factors might have contributed to Maelgwyn's evil? How much of his abuse of Elise is based on fear of her power? How much might be based on a fear of women in general? Do you think he is truly pious? Do you feel any sympathy for him?

8. In the Middle Ages, medicine was more superstition than science. When the doctor visits Gwydion on his sickbed in Llanrhychwyn, he suggests a number of incredibly painful-sounding treatments. In fact, Gwydion himself is less than interested in the doctor's cures. Why do you think medieval communities were willing to accept torturous treatment from male doctors as opposed to the traditional herbal remedies of local "wise women"? Can you name some of the political implications that caused and were caused by this shift?

9. Though Annora is her servant, Elise treats her as a friend. Elise's treatment of Annora might have been considered unusual by other members of the noble class. What do you think Elise's behavior toward her beloved servant says about Elise herself? Would she have treated Annora differently if she were happily married instead of living in a hostile environment and in need of an ally? What role does Annora play in Elise's life and in the unfolding story?

Q&A with Jane Guill

1. **Though it shares a landmass with England, Wales is often underrepresented in fiction, especially historical fiction. What made you choose Wales as the backdrop for *Nectar from a Stone*?**
   I love Wales. It always surprises me that many people seem so unfamiliar with its history or even its location. I suppose I chose it as my backdrop, in part, to help redress that.

2. **The landscape of Wales really comes to life in *Nectar*. You paint its loneliness and sweetness so vividly. How much time did you spend on location in preparation for writing the novel? What settings did you actually visit?**
   I visited nearly all the places in the novel. One day, I recall, I slogged up a muddy hill near Llanrhychwyn. I had a terrible cold, it was drizzling and chilly, and I thought I might die. On days like that, my husband bracingly says the atmosphere is "very medieval." Speaking of atmosphere, the Migneint Moor truly is bleak and lonely, a place where anything might happen. For a more festive outing, the Conwy Honey Fair is great fun. Nearby Deganwy was virtually wiped out by the fourteenth century plague, but these days it's flourishing, with a new marina, condos, and pubs. And it still looks out across the estuary to Conwy Castle.

3. ***Nectar* is set in the fourteenth century, which was rife with turmoil. What about the 1350s attracted you? Did it give birth to Elise's story, or was it just the perfect vehicle?**
   A psychic once approached me (at an airport, out of the blue) to casually inform me I'd died of the bubonic plague in the eleventh century. "Uh, well," I said, as she strolled away, "that's nice to know." Strange. I've had other odd "spiritual" encounters, but if I recounted them all, people might think I'm a regular lunatic. Suffice it to say, some of my experiences led me to write about a woman who has visions. Besides that, I really do

love medieval history—it's beguilingly strange, yet somehow familiar.

4. **Your main characters are fabrications, but there are several historical figures in the novel as well. Can you point them out to us?**

Raoul de Brienne, Count of Eu, met the same fate in life as in the novel. Charles of La Cerda also played a small role in the Hundred Years' War and was reportedly a nasty man. Ednyfed Fychan is mentioned as Gwydion's ancestor; he was seneschal to Llewelyn the Great. The Tudors were distant descendants of Ednyfed. In the 1340s one Thomas Upton really served as mayor of Conwy and constable of Conwy Castle (or Conway, to give it the English spelling). Finally, the story of Joan, the adulterous princess, has a firm foothold in reality. She was the beloved wife and confidante of Llewelyn the Great and the illegitimate daughter of King John, John Lackland, the brother of Richard the Lionheart. Joan succumbed to the charms of William de Briouze (or de Braose), an English hostage at her husband's court. But Llewelyn found out. Welsh law dictated de Briouze be hung for the offense, and he was, in 1230. Things must have been tense for a long while afterward, I always imagine, in Llewelyn and Joan's royal household.

5. **How do you choose what historical fact to include and what to create for the story?**

Some of it is whimsy, but certain historical facts lend themselves to the story or characters. For instance, here are a few facts: phallic gewgaws like the pilgrim badge Nicolas sported were popular in the Middle Ages; the Knights of Saint John, the Hospitallers, did have a hospice at Ysbyty Ifan; there was (and still is) a holy well at Penmon Priory; a robust medieval market existed for spurious relics, saints' body parts, and bones; herbal remedies Elise and Annora discuss are all drawn from medieval sources and folklore. There's so much fascinating material in obscure old books and reference works that it can be overwhelming. The fun part is plucking out the best bits and weaving them into the tale.

6. **You have your own Welsh love story. Will you share it with us?**
On my first trip to Wales, I visited a partially excavated four-thousand-year-old copper mine that is run as an educational site. The quiet, handsome geologist who acted as our underground guide was one of the mine's founders and, coincidentally, a friend of the people with whom I was staying. That geologist and his mining colleagues came to my friends' house for dinner a few nights later. My hostess, a shameless matchmaker, politely coerced him into taking me walking up on the Roman Road the next day. Well . . . he's brilliant, but shy, and I'm practically hopeless, but despite a thunderstorm our walk went amazingly well. We met again for dinner. And the following night. We were somehow drawn to one another and I found his love for Welsh history contagious. Over the next days we spent hours and hours talking. But then I had to go home to the States—and I felt completely bereft and heartbroken. Fortunately, he phoned unexpectedly a week later and saved my sanity. We had a long-distance romance for four years and married at Conwy Castle in 1996. For the record, I still think he's handsome and brilliant.

7. **What do you want people to take away from *Nectar from a Stone?***
I hope readers will want to know more about medieval history and mind-set, and about Wales. Do people really change or only customs? Those are the things I wonder about and I hope readers will wonder too.